THE ORPHAN UPRISING

Book Three in The Orphan Trilogy
(Sequel to The Ninth Orphan)

**James & Lance
MORCAN**

THE ORPHAN UPRISING

Published by:
Sterling Gate Books
78 Pacific View Rd,
Papamoa 3118,
Bay of Plenty,
New Zealand
sterlinggatebooks@gmail.com

In this work of fiction, the characters, places and events are either the product of the authors' imaginations or they are used entirely fictitiously.

National Library of New Zealand publication data:

Morcan, James 1978-
Morcan, Lance 1948-
Title: The Orphan Uprising
Edition: First ed.
Format: Ebook
Publisher: Sterling Gate Books
ISBN: 978-0-473-52104-2

Prologue

Downtown Chicago's streets were gridlocked and the Friday evening rush hour even more chaotic than usual as a result of three events that occurred simultaneously in the busy Loop district – an afterhours bank heist in State Street, a burst water main on Wabash Avenue and a fire callout to a hotel in Madison Street.

The heist ended almost before it began when the would-be robber accidentally shot himself in the thigh and had to be rushed to hospital for emergency surgery; the water main was brought under control within minutes and the fire turned out to be a false alarm. However, the unfortunate timing of these events ensured that Chicagoans had a long wait before the streets would be cleared and they reached home, or wherever it was they were heading. To add to their misery, the Windy City was living up to its name: a gale was blowing.

On nearby Michigan Avenue, commuters and pedestrians were too concerned with their own problems to notice a solitary blonde-haired woman who sat rocking, as if in a trance, on a bench on the sidewalk. She seemed oblivious to the cold wind that tore at her clothes. Had anyone observed her, they'd have thought she was a junkie or a homeless person, or both.

The woman was thirty-one-year-old Jennifer Hannar, though few from her past knew her by that name. Her official birth name was *Number Seventeen* – appropriate considering she was the seventeenth-born product of a top secret genetic experiment called *The Pedemont Project*.

There were twenty-two others like her, and like her they were all elite intelligence operatives – the beneficiaries of carefully selected genes that ensured they were superior in almost every way, physically and mentally, to the average human being. *The Pedemont Orphans*, as they were known, were all born within two years of each other. Each carried the genes of some of the world's most intelligent men whose sperm donations had been stolen from another medical experiment called the *Genius Sperm Bank*. Its purpose was to advance the breeding of super-intelligent people.

While the orphans each had one mother, they all had numerous fathers. Their employer was the Omega Agency, a secretive outfit whose primary goal was to establish a New World Order. It was well on the way to achieving exactly that.

Seventeen recalled none of this. She hovered precariously on the brink of sanity and insanity – a result of something traumatic that had happened to her. Something that eluded her fragile memory. The former orphan-operative couldn't even remember how she'd come to be sitting on the bench or how long she'd been there.

Memory flashes skittered through her brain like the lightning that now flashed across the dark sky above. She had brief recollections of being dismissed from the Omega Agency. Something to do with another botched assignment, they'd said. Fleeting memories of a drug-induced trip to a hospital, or was it a laboratory? Painful jabs from needles. Another trip, by train this time or perhaps by air. She wasn't sure.

Try as she may, Seventeen couldn't focus on her fleeting recollections long enough to make sense of them. She feared she was going mad.

However, for no apparent reason she had a clear memory of one thing: a street on Chicago's Far South Side. What its significance was she hadn't a clue, but something told her she had to find out. It was as if her life depended on it.

The traffic was moving again and Seventeen hailed a passing cab. It stopped and she climbed into the back seat.

"Where to?" the middle-aged African-American cabbie asked.

Seventeen's mind went blank. The headlights of approaching vehicles momentarily blinded her, causing further confusion. Then it came back to her. "South Street, Riverdale," she said hesitantly.

"Got a number?"

"I'll know it when I see it."

The truth was Seventeen hadn't a clue what was drawing her to South Street. She couldn't remember it was the location of the former Pedemont Orphanage, the only home she and her twenty-two fellow orphans had ever known up until their late teens. The orphanage had long since been demolished. Aside from the occasional brief flashbacks, Seventeen had no recollection of her childhood at all. For the moment, she could only think of one thing: getting to South Street, Riverdale.

Heavy traffic ensured the journey south was a slow one. When the cab reached Riverdale, Seventeen retrieved a small mirror from her handbag and studied her reflection. She hardly recognized herself. Her normally icy blue eyes were bloodshot, her hair straggly and her face pinched and drawn. She went to work with lipstick and blusher to make herself presentable – for who exactly, or what, still evaded her.

"We're here," the cabbie announced as the taxi pulled into a drab suburban street.

Seventeen looked at a street sign. It read: *South Street*.

"Let me know when you see it," the cabbie ordered. He drove slowly to allow his fare time to study the houses on both sides of the dimly lit street.

Seventeen delved into her memory banks to try to remember what it was that had drawn her to this particular street in one of the poorest neighborhoods in Chicago. Nothing came to her. Then she saw it: a large, vacant section. "Stop here."

The cab pulled up opposite the section. Nestled between two old houses, the property backed onto a block of apartments which, like the surrounding homes, had seen better days.

"Wait here," Seventeen said as she climbed from the cab, crossed the street and stood on what was once The Pedemont Orphanage's front lawn. Pulling her coat around her to help ward off the rain which was now falling, she studied the section and the surrounding homes. *Why am I here?* Nothing came to her.

A towering sycamore tree at the rear of the section caught her attention. The remains of an old tree hut could just be seen in its lower branches.

Seventeen could suddenly picture a young boy sitting in the tree hut with a white dog. Fragments of memories came to her. She remembered the same boy, binoculars in hand, climbing the tree.

Feelings of regret washed over her. Why, she couldn't

imagine. Another memory came to her. In her mind's eye she could see an old man sitting on the front step of a neat bungalow. But it wasn't here. It was in a plush part of town.

Seventeen turned and marched back to the cab. "Next stop the western suburbs," she said to the cabbie as she climbed into the back seat.

"Got an address this time?"

Seventeen didn't hesitate. "One Twenty Three College Ave, Glen Ellyn." As before, she hadn't a clue what was significant about the address or who lived there.

Forty-five minutes later, the cab pulled up outside a neat bungalow in Glen Ellyn.

The cabbie looked at the meter then astutely studied his passenger in the rear-vision mirror. "Seventy-five dollars," he said.

Only now did Seventeen pay any heed to the matter of payment. In her disorganized state, she'd overlooked the fact she had no cash or credit cards on her. She only remembered that when she looked into her empty purse. "I'm sorry, I don't seem to have any money," she mumbled.

"Goddammit, lady!" The cabbie reached over and snatched Seventeen's purse from her. He quickly established she was telling the truth.

Before the irate cabbie could remonstrate further with her, Seventeen slipped the ruby ring she wore off her finger and handed it to the cabbie. "Will you take this instead?"

Still fuming, the cabbie studied the ring. He quickly calmed down when he realized it could be quite valuable. "Okay, but you better get out before I change my mind."

Seventeen thanked the cabbie, climbed out and stood in the rain watching as the cab sped away. She then walked slowly up the concrete path leading to the bungalow's front door. The place was in darkness, its occupant either asleep or away. Asleep she hoped. By the time she reached the door, she was crying. About what, she didn't know.

It felt like a new experience for her. Seventeen couldn't recall ever having cried before, nor could she make sense of the tears which now cascaded down her face.

Reaching the door, she rang its bell. No answer. She rang

again for the same result. Still crying, she began banging on the door with her fist.

Finally, an interior light came on. Sounds of faint shuffling came from inside followed by the sound of someone fumbling with the door key. The door opened to reveal an elderly man. He was brandishing a walking stick, which he looked ready to use.

"Who the hell are you?" the old man asked.

"I'm Jennifer Hannar," Seventeen sobbed. "Are you Sebastian Hannar?"

1

A man and a small boy knelt before a large, golden Buddha statue inside a temple and recited an affirmation in well practiced unison.

I am a free man and a polymath.

Whatever I set my mind to, I always achieve.

The limitations that apply to the rest of humanity,

Do not apply to me.

A hundred flickering candles added to the tranquility of the setting. They'd been lovingly prepared by an elderly Buddhist monk who sat cross-legged just inside the temple door as he waited for his two guests to finish their devotions.

The distant sound of children playing outside carried to them on a gentle tropical breeze. Unfortunately, the breeze did little to alleviate the humidity, which was already oppressive even though the sun had not long risen. The temple's occupants were drenched in sweat, but they were used to it: heat and humidity were part of everyday life in the Pacific Islands.

Finally, the guests arose and walked hand in hand toward the exit. The man was Sebastian Hannar, or *Number Nine* as he'd been unceremoniously labeled by the Omega Agency when he was brought into the world thirty-six eventful years ago; the boy was his five-year-old son Francis. They enjoyed the temple's peaceful atmosphere and the togetherness they experienced within its confines, and so such visits had become a regular occurrence of late.

The affirmation they'd just recited was similar to one that Nine had been forced to recite every day of his life alongside the other twenty-two orphans raised at Omega's Pedemont Orphanage in Riverdale, Chicago. Since breaking free of the agency five years earlier, Nine had changed the affirmation's opening line from *I am an Omegan and a polymath* to *I am a free man and a polymath*.

Although the affirmation reminded him of a past he'd rather

forget, it also served to remind him that not everything he'd experienced at the orphanage had been bad, and many of the lessons learned could be applied to everyday life.

As father-and-son approached, the elderly, bald-headed monk stood to receive them. Luang Alongkot Panchan, a native of Thailand, couldn't help thinking how alike Nine and Francis were. Living in the tropics had darkened their skin so that they were hard to distinguish from the Marquesas Islanders who made up the bulk of the population in this remote corner of French Polynesia.

When the pair reached Luang, they bowed to him. He and Nine exchanged pleasantries. The ninth-born orphan treated the kindly monk with respect bordering on reverence. He viewed Luang as his adopted spiritual master.

Nine's startling green eyes locked with Luang's all-knowing eyes. There was much between them that was unsaid. Over the years, they'd come to know each other so well they could communicate without even speaking. Nine felt it was as if his friend could look into his innermost being and know him better than he knew himself.

Luang could see that Francis was straining to get outside and play, so he stepped aside and smiled at Nine. "Remain in light, my friend," Luang said, bowing deeply with hands clasped in prayer.

"And you, my friend," Nine said responding in kind.

The former orphan-operative allowed Francis to pull him by the hand outside. Though it was still early morning, the sun's rays hit them like a furnace, serving as a rude reminder how hot it could get in the islands.

A cluster of frangipani trees some fifty yards away beckoned them, and the pair hurried toward the trees and the heavily pregnant woman who waited for them in the shade. She was Nine's French-born mixed-race wife Isabelle, the mother of Francis.

"Race you!" Francis challenged his father.

"You're on!" Nine said. "On three. One, two--"

The boy knew this game well and set off before Nine finished counting.

"Three, go!" Nine said. "Hey!" He took after his son whose athletic little legs were pumping like pistons. Nine quickly made up the lost ground, but slowed to make a race of it.

By now Francis was shrieking with laughter, alerting his mom to the imminent arrival of the two favorite men in her life.

"Faster, Francis!" Isabelle shouted in French.

Before the boy could reach his mom, Nine scooped him up with one arm and collapsed, panting, beside Isabelle. They were all laughing now.

As soon as he'd regained his breath, Nine kissed his wife tenderly. "Miss me?" he asked in English. As they'd done since first meeting, they effortlessly switched between English and French whenever they conversed with each other.

"Yes and so did our daughter," Isabelle chuckled, rubbing her pregnant belly. This time she, too, spoke English, but there was no hiding the strong French inflection.

Nine placed his palm on her belly and immediately felt the baby kick. At the same time, he observed his wife lovingly. *What a goddess.* He never tired of her beauty. Thirty-three-year-old Isabelle's French-African heritage combined with her strong accent gave her an exoticness that excited him even in her current state. Nine was convinced she looked more radiant than ever. It was obvious that motherhood and years of island living agreed with her.

"I'm thirsty," Francis announced, breaking the mood.

Isabelle laughed and immediately produced a tumbler of freshly squeezed pineapple juice from a cooler, which the thirsty boy gulped down.

Squeals of delight carried to them from a nearby grove of coconut trees. Local island children were playing tag while their mothers looked on. The children didn't seem to notice the heat. Beyond them, fishermen could be seen casting their nets into the turquoise waters of the bay. It was an idyllic scene so typical of this part of the world.

Francis recognized a couple of the children. "Can I go play, mama?"

"Of course you can, but don't outstay your welcome!" Isabelle chuckled in French.

Francis ran off to play. His doting parents watched as he unabashedly introduced himself to the children and joined in their play.

"He makes friends so easily," Isabelle said.

"Yes he does," Nine agreed. "He gets that from you."

"And from you," Isabelle countered.

Nine shook his head. "No he has made more friends in the past year than I did in the first thirty years of my life."

"Well, there's a good reason for that, my love." Isabelle kissed him tenderly.

"I guess." Nine smiled. His eyes were drawn to the ruby that hung from the silver necklace Isabelle wore. He had inherited it from the mother he'd never known and had given it to Isabelle as a declaration of his love for her.

Isabelle noticed the object of his attention and reflexively touched the ruby. For some reason, its touch brought her comfort, as it had Nine when he'd worn it.

"Well, I must love you and leave you," Nine announced.

Isabelle watched as her husband donned a pair of running shoes in preparation for his daily training run. "Don't overdo it in this heat," she warned.

"No, mother."

"I mean it, Sebastian!"

"Don't worry." Smiling mischievously, Nine set off at a gentle pace. As always, he would pick the pace up as soon as he was out of his wife's sight.

Isabelle's concern was not without good reason. Nine had developed a heart condition, which his specialist had diagnosed as a relatively common complaint called *stenosis* – a narrowing of one of the heart valves.

The former operative had become aware all was not well soon after he and Isabelle had arrived in the tropics from France. Chest pains had prompted him to seek professional advice. The specialist had prescribed physical activity and a heart-smart diet, but warned an operation would be required if Nine's condition deteriorated. That had been four-and-a-half years ago, and so far so good. Sensible food and exercise had seen no recurrence of chest pains. Even so, Isabelle had insisted Nine keep to the recommended schedule of quarterly visits to the specialist. A major inconvenience considering the specialist was based in Tahiti, nearly a thousand miles away.

A caring Isabelle watched Nine as he jogged away. She noted for possibly the hundredth time how different he was to the man who had abducted her while on the run in Paris. Apart from a few gray hairs around the temple, she thought he looked as youthful and vibrant as ever. There was a certain calmness surrounding him – proof of the peace he'd found. Proof also that he'd finally banished the inner demons that had plagued him since his unusual and some would say abusive upbringing at the Pedemont Orphanage.

Once out of sight of Isabelle, Nine strode out. Though not in the same peak condition as when an elite operative with the Omega Agency, he was still a fine physical specimen – a shade over six foot and toned like an athlete. He moved like an athlete, too. Soon he was breathing hard and sweating even more profusely.

As he ran, Nine reflected on how content he was with his life. After many years as a virtual prisoner of the Omega Agency, constantly traveling the globe and killing at the whim of his Omega masters, he finally had the life he'd always wanted – a family and a normal existence. It was, he reminded himself, a far cry from the dark days working as an operative. *An assassin more like it*. He used to have nightmares about those days, but no more.

After he'd broken away from Omega, he and Isabelle had fled France and settled on an isolated and unoccupied island he'd inherited in the Marquesas Islands, effectively getting off the grid. Their stay there had been short-lived. The onset of Nine's heart condition and other circumstances had conspired to prompt their relocation to the main settlement of Taiohae, on the island of Nuku Hiva, elsewhere in the Marquesas group.

A difficult pregnancy with Francis meant Isabelle had required ready access to medical assistance – assistance that wasn't available on their former island paradise. And she and Nine also wanted Francis and any future offspring to receive proper schooling.

So the move to Taiohae had been almost inevitable. It had worked out for the best. The couple, who married soon after they relocated, had been readily accepted by the locals and had made many good friends. Francis had also adapted well to life at school. The boy spoke French and English equally well, and could even communicate with the islanders in their native tongue.

In material terms, life was treating the family pretty well, too. Some shrewd offshore investments had seen Nine increase his not-inconsiderable wealth several times over, so money wasn't a problem.

Nine was following a well worn path that took him high into the steep hills overlooking Taiohae Bay. He could just make out his wife and son down near the waterfront. Francis was playing an impromptu game of soccer with his newfound friends while Isabelle and the other mothers sat in the shade, looking on.

The sweat was pouring off him as he ran up a steep incline. Sudden shortness of breath prompted him to slow to a walk. He thought nothing of it, putting it down to the heat. *You're getting old, Sebastian.*

Still looking down at Taiohae Bay, he noticed an inflatable craft approaching the distant waterfront at speed. It was manned by two men and appeared to have come from a floatplane Nine had seen touch down on the water a short time earlier out in the bay. He watched as the inflatable nosed up onto the beach and two men jumped out. They began walking purposefully toward where Francis and the other children played.

Something about the pair bothered Nine. He couldn't put his finger on it, but it didn't seem right. Even from a distance, he could see the two weren't your average tourists. Besides the dark sunglasses they wore, there wasn't a camera, sun hat or beach towel in sight. They looked more like business executives in their white shirts and long, dark trousers. One even wore a tie.

Nine found himself growing apprehensive as he continued to watch the pair closely.

2

The former operative didn't know it, but he wasn't the only one observing the two men. His spiritual master, Luang, had noticed them around the same time Nine had. The elderly monk was watching from the entrance of the temple Nine and Francis had visited a short time earlier. Like Nine, he thought the two strangers seemed out of place.

Luang's suspicions grew when the men purposefully marched up to one of the boys. He recognized the boy as Nine's son. "Francis!" he shouted.

The boy, who was now playing quite close to the temple, looked at the monk and innocently waved.

Luang motioned to him with his hand. "Francis, come!" He motioned to him again.

Francis suddenly noticed the two strangers approaching. They were only a few yards away. Sensing they meant him harm, he sprinted toward the kindly monk and the sanctuary of the temple. The men began running after him.

Only now did Isabelle and the other mothers notice anything untoward from where they sat some distance away. Immediately concerned, they hurried to investigate. The island women began shouting at the strangers. Isabelle screamed when she realized it was Francis the men were chasing.

Fear drove Francis' legs. The terrified boy ran as if his life depended on it. He reached Luang just before the strangers could catch him. The monk took Francis in his strong, wiry arms and threw him inside the temple. "Hide!" he ordered.

Francis ran to the rear of the temple and hid behind the statue of Buddha while Luang drew a long ceremonial sword from its scabbard that hung just inside the temple's entrance. An exponent of the Muay Thai martial art, Luang was no slouch with a sword either – as the two strangers were about to find out.

The first man to enter the temple was the younger of the two.

Confident the monk would offer no resistance, he hadn't bothered to draw the pistol he carried on him as he stepped inside. He didn't even see the steel blade that slashed his arm open to the bone. Screaming in pain, the wounded man threw himself to one side just in time to avoid a second slash that would have taken his head off.

Luang turned to face the second man too late to avoid the gunshot that ended his life. The monk was dead before he hit the temple's concrete floor.

The sound of the gunshot galvanized Isabelle and the other women into action. Shouting to attract the attention of menfolk in the vicinity, they started running toward the temple. In her pregnant state, Isabelle was left far behind.

The women were still some distance from the temple when the older of the two men emerged with a struggling Francis under his arm. He was followed by the younger man whose wounded arm hung limply at his side. His once white shirt was blood-soaked. The older man pointed his pistol at the advancing women who by now were swearing obscenities at the pair. The sight of a pistol had no effect on the women, so he fired a warning shot above their heads, stopping them in their tracks.

Only Isabelle wasn't deterred. "Francis!" she screamed as she ran toward the men whom she now knew were intent on abducting her son.

With a squirming Francis still under his arm, the older man ran off toward the beached inflatable craft, closely followed by his wounded partner.

"Mama!" Francis screamed.

Isabelle tripped and fell heavily. By the time she struggled to her feet, the men were already pushing their inflatable into the water. She was powerless to resist as they fired its engine into life and sped off toward the waiting floatplane.

"Mama!" Francis' plaintiff cries reached his mother, but she was powerless to help.

High in the hills above the bay, Nine had started running as soon as the men began chasing after Francis. By the time they'd bundled the boy and their inflatable into the floatplane, Nine was already down at sea level and sprinting toward the waterfront. His lungs were burning and his legs felt like lead, but he ignored that.

All he could think of was Francis.

The previous few minutes had seemed like a nightmare to Nine. There was no obvious explanation for what he'd just witnessed. Falling back on his training, his mind worked at a thousand clicks per second as he tried to figure out what was happening and who was behind it. *It could only be Omega!* He figured the Omega Agency must have discovered his whereabouts. *But how? And why Francis? Why not me?* There were so many questions and no answers.

Nine drove himself to run faster.

As he neared the waterfront, he felt a searing pain in his chest. Nine knew immediately what was happening. He was having the heart attack his specialist had warned he'd have if he overdid things.

Despite his condition, he had the presence of mind to note the description of the plane that was now taxiing out into deep water in preparation for take-off: it was a de Havilland Canada DHC-3 Otter floatplane of the type favored by the Air Command of the Canadian Forces because of its excellent search and rescue capabilities.

The floatplane was the last thing Nine saw before everything went black.

3

The next few hours were like a blur to Nine. With a distraught Isabelle at his side, he was rushed to Taiohae's medical center where the duty doctor attended to him. After a battery of tests, which included an ECG, the doctor confirmed his patient had indeed suffered a heart attack, albeit a mild one. Nine was ordered to rest up at home until the doctor considered him fit enough to fly to Papeete to consult with his heart specialist.

Drugged to the eyeballs with medication the doctor had prescribed, Nine was in no position to argue. He felt woozy and couldn't focus long on any one thing. Every time his thoughts turned to Francis, other thoughts and memories intruded, pushing his son's abduction to the back of his mind.

Isabelle took over. The Frenchwoman knew, for the moment, she had to be the strong one. For so long she'd relied on her Sebastian to make the hard decisions. Now it was her turn.

First, she had to give a statement to one of the gendarmes charged with investigating Francis' abduction and Luang's murder. The gendarme seemed as bewildered by it all as Isabelle felt, which didn't inspire her with confidence. Next, she gave an interview to a persistent reporter from the local newspaper in the hope that the resultant publicity could lead to a sighting of her missing son.

Finally, armed with a small carton of drugs for the patient, Isabelle drove Nine to their home on the settlement's outskirts. There, she put him to bed. He was asleep as soon as his head touched the pillow.

Then she ran outside and into a nearby palm grove. Near collapse, she raised her head to the sky and screamed. It was a long, heartfelt scream – a scream of anger, frustration and fear. Fear that she may never see her son again.

#

Isabelle spent the next few hours hosting a stream of concerned friends and well-wishers who commiserated with her and offered their love and support. Many of them were mothers, like her, who could relate to the loss of a child. They kept coming and going until well after dark.

Finally, toward midnight, an exhausted Isabelle made it to bed. She slept fitfully, waking to check on Nine every so often and worrying about Francis.

#

Nine woke to find Isabelle asleep in a bedside chair. How long she'd been there, he could only guess. Her tear-stained face told him she'd been crying in her sleep. The early morning sun streamed through a gap in the curtains, casting a golden glow over the bed. Everything seemed peaceful.

For a moment, the still groggy Nine remembered none of the previous day's terrible events. Then it all came flooding back to him: the abduction, the murder, the heart attack. He sat bolt upright. "Francis!"

Isabelle awoke, startled. "What is it?"

"Sorry, didn't mean to wake you." Nine was already dressing.

Isabelle tried to force him back to bed. "The doctor said--"

"Forget what the doctor said," Nine snapped. "I have to find our son."

Isabelle was momentarily taken aback by Nine's cold manner. She hadn't seen this side of him since he abducted her in Paris while on the run from Omega five years earlier.

Now fully dressed, Nine gently but firmly sat his wife down on the edge of the bed then sat beside her. "I need you to listen very carefully, Isabelle." He stared hard into her eyes.

For a second Isabelle almost didn't recognize Nine. He had his game face on now. The loving husband and father had been displaced by the ruthless, dispassionate operative she once knew.

Nine continued, "Who took Francis, and why, I can only guess. I have a few ideas, but nothing concrete." He spoke almost in a monotone voice, as if reciting a script. In a way he was. Nine was falling back on his years of training to become an elite operative with the Omega Agency. In his mind's eye he could see his old mentor, Special Agent Tommy Kentbridge, lecturing him and the other orphan-operatives on what to do in just such a situation; he could almost hear him speaking. *For every problem, there's a solution.* Nine just hoped that was true.

Isabelle went to interrupt, but thought better of it.

"I have to act now. The longer I wait the less chance we have of finding him."

"Oh Sebastian, what are we going to do?" Isabelle collapsed sobbing into his arms.

Nine caressed her, but his mind remained detached and on the problem at hand. A plan was beginning to form. He held Isabelle out at arm's length. "Whoever it was who took Francis will have spirited him out of the islands."

Isabelle looked mortified. She hadn't considered that her beloved son could have been taken away from the Marquesas Islands.

Nine continued, "I suspect they've taken him to the States."

"America? But why? And who are they?" She hesitated for a moment. "It's Omega, isn't it?"

Nine sighed. *She's reached the same conclusion I have.* He stood up. "I don't have any proof, but yes it could only be Omega."

Isabelle became hysterical. She'd witnessed first hand the agency's ruthlessness. The thought of Francis being in Omega's hands terrified her. Nine tried to calm her, but she screamed over top of him. "We must tell the authorities it's Omega!"

"No!" Nine could feel his patience running out. The last thing he needed now was a hysterical wife trying to run the show. He knew the job ahead of him would be difficult enough without that. "Omega doesn't even officially exist, Isabelle."

"But surely somebody can do some research and--"

Cutting her off he said, "Remember, Omega is above the police, the FBI, the CIA, even the President. And it has eyes and ears everywhere. If I lodged an official complaint with any of the law enforcement authorities, I'd be apprehended and handed over to the agency before I could blink."

"But they'll kill Francis!"

"No they won't!" Nine had to shout to make himself heard. Not wanting to precipitate another heart attack, he forced himself to calm down. "If they wanted to kill him, they'd have done that already," he said quietly. He reminded Isabelle of the lengths the two men had gone to, to abduct their son. "Those weren't the actions of people out to kill him."

That got through to Isabelle. She calmed herself down enough to take a breath. "I'm sorry. You're right of course."

"No, it's me who should be sorry. If I hadn't once been part of Omega, we wouldn't be in this terrible situation." He kissed her forehead.

"What will you do?"

"I have to get to the States. I can't explain every detail to you, my darling. What I need is for you to trust me. Can you do that?"

Isabelle nodded. In such matters, she trusted him implicitly.

"Good. Get dressed and packed. You're coming with me to Papeete." Nine considered it likely the floatplane had flown to Tahiti. That was within its flight range whereas mainland USA, and even Hawaii, was well beyond it. But that wasn't why he was going to Papeete. He had something to do in the Tahitian capital before continuing to America.

Isabelle sprang into action. She dressed quickly then began packing. As she packed, memories of what Omega had done to her, and her deceased parents, replayed over and over in her mind. Her fears were increasing by the minute.

4

While Isabelle finished packing, Nine walked down steps leading to the bungalow's basement. There, behind a false wall panel, he retrieved a variety of items he'd stored for just such an emergency. They included disguise-aids such as a fake moustache, cosmetics, hair dyes, contact lenses and facial prosthetics. He scooped these up and placed them inside a long black makeup kit designed to be strapped to his chest. Other items included several falsified passports he'd acquired during and since his days as an active Omega operative.

Nine returned to the bedroom upstairs and found Isabelle sobbing uncontrollably as she studied a framed photograph of Francis. Nine took her in his arms and held her tight. Gradually,

Isabelle's sobbing subsided. "You okay?" he asked somewhat lamely.

"What do you think?"

Nine had no answer. He could see his wife was beside herself with worry, but he was now in operational mode and his mindset was such he had no time for histrionics. "Did you speak to the police yesterday?"

Pulling herself together, Isabelle nodded. "Yes, I spoke to the local gendarme and to a reporter from the paper." She described in detail what she'd told the gendarme.

Nine then phoned the gendarmes' office. After two attempts, he got hold of the same gendarme who had interviewed Isabelle the previous day. Within minutes he learned the local authorities hadn't a clue who had abducted Francis. Nor had there been any sightings of the floatplane since local fishermen had reported seeing it depart Taiohae Bay soon after Francis' abduction.

Nine quickly relayed his description of the plane to the gendarme and asked him to alert the Tahitian authorities of its likely arrival there. The gendarme assured him that had already been done. He and his colleagues had also concluded that Tahiti was the plane's likely destination. If they were right, Francis and his abductors had long since reached Tahiti and, in all probability, were already in or on their way to America – or wherever it was they were bound.

#

Nine and Isabelle caught a mid-day flight to Papeete. She used the two-hour flight to catch up on lost sleep while he used the time to try to make sense of the recent events and also plan his next steps.

Fighting against the tiredness that threatened to overwhelm him – a side-effect of the cocktail of drugs the doctor had prescribed – Nine reviewed what he knew and what he suspected. He knew professionals had abducted his son for he came from their world and recognized the signs; he knew they'd targeted Francis for they sought him out amongst all the other children; and he knew they'd taken him away in the floatplane.

That was the extent of what he knew. There were still so many unanswered questions. *Why has Omega come back for me now after so many years? Why did they take Francis and not me? What do they hope to gain?*

"A drink, sir?"

Nine's thoughts were interrupted by an airline hostess pushing a drinks trolley along the aisle. He ordered a strong black coffee, hoping that would help keep him awake.

Once served, he turned his attention to his next step. Something told him he needed to contact his old nemesis Andrew Naylor, the head of the Omega Agency. *If Omega's involved, he'll know about it.* After all, the Pedemont Project and the Twenty Three orphan-operatives who had evolved out of that groundbreaking experiment was Naylor's brainchild.

Thinking of Naylor reminded Nine how much he hated the man. He blamed him personally for the years he spent as a prisoner of Chicago's Pedemont Orphanage, being trained to become an elite operative; he also blamed him for the deaths of his mother, Annette Hannar, his mentor, Tommy Kentbridge, Isabelle's parents, and his childhood sweetheart, Helen Katsarakis, whose only crime was that she had befriended him.

Nine thought back to his last sighting of Naylor. That had been at the off-limits Bilderberg conference at Saint Michael's Mount, in Cornwall, England, just before he'd gotten off the grid. It turned out Naylor was also a senior Bilderberger.

On that occasion, Nine had convinced Naylor he knew all about the Omega Agency's horrific scientific experiments on children at a secret medical laboratory, or orphanage, in Germany's Black Forest. He'd produced graphic photographs to back up what he was saying, and advised that copies of those, together with other incriminating documents, had been left with attorneys in Berlin and London. That had given him the leverage he needed to escape Omega's clutches. He'd warned Naylor that his attorneys had been instructed to release the documents to the media should anything untoward ever happen to himself or Isabelle. Naylor had been only too happy to agree to his terms.

What has changed in the last five years?

Nine couldn't imagine what had so emboldened Naylor that he'd suddenly be prepared to risk everything he and Omega had worked so long and hard to achieve. Naylor had always been paranoid about protecting the agency's secrecy. While the former orphan-operative had the option of contacting his attorneys and ordering the release of the incriminating documents, he realized that wouldn't leave him with any leverage when he confronted Naylor over the whereabouts of his son. Worse, he'd almost certainly never see Francis again.

It gradually dawned on Nine that Francis' abduction could somehow be connected to the Black Forest orphanage or one of the other underground medical labs Omega was rumored to be operating elsewhere in the world. Whilst with Omega, Nine had heard the rumors that the agency was conducting illegal scientific experiments on genetically enhanced children at various isolated labs. He'd seen it for himself in Germany, and didn't doubt for a minute there could be others.

Nine shuddered at the thought of Francis ending up in such a place. He tried to dispel the memories of the grotesque and zombie-like children he'd seen at the Black Forest orphanage. The memories persisted. *Why Francis?* Connecting the dots, he knew it would be common knowledge within Omega that his son shared some of his unique genes. As far as he knew, he was the only one of the Pedemont orphans who had a child.

He kept coming back to the same conclusion: if Omega had become aware of Francis' existence, they'd abducted him for some scientific experiment. It didn't bear thinking about.

Finally succumbing to his tiredness, Nine fell asleep only to be immediately wakened by an announcement over the intercom that the plane would soon be landing in Papeete.

5

fter Taiohae, the main street of Tahiti's capital Papeete always seemed more like Paris's iconic Avenue des Champs-Elysees to Nine and Isabelle. Tourists and locals competed for space as they paraded up and down the busy street. The cab that the pair traveled in even had to negotiate a minor traffic jam as they were ferried from Faa'a International Airport to their hotel.

While Nine was desperate to fly to America to begin his search for Francis, he had some urgent matters to attend to first. His first priority was to ascertain what the Tahitian authorities were doing, if anything, about Francis' abduction and whether they had received any reported sightings of him or the floatplane.

A phone call to the offices of both the French National Police and the Gendarmerie confirmed there had been no sightings of Francis or the plane, and until there was they were powerless to act.

Ending the call, Nine pocketed his cell phone. He couldn't bring himself to look at Isabelle who had been hanging on to every word, choosing instead to look out the cab's rear window at the sights of Papeete.

"Nothing at all?" Isabelle asked.

"Nothing," Nine mumbled.

Isabelle began weeping silently. Nine put one comforting arm around her as he tried to make sense of the fact that the floatplane had not been sighted in Tahitian waters or airspace. He considered various scenarios. *The plane could have crashed. It could have flown to another island. It could have transferred Francis to a boat out at sea.* He knew all were possibilities, but kept his thoughts to himself.

Nine's next priority was to ensure his wife's safety before departing Tahiti. He realized he couldn't take her with him, especially not in her pregnant state. She was already entering her eighth month and the baby could arrive any day.

Isabelle had also insisted that Nine consult with his heart specialist while they were in Papeete. He'd reluctantly agreed after she made it abundantly clear she wouldn't take no for an answer. So the specialist's clinic would be his next port of call after they checked in at their hotel.

As Nine paid the cabbie and escorted Isabelle into the hotel, he didn't notice they were being observed. If he had, he'd have been concerned. His observer was a fellow orphan-operative from the Omega Agency.

Number Twenty Three, who was the youngest of the Pedemont orphans, recognized Nine immediately. Living and training with each other day in, day out for the best part of eighteen years at the orphanage meant it was improbable any would forget their fellow orphans.

Omega Director Andrew Naylor had ordered Twenty Three to fly to Tahiti to look out for the rogue operative. He had anticipated Nine would act quickly to find his son and Papeete would be his first port of call. Naylor wanted to keep tabs on

Nine's movements at all times as he knew how troublesome he could be.

Twenty Three, a suntanned and fit-looking individual who dressed casually to fit in with the locals, was getting to know Papeete well. This was his third visit to the Tahitian capital since a fellow orphan-operative had spotted Nine arriving for one of his quarterly consultations with his specialist. That had been a year earlier. Since then Twenty Three had been tasked with keeping tabs on Nine.

As soon as Nine and Isabelle disappeared from view, Twenty Three fished his cell phone from the pocket of his floral shirt and speed-dialed a number. "It's Sandy Phipps." He used the nom de plume of his current character. Omega's orphan-operatives never traveled as themselves. "I've seen our Mister Darrell Royden," he said, using Omega's code name for Nine. "He's traveling under the name Sebastian Anderson."

Nine had adopted the name *Sebastian Anderson* soon after fleeing the Omega Agency. Even at the risk of being tracked down, he'd refused to forsake his Christian name. After all, that was the name his mother had given him.

Twenty Three finished relaying his information then set up a watching brief from a café opposite the hotel's front entrance.

#

Omega boss Andrew Naylor sat alone with his thoughts as he digested the news he'd just received from Twenty Three. It was as he'd expected: Nine's search for his son had begun.

The hard-nosed, sixty-three-year-old was in his office at the agency's headquarters in southwest Illinois. Omega HQ was a subterranean facility hidden deep below an abandoned hydro dam. It wasn't to be found in any telephone directories. Few in the US federal government knew of its existence, and even fewer outside it knew – such was the level of secrecy that surrounded this, the world's most powerful and influential intelligence agency.

A recent image of Nine filled a large video screen set into the wall facing Naylor's desk. It had been taken by Twenty Three during Nine's previous visit to Papeete three months earlier. The former operative looked tanned, happy and relaxed.

Staring at the image, Naylor was worried. He feared that

Nine could do what he'd threatened to do years ago and instruct his attorneys to release information that would make life extremely difficult for him and for Omega. That information included evidence linking Naylor and the agency to illegal scientific experiments on children at the Black Forest orphanage in Germany.

While he'd ordered the immediate destruction of the lab, the possible repercussions resulting from the release of such information made him shudder. The good name he'd forged for himself as recently retired Director of the CIA, and chairman – past and present – of numerous major organizations, would be subjected to the minutest scrutiny. If the allegations were ever proven, he'd be vilified and imprisoned.

However, Naylor had considered all that. He'd thought of little else since learning of Nine's whereabouts and his family situation a year earlier. The gains to be had from adding Francis, with his unique set of genes, to Omega's secret medical program outweighed the risk of Nine going public. And to the best of his knowledge, the former operative never knew the existence of, let alone the whereabouts, of the other underground labs Omega operated around the globe.

Naylor was gambling that Nine would realize he'd never see Francis again if he ordered the release of the so-called evidence. He hoped the rogue operative would be aware that Omega would terminate Francis and the other children under its control if he went public.

As always when he was worried or stressed, Naylor could feel his lazy eye start to twitch. He cursed his lazy eye: it had made him the butt of private jokes within the agency and it advertised to all and sundry that he was under pressure. The damned twitch had ensured he rarely succeeded at poker – a game he'd had a lifelong love affair with but which had never returned him a decent dividend.

There was a knock on the door and a prim secretary looked in. "Marcia Wilson is on the line for you, sir."

"Thank you." Naylor waved his secretary away then pushed a button on a control panel on his desktop. On the video screen before him, the image of Nine was replaced by a live video feed from the office of his successor at the CIA. There was no sign of firm's newly appointed director, though she could be heard talking to her personal assistant off screen. All that could be seen for the moment was Marcia's desk and chair. The paperless desktop supported a laptop, three color-coded telephones and a miniature American flag.

The static scene reminded Naylor he'd sat behind that very desk not that long ago. That was before Marcia had succeeded him. He'd personally groomed the no-nonsense, fortysomething African-American to take over from him as Director of the CIA ever since she'd made her mark as a senior agent at the Omega Agency. Of all the moles Omega had in high places, she was the standout success.

Finally Marcia came into view. She sat down behind her desk and nodded to the camera. "Hello Andrew. Good news I hope?"

"Yes." Naylor proceeded to update Marcia on the latest developments concerning Nine and his son. Marcia seemed relieved all was going to plan. Before ending the call, Naylor reminded her of an earlier arrangement they'd made. "You will help us find Darrell Royden, right?"

Marcia knew that Naylor was using the codename allocated to Nine. "As soon as you give me his flight details and ETA, I'll send people to the airport."

"Okay, but they're to tail him only. They're not to touch him until I give the word."

Marcia was aware Naylor was still worried about the information Nine had on the Black Forest lab. "Understood." She wondered what Naylor had planned for the rogue operative once he was apprehended.

As if reading Marcia's mind, Naylor added, "When the time's right, we'll take care of the problem."

Marcia was in no doubt what Naylor meant by that.

6

Isabelle sat alone in her hotel room watching an early evening news report on television. In a pre-recorded interview, a gendarme was talking to a female reporter about Francis' abduction. He expressed grave concerns for the boy's safety and acknowledged the authorities had no clues to follow.

A photo of a de Havilland Canada DHC-3 Otter floatplane, like the one that took Francis away, filled the screen. When it was replaced by a recent photo of her son, Isabelle broke down. She had to turn the volume up using the TV remote so that she could hear the rest of the interview above her sobs. The interview ended with the gendarme asking the public to report any sightings of the boy or the floatplane.

Isabelle muted the volume and resumed reading the latest issue of Tahiti's daily newspaper, *Les Nouvelles*. Francis' abduction was the lead story. Again, a photo of Francis added to Isabelle's grief.

She was still crying several minutes later when Nine walked in. He'd been to see his heart specialist, keeping the earlier promise he'd made to his wife.

"Sebastian!" Isabelle stood up and stumbled into Nine's arms.

Nine's eyes strayed to the photo of Francis on the newspaper's front page. He didn't need to ask what was causing Isabelle's distress.

Finally, Isabelle made an effort to pull herself together. Drying her eyes, she asked, "What did the specialist say?"

"He confirmed what our doctor back home said," Nine lied. "I had a mild heart attack and shouldn't over-exert myself." He pointed to several bottles of heart pills he'd placed on a tabletop a few seconds earlier. "As you can see, he has given me more medication."

Nine was making a good fist of shielding Isabelle from the truth. His specialist had confirmed he'd only suffered a mild heart attack, but he'd also warned that Nine needed an operation to mitigate the risk of another more serious attack. And he needed it sooner rather than later. However, Nine saw no point in sharing any of that with Isabelle. It wouldn't help her. Nor would it help him find Francis.

What Nine did share was his latest plans: he told Isabelle he'd arranged for her to stay with Thai friends who lived in a commune a short drive from Papeete. They were related to Nine's former Buddhist master, Luang. Although the monk's family members were mourning his violent death, they were only too happy to offer sanctuary to Isabelle.

"It's important no-one knows where you are," Nine said. He didn't need to explain that Omega could use her to get to him if she fell into their hands. "Chai will collect you later tonight."

Isabelle nodded, indicating she understood. She and Nine knew Chai well. He was Luang's nephew.

Isabelle realized Nine would not be able to communicate

with her due to Omega's advanced global surveillance network. She suddenly became concerned at the thought of not knowing if her husband was okay or whether he'd rescued their son. "How will I know what's going on?"

"I'll risk sending one email when I've found Francis." He handed Isabelle a slip of paper. "As you can see, I've set up an email account for you under an assumed name. Memorize that in case you lose it. It's your user name and password."

Isabelle took the slip of paper from him.

Nine continued, "In two or three days, you should start checking your emails every couple of days, but only at an Internet café. Nowhere else. And never the same place twice."

Isabelle wasn't happy, but she resigned herself to being kept in the dark until Francis was found.

There was more bad news to come. Nine sat Isabelle down and looked into her eyes. "There's something else you need to know."

Isabelle braced herself.

Nine took a deep breath. He knew this wasn't going to go

down well. "We'll never be able to return home. They know where we live now, so we will always be at risk in this part of the world."

That came as a shock to Isabelle. Since relocating to French Polynesia, she'd never envisaged living anywhere else. It was Utopia as far as she was concerned. "Where will we go?" she asked.

"I've made arrangements."

"Where, Sebastian?"

"Vanuatu."

Isabelle looked at Nine in horror. The Frenchwoman knew little about Vanuatu other than that it was an island territory somewhere near Papua New Guinea on the other side of the Pacific. She seemed to recall it was inhabited by fierce cannibal tribes, but wasn't sure.

7

Toward midnight, Nine secreted Isabelle out the hotel's rear door, away from any prying eyes that may be monitoring the establishment's front entrance. Although he hadn't spotted anything untoward, he knew it was possible that Omega had someone on the ground in Papeete watching out for him.

The couple followed a path leading away from the town. They walked slowly to allow for Isabelle's pregnant state. Nine supported her as best he could given he was also carrying her suitcase and extra travel bag.

After several minutes, they reached the main road where a Jeep awaited them. Nine led Isabelle straight to it.

A wiry Thai youth jumped out of the vehicle and opened the

front passenger door for Isabelle. He nodded respectfully to Nine while helping Isabelle climb into the Jeep. Nine threw her luggage onto the back seat.

No introductions were needed for the youth was Luang's nephew Chai, and they'd socialized with him and his family on many occasions. Chai lived with family members in a small, self-contained commune for other Thais and expatriates. It was half an hour's drive inland – close enough to civilization should Isabelle need to get to hospital, but isolated enough to escape prying eyes.

As Chai climbed back behind the wheel and prepared to drive away, Nine reached inside and held Isabelle. "Don't worry, everything will work out."

Isabelle kissed him fiercely as if for the last time. "Find Francis!" She clung to her husband tightly.

Nine had to physically prize her fingers from around his arms. "You must leave now before someone sees you." He turned to their Thai friend. "Look after her, Chai. And thank you."

The Jeep drove off into the night, leaving Nine staring after it and its precious passenger. He hoped he'd see his wife again, but the ninth orphan had a sickening feeling that he may not. With his heart condition, Isabelle's pregnant state and Francis' abduction, Nine knew something had to give. He sensed it would be impossible to succeed on every single front in this mission: either he'd be terminated or his wife and son would be harmed, or worse, killed.

In the front seat of the departing vehicle, Isabelle looked back until her beloved Sebastian was swallowed up by the darkness. She touched the ruby that hung from the silver necklace Nine had given her and uttered a silent prayer.

Nine stood on the side of the road listening until the sound of the Jeep's engine completely faded. He suddenly felt very lonely. The feeling took him back to when, as an operative in Omega's employ, he had experienced such utter loneliness he'd been driven to despair. That had all changed when he met Isabelle and they had a child. Now Omega had separated him from them both.

The feeling of loneliness was gradually replaced by another feeling. It burned like hot coals in his gut. At first he didn't recognize the feeling. It gradually intensified. Now he recognized the feeling: it was anger. Nine welcomed it. He embraced it and vowed to channel his anger to enable him to find his son and destroy those who had taken him away.

#

Elsewhere in the Pacific at that moment, in a different time zone, Francis was about to be transferred ashore from a freighter. The location was Honolulu Harbor, on the main Hawaiian island of Oahu, and the freighter was the Liberian-registered *Seven Seas*.

After Francis was abducted in Taiohae, the floatplane had flown north toward Hawaii, not south to Tahiti as Nine had presumed. It had flown almost to the limit of its fuel reserves before landing at sea to rendezvous with a vessel. After refueling at sea, it had continued its flight north and rendezvoused with the *Seven Seas*, which took delivery of the abducted boy. The seaplane had refueled again and continued to Honolulu followed by the freighter and its human consignment.

In the sick bay aboard the *Seven Seas*, a sedated Francis was being attended to by a nurse in Omega's employ. Sixtysomething Nurse Hilda had cared for Nine and the other orphans as young children and then as teenagers at the Pedemont Orphanage. The irony of caring for the son of one of them wasn't lost on her. She was aware Francis had been abducted.

In Francis' drugged state, conversation with him had been limited to a few words. He'd asked when he could see his parents, and Nurse Hilda had assured him he'd be reunited with them soon. The nurse knew that was unlikely. While her low level security rating meant she was not privy to many of Omega's dark secrets, she knew enough about its scientific experiments on children, and the clandestine experimental labs it operated around the world, to know that Francis would be considered a prize catch by her Omega masters. With the superior genes he'd inherited from his genetically engineered father, it was a no-brainer those same genes could be used in the cloning of more *perfect* human beings.

Although the agency's scientists had long since mastered the science of cloning, they'd never had access to the progeny of any of the Pedemont orphans before. To Omega's knowledge, Nine was the only orphan-operative to have had a child. An experimental drug the agency had given to the other orphans –

after Nine had fled Omega five years earlier – had inadvertently rendered them infertile. The drug had been intended to enhance mind-control prompts Omega had imbedded in the minds of each in their childhood. While it had the desired effect, it had also had unfortunate side-effects of which infertility was one.

Fortunately, Nine had escaped all that. Even more fortunate, from Omega's perspective, his wife had given birth to a child.

Nurse Hilda was also aware that Francis' DNA would be useful in some of the illicit scientific experiments the agency's medical people were carrying out on human guinea pigs in its various underground labs. One of its many legitimate businesses, *KaizerSimonsKovak*, just happened to be the world's number one pharmaceutical company, and Omega was anxious to protect its market share and the huge revenues it generated. Those same revenues helped finance Omega's activities.

Like all companies in the legal drug trade, *KaizerSimonsKovak* needed to test new drugs before releasing them onto the market. While its competitors tested their new drugs mostly on rats, mice and monkeys, *KSK* had the advantage of being able to test them on humans. No *KSK* employee, or indeed anyone outside Omega, was aware of that, however. All testing was contracted out – to another Omega-owned company. And its modus operandi was far from legal.

Francis drifted off to sleep, prompting Nurse Hilda to study the boy's angelic face. She brushed a strand of his dark, curly hair from his forehead. The nurse had no children of her own. She'd lost a child – a son – in childbirth. Even though that had been thirty years ago, she still had strong maternal instincts and these were being aroused now.

Nurse Hilda tried not to think about what was in store for Francis. She busied herself preparing a change of clothes for him to wear later.

A wall-mounted telephone rang. The nurse answered it.

The caller was her immediate superior, Doctor Andrews, who ran the agency's cloning initiative and also its underground labs around the world. He was calling from Omega's HQ. "How's our patient?" Doctor Andrews asked.

"He's fine. Sleepy but fine."

"Good. He's to be kept sedated for the transfer to the airport."

"Of course."

"Stay close to him. Naylor doesn't want any slip-ups." The line went dead.

Nurse Hilda knew Francis was to be flown to his final destination – wherever that may be – aboard a private jet, which had arrived in Honolulu around the same time as the freighter. If the rumors she'd heard about the experimental labs were even half true, she thought it likely the boy would never reach adulthood – certainly not with all his faculties intact.

The nurse looked down at Francis, and her heart went out to him.

8

apeete's Faa'ā International Airport was already bulging at the seams when Nine arrived to catch his mid-morning Air Tahiti Nui flight to Los Angeles. His arrival at the airport coincided with the arrival in quick succession of three international flights and the delayed departure of two international flights including the one he was booked on; he was resigned to further delays.

While Nine was booked to continue on to Chicago after a two-hour stopover in Los Angeles, he had no intention of being on that particular flight. He suspected people would be looking out for him and he didn't intend making it easy for them.

After reporting to the Air Tahiti Nui check-in counter and handing over his suitcase, he chose to wait in the busy Public

Lounge rather than going through to the more private Departure Lounge. This suited Twenty Three who was at that moment observing Nine from a distance. He was under orders to report back to Omega as soon as the former orphan-operative boarded his flight.

Twenty Three made sure he kept several people between him and his mark at all times. Even if Nine had looked directly at his former colleague he probably wouldn't have recognized him: Twenty Three was disguised as a hippy complete with dreadlocks and droopy moustache, and he even carried a guitar which hung by its cord over one shoulder. Even so, Twenty Three wasn't taking any chances.

Like all Omega's orphan-operatives, the twenty third-born orphan was an accomplished shapeshifter, adept at taking on new guises at short notice. It was an art they'd had to perfect as they traveled the globe, usually to hostile places and often to terminate someone. Their lives depended on it.

Twenty Three was relieved Nine hadn't resorted to disguising himself. The ninth orphan was acknowledged among his former colleagues as being without peer in the art of shapeshifting. A *human chameleon*, his former Omega masters had called him. The fact that Nine was traveling as himself flagged to Twenty Three that he didn't believe Omega would be looking for him, or he didn't care.

Closer to the delayed departure time, Nine disappeared into a men's restroom, carrying an airline travel bag. Twenty Three thought nothing of it, but when his former colleague hadn't re-emerged after ten minutes, he began to fret. After another five minutes, he was sure something was wrong and hurried to investigate. His heart sank when he found the restroom unoccupied.

Twenty Three discovered Nine's discarded travel bag in one of the vacant cubicles. It was stuffed full of the former operative's discarded clothing. A quick inspection of the contents revealed Nine had replaced his shirt, jacket and even his shoes.

Nine had vacated the restroom ten minutes earlier. Not as himself, but as an elderly man. Five minutes was all he'd needed to effect his new guise. Making full use of the disguise aids he carried on his person and in his travel bag, he could now pass for an eighty-year-old. His smart casual gear had been replaced by grey trousers and matching grey cardigan, which he wore over a white shirt and striped tie; his fashionable slip-ons had been replaced by black lace-up shoes; he wore spectacles, and colored contact lenses ensured his distinctive green eyes were now brown.

To top off his disguise, Nine walked with a stoop and appeared reliant on a walking-stick he used with practiced precision. It was a telescopic stick he'd secreted into the restroom in his travel bag.

Cursing, Twenty Three hurried from the restroom and frantically searched the faces of people in the Public Lounge. He didn't realize it, but he'd looked straight at Nine as he emerged from the restroom earlier.

While Twenty Three was pursuing a lost cause in the Public Lounge, Nine had already checked himself in again, but this time as a Mister Charles Morris, the fictional resident of a Los Angeles rest home for the aged. And this time he was booked to fly to Honolulu, not Los Angeles, and he was flying Air New Zealand, not Air Tahiti Nui.

While Nine was anxious to get to mainland America to pick up his son's trail, he knew Omega would be expecting him to do exactly that. So he'd opted to fly to Honolulu first. It would add a few hours to his flight, but it would help keep Omega off his scent.

Minutes later, as a frustrated Twenty Three unsuccessfully tried to identify Nine among the passengers boarding the Air Tahiti Nui flight to Los Angeles, the former operative was boarding the Air New Zealand flight to Honolulu.

Twenty Three realized he'd been duped. Fishing his cell phone from his shirt pocket, he speed-dialed a number. Omega boss Andrew Naylor answered the call. Twenty Three proceeded to deliver the bad news to Naylor. He had to hold the phone away from his ear until Naylor finished shouting at him.

Meanwhile, aboard the Air New Zealand plane that was now preparing for take-off, Nine allowed himself to be assisted to his Business Class seat by a pretty Maori hostess who was keen to ensure the elderly traveler didn't have a mishap. Safely seated, he thanked the hostess and smiled to himself: he considered the sacrifice of the empty suitcase he'd handed over at the Air Tahiti Nui check-in counter, and the travel bag he'd left behind, a small price to pay for his anonymity.

As the Air New Zealand flight took off, Nine had no way of knowing his sleeping son was being stretchered aboard a private jet that was about to depart Honolulu International Airport at that very moment.

9

While Francis and his father were being whisked across the Pacific in separate aircraft, Nine's former colleague and fellow orphan, Seventeen, was sitting down for dinner with her elderly grandfather in the neat bungalow they shared in Glen Ellyn, in Chicago's upmarket western suburbs.

Eighty eight-year-old Sebastian Hannar had aged alarmingly since Seventeen had arrived unannounced on his doorstep on a windy winter's evening four years earlier. Frail then, he'd deteriorated to the point where his doctor considered he should now be in a rest home. However, Seventeen, now thirty-five, wouldn't hear of it. She credited her grandfather with saving her life, and had vowed she wouldn't hand over responsibility for caring for him while she was still able to draw breath.

However, looking at him now as he pecked at the dinner she'd lovingly prepared, she knew his days were numbered. Sebastian suffered Alzheimer's and had advanced osteoporosis. The former had rendered his memory almost useless and the latter had left him permanently stooped and confined to a wheelchair. With each passing week, his symptoms worsened and his quality of life waned.

Despite all that, prescription drugs kept him largely pain-free, and Seventeen imagined that deep down, on some level, he enjoyed his granddaughter's company and the comforts of home, though he couldn't articulate that: his utterances were monosyllabic these days.

The bungalow they shared was at least half a century old and small, but it was comfortable and all either of them needed or desired. For Seventeen, it was a refuge from a world that frightened her – a world she no longer felt part of.

Over the past four years, Seventeen had largely gotten herself together with the help of her grandfather in the first couple of years. Physically, she was almost back to her old self: her icy, blue eyes were clear, her blonde hair shone and her body was still toned and athletic. Mentally, she had somehow pulled herself out of the abyss she'd fallen into, and had managed to retain her sanity.

She had never regained her old confidence, however, and seldom ventured out of the house except to shop for essentials or take Sebastian to the doctor. Occasionally, she'd work out at a local gym or go to a movie, but such outings were becoming less frequent.

Seventeen had often tried to make sense of what happened to her before she'd landed on her grandfather. She remembered snippets of her years as an elite operative with the Omega Agency, and prior to that as an orphan at the Pedemont Orphanage, but the memories were hazy.

The memories, and the nightmares, were also disturbing. Flashes came to her at the oddest of times: in the shower, watching television, baking, gardening. They included assassinations – shootings, knifings, strangulation, poisoning – she'd carried out for Omega. She could remember the victims' faces, and occasionally their names, but couldn't recall why she'd killed them.

Seventeen had given up trying to banish the ugly memories. She accepted they were part of who she was, and had decided to get on with life as best she could.

For some reason, memories of her years at the orphanage over on Chicago's South Side were clearer. She could recall nearly every one of her fellow orphans and much of the relentless training regime they were forced to follow in order to graduate as Omega operatives.

One orphan in particular stood out whenever she thought of them: Number Nine. Seventeen also knew him as Sebastian, for Nine had confided in her that their mentor, Special Agent Kentbridge, had advised him of the Christian name his mother had given him before she'd had to give him up to Omega.

What Seventeen couldn't remember was that Nine's mother was also hers. While they came from the sperm of numerous fathers as part of *The Pedemont Project*, they shared the same mother, Annette Hannar, which meant they were siblings. Nine was aware of that as Kentbridge had told him. That meant

Annette's father, Sebastian Senior, was grandfather to both Seventeen and Nine, though the latter had no idea of his existence.

How Seventeen had learned of Sebastian Senior's existence, or where he lived, she couldn't recall. What she could recall was how grateful she'd been to be taken in by him. He'd nursed her back to health and, she truly believed, had saved her from going completely insane.

Seventeen had obviously registered that her grandfather and Nine shared the same Christian name, but had considered that nothing more than one of life's coincidences.

Looking at him now, as he slept in his wheelchair, Seventeen felt she'd burst with love and devotion for him. Sebastian was the only real family she'd ever known. Before he'd developed Alzheimer's, he told Seventeen about her mother, about how fun-loving she'd been as a girl and what a beautiful young woman she'd grown into. Every day, he'd assured his granddaughter that she reminded him of Annette.

Seventeen's gaze went to the faded color portrait photograph of her mother that had pride of place on the dining room mantelpiece. She never tired of looking at it, and wished she'd known the beautiful, dark-haired woman whose striking green eyes seemed to look right into her soul.

As she often did when she looked at her mother's photo, Seventeen looked wistfully at the index finger of her left hand. It had once displayed a ruby ring – the only thing she'd inherited from her mother. She couldn't remember what had happened to it.

Omega boss Andrew Naylor had given Seventeen the ring in another lifetime. That was back when she was the agency's golden girl. Naylor had told Seventeen it was her mother's. He'd also told her that Annette had died of a drug overdose a year or two after giving birth to her.

The first part at least was true: the ring had belonged to her mother. However, Annette hadn't died of an overdose. She'd been terminated on Naylor's orders.

10

Although Seventeen hadn't a clue what had caused her memory loss, her meltdown or her dismissal from the Omega Agency, there was someone who did.

Andrew Naylor knew very well what had gone down. It was on his orders that Seventeen and all her fellow orphans be subjected to an insidious mind control program while still only children. Known as *MK-Ultra*, the program allowed the orphans' controllers to put their young charges into a mind-controlled state by using voice-commands. The same program was widely reported by mainstream media to have been used by the CIA, using American soldiers as guinea pigs – a fact the firm later admitted.

As it transpired, MK-Ultra was never actively used long-term on any of the Omega orphans – with one notable exception:

Seventeen.

Naylor, who had always lusted after the seventeenth-born orphan, had misused his powers and treated the blue-eyed blonde as his personal sex slave. He'd resorted to using the MK-Ultra voice-commands to induce her to do whatever he asked. No-one else was aware of this. Not even his victim. In the process, after years of abuse, Seventeen had finally cracked. In medical terms, she had suffered a mental breakdown; in truth, she'd become yet another victim of MK-Ultra, and of Naylor.

Although he was the cause of Seventeen's miserable state, Naylor had not a shred of conscience. In his own words, he didn't *do* conscience.

After Seventeen had botched her last two assignments for Omega, Naylor's first instinct had been to order her termination. Only the timely intervention of Marcia Wilson had dissuaded him. That was back when Marcia was Naylor's second-in-command at Omega and before she took over directorship of the CIA from him. Marcia had cautioned that Seventeen could be useful should her brother, Nine, ever come out of hiding and cause Omega any problems.

Naylor had immediately seen the wisdom in that, and took steps to release Seventeen into the custody of her grandfather whose existence he'd known of since he'd recruited the orphan's mother for *the Pedemont Project*. Using MK-Ultra for the last time, Naylor programmed Seventeen so she would remember her grandfather's Glen Ellyn address even though she'd never been there and had no knowledge of the old man's existence.

Thus it had been almost inevitable that Seventeen would end up at 123 College Avenue, Glen Ellyn.

Naylor hadn't thought about Seventeen in a while. Only the unexpected reappearance of Nine had reawakened his interest in the woman. Truth be known, he still harbored lustful feelings for her.

For now, though, his focus was on Nine and his son Francis. Three days had elapsed since the boy's abduction and two days since the last sighting of Nine at Papeete's Faa'ā International Airport. Isabelle's whereabouts were unknown also as she hadn't been seen since she and Nine checked in at the hotel in Papeete.

Naylor was certain that Isabelle was still in Tahiti, and had ordered Twenty Three to find her. She would give him leverage if Nine caught up with him or otherwise caused problems. Naylor knew the best disguise in the world wouldn't hide Isabelle's pregnant state and she'd be spotted if she tried to fly anywhere as Omega had *eyes* at all the airports.

The Omega boss was also certain Nine was coming for him. Nine would know that he had ordered Francis' abduction and therefore would assume he knew where the boy was being taken. In anticipation of that, Naylor had turned his castle-like mansion in rural Illinois' Saint Clair County into a veritable Fort Knox and was guarded around the clock by handpicked Omega operatives. He traveled with an armed escort to and from his place of work at Omega's nearby underground headquarters, and made sure he was never alone.

In the past twenty-four hours, the Omega boss had come round to the idea that Nine should be terminated at the first opportunity. While Naylor remained nervous about the inevitable scrutiny he and Omega would be subjected to if and when the

Black Forest lab documentation was released, he'd realized that Nine, alive, presented a greater risk. The bottom line was the evidence had been destroyed and the allegations could never be proven.

As for Francis, he'd been delivered safely to another of Omega's underground medical labs the previous day after a full physical assessment by Doctor Andrews. The doctor had given the boy the all-clear, confirming he was in good health and, more to the point, a perfect candidate for the experimentation that awaited him.

Yawning, Naylor's thoughts turned to bed, or more accurately they turned to what awaited him there. He'd been burning the midnight oil in his den. Despite the late hour, it was hot and humid. Sweat rolled down his brow and he dabbed at it with a handkerchief. Not for the first time that day, he cursed Illinois' summers. They were long and hot. Naylor was already looking forward to the fall, and it wasn't even mid-summer yet.

Before retiring, he made a quick call to the cell phone of one of the three operatives he knew were currently on duty either inside or outside his home. "Leroy, this is Naylor," he said into the phone. "Everything alright?"

"Yessir," the answer came back loud and clear.

"Good. I'm turning in." Naylor hung up then hurried upstairs. Long-since divorced, he was anxious to entertain the latest piece of skirt to have taken his fancy – a sultry, teenage, Asian hooker who had been chauffeured to Naylor's home earlier by another long-suffering Omega staffer.

An excited Naylor found the hooker stretched out and near-naked on his bed. A whirring overhead ceiling fan did little to ease the humidity. Both Naylor and his young companion were sweating and they hadn't even done anything yet. As he threw off his dressing gown and prepared to join the hooker between the sheets, he found himself thinking about Seventeen.

Later, after a frenzied bout of lovemaking aided in no small way by the Viagra pills Naylor took religiously, he found he was still thinking about Seventeen. It hit him like a bombshell: he still lusted after the former orphan-operative with the blonde hair and icy blue eyes. He vowed to do something about that.

The female CIA agent didn't give the portly clergyman a second glance as he entered the Arrivals Lounge in the company of other travelers at Chicago's Midway Airport. If she'd known the clergyman was the man she was looking out for, she would have taken a little more interest.

Nine had adopted his latest guise after arriving in Los Angeles from Honolulu. A believer in never using the same disguise twice, he'd forsaken his elderly gent's guise for that of a middle-aged clergyman for the flight to Chicago.

Safely past the CIA agent whom Nine had spotted the minute he entered the Arrivals Lounge, the former operative headed for the nearest car rental counter. He was planning to drive to Saint Clair County to confront Naylor about Francis' abduction. Nine would have preferred to fly, but he knew Omega would have people looking out for him at every airport, large and small, in Illinois. It would be safer to drive.

While he knew every minute counted if he was to rescue his son, he was mindful of the fact he'd be of no use to Francis if

Omega took him out of circulation, permanently or otherwise. *More haste, less speed.* At the Avis counter, he booked a mid-size family sedan so as not to draw attention to himself when on the open road.

Within ten minutes, he was safely out of the terminal and driving toward downtown Chicago. En route, he stopped at a shopping mall where he purchased clothes and footwear.

In the mall's outdoor car park, as he loaded his newly purchased items into the rental car, he experienced a sudden sharp pain in his chest. It passed as quickly as it came, but it served as a timely reminder that he'd been neglecting to take the heart medication as often as his specialist had prescribed. In fact, it had been over a day since he'd taken anything. Erring on the side of caution, he popped four of the little yellow heart pills rather than the prescribed two.

The ninth-born orphan shook his head as he thought about the irony of his heart condition. He was supposed to have *perfect* genes and yet here he was enduring a potentially fatal disease at the age of only thirty six.

Nine sat quietly behind the wheel to allow the pills to take effect. He knew from experience, they acted quickly. Already he imagined he was feeling better. *Psychosomatic!* The somewhat frightening experience reminded him of his mortality. He was aware he needed an operation, but was resigned to finding Francis first. The rogue operative promised himself he'd take his medication as prescribed from now on.

Dusk was falling as a revived Nine drove out of the car park and continued into the city center. He had something else to do before driving to Saint Claire County.

11

There was no sign of life in the apartment Nine had been studying for the past few minutes in Chicago's busy Loop district. Still in his clergyman's guise, he was standing on the pavement opposite the upmarket apartment building. The apartment he studied – one of five on the third floor – was the only one on that floor in darkness. He hoped that meant it was unoccupied.

Nine would have been surprised if there had been signs of occupation. After all, he owned the apartment. He'd purchased it under an assumed name before he'd left Chicago five years earlier. That had been just before he'd opted out of the Omega Agency. Since then, he'd kept all rates and levies up to date to ensure the unused property didn't come to the attention of the local authorities.

Reasonably satisfied the apartment wasn't occupied, Nine strode across the street and entered the apartment building. He took the elevator to the third floor and let himself into the apartment using his own key. Inside, he closed the curtains and switched on the lights. A quick scout around confirmed the place was as he'd left it: unlived-in and unfurnished apart from a stretcher bed resting against one wall of the main room. A never-used sleeping bag and pillow, still in their original plastic wrapping, lay atop the stretcher.

Nine had purchased the apartment as an insurance policy. Now he had come to collect. He'd always viewed it as his own personal safe house. A sanctuary to crash in if he needed somewhere to hide in the event of his ever returning to Chicago for any reason. It also served as a place to stash a few emergency items.

Walking through to the smaller of the two bedrooms, Nine opened a wardrobe door and entered the walk-in wardrobe. He pulled up the carpet to reveal a locked trapdoor, which he unlocked using the same key he'd used moments earlier. He raised the trapdoor and reached in to retrieve a leather bag he'd stored there. Then he returned to the main room and dropped the bag on top of the stretcher. Kneeling down, he unzipped the bag and inspected its contents.

The contents included more falsified passports and disguise aids, plus maps, a pen-torch, first-aid kit, flick-knife, and a Glock 18 machine pistol with ammunition. There was also a wad of hundred dollar bills. Satisfied everything was as he'd left it, Nine returned the items to the bag before changing out of his clothes and dispensing with his clergyman's collar.

Stripped down to his undershorts, he removed the black kit he wore strapped around his chest. It contained mini-dispensers of cosmetics and other disguise-aids. As an active operative, it had been an indispensable part of his modus operandi, allowing him to literally change guises on the run. The contents of such kits had helped save his life more than once. He never dreamed he'd have cause to use them again.

After showering, he adopted the guise of a bespectacled

tourist complete with a false moustache, Hawaiian shirt and fake suntan. Nine then returned to the rental car he'd left parked nearby and began driving south toward Saint Clair County. As the miles passed, he could think of nothing else except the wife and son he'd been separated from.

#

While Nine was driving toward Naylor's residence, Omega orphan-operative Twenty Three entered an afterhours medical center in downtown Papeete, in Tahiti. He approached the duty nurse in reception and showed her a recent photo of a pregnant Isabelle. Speaking fluent French, he asked if she'd seen anyone resembling Isabelle. The nurse assured him she hadn't.

Undeterred, the operative left the center and drove to Papeete's public hospital. Entering the hospital's maternity ward, he asked the male duty nurse if he'd seen anyone resembling the pregnant woman in the photo. The nurse laughed, pointing out that the ward's patrons were all pregnant woman, so, yes he had seen someone resembling her.

Twenty Three wasn't amused. He strongly advised the nurse

to study the photo closely. Something about the visitor unsettled the nurse so he studied the woman in the photo. Still he didn't recognize Isabelle. Twenty Three cursed and marched from the ward.

The operative was beginning to feel frustrated. He'd shown Isabelle's photo to scores of people and not one had recognized her. Not for the first time that night he questioned what was so damned important about the woman, or her baby for that matter. Naylor had told him he wanted mother and baby, alive, but he hadn't said why.

Twenty Three lamented the fact that this is what his life had come to. He knew any half-trained private eye could do what he'd been tasked with. Yet here he was, an elite operative with perhaps thirty kills to his name, and he'd been relegated to working all day and night to find some pregnant woman.

12

An urgent after-hours board meeting Andrew Naylor had called for was taking place at Omega HQ in south-west Illinois. Every chair around the large table in the agency's boardroom was occupied except for one – Marcia Wilson's. However, the CIA Director was still present courtesy of a live holographic video feed from her office in Langley, Virginia. Her life-size image was so lifelike it was as though she was there in the flesh.

At the head of the table, Naylor rose to speak. He paused theatrically for a moment to ensure he had the attention of everyone present. The twelve people who made up his audience included all of Omega's directors as well as Doctor Andrews, the only non-director present. "We all know why we are here," he said without preamble.

The directors nodded. They had all been well briefed before the meeting. Among them were Omega's remaining four founding members. Besides Naylor, they included billionaire Fletcher Von Pein, pharmaceutical magnate Lincoln Claver and computer software designer Bill Sterling.

The other eight founding members had either died, resigned or in two unfortunate cases disappeared mysteriously without trace. Naylor had personally led the investigation into their disappearance, but gotten nowhere. Marcia and another director had misgivings over the manner in which Naylor had conducted the investigation, though they didn't voice their criticisms too loudly. The incident served as a reminder to the directors that no-one was indispensable.

Naylor continued, "Before we get into that, I'm pleased to report the boy arrived at the school in good health." Everyone present was aware *the school* was a euphemism for one of the agency's underground medical labs. Naylor turned to Doctor Andrews who sat at the far end of the table. "Doc. Over to you."

The stern-looking doctor, who was spearheading the agency's cloning activities, stood up and pressed a button on a remote control device. Video images appeared on a screen on the wall behind him. "This footage was taken last night. It shows the boy arriving at the school."

Every eye in the room was fixed on the video that showed a sleepy Francis being carried into an austere, hospital-like facility by a burly, white-coated orderly. He was placed on a bed and immediately subjected to a physical inspection by a team of white-coated doctors and nurses. Behind them, more white-coated personnel scurried back and forth as they went about their everyday business.

As he was prodded and probed, a wide-eyed Francis reacted as any five-year-old would, and began howling for his mother. A nurse jabbed him with a needle and the boy soon quietened.

Throughout all this, Doctor Andrews kept up a steady patter, assuring the Omega directors that the boy had suffered no ill-effects from his sudden separation from his parents.

"Get to the point, Doc."

The interjection came from one of the agency's founders. Fletcher Von Pein, who was appropriately seated at Naylor's right hand, was known for his directness. A former Federal Reserve majority shareholder, the elderly but still dynamic Von Pein wasn't one to mince his words. "What do our friends at KSK think of our latest acquisition?"

Doctor Andrews knew Von Pein referred to Omega's pharmaceutical company, *KaizerSimonsKovak*, and the *acquisition* he referred to was Francis. "They're delighted by the initial test results."

"That seems very quick," a sceptical Von Pein commented.

"Blood samples were taken from the boy in Papeete and immediately air-freighted to the school," Doctor Andrews explained. "KSK's people confirmed the results showed the boy's DNA is unique. It's like nothing they've seen before."

Noting the bemused looks on the faces of several directors who had not been privy to the decision to seize Francis, Naylor instructed the doctor to outline the reasons for the boy's abduction.

"Certainly." Doctor Andrews was now in his element,

lecturing on cutting-edge medical matters. "As the progeny of one of the original Pedemont orphans, the boy obviously inherited his father's superior genes. Those genes will help fast-track Stage Three of our cloning program to create more perfect human beings."

The directors hung on his every word. They were very aware of the spectacular success he'd had in recent years in the cloning field – success that was already translating to huge revenues for the agency.

Doctor Andrews continued, "The boy will also be a good test subject." He deliberately avoided using the term *human guinea pig*, preferring *test subject* to convey what was in store for Francis. It sounded more benign. "KSK have a new cancer drug our testers are currently testing on monkeys." The directors knew the *testers* he referred to were the illicit drug testers the agency used to shield its legitimate KSK operation from any accusations of wrongdoing. "Our testers can't wait to put the boy on a course of the new drug to see how he responds."

"How are the monkeys doing?" Von Pein asked.

Doctor Andrews shuffled uncomfortably. "None have survived to date, but our scientists are confident humans will prove more resilient."

Von Pein didn't look convinced, but he refrained from further comment.

The other directors fired a barrage of questions at Doctor Andrews, which he fielded to the best of his ability.

As the discussion ran its course, Marcia Wilson spoke for the first time, diverting attention from the doctor to her holographic image. "What about the boy's mother?"

Naylor motioned to Doctor Andrews to leave the boardroom. The doctor gathered up his files and quickly departed. Naylor waited until the door closed behind the departing doctor before addressing Marcia. "Isabelle Hannar is in the advanced stages of pregnancy and we believe she's still in Tahiti," Naylor said. "Twenty Three is there looking for her now and I've sent another operative to help him. We should have her soon. It's a small island."

"And the boy's father?" Marcia asked.

"There's been no sighting of Nine since he checked in at the airport in Papeete," said Naylor, "but it's a safe bet he's in the States now."

"You know he's coming for you, don't you Andrew." Marcia said. It was more a statement of fact than a question.

"Yes, I've already worked that out," Naylor said dryly. "Some of our operatives have been assigned to watch out for me."

"I'd put our elites on the case," Marcia suggested, referring to the agency's orphan-operatives. With their superior genes and advanced training, she knew the *elites* had no peers in the murky world of espionage

"I agree with Marcia," Omega co-founder Lincoln Claver volunteered. "We can't take any risks with that maverick operative."

Naylor didn't need any persuading. He vividly remembered how disruptive, and deadly, the renegade ninth-born orphan could be. "Alright, I'll call a couple of them in from the field."

"Call in half a dozen," Von Pein said. "This has to take priority over anything else we've got going on right now. He has to be hunted down and shut down before he can cause any trouble."

Naylor nodded. He agreed with Von Pein. The revenues Omega stood to make, directly and indirectly, from Francis' highly unique genes were potentially massive. Naylor knew every effort had to be made to ensure Nine didn't jeopardize what had been started. "I'll call them in as soon as the meeting's over."

As Naylor pondered the situation for a moment, he realized a part of him was actually enjoying the prospect of Nine returning to the scene. It was a challenge and he hadn't experienced too many of those of late – not since the Omega Agency had all but achieved its New World Order goal. Things had been running very smoothly and even though the agency had reached the promised land in terms of global domination, Naylor often found himself getting bored.

The more he thought about Nine, the more Naylor realized he lived for this stuff and loved orchestrating events in Omega's favor. Working in this hyper state was like a grandmaster's game of chess to him where every move or every decision often meant the difference between success and failure.

Naylor came out of his reverie when he noticed Von Pein staring at him. The old man was frowning.

13

It was well after midnight and Nine was beginning to think it unlikely Naylor would be returning home that night. Still disguised as a bespectacled tosurist in his Hawaiian shirt and fawn khaki trousers, he'd been observing the Omega boss's mansion from a stand of trees on a nearby hilltop for some time. He was grateful it was a summer's night. Had it been winter, he'd be frozen stiff by now.

In the bright moonlight, the house was clearly visible – as was the four-wheel drive vehicle parked outside it. The vehicle belonged to one of the three Omega staffers Nine knew were currently inside the house. He'd glimpsed each of them periodically as they did their rounds, inside and outside, over the past few hours. Their physiques, and the way they carried themselves, flagged to him they were operatives. He thought one or possibly two of them looked familiar.

Naylor's non-appearance prompted Nine to wonder if Naylor suspected he was in immediate danger. *You know I'm coming for you, don't you, you old bastard.* When two staffers emerged from the house and drove off, that confirmed it for Nine: his mark had gone to ground. He knew if Naylor was returning home, all his people would have stayed put to ensure he had protection.

Faced with the realization he wouldn't be able to confront Naylor that night, a disappointed Nine decided to break into the house anyway to see what he could find. He left the cover of the trees and jogged silently down the hill.

Mindful that one man remained inside the house, he kept to the shadows and moved silently. He was grateful the man's colleagues had left all the exterior lights on when they'd departed. That had rendered the property's security lights temporarily surplus to requirements.

Just before he reached the house, the headlights of a fast-approaching vehicle warned him he'd soon have company. Nine hid behind a garden shed as a late model Volvo slid to a halt in front of the house. Peering around the corner of the shed, he was pleasantly surprised to see Naylor climb out of the Volvo. The Omega boss was closely followed by his driver, a young man who looked as though he came from the same mould as his recently departed colleagues. The pair disappeared inside the house.

Nine decided to give Naylor time to turn in before breaking in. He didn't have long to wait. The upstairs lights were extinguished within ten minutes, signalling in all likelihood that Naylor had gone to bed. Then the front door opened and a man Nine had never seen before emerged and began patrolling the grounds. A tough-looking individual, he moved like the prizefighter he once was.

Aware the house would be protected by the most sophisticated security alarms known to man, Nine had been racking his brains how to gain entry without alerting anyone. The answer came when Naylor opened his bedroom window. However, that fleeting opportunity passed by when the observant staffer patrolling outside whistled to his boss and signalled to him to shut the window. Naylor closed it immediately.

Nine's eyes scanned the top of the house. Its castle-like battlements concealed the roof, but the rogue operative was willing to bet it contained solar panels or a skylight, or both. Picking his moment, he scaled a drainpipe and hauled himself up and over the battlements. *Bingo*. The skylight he'd hoped to find was almost at his feet.

Retrieving a screwdriver he'd brought along for just such a purpose, he quickly unscrewed the skylight and lowered himself down into the attic. There, he produced his pen-torch and quickly located a trapdoor, which he assumed would lead to the house's top floor and to Naylor's bedroom. It did. In no time, Nine found himself outside Naylor's bedroom. The old man was fast asleep. His features were just discernible in the moonlight that filtered through the curtains, and his snores could be heard above the whirring overhead fan.

Nine knew what he had to do. He needed to get information out of Naylor, but before that he needed to ensure the staffer on duty inside the house wouldn't cause him any problems.

Anxious that Naylor didn't wake and sound the alarm, Nine glided over to the sleeping man. He reached out and his strong fingers tightened around the vagal nerve in Naylor's neck. The old man woke, but he only remained awake for a second. In that time, Nine saw fear in his startled eyes.

Naylor appeared to be sleeping again, but Nine new differently. He was actually unconscious and would remain that way for several minutes at least. Now the former operative could turn his attention to dealing with the Omega staffer whom he guessed was downstairs.

A quick search revealed the staffer was in the kitchen. Nine wasn't surprised to see it was the young driver who had delivered Naylor to the house a short time earlier. He was making a coffee for himself. Nine had no doubt the man was an operative. Tall and lithe, he had the air of someone who knew how to take care of himself.

Not willing to risk a physical confrontation, Nine drew out his Glock 18 machine pistol from the holster hidden beneath his loose-fitting Hawaiian shirt and stepped into the kitchen. The young operative did a double-take and immediately reached for his firearm.

"Don't do it," Nine warned.

The surprised operative deliberately placed both hands on the tabletop in front of him so as not to prompt the stranger with the gun to do anything silly – like shoot him. "Who the hell are you?"

"I'll ask the questions," Nine said. "Stand up and turn around. I wanna search you."

The young operative did as he was told. He stood up and turned, expecting to be frisked. Instead, Nine reversed his grip on the pistol and whacked his opposite across the back of the head. He caught the unconscious operative before he hit the floor so as to minimize the noise and not attract the attention of the staffer patrolling outside. That done, he tied the operative up using a dressing gown cord he'd brought from Naylor's bedroom, and he gagged him using his own handkerchief. As a precaution, he removed the operative's firearm, a Magnum .44 revolver, from its holster and hid it in a cupboard.

Nine had planned to deal with the other staffer outside, but changed his mind. He wanted to get back to Naylor, and was prepared to gamble that he could extract the information he needed from the old man and depart the premises before the other staffer knew anything was amiss.

The former operative quickly returned upstairs armed with a jug of cold water he'd poured from the tap over the kitchen sink. Reaching Naylor's bedroom, he tipped the water over the still unconscious man, waking him. Startled, Naylor tried to sit up, but Nine restrained him. "Just catch your breath for a minute," Nine said quietly. He knew from experience it would take a few moments for Naylor to come round fully.

As his senses slowly returned, Naylor could only stare up at Nine and wonder what the rogue operative had in store for him. He didn't have to wait long to find out.

"You know why I'm here." Nine didn't wait for a response. "You took my son and I want to know where he is."

"I don't know--"

Nine rammed the end of his Glock's barrel into Naylor's open mouth. "Don't tell me you don't know where he is!" he hissed.

Naylor's eyes bulged with fear. Unable to speak, he could only shake his head impotently.

Nine withdrew the pistol from Naylor's mouth. "You have one more chance to tell me the truth. Otherwise you're dead."

"I have some files down in my den!" Naylor blurted out, his lazy eye twitching violently.

Nine yanked Naylor out of bed. Only now, did he realize the old man was naked. Screwing up his nose in disgust, he retrieved Naylor's dressing gown from the foot of the bed and threw it at him. "Put that on before I'm sick."

Naylor hurriedly donned his robe.

Nine then pushed him out of the room toward the stairs. "You lead the way. And quietly."

As Naylor led Nine down to the den, he wondered why his staffer wasn't coming to his rescue. He had his answer when they walked past the kitchen. Through the open door, he saw the young operative – trussed up and still unconscious.

14

O n reaching Naylor's den, Nine quickly checked that there were no windows or other openings to the outside of the house. He needn't have bothered: the den was below ground level. Satisfied, he switched on the light and motioned to Naylor to sit down.

By now, Naylor had recovered some of his composure. As he sat down behind his desk, he looked pointedly at the machine pistol levelled at his gut. "Any shots from that thing will be heard for miles around. My men outside will be onto you like a ton of bricks."

"There's only one man outside," Nine countered, "and you'll be dead so it won't matter a damn to you what anyone else may or may not do to me."

Naylor suddenly remembered something and looked at Nine triumphantly. "Mercury, Venus, Earth, Mars, Jupiter, Saturn--"

"Uranus, Neptune, Pluto," Nine finished the sentence for him. The former operative then shook his head at Naylor. "Nice try, but I got myself deprogrammed from MK-Ultra long ago."

There was a long, drawn out silence as the two arch enemies surveyed each other. Scanning the den, Nine's eyes rested on a small, framed photograph of a young, blonde woman on a bookshelf behind Naylor. The woman seemed familiar. Looking closer, he realized he was looking at Seventeen. *What the hell?* He guessed the photo would have been taken around ten years earlier. It dawned on him that Naylor must be carrying a torch for his fellow orphan-operative. *You dirty, old man.* Finally, Nine returned his attention to his captive. "Okay, where is he?"

Resigned to giving his rogue operative some information, Naylor started talking. "Francis has been taken to one of our medical labs."

"The Black Forest lab?"

"No, we shut that operation down years ago." Naylor said.

That made sense to Nine. He guessed Naylor wouldn't have risked doing anything to prompt him to release the incriminating evidence he'd gathered if the Black Forest lab was still operating.

"We have secret labs in Greenland and the Democratic Republic of the Congo," Naylor continued, "so he'll be interned in one of those."

"Which one?" Nine was losing patience.

"That I don't know." Ignoring Nine's disbelieving look, Naylor hurried on. "A lot has changed since you were with the agency."

"I don't doubt that, but let's not pretend you don't have your finger on the pulse."

"The chain of command has shifted." As Naylor spoke, he slowly opened his desk drawer and reached for the loaded pistol he kept there. "Our operation is now run by Omega splinter groups and other shadow organizations which have links to elite, secret societies."

As Naylor's hand closed around his pistol, Nine leaned across the desk and slammed the draw against the old man's wrist.

Naylor yelped in pain. Nine then reached into the drawer and pulled out the weapon. Extracting the cartridge, he threw the pistol into a wastepaper bin and continued as if nothing had happened. "Exactly where are these labs?"

"I can show you," Naylor grunted as he massaged his injured wrist.

"Okay, but no more tricks. You can't fool me, so don't even try."

Naylor stood up and walked to another desk that supported a computer. He booted it up, entered his personal password and brought up two files marked *Confidential*.

Nine looked on over Naylor's shoulder as the Omega boss opened the first of the files. It related to the agency's lab in Greenland and was headed *Medical Laboratory #3*. Nine immediately pointed that out to Naylor. "You said there were only two labs."

"There are now that the Black Forest lab has been closed," Naylor said. "The Greenland lab was established while the one in Germany was still functioning."

Nine studied his opposite closely. For once, he seemed to be telling the truth. He motioned to Naylor to move over. The old man gave up his seat for Nine who resumed reading, scrolling through the file's contents at the rate of a page a second just as he'd been taught to do as an operative-in-waiting at the Pedemont Orphanage.

With every page, his concern for Francis grew. The document contained a litany of medical horrors that ranged from never-before attempted organ and face transplants to unsanctioned cloning procedures and flat-lining experiments. Medical and scientific text was supported by graphic photographs of subjects – children and teenagers – who had been subjected to these experiments. Some were grotesque in the extreme.

Nine opened the second confidential file. It was headed *Medical Laboratory #1* and related to Omega's secret lab in DRC, or the Democratic Republic of the Congo. Scrolling through the pages of this file, the former operative could see it made for equally gruesome reading. If anything, the scientific experiments being conducted at the DRC lab were even more horrific than at the lab in Greenland.

Naylor fidgeted nervously as Nine continued reading. He could imagine what was going through his rogue operative's mind.

The awful reality of what Francis was going to be subjected to slowly dawned on Nine. It was clear he'd been abducted for some sort of experiment. *But what?* He looked up at Naylor and pointed his Glock at his head. "Talk old man. And make it good. Tell me why you took my son." With that, he pulled a mini-digital recording device from his pocket and placed it on the desktop between them. A red light indicated it had been recording all along. "You've already hung yourself, so you might as well tell me everything."

Naylor's eyes were drawn to the recorder. Tearing his eyes away from the device, he could tell from the expression on Nine's face that there was murder in his heart. He had to control the sudden pressure in his bladder to prevent himself from pissing where he sat. "I can explain." He took a deep breath. "You're the only one of the Pedemont orphans who has a child. Coming from a mixture of your exceptional genes and your wife's regular genes,

Francis has unique DNA. He's a one-of-a-kind."

"What will be done to him exactly."

Naylor hesitated. Nine waved his Glock menacingly, prompting him to continue. "He will assist our cloning program," Naylor continued. "He'll undergo a range of tests--"

"Tests? What tests?" Nine was growing more alarmed by the second.

"I don't have specifics, but they'll be scientifically conducted and monitored by Doctor Andrews' team."

Nine could feel his disbelief and anger growing in equal measure. He felt like his head was about to explode. Irate beyond words, he jumped to his feet and pistol-whipped Naylor, leaving the old man's face cut and bloodied. "You bastard!" Nine swore at the Omega boss who now lay groaning on the carpet. "Just what gives you the right to play God with my son?"

As Nine remonstrated with Naylor, he didn't hear the faint sound of someone behind him until it was too late.

15

The first that Nine realized something was wrong was when he tried to sit up. He couldn't. And he had a splitting headache. When he attempted to open his eyes, the light was blinding and everything seemed to be spinning.

As normality slowly returned, Nine realized he was lying on the floor of Naylor's den. It dawned on him he'd been ambushed and he cursed that he hadn't been more attentive.

The staffer he'd seen outside was now standing alongside Naylor, talking to someone on his cell phone. He was holding Nine's Glock in his other hand and he surveyed the intruder as he spoke. Naylor was gingerly dabbing at his bloodied face with a tissue.

"He's conscious now," the staffer said into his phone. "Don't worry, he won't give us any more trouble."

"Tell them to get here fast," Naylor said, glaring at Nine. "I want this son-of-a-bitch in secure confinement at HQ."

"Get here quick," the staffer said before ending the call. He turned to Naylor. "They're only ten minutes away."

Nine guessed the staffer was referring to reinforcements from Omega. The former operative knew once he was interned at Omega's underground HQ, he'd never be seen again. And neither would Francis. He realized he had to escape within the next minute or two. *How to distract them?* A desperate plan came to mind.

Naylor remembered the mini-recorder on the desktop. Its red light indicated it was still recording. He picked up the device and hurled it against a wall, smashing it.

Nine chuckled. "You realize I'm also wired," he lied.

Naylor looked down at him, horrified. He hadn't considered that someone on the outside could have been listening to the conversation these past few minutes. If that was the case, he knew he was finished. Naylor turned to his staffer. "Search him."

The staffer handed the Glock to Naylor. "Shoot him if he

tries anything, sir."

Naylor trained the Glock on Nine as his staffer bent down to frisk the intruder. That was the opening Nine had been waiting for. He reached up, grabbed the staffer by his ears and pulled his head down. At the same time, he raised his own head sharply off the floor, effectively delivering a head-butt that knocked the man out cold.

Lying beneath the now unconscious staffer, Nine prayed that Naylor wouldn't shoot for fear of hitting his own man. If he did shoot, he was aware the Glock's kick was such the bullet would go right through the staffer and through him as well. Fortunately, Naylor didn't shoot. That hesitation was all Nine needed. Pushing the staffer off him, he rolled beneath Naylor's desk. Only now did the Omega boss shoot. The bullet travelled through the desktop and missed Nine by a whisker. The former operative thought he felt the wind of the bullet as it passed his left ear, but couldn't be sure.

Before Naylor could loose off a second shot, Nine hurled the desk forward, crushing the old man between it and the wall. Naylor slumped to the floor unconscious.

The efforts of the past few minutes caught up with Nine. Breathing hard, he sat down as the now familiar chest pains coursed through him. He prayed he wasn't having another heart attack. Fumbling in his trouser pocket, he retrieved the small container of pills he now carried on his person permanently. Popping two into his mouth, he waited for them to take effect. It wasn't long before the pain passed.

Retrieving his Glock, Nine quickly tied the hands of both men behind their backs. He used his own belt to tie the staffer's hands then removed the staffer's belt and used it to tie Naylor's.

Nine then returned to the computer and, using a flash-drive he'd brought along for just this purpose, downloaded the contents of the two classified files he'd read earlier. He would print them out later to study in more detail.

The former operative was about to extract the flash-drive from the computer when he hesitated. Operating the computer's mouse, he noticed another confidential file on the monitor. The file was labelled *Pedemont Orphan Number Seventeen*. He opened it and speed-read its contents in a matter of seconds. So surprised was he by what he learnt about Seventeen, he re-read the file, but more slowly this time.

Finally, he downloaded the file to his flash-drive then extracted it and returned it to his pocket. Not wanting to advertise the fact that he'd accessed that particular file, he clicked out of it.

An audible groan alerted him to the fact the Omega staffer was coming round. Nine delivered a swift punch to the staffer's jaw, rendering him unconscious once again. A glance at Naylor confirmed the old man was still out to it. Aware he had a couple of minutes at best to make his escape, Nine left the house via the back door.

16

It was mid-morning before Nine reached the outskirts of Chicago. Tired and unshaven, he'd driven through the night since his hurried departure from Naylor's house. He'd dispensed with his tourist guise, but wore dark glasses and a baseball cap as a precaution against being identified by someone who may not have his best interests at heart.

The former operative was aware if he wasn't a marked man before, he certainly was now. He was in no doubt Naylor had believed him when he'd said he was wired. The old man would be paranoid that whoever was listening in at the other end had recorded the conversation and could release it to the media any time – and that would be disastrous for Omega and for Naylor personally. For a start, it would turn the spotlight on Omega's illicit medical labs. From Naylor's perspective, the fallout from that wouldn't bare thinking about.

Nine wasn't happy about the outcome of the raid on Naylor's house. While he had downloaded the confidential files on the overseas labs, he hadn't a clue which one Francis had been sent to. And he wasn't sure Naylor had been telling the truth about the labs. For all Nine knew, there could be others. He couldn't even be sure the Black Forest lab had been closed down.

However, he was aware that was all the information he was likely to get, and he had to make the most of it and hope it would lead him to Francis.

Nine was straining at the leash to start searching for his son at Omega's orphanages, but first he had something even more urgent to do: he intended to visit Seventeen. A plan was forming in his mind. For it to work, he needed someone to help him – and his sister was the only one he could turn to. He had no other allies. Not with her skills at least.

The former operative had often thought about Seventeen since he'd fled the agency. After all, she'd been his nemesis throughout his formative years and had left him for dead on their first major overseas assignment. That had been in the rainforests of Guyana, and he'd been fortunate to survive that mission. She'd also killed Isabelle's parents in France and had come close to killing Isabelle herself at a CIA detention centre in Andorra while trying to get to him.

But those weren't the only reasons he'd thought about Seventeen. Nine had often recalled the eerie moment they'd shared together in Paris shortly before he'd extricated himself from Omega. On that occasion Seventeen had had the opportunity to kill him, but chose not to. While looking into his sister's eyes on that winter's day, Nine felt certain he had seen a different side to Seventeen – a more human and merciful side.

He'd learned from reading the contents of her file that Seventeen was the only other orphan no longer working for Omega. The file had seemingly included every detail of her life – from childhood through to her forced departure from the agency. Her mental breakdown and subsequent expulsion from Omega were covered in minute detail.

There was even a reference to MK-Ultra and to possible side-effects of a mind-control experiment Seventeen had been subjected to, though there was no mention of Naylor's misuse of that particular tool. Nor was there any mention of Naylor's sexual abuse of Seventeen while she was under the spell of MK-Ultra.

The reference to mind control had gotten Nine wondering. If he had to bet, it was MK-Ultra that had caused Seventeen's spectacular meltdown. The file had also confirmed Seventeen had been under the influence of insidious mind control technology when she'd killed their mentor, Tommy Kentbridge, and Isabelle's parents.

Nine knew about Omega using MK-Ultra on the Pedemont Orphans because Kentbridge had confided in him about it when they'd visited the Black Forest orphanage. Kentbridge had even demonstrated its use by subjecting both him and Seventeen to mind control in order to extricate himself from a tricky situation.

However, the most interesting thing Nine learnt from reading the file was Seventeen had a grandfather. That meant he, too, had a grandfather – a direct link to his and Seventeen's mother. That revelation had hit him like a bombshell.

For now, though, he had more important things to think about. Like finding his son. He was sick with worry, but forced himself to think like an operative and put his emotions to one side. Kentbridge's old catch phrase came to him once more: *For every problem there's a solution.* Nine wondered what Kentbridge would advise were he still alive.

The return to Chicago brought back a lot of memories for Nine – memories he'd tried to suppress. As always, he attempted to force them from his mind, but that never completely worked. Somehow, they always resurfaced.

Entering Glen Ellyn, Nine focused on what he was about to ask Seventeen to do. He stopped the rental car several properties short of the bungalow he'd learnt was home to his sister and their grandfather.

Nine observed the neat home for a good five minutes to satisfy himself no-one else was watching it. While waiting, he took the opportunity to shave, using an electric shaver he'd brought with him. He wanted to at least look half-presentable when meeting his sister and grandfather.

Leaving the car where it was, Nine walked along the sidewalk and continued right by the bungalow. Surreptitious surveillance of the property confirmed that nothing seemed out of place. Nine immediately retraced his steps and approached the bungalow's front door. The sound of a radio reached him from inside. He could hear a radio host warning Chicagoans the Windy City was in for another scorching day.

Nine knocked on the door. No answer. He knocked again. Eventually, the door opened.

Nine recognized Seventeen immediately. Physically, she was just as he remembered, although there seemed to be a vagueness about her – almost as if nobody was home. He forced a smile. "Hello, Jennifer."

Seventeen didn't recognize him at first. It wasn't until he removed his sunglasses and baseball cap that it dawned on her she was looking at the ninth orphan – her long-time rival and the colleague she'd once left for dead in Guyana. "Sebastian?"

Nine simply nodded. Brother and sister stood staring at each other, awkwardly, for several drawn-out moments.

"I suppose you'd better come in," a bemused Seventeen said. She led Nine through to the dining room.

Nine immediately spotted the framed photograph of Annette Hannar, their mother. Nine walked over to the photo and stared at his mother intently.

Seventeen looked strangely at him. "You know her?"

Her response telegraphed to Nine that she'd forgotten they were siblings. He debated whether to break it to her gently, but decided to go for the shock factor. "I should know Annette. She's my mother."

Seventeen was visibly shaken. "So that makes us…"

"Siblings. I'm your brother. Well, half-brother at least. We have the same mom, but many different fathers thanks to the Pedemont Project."

As Seventeen digested this information, Nine assessed her. What he observed didn't inspire him with confidence. It was clear she was damaged goods – a shadow of the elite operative she'd once been. *What did they do to you?* Having read her file, he already knew the answer to that. The link between MK-Ultra and her current state of mind was depressingly evident.

However, the bigger question was: could she help him?

17

Seventeen was feeling confused. This was her first contact with anyone from her past in four years.

"I hear we have a grandfather," Nine said.

"What? Oh, yes. Sebastian Hannar."

That was the first time Nine had heard his grandfather's name. He realized he must have been named after him. Nine glanced around. "Where is he?"

"He's asleep. I always make him breakfast in bed and he usually snoozes through to lunch."

Again the conversation lapsed.

Finally, Seventeen asked, "What brings you here Nine . . . I mean Sebastian?"

Nine steeled himself for what he was about to ask. *Here we go*. He'd rehearsed in his mind many times what he was going to say, but now that it was time to say it, he wasn't feeling at all confident. "After I disappeared off the grid, I got married. Her name's Isabelle. Isabelle Alleget. You met her. Remember?" *How could you forget? You tortured my wife and murdered her parents.* He waited for a reaction.

Seventeen shook her head. She genuinely appeared to have no recollection of having met Isabelle.

Nine pressed on. "We have a son. Omega has taken him from us." He paused to allow time for this to sink in.

Seventeen heard what Nine was saying, but was having trouble digesting the information. In her present state of mind, it was too much to take in, in one hit. "You have a son?"

"Yes. His name's Francis."

"Where have they taken him?"

"To one of Omega's new orphanages, a secret offshore medical lab somewhere. I don't know which one of the orphanages it is, but I aim to find out."

"Why did they take him?"

"For scientific tests and medical experimentation. His unique DNA means he's of interest to Omega's medical gurus. Apparently, testing Francis will help fast-track the agency's cloning operations."

Seventeen frowned as she disseminated this. The information revived hazy memories of her time with the Omega Agency and with the Pedemont Orphanage before that.

Nine could almost see Seventeen's mind racing to come up to speed. He knew he was loading a lot onto her, but now that he'd started he couldn't stop. "I need you to help me."

"Me? What can I do?"

"You can protect Isabelle to ensure Omega don't abduct her as well." Having caught up with Seventeen, Nine wasn't sure she could protect herself let alone Isabelle. But he pressed on.

Over the next few minutes, he quickly explained how he'd left Isabelle with friends in Tahiti, but was afraid Omega would get to her before he found Francis. Nine said if that happened, the agency could use her as leverage to force him to stop searching for Francis. He also mentioned that Isabelle was in the advanced stages of pregnancy.

At the mention of Isabelle's pregnancy, Seventeen looked up sharply. "So they'll want to take the baby, too." It was a statement more than a question.

Nine was impressed that Seventeen was sufficiently with it to recognize the danger Isabelle was in. *Hallelujah! There's hope yet.* He pressed on. "Yes, I don't doubt they'll want the baby as well." *That's it. That's my final card.* Nine sat back and awaited Seventeen's answer. He didn't have long to wait.

Seventeen had made up her mind as soon as she'd learned Nine wanted her help. He was asking her to re-enter the ugly world of espionage – a world she'd left far behind. She feared that to revisit that world would cost her, her sanity. Even now, listening to her brother, she felt as if she was on the verge of another breakdown. "I'm sorry, I can't help you." She shook her head.

Nine had feared that would be her answer. In the five years since he'd last seen her, she'd changed from an operative without peer – a trained killer with a mind like a steel trap – to someone else altogether.

The old Seventeen would have been a great ally to have in his current predicament, but this new Seventeen was different. She'd obviously settled for living in the suburbs, caring for their grandfather, and she had no intention of returning to her former life. Deep down, he couldn't blame her.

The strained silence between them was interrupted by the sound of a bell ringing from another room.

"That's Grandpa," Seventeen said. She sounded relieved. "He'll be ready to get up. Excuse me a minute." She hurried from the room.

Alone, Nine debated whether to stay or go. He'd already reached the conclusion that Seventeen's mind wouldn't be changed. Having observed her, he wasn't sure she'd be of much use anyway. She seemed out of touch with the real world.

Nine was about to leave when Seventeen returned to the room wheeling a frail Sebastian Hannar.

"Grandpa," she said, "this is Sebastian, your grandson."

Sebastian Senior looked up from beneath bushy eyebrows and surveyed the stranger who had arrived unannounced in their midst. "You must be Annette's son," he rasped.

Seventeen gasped in amazement. "Yes Grandpa, this is mom's son." She turned to Nine and smiled. "That's the first time he has said more than one word in months," she whispered.

Nine suddenly felt overwhelmed. After a lifetime of being separated from people he was related to by blood, here he was in the presence of his grandfather and sister. Nine studied the old man and approached him with something bordering on reverence. He extended his right hand. "Pleased to meet you, sir."

Sebastian Senior took his grandson's hand in his bony hand and shook it. His other hand remained clasped around a trusty walking stick, which he carried with him out of habit. Nine waited for him to speak further, but nothing more was forthcoming.

Assessing his grandfather, Nine could tell there was an inner strength behind his physical frailty. He could see steel in his blue eyes and guessed he would have been a man to be reckoned with once upon a time.

Seventeen wheeled Sebastian Senior over to the dining table. She turned back to Nine. "Join us for a bite, Sebastian?"

Before Nine could reply there was a loud knock on the front door.

"Excuse me." Seventeen went to answer the door.

"Wait!" Nine ordered. He hurried to the window and peeked through a gap in the curtains. A four-wheel drive vehicle, not dissimilar to the one he'd seen outside Naylor's house, was parked out front. He suddenly had a bad feeling. Turning to Seventeen, he whispered, "I'm not here and you haven't seen me."

Seventeen nodded and left the dining room to answer the door. Nine hurried from the room and hid in the first bedroom he came to. The musty smell and dated décor indicated it was Sebastian Senior's room. As a precaution, he drew his Glock from its holster.

18

Nine kept the door slightly ajar in order to listen. He could hear Seventeen talking to someone. A man's voice carried to him, then another, confirming there were at least two men at the door.

"I assure you, I haven't seen or heard from Number Nine in years," Seventeen could be heard saying.

The hairs on the back of Nine's neck came erect. He knew now the men were from Omega. Only the agency knew him by his number.

"You don't mind if we look inside, do you?" a man with a deep voice asked.

"I most certainly do," Seventeen replied. "Hey!"

There were sounds of a commotion as the visitors burst in. A second later, there was a gunshot followed by the sound of Seventeen screaming.

Nine ran to investigate. He burst into the room to find his grandfather lying motionless on the floor. Blood from the bullet lodged in his chest stained his shirt. He was clearly dead. Nine would learn later that the old man had risen to assist his granddaughter and had been shot when one of the intruders had mistaken his walking stick for a firearm.

It took Nine only a split second to assess the situation. Both the intruders were armed and they were obviously under orders to shoot first and ask questions later. Virtual clones of the staffers Nine had clashed with at Naylor's, they were obviously Omega operatives. The older one had his back to Nine while the other had his pistol trained on a distraught Seventeen.

The older operative spun around too late. Nine shot him stone cold dead with a clean head shot then deliberately shot his companion in the thigh. The wounded operative dropped his weapon and clutched his thigh as he fell to the floor. Nine was onto him in a flash, kicking the fallen weapon out of reach and delivering a savage kick to the operative's head for good measure.

Satisfied the two operatives were out of commission, Nine looked around to see Seventeen kneeling beside their grandfather. She sobbed uncontrollably as she cradled the old man in her arms. Nine went to her side.

Seventeen looked up at him through tear-filled eyes. "They killed him," she said. "Why did they do that?"

"Because I was here," Nine said. The former operative felt as flat as he sounded. He knew their grandfather would be alive if he hadn't visited. He also realized he'd just killed a man. Once that wouldn't have bothered him. Now it left him feeling shaken and on the verge of throwing up.

Nine had a feeling he'd have to kill more men if he was to find Francis. A groan alerted him that the wounded operative was coming round. Nine returned to his side. He could see he was in a bad way. Blood from the wound in his thigh stained the carpet. The operative grimaced as Nine pulled him up into a sitting position.

"Who sent you?" Nine asked.

The operative spat at his interrogator.

Nine pushed his finger into the bullet hole in the operative's thigh. The wounded man screamed in agony.

"Who sent you?" Nine asked again, reinserting his finger into the hole.

Screaming, the operative said, "Andrew Naylor!"

Nine withdrew his finger from the bullet hole. "Good. Now that wasn't hard, was it?" Before the operative could answer, Nine knocked him out again – this time with a blow to the head with the butt of his machine pistol. He turned back to Seventeen. "You okay?"

Seventeen was too distraught to answer. She could only sob as she cradled Sebastian Senior in her arms.

Nine realized he should share Seventeen's grief. However, when he looked at his grandfather he felt like he was looking at a stranger. He'd never had the chance to bond with Sebastian Senior. That made him angry. He blamed Omega for that state of affairs. They had raised him to believe he had no family. It was only later in life he'd learnt he had blood relatives.

The irony of meeting his grandfather and then losing him in

the space of a couple of minutes didn't escape him. Nine could feel his anger reaching boiling point.

Seventeen's unabated sobbing suddenly got on his nerves. "Stop that!" he ordered.

Startled, Seventeen looked up at him. She stifled her sobs, pushed herself to her feet and looked at her brother as if in a trance.

Nine realized he must leave immediately. He was aware neighbors would have reported the gunshots and it was likely the police would be arriving soon. Returning to the front window to see if there was any activity outside, he wasn't surprised to see a small group of people had gathered on the sidewalk across the street. They were obviously alarmed by the gunfire.

The former operative was about to head outside when Seventeen reached out and touched his arm. "I'll help you," she whispered.

"What?"

"I'll do as you ask."

19

Nine had given up on any thought of his sister assisting in his quest to find Francis. He'd considered her a lost cause. Now he could see she'd stopped crying and had regained some of her poise. And he could see a glimmer of something in her eyes he hadn't seen for many years. "You'll help me?"

Seventeen nodded. "Yes. There's nothing left for me here."

Nine debated whether to accept her offer. He was aware it'd be a huge risk sending Seventeen to Tahiti to be with Isabelle. However, Nine felt it would be an even bigger risk to leave his wife alone as Omega would most certainly want the unborn baby. He just hoped blood really was thicker than water and that his sister wouldn't return to being the spiteful individual he remembered from his childhood.

As Nine looked Seventeen in the eye, his gut told him to give her a chance. "Okay. Get your things together. We have to get out of here."

"What about Grandpa?"

"There's nothing we can do for him. The authorities will ensure he gets a proper burial."

Seventeen looked over at the wounded operative who was still unconscious. "And him?"

"We'll leave him for the authorities to deal with also. He can explain to them why he and his buddy broke into your home with guns blazing." Nine looked hard at his sister. "You sure you want to help?"

Seventeen nodded. "Just give me a minute." She returned to her room. There she threw clothes and toiletries into an overnight bag, and retrieved a false passport, disguise aids and other emergency items she'd hidden for just such an emergency as this.

When Seventeen returned to the dining room, she found Nine speaking in hushed tones on a cell phone.

Nine ended the call quickly and motioned to her to follow him outside. As soon as they stepped outside the bungalow, they saw the ranks of concerned neighbors had grown considerably. At least twenty people had gathered across the street. Nine placed a protective arm around his sister as he steered her toward his waiting rental car. "Say something to them," he whispered.

Seventeen looked at her neighbors. "Home invaders have just killed grandpa," she shouted. "My friend is taking me to hospital."

"She's been shot," Nine added.

The horrified neighbors seemed to accept that. Already, the sound of sirens could be heard in the distance.

Nine bundled Seventeen into the car, jumped in behind the wheel and accelerated away. As he drove, he imagined it wouldn't be long before Naylor sent someone to investigate what had happened to his two operatives. He wondered how Naylor knew he'd be at his sister's residence. Then he recalled the Omega boss had noted his interest in the photo of a younger Seventeen in his den. He realized Naylor had probably suspected he'd read the file on his sister and noted her home address.

Approaching the city centre, Nine studied Seventeen next to him in the front passenger seat. His sister had been sobbing since they'd left the bungalow. Nine could see she was a mess and rebuked himself for even thinking of recruiting her to help him. But there was no-one else he could turn to, to protect Isabelle. Not with Seventeen's skills at least.

Casting his misgivings aside, he turned to his emotional passenger. "We need to talk."

Seventeen rallied herself. Drying her eyes, she looked at Nine and waited to hear what was on his mind.

Nine just hoped what he had to tell her wouldn't push her over the edge. *Steel yourself, sis.* He said, "When I was at Naylor's, I read a confidential file he had on you."

Seventeen remained silent, willing Nine to continue.

"I have reason to believe he had sexual relations with you without your realizing it."

"Sex with Naylor? You have to be joking. D'you think for a minute I could have had sexual relations with that dirty old man and not remember?"

Undeterred, Nine continued. "I assume you've heard of MK-Ultra?"

Seventeen nodded. "What does that have to do with anything?"

"When we were youngsters, you, me and all us Pedemont orphans were programmed as part of an MK-Ultra mind control initiative." Seventeen shook her head in disbelief, but Nine ignored her scepticism. "The program was discontinued after the CIA's involvement was leaked to the media, but the control codes remain dormant in each of us. Except for me. I got myself deprogrammed after I found out about it."

"How did you find out?"

"Tommy told me that time you tracked us down in the Black Forest. He used mind control on you when you were about to shoot me." Nine could see Seventeen was trying to recall the event, but it eluded her. "He even tried to use it on me and almost succeeded."

"What does all that have to do with Naylor abusing me?"

"The file contained some pretty damning evidence."

"Go on."

"There were references to you being subjected to mind control experiments during your last year or two with the agency, and there were photos of you in various stages of undress."

Seventeen gasped.

"Naylor even keeps a framed photo of you on his bookshelf."

As Seventeen struggled to disseminate this shocking information, she began to understand what had caused her fall from grace during her final two years with Omega. "So I was under MK-Ultra all that time?"

"You still are. And Naylor used the program's codes to exercise mind control over you to keep you as his personal sex slave by the looks."

"The bastard!" Seventeen felt violated. She wanted revenge. "I'm going to kill him."

"Do what you want to him," Nine said, "but first we need to get you deprogrammed. You still have the control codes embedded in you."

"How do I get deprogrammed?"

"I happen to know someone." He was referring to one Clarence Fisher-Tinbull, an old FBI contact who knew everything there was to know about MK-Ultra. He'd phoned the man on Seventeen's behalf from her bungalow forty minutes earlier. Clarence had deprogrammed Nine during a rare visit to mainland USA after he and Isabelle had settled in the Marquesas Islands.

"Is that necessary?"

"Yes. You won't be any help to me, or Isabelle, if Naylor or anyone else in Omega can still control your mind."

"He'd have to catch me first."

"A simple phone call would suffice. All he'd have to do is reach you by phone and recite the voice prompts, or codes, and you'd be under his control." Nine could tell by the expression on Seventeen's face that she agreed with his rationale.

"Okay. Make the arrangements."

Nine smiled for the first time in a while. "I already have."

They drove several blocks in silence. Nine suddenly remembered something he shouldn't have overlooked. He angrily thumped the steering wheel. "Goddamn it!"

"What?"

Nine looked at Seventeen. "Your microchip," he said referring to the miniature electronic tracking device Omega had surgically embedded in the forearm of each of the Pedemont orphans when they were youngsters. It enabled their Omega masters to keep track of them no matter where in the world they were at any time.

"Relax," Seventeen said. "They removed mine when they dismissed me. Obviously, I was such a mess they considered I'd never be a threat to them, or anyone else for that matter."

That came as a relief to Nine. He was aware if his sister was still *on the grid*, Naylor would know where they were at that very moment.

20

Half an hour later, Nine and Seventeen were safely parked in the basement of an inner city car parking building. Aware they would now both be on Omega's *wanted* list, they were adding the finishing touches to new disguises they'd adopted.

Nine was in the front seat, studying his new look in the car's rear vision mirror, while in the back seat Seventeen added blusher to her face with the aid of a hand mirror. Like her brother, she, too, had a portable kit containing various disguise aids. Working within the car's confines, it was slow going – especially for Seventeen who had never been the most proficient of the orphan-operatives when it came to shape-shifting and adopting new guises.

By the time they'd finished they resembled a posh business

couple who could pass for bankers or attorneys, or successful members of any profession for that matter.

Nine now wore his hair parted in the middle. He sported a fashionable stubble while blue-colored contact lenses hid his startling green eyes. Clever use of makeup made him look extremely pale-skinned. Blonde Seventeen was now a brunette and she wore her wig tied up in a bun. Rouge gave her cheeks a pink glow and fashionable dark-tinted spectacles hid her icy blue eyes.

Never a fan of resorting to different guises – though she'd had to use them often enough when an active Omega operative – Seventeen had protested when Nine said they must disguise themselves. She'd quickly backed down after her brother reminded her that the agency would be watching out for them and would have guessed the siblings were now in cahoots.

Nine surreptitiously studied his sister in the mirror. He could see she was still a mess – not physically so much, but mentally. Sebastian Senior's death had left her shattered and even more befuddled than before. Nine knew some drastic action was needed if she was to keep her sanity and be of any use to him. He'd explained to Seventeen what was in store for her. She'd seemed to accept it, but he couldn't be sure.

Satisfied with their appearance, they left the car and walked up a flight of steps that opened out into Michigan Avenue. It was mid-afternoon and the inner city was predictably busy, which suited them just fine. They quickly merged with the crowds.

Their destination was the office of former FBI agent-turned consultant Clarence Fisher-Tinbull. It was conveniently a stone's throw from the parking building they'd just left. Exactly who Clarence consulted for, Nine wasn't sure, but judging by the trappings of wealth that surrounded him, consulting paid handsomely.

As Nine led Seventeen through the ground floor entrance of an office tower, she hesitated. "Can we trust this man?"

"We can trust him. He helped me out before, remember?"

After an elevator took them to the top floor suite, the siblings found themselves in a spacious reception room in the offices of *Clarence Fisher-Tinbull Consultancy*. A secretary told them to wait while she advised her boss his next appointment had arrived.

Nine could see Seventeen was becoming increasingly stressed over what she was about to undergo. "Don't worry," he whispered. "It's a breeze." He concealed the lie behind a smile.

Seventeen wasn't convinced. She appeared ready to flee.

The office door opened and Clarence Fisher-Tinbull entered the room. Nine almost didn't recognize him at first. In the intervening years since he'd seen him, the once-fit FBI agent was now decidedly rotund with a set of jowls to match.

Nine stood and extended his hand. "Hey, old-timer. What have you done to yourself?"

Clarence didn't recognize Nine even though he'd been expecting him. He shook the extended hand. "Hell, is that you, Sebastian?"

"Afraid so," Nine chuckled.

Clarence glanced at Seventeen.

"Let's complete the introductions in your office, shall we?" Nine was anxious not to draw any more attention to Seventeen and himself than necessary. Clarence's secretary was already showing interest in them.

"Of course." Clarence ushered the couple through to his office. As soon as he'd closed the door, Nine introduced Seventeen. Clarence gave her a perfunctory nod then turned to back Nine. "Forgive me, but can you prove you are who you say you are? I need to be sure."

It was clear to Nine that Clarence wasn't yet convinced he was who he claimed to be. That was a comforting reminder of how effective his latest disguise was.

Nine thought of something his opposite would be aware only he could know. "You once said the thirty minutes it took you to deprogram me was a record. Has anyone broken that record yet?" He was referring to when Clarence had deprogrammed him after he'd learnt he was part of Omega's MK-Ultra mind-control program. The then-FBI agent had told him it usually took at least an hour to deprogram *victims*, as he so aptly called them, of MK-Ultra.

"So it really is you." Clarence looked relieved.

"Who else?"

Clarence returned his attention to Seventeen. He knew why

she was there, having been briefed over the phone by Nine. Clarence invited Nine to make himself at home in his office then ushered Seventeen through to an adjoining room.

Nine flashed an encouraging smile at his sister before Clarence closed the door, leaving him alone. He felt more than a little nervous for Seventeen, for he knew what she was in for.

Four years earlier, in these very offices, Nine had entrusted himself to Clarence's deprogramming skills. Then, as now, the former FBI agent was the only person in the world he could have turned to for the deprogramming services he provided. After all, Clarence's knowledge of MK-Ultra was second-to-none. He'd been directly involved in the controversial use of MK-Ultra mind control among Gulf War veterans and, later, in the deprogramming of many of those same veterans.

While the procedure had only taken thirty minutes in Nine's case, he swore it was the longest thirty minutes of his life. In that time, Clarence had hypnotized him and forced him to relive some of the worst experiences he'd had when growing up at the Pedemont Orphanage and, later, when an operative in the field.

Because Seventeen had been subjected to active mind control over a long period, Clarence had confided that her deprogramming would be more difficult. And so it would transpire.

Helping himself to Clarence's computer and printer, Nine put his time to good use and printed out copies of the confidential files he'd downloaded to his flash-drive at Naylor's residence. He then started reading Seventeen's file at a more leisurely pace than before.

21

While Nine and Seventeen were at Clarence's office, three Omega operatives were waiting for them in the basement of the car parking building the pair had left the rental car in earlier. Smart detective work by one of Omega's IT people had connected the troublesome siblings with the car as they left Glen Ellyn after the violent incident at Seventeen's residence.

The car and its two occupants had been spotted during real-time surveillance of security camera footage back at Omega HQ. That same footage revealed the route the car followed and the parking building it entered.

As soon as the information had been forwarded to Naylor, he ordered his operatives to stake out the building and await the return of Nine and Seventeen. Their orders were to shoot to kill.

Nine would have been interested to know his earlier assessment of Naylor was correct: the Omega boss did believe Nine had been wired when he'd accosted him in his home, and he was paranoid that whoever had been listening in at the other end had recorded the conversation. Naylor wanted Nine dead, and if that mean putting every last one of his still-active, elite orphan-operatives on the case, he'd do it.

#

Ninety minutes later, Nine was still waiting for Seventeen's deprogramming to finish. He'd been pacing for much of that time. The clock was ticking and every minute's delay was agony for him.

Curiosity got the better of him and he quietly walked over and placed his ear to the wall of the adjoining room. He could hear Clarence repeating the names of the planets of the solar system over and over in a calm, monotone voice.

"Mercury, Venus, Earth, Mars," Clarence said, "Jupiter, Saturn, Uranus, Neptune, Pluto."

Nine knew from experience his friend was reciting the MK-Ultra voice-commands to de-activate the mind-control program Seventeen had been subjected to. The irony was they were the same commands as those recited to activate the program. As Clarence had once explained to him, continuous repetition of the commands was required to desensitize the subject and to successfully and permanently deactivate MK-Ultra.

Resigned to waiting, Nine sat down again.

Finally, the door to the adjoining room opened. Clarence entered the office and closed the door behind him. He quietly advised Nine that the deprogramming had been successful. However, he said the procedure had taken a lot out of Seventeen and recommended she get some rest. Nine concurred, but privately thought that rest was a luxury neither of them was likely to experience in the coming days.

"Oh, one other thing," Clarence said. "She may never fully recover her memory."

"Why? I did."

"Yes, but you weren't subjected to prolonged mind control

like she was. She will have to face the fact that she has amnesia and may always have it."

As Nine digested this news, the door opened and an exhausted Seventeen joined them. It was obvious she'd been crying. Her appearance reminded Nine how he'd felt after he'd undergone the same procedure. He could only imagine how Seventeen must be feeling, having endured such a lengthy session.

Nine paid Clarence the pre-agreed rate, in cash, and thanked him profusely for his assistance. Anxious to be on his way, Nine led a subdued and shaken Seventeen from the building. Outside, on the sidewalk, he looked at her. "You okay?"

She nodded. Even the effort of speaking was beyond her for the moment.

Nine hailed a passing cab. He'd figured it was time to leave their rental car behind. *No point in taking unnecessary risks.* The cab stopped and the siblings climbed into the rear seat.

"Where to?" the cabbie asked.

"The Loop thanks," Nine said.

#

Omega boss Andrew Naylor presided over a meeting he'd called at short notice. It was being held in the boardroom at Omega's underground headquarters. Naylor's audience comprised seven male operatives – *elites* all of them.

Like Nine and Seventeen, the operatives had been raised at the orphanage in Riverdale on Chicago's South Side and were graduates of the Pedemont Project. They knew the two former orphan-operatives as well as any siblings knew each other. After all, they'd spent all their formative years living with them day and night, and since then had often worked on field assignments together.

While none of the Pedemont orphans had fond memories of the ever-competitive and cold Seventeen, several had been friends with Nine and all respected him. Or they had respected him until he'd turned his back on them and fled the agency.

Naylor, whose face still bore the fresh scars of his run-in with Nine, was aware there could be divided loyalties among the orphan-operatives. After all, this would be the first time since Seventeen had been tasked with killing Nine that any of the elites had been asked to go up against one of their own.

For this reason, Naylor had solicited Doctor Andrews to reactivate MK-Ultra mind control in all seven elites. Reactivation had been successfully carried out a short time before the meeting. A quick hypnosis session with each was all it took. Now, as he addressed his elites, Naylor was certain they wouldn't hesitate to carry out his orders to the letter.

Six of the operatives were ordered to catch the first available commercial flights to one or other of the agency's offshore orphanages. Their assignment was to intercept and terminate Nine and Seventeen should either show up. Naylor was in no doubt Seventeen was now working with her brother. He stressed that one or both would be heading for at least one of the orphanages at that very moment, and reminded the elites that the pair were masters of disguise.

Naylor didn't consider it likely that Seventeen would be headed for Tahiti to help protect Isabelle. It had crossed his mind, but he thought Nine would be so worried about Francis he'd have recruited her to help find the boy.

The fifteenth operative, appropriately named Fifteen, was ordered to fly to Tahiti to help TwentyThree find the pregnant Frenchwoman and take her and her unborn child into custody. Naylor didn't explain what Omega's interest was in the baby.

Fifteen, a strapping Latino, was one of those who had considered Nine a friend when they were growing up at the orphanage. Normally, he'd have had serious misgivings about what he was being asked to do. Under the effects of Mk-Ultra however, he had no misgivings at all.

22

As Naylor continued to make plans to thwart the two siblings, Nine and Seventeen were safely ensconced in the former's apartment in The Loop, in downtown Chicago. They were filling in a couple of hours until their respective flights departed from nearby O'Hare International Airport.

The siblings sat on the carpeted floor of the main room, pouring over the contents of the confidential files Nine had printed out earlier. Having showered, changed and then eaten a pizza together, they were finalizing their plans for the coming days and possibly weeks.

Nine was delighted by the transformation he'd witnessed in Seventeen: she was becoming more like her old self. The deprogramming had done the trick. Either that or their grandfather's murder had galvanized something inside Seventeen and revived her killer instinct. Nine suspected it was a bit of both.

As Clarence had warned, there were still big gaps in Seventeen's memory, and her ability to recall events was shaky at best, but the mental improvement in her was undeniable.

The documents Nine had printed out included three maps. On two of them, *X* symbols marked the location of Omega's underground medical labs in Greenland and the DRC, while on a map of Tahiti an *X* marked the location of Isabelle's safe house near Papeete.

Seventeen's willingness to fly to Tahiti to help protect Isabelle had come as a huge relief for Nine as he was desperately worried for his wife's safety. Knowing Seventeen would be looking out for her meant he could focus solely on the all-important task of finding and rescuing Francis.

After going over their plans for the third time, Nine asked, "So, is everything clear?"

"Yes," Seventeen said without hesitation. "Isabelle and I will sit tight until we hear from you."

"Good." Nine was beginning to trust his sister more and more. It felt like he had a real ally on board now that Seventeen had pulled herself together. He looked at her intently. "This mission means everything to me, Jennifer."

She returned his earnest stare. "Me too, Sebastian. You are the only family I have now. And your son, Francis, is my nephew, right?"

Nine nodded then smiled at his sister.

It was a watershed moment. Each felt they'd connected with their sibling for the first time in their lives.

Nine reached out and took Seventeen's hand in his. "How much do you know or remember about our mom?"

"Grandpa filled me in on her early years, but he said he lost contact with her when she fell into bad company."

Nine smiled grimly. "Yes and I have a good idea who, or what, that bad company was. Omega."

"I vaguely remember Naylor telling me that mom died of an overdose when she went back on the drugs a short time after I was born. Grandpa confirmed that."

"Well Naylor was lying, and Grandpa obviously believed the official story. Naylor had our mother terminated and concocted the story about a drug overdose."

A shocked Seventeen asked, "Why?"

"You remember Yannie Hertzog?"

Seventeen looked blank.

"Omega's man in Cape Town," Nine continued. "He confided in me that Naylor had mom terminated because she was considered a security threat."

"A security threat? How?"

"Not sure. Hertzog thought it could have been something to do with her threatening to go to the authorities if she couldn't have contact with us."

A suddenly emotional Seventeen leaned forward and rested her head on Nine's shoulder. Before she knew it, she was crying as a myriad of emotions erupted within her.

Nine stroked her blonde hair tenderly.

"Oh Sebastian, look what Omega did to our mother. And

now Grandpa," she sobbed. "And we can't even arrange a funeral for him."

There was nothing he could say that would comfort her. Besides, Sebastian Senior was dead, but Francis was very much alive. Nine was very aware if what Naylor said was true Francis would soon be subjected to cutting-edge medical experiments. *All in the name of science*. With every passing hour, the risk to his son increased.

Nine suddenly noticed Seventeen looking at him anxiously. "What is it?" he asked.

"How will Isabelle receive me?"

Nine knew from their earlier discussions that Seventeen had no recollection of murdering Isabelle's parents. Nor did she recall having interned Isabelle in the CIA detention center in Andorra. After the recent traumas she'd been through, he wasn't sure she could handle learning the truth.

However, Nine realized he'd have to tell her what happened before she left for Tahiti. *It might as well be now*. He looked at her seriously. "There's something I need to tell you."

For the next ten minutes, Seventeen listened in shocked silence as Nine related how she'd killed Mister and Missus Alleget, and tortured Isabelle in a CIA detention center as part of an Omega operation to try to capture Nine. By the time he'd finished, Seventeen was shaking her head in disbelief.

"But I remember none of this," she whispered ashen-faced.

"Of course you don't. One of the side-effects of MK-Ultra is memory loss."

Seventeen couldn't speak for some time. She just sat there, staring into space, as she tried to make sense of the awful news Nine had just delivered. Finally she whispered, "Isabelle must hate me."

"She does," Nine conceded, "but she'll also recognize she needs your help." He put as positive a spin on it as possible, but wasn't sure he even believed it himself. "Plus, you can explain to her you were under the spell of MK-Ultra when you killed her parents."

Seventeen shook her head sadly. "I was a really bad person, wasn't I?"

Nine looked at his sister in a new light. He was seeing signs of a conscience in her he'd never seen before. "We were both forced to terminate many innocent people, Jennifer."

23

Seventeen had mixed emotions as she entered the Business Class compartment of the Air Tahiti Nui flight that would deliver her to Papeete. Still grieving over the loss of her beloved grandfather less than twenty-four hours earlier, she nevertheless felt more alive and invigorated than she had in a long time.

The former operative, who was traveling in the guise of a Dutch tourist, felt as though she was embarking on a mission as a working agent. In a way, she was. Only this time she was working against the Omega Agency, not for it. After how Naylor had treated her, that made her feel good.

Seventeen also felt guilty. Guilty that she should feel so alive and exhilarated so soon after her grandfather's death. She tried to put that out of her mind as she looked for her seat number. Then she saw it: seat number 9. She took it as a good omen she'd been allocated the same number her brother had been allotted by their Omega masters at birth.

As Seventeen placed her hand luggage in an overhead compartment, a familiar face caught her eye. She started when she realized she was looking at Fifteen, her former Omega colleague. The Latino, who was already sitting in an aisle seat several rows behind Seventeen's seat, looked briefly at her as he scanned all his business class traveling companions – just as he'd been trained to do.

Fifteen returned his attention to the attractive woman several rows ahead as she closed the door of the overhead compartment. Not because he'd recognized her, but because he found her easy on the eye.

Seventeen turned her back on him and sat down as quickly as she could without attracting any more attention than she already had. Mercifully, she had a window seat, so she was hidden from Fifteen for the moment at least. She found her heart was hammering away. A hundred unanswered questions raced through her mind. *Did he recognize me? Is he going to Papeete or getting off at Los Angeles? Is he looking for Isabelle too?* Then she remembered she was disguised and unrecognizable. So that took care of the first question, she hoped.

The former operative knew her other questions would be largely answered when they reached Los Angeles where their flight had a scheduled one-hour stopover before continuing to Papeete. If Fifteen remained on board for the entire flight, she could be certain he'd been sent to look for Isabelle.

Seventeen could feel her competitive juices flowing. She hadn't experienced that since her days as an active operative. All of a sudden, she was relishing the idea of pitting her skills and wits against her fellow orphan-operatives. Why the renewed confidence, she couldn't be sure, but she assumed it had something to do with Nine and the deprogramming he'd arranged for her.

An hour into the flight, Seventeen had to use a restroom. She opted to use one of the restroom cubicles toward the front of business class. That meant Fifteen would see her face when she returned to her seat. Better that, she figured, than walking right by him to use a cubicle to the rear. Steeling herself, she stood up and walked to the nearest cubicle.

Inside the cubicle, Seventeen checked her disguise. She couldn't fault it. Her blonde hair was now dyed red. Generous use of an artificial tanning agent ensured her normally pale skin looked tanned and clever use of makeup added ten years to her actual age.

Satisfied, Seventeen emerged from the cubicle and walked as casually as she could back to her seat. She'd hoped Fifteen would be sleeping, but he wasn't. Without looking directly at him, she could see he was wide awake and surveying her as she walked down the aisle. By the time she reached her seat and sat down, she was shaking. Seventeen prayed yet again that Fifteen hadn't recognized her.

#

As the Air Tahiti Nui flight crossed America's Midwest, Twenty Three was doing the rounds of maternity shops and baby's clothing stores in Papeete. He was showing Isabelle's photo to managers and staff, and even to customers, in the hope he could find someone who recognized her. However, he had no more luck than when he'd visited most of the town's restaurants earlier that day or the hospital and medical centers the previous night.

Twenty Three was almost certain Isabelle wasn't in Papeete. He'd searched high and low. He vowed he'd expand the search for her beyond the municipality as soon as Fifteen arrived. The extra manpower would enable him to search the entire island of Tahiti while Fifteen could start searching the outer islands. Meanwhile, he was resigned to more legwork as he still had more venues to visit in Papeete.

#

At the same time, less than an hour's drive away, the woman that Twenty Three was scouring Papeete to find was resting in the shade of a covered veranda at the home of her Thai friends. Still worried out of her mind, she was unable to admire the view the veranda afforded.

The home was one of a dozen modest bungalows that made up the small, self-contained commune that had been home for Isabelle since Chai, the nephew of their old friend Luang, had collected her in the middle of the night in Papeete. That had been several days ago.

In that time, no outsiders had visited the commune. It was at the end of a gravel road and well off the beaten track. The only comings and goings were those of the residents themselves. Chai and his co-workers took turns to take a van-load of freshly picked vegetables into Papeete early each morning to sell at the local markets.

The commune was situated in a narrow valley. High, jungle-covered mountains rose up on either side of the valley, giving it a Shangri-La sort of feel.

Most of the commune's residents were market gardeners. Rows of neatly tended vegetables stretched almost the entire width of the valley. One end of the valley opened up into banana plantations owned and operated by local Tahitians, and beyond these the Pacific Ocean could be seen – a sparkling slither of blue in the distance.

Under normal circumstances, Isabelle would have relished her stay in such an idyllic location. However, circumstances were far from normal and she felt she was going up the wall. While the gated commune was secure and comfortable enough, and her friends were the most hospitable of hosts, Isabelle feared she may never see her husband or son again. She was beside herself with worry.

Thinking of Nine prompted Isabelle to reach for the ruby he'd given her. It hung as a permanent adornment from the silver necklace she wore.

Isabelle was fearful for the wellbeing of her unborn child, too. The knowledge that people were looking for her so that they could take her baby, as they had Francis, terrified her.

#

As Seventeen queued to pass through Customs at Papeete's Fa'a'ā International Airport, she made sure she remained behind Fifteen in the queue. And she ensured she kept several other passengers between herself and the operative at all times. Not just because she wanted to minimize the risk of being seen and possibly identified, but because she wanted to observe him without being at all obvious. She was keen to see whether anyone was at the airport to meet him.

Seventeen had established that Fifteen was continuing on to

Papeete when he'd remained on board the Air Tahiti Nui flight during its one-hour stopover in Los Angeles. That had been a sobering moment, confirming that she'd be matching her wits against at least two Omega operatives – Fifteen and Twenty Three – in Tahiti. She assumed the latter was still there.

The former orphan-operative didn't have long to wait to find out. She and the other new arrivals were soon through Customs.

Seventeen emerged into the Arrivals Lounge in time to see Fifteen being greeted with a handshake by Twenty Three. Observing the pair took her back to when she was an active Omega operative. She couldn't help thinking how times had changed. When she was in the field, all the orphan-operatives – or the *elites* as Naylor insisted on calling them – nearly always traveled in disguise.

The former operative wondered if standards were slipping at the agency.

#

The following morning, Isabelle didn't recognize the tanned, red-headed tourist who arrived unannounced at the commune in a rental Jeep. Watching from the kitchen window of her bungalow, she tensed when she heard the visitor ask for her by name.

Isabelle's first thought was that the woman was an Omega operative. Remaining out of sight, she listened as the visitor spoke to the Thai market gardener who had greeted her.

"Sebastian has sent me to find Isabelle," the visitor said. "I am Sebastian's sister, Jennifer Hannar."

Isabelle thought she was hearing things. The visitor didn't remotely resemble the operative who had interned her in Andorra after killing her parents. Nor had Nine mentioned he would be recruiting her services. Isabelle studied the woman closely, looking for some sign she was who she claimed to be.

"I have a note for Isabelle from Sebastian," the visitor said, waving an envelope.

That decided it for Isabelle. Against her better judgment, she walked out onto the verandah. "You are looking for me?" she called out.

The visitor headed straight for her. As she neared, Isabelle thought there was something familiar about the way she moved.

"Hello, Isabelle," Seventeen said. She held the envelope out. "Sebastian asked me to give this to you."

Shaking, Isabelle took the envelope from the woman who claimed to be Jennifer Hannar. She opened the envelope and instantly recognized Nine's handwriting. "It is you!" she said, looking back at Seventeen.

The former operative smiled. "As you can see, my brother sent me to look after you."

Isabelle read the note quickly. In it, Nine confirmed he'd sent Seventeen to protect her. He also asked her to trust his sister and he reminded her that Seventeen had been under the insidious influence of MK-Ultra mind control when she'd terminated her parents.

Reading the note again, the Frenchwoman felt sick to her stomach. She couldn't believe her husband had recruited the services of the one person on earth she truly hated.

Seventeen thought she could read what was going through her sister-in-law's mind. She imagined she could feel the vibes of resentment Isabelle was directing her way.

"I'm sorry," Seventeen said.

"You're sorry?" Isabelle replied sarcastically in French. "Exactly what are you sorry about? Arriving unannounced or murdering my parents in cold blood?"

Seventeen had no answer and couldn't even look at Isabelle. She'd warned Nine this would be his wife's reaction – and so it had turned out.

24

Nine's arrival in Greenland was a first for him. Of all fifty-three countries he'd visited while an active operative with Omega, he'd never been to the mysterious, scenic land of Erik the Red and the other infamous Viking explorers and plunderers.

However, Nine wasn't here for the scenery or the history. The former operative was here for the sole purpose of finding his son, or at least confirming that Francis hadn't been sent to Greenland. He hoped it was the former as he was conscious he needed to find the boy quickly – before Omega's scientists had their way with him, if they hadn't already.

Nine had already lost valuable time as he'd flown via a brief stopover in Zurich. From there, he'd driven across the Swiss-

German border into the nearby Black Forest to confirm to his own satisfaction that the secret orphanage Omega operated there had in fact been closed down. He'd been confident it was as Naylor had said. Even so, he wanted to see for himself so that he could cross it off his list of possible places Omega could be holding Francis.

The former operative had soon confirmed with his own eyes that the Black Forest medical laboratory no longer existed. A forest ranger he'd had the good fortune to meet recalled that a colleague had personally witnessed the lab's destruction. The ranger couldn't remember the exact date, but by all accounts it was soon after Nine had blackmailed Naylor with the incriminating evidence he'd gathered on the orphanage.

Before returning to Switzerland, Nine had checked into an Internet café where he quickly established a new Yahoo account under an assumed name. Using an agreed codename, he'd emailed his attorneys in London and Berlin. They were the same attorneys he'd supplied with the evidence relating to the Black Forest orphanage five years earlier. He had retained them as his European legal representatives, though he'd had no cause to contact them again until now.

Nine had forwarded the two confidential files he'd downloaded at Naylor's together with new instructions. These included a directive to release the files far and wide, to the media and to appropriate authorities, should anything untoward happen to himself or to Isabelle.

Before leaving the café, he'd considered emailing Isabelle from his new account, but he resisted the temptation. While he was confident he couldn't be traced, the same couldn't be said of Isabelle, and he didn't want to expose her to any more danger than she was already in.

Nine had flown from Zurich to Greenland's main international airport at Kangerlussuaq via another stopover – this time in Copenhagen. During his short time in the Danish capital, he'd re-established contact with an underworld connection dating back to his Omega days. In return for a tidy bundle of cash, that shady individual had organized the contacts, permits and security passes Nine required for what he was planning to do in Greenland.

For the five-hour flight from Copenhagen to Kangerlussuaq,

he'd travelled in the guise of one Johannes Petersson, a Danish photo-journalist ostensibly on assignment for *National Geographic Magazine*. Blue contact lenses, a rouge-ruddy complexion, a curly, ginger-colored wig and matching false beard rendered him unrecognizable while a fluent understanding of Danish and an ability to speak the language flawlessly helped ensure his adopted persona appeared totally authentic.

The former operative had his Omega upbringing to thank for his fluency in Danish and, indeed, in the numerous languages and dialects he'd mastered during his exhaustive studies at the Pedemont Orphanage. In the orphanage's Spartan surroundings and university-like atmosphere, he and his fellow orphans had been raised from birth to be polymaths, or veritable walking encyclopaedias. Their education had been fast-tracked by a learned ability to speed-read and by being exposed to a succession of handpicked tutors who were, without exception, the best in their individual fields of expertise.

Nine's official reason for visiting Greenland was to photograph and report on the impact on wildlife caused by US Air

Force jets operating from Thule Air Base in the far northwest of the country. If the information he'd extracted from Naylor was correct, one of Omega's underground orphanages was located at Thule. Nine was reasonably confident the information was correct. After all, its accuracy had been confirmed by the confidential files he'd uplifted from Naylor's residence. Access to the Air Force base had also been organized by his Copenhagen contact.

Nine was in no doubt Omega would be looking out for him at Thule. *And probably here at Kangerlussuaq International Airport, too.* Naylor would have seen to that. The former operative reflexively glanced around at the baggage handlers and Customs officials as he queued to collect his luggage. No-one seemed to be taking any notice of him.

It was mid-morning by the time he passed safely through Customs, and he had several hours to kill before the scheduled departure of his early afternoon flight to Thule. While anxious to keep moving, Nine was thankful for the spare time as he had some important business to attend to.

A cab ride to the centre of Kangerlussuaq township delivered him to the ramshackle home of one of the contacts his Copenhagen confidant had organized. He asked the cabbie to wait then walked to the front door of the house. There, he was greeted by a heavily tattooed, twentysomething local woman whose features were distinctly Inuit. Her eyes were glazed and the smell of marijuana hung heavy in the air. Nine guessed she was half stoned.

"Who are you?" the woman asked in Greenlandic, the country's official tongue. Her words were distinctly slurred.

Unfamiliar with Greenlandic, Nine addressed her in Danish, the country's colonial language. "Is Lars Khader here?"

Switching to hesitant Danish, the woman asked, "Who wants to know?"

"I'm Johannes Petersson. He's expecting me."

The woman pointed down the street to a hotel. "He's at a meeting at the Kangerlussuaq."

Nine saw the hotel was only a couple of hundred yards away. He turned back to thank the woman, but she'd already retreated inside. The former operative returned to the cab. "To the Kangerlussuaq," he said as he jumped into the back seat.

The cabbie drove off. As it trundled the short distance to the hotel, Nine observed the passing homes. He was struck by their quaintness. Most were painted in bright colors, not dissimilar to homes he'd seen in townships in Norway. One was bedecked in reindeer antlers, which hung from the chimney, the roof and the balcony, and even adorned the letterbox.

Moments later, as the cab pulled up outside the hotel, Nine noticed a dozen Harley-Davidson motorcycles parked in the establishment's parking lot. "Tourists?" he asked in Danish, knowing full well who the bikes belonged to.

The cabbie shook his head. "No. Hell's Angels, would you believe?"

"Hells Angels? I wouldn't have thought there's enough open road for them here."

"There isn't. These lowlifes are the nearest we have to organized crime. They control the imports of illegal drugs."

Nine feigned surprise though he'd learned nothing he didn't already know. His Copenhagen confidant had fully briefed him. Pulling out a wad of dollar bills, he handed some to the cabbie.

"I'll get you to wait for me here, too."

"Be careful. These bikers don't take kindly to outsiders." The cabbie switched off the engine and waited while his fare entered the hotel.

25

Inside, the hotel's duty manager directed Nine to a small conference room at the rear of the premises where Hells Angels gang members were meeting. Approaching the room, Nine found a young, pimply-faced biker stationed outside the closed door. The gang's skull logo and death's head insignia were emblazoned on his leather motorcycle jacket, but that's where any resemblance of a Hells Angels biker ended. Nine adjudged the youth to be no taller than five foot three and eight stone in his stockings if he was lucky.

When the youth saw Nine approach, he folded his arms across his sunken chest and tried to make himself look taller. "Where do you think you're going?" he asked gruffly in Greenlandic.

Nine simply handed him a fake business card and replied in Danish, "Johannes Petersson to see Lars."

The youth looked suspiciously from Nine to the card and back to Nine. Without a word, he opened the door behind him and entered the conference room, leaving Nine alone in the passageway. The distinctive odour of marijuana carried to him.

Moments later, the youth returned in the company of Lars Khader, a Dane and self-appointed leader of the Kangerlussuaq Chapter of Hells Angels. Nine knew it was Lars from the photo his Copenhagen connection had shown him.

Lars Khader was as big as the pimply youth was small. At six foot six inches, he towered over his subordinate and was a good five inches taller than Nine. His flaming red hair and beard were even brighter than the former operative's ginger hair and beard. Nine fleetingly wondered if the biker was a throwback to Erik the Red. Lars studied the business card the youth had given him then looked suspiciously at the visitor standing before him.

Nine wasn't sure what to expect. He was taken by surprise when Lars' weather-beaten face suddenly creased into a huge grin.

The big biker extended his right hand. "I've been expecting you," he announced in Danish. They shook hands. Before Nine could speak, Lars swept one strong arm around him and steered him into the conference room. "We'll talk in here."

In the conference room, ten other gang members – most of whom were smoking joints – studied Nine critically as he appeared in their midst. Lars quickly dismissed them, indicating the meeting was over. They departed without debate. It was clear who was boss.

As soon as the pair were alone they sat down, facing each other across a table.

Lars got straight to the point. "I understand you've got some cash for me." It was evident the biker had been well briefed and their mutual Copenhagen connection had assured him Johannes Petersson was prepared to pay well for the specialist services he was able to provide.

"You understand correctly," Nine said, speaking for the first time. He fished out a thick wad of notes from his jacket pocket and placed it on the table-top in front of Lars. "There's your down-payment."

Lars eyed the cash greedily. Scooping the notes up, he counted them then placed them in his jacket pocket.

In the course of the next hour, Nine outlined his travel plans and likely requirements over the next twenty-four to thirty-six hours. Various contingencies were covered in depth in the event that something went wrong.

While Nine didn't explain what had brought him to Greenland, or what he hoped to achieve, he still had to tell Lars quite a lot. That made him nervous. It went totally against all his training and his instincts, but he realized he didn't have any choice. What he planned to do in the next day or so couldn't be done without outside help.

Nine just hoped the hundred grand Lars had negotiated as his payment would be enough to buy his loyalty and guarantee his silence. While half that amount would go on expenses, including helicopter and speedboat charters and the like, that still left a fifty grand profit for the gang leader.

The former operative watched as Lars reached beneath his

jacked and pulled out a pistol. Nine saw at a glance it was a USP semi-automatic weapon of the type favored by German police. He'd asked his Copenhagen contact to organize just such a weapon for him.

"I believe you ordered this," Lars said, sliding the pistol across the table top to Nine. "It's loaded." From a jacket pocket, he then produced a spare clip and a small box of ammunition, and placed them in front of his client.

"Thanks." Nine quickly established that the pistol was loaded then pocketed the weapon and scooped up the ammunition. "Any questions before I go?"

"Nope." Realizing the meeting was over, Lars stood up. "I just wait to hear from you then call in the chopper." He flashed his trademark grin.

Nine stood and shook hands with his opposite. While he didn't approve of the murky business Lars was in, he couldn't help but like the big fella. *But can I trust you?* Lars tried to disengage from the handshake, but Nine held on, squeezing the other's hand. The two stood like that for several seconds, staring each other down.

Lars' grin faded as he realised his client was testing him. He increased the pressure of his own grip.

Nine pulled the pistol from his pocket with his free hand, released the safety and held the barrel to Lars' forehead. "You double-cross me and I'll come looking for you. Do we understand each other?"

Lars could only nod, his eyes transfixed on the weapon.

Now it was Nine's turn to smile. He pocketed the pistol, released Lars' hand and slapped him on the back in friendly fashion. "Good man. Be ready for my call." He winked at the biker and strode from the room.

Behind him, Lars quickly reassessed his original perception of his client. He'd adjudged him to be a hard man. Now he knew he was dealing with hard man who was also a stone cold professional who wouldn't hesitate to kill. He told himself to tread carefully around the man who called himself Johannes Petersson.

26

From the shade of the veranda of the bungalow they now shared, Isabelle and Seventeen maintained an uneasy silence as they watched Chai and members of his family tend their vegetable plots. It had been like this since Seventeen had arrived in Tahiti and driven to the commune two days earlier.

The former operative hadn't expected a warm welcome from Isabelle. Not even if Nine had convinced her that Seventeen had terminated her parents whilst in a mind-controlled state and to this day had no recollection of the event. But she'd hoped her sister-in-law would at least try to be communicative. After all, she'd risked her life coming to protect her.

However, Isabelle wasn't prepared to cut Seventeen any

slack. On top of the murder of her parents, the memory of her treatment at the hands of Seventeen while interned at the CIA detention center in Andorra was still fresh in her mind. So she had done her best to ignore her uninvited guest since she'd arrived.

Before Seventeen had driven up to the commune's locked gate in her rental Jeep, she'd been intent on relocating Isabelle. The fact that the commune was so close to Papeete had worried her. She'd believed it would only be a matter of time before her former Omega colleagues found the Frenchwoman.

After arriving at the commune and seeing for herself how secure and self-contained it was, located as it was in a remote valley, she'd changed her mind. She now believed Isabelle was as safe here as anywhere in Tahiti – for the moment at least.

Under normal circumstances, Seventeen would have taken Isabelle to one of the remote outer islands in French Polynesia. However, given her advanced pregnant state, that was out of the question. She needed to be close to a hospital in the event of complications.

Now into her eighth month, Isabelle was extremely

uncomfortable. Her swollen belly felt tight and distended, her lower back constantly ached, her feet and knees hurt, she was always hungry and she had trouble sleeping.

The heat and humidity only added to Isabelle's discomfort – and Seventeen's. Although the two women were sitting in the shade, they were sweating profusely. Humidity levels were already high and it was not yet mid-morning.

Seventeen looked at her companion. "Feel like a cold drink?"

"Non."

That was another thing that irked Seventeen. On the odd occasion Isabelle did deign to speak to her, she spoke French. The former operative shrugged and disappeared inside.

In the bungalow's kitchen, as she poured herself a pineapple juice from the fridge, Seventeen wondered how long she'd have to put up with the cold-shoulder treatment from Isabelle. *Surely she'll realize her survival, and the baby's, depends on me no matter what I may have done to her in the past.* She drained the glass and closed her eyes as the ice-cold juice slid down her parched throat.

\#

If Seventeen had known how close one of her former Omega colleagues was at that moment, she'd have been more than a little concerned. Twenty Three was only a few miles away, working his way up the same gravel road the commune was on. He was calling in at every holding along the road to ask if anyone had seen a pregnant woman matching Isabelle's description.

Elsewhere on the island, Fifteen was following the same modus operandi, showing an identical photo of Isabelle to local residents.

So far, the two operatives were having no more luck than Twenty Three had when he was working alone. However, both men were feeling confident. They were convinced Isabelle was still on the island. And they had eyes everywhere since setting up a network of informants – local islanders who were being paid a handsome retainer to look for Isabelle and who stood to make a small fortune, by their standards at least, if they found her.

#

In his office at Omega's subterranean headquarters, Naylor sat, alone, massaging his temple. It was late and apart from a dozen or so personnel working the night shift on other floors he just about had the place to himself.

The Omega boss had been studying maps and photos of the agency's secret orphanages in Greenland and The Congo – the two medical labs whose existence the ninth-born orphan Sebastian Hannar was now aware of.

Just thinking of Nine gave Naylor a headache. That was why he was massaging his temple. Since the rogue orphan had physically assaulted him in his home, he'd suffered headaches. His doctor had assured him they'd pass, but here he was, several days later and they were as bad as ever.

For perhaps the tenth time that day, Naylor cursed the ninth orphan. The old man remained fearful his nemesis would go public with the information he had. He and his fellow directors would be in the hot seat if that happened and he knew it. However, with each passing hour he breathed a little easier. Naylor hoped Nine would realize he'd be saying goodbye to any hope of finding his son if he went public with what he knew. He would make sure of that.

Naylor returned his attention to the documents spread out

before him. He had no doubt whatsoever that if Nine wasn't there already, he would be on his way to one of Omega's two offshore medical labs in his search for his son. Which one, he had no way of knowing.

There had been no reported sightings of Nine since video surveillance cameras had filmed him driving into the car park building in downtown Chicago several days earlier. Nor had there been any sightings of Seventeen.

Using his secure line, Naylor had just phoned one of the orphan-operatives he'd sent to the orphanage in the DRC, in Africa. The operative had reported all was quiet.

Now he was in the process of placing a call to the operatives he'd sent to the lab in Thule, Greenland. The call was answered by Number Three, a mixed-race individual of African-American and Arab descent known for his mastery of Teleiotes, a deadly martial art. All of Omega's orphan-operatives had been drilled in Teleiotes since early childhood. However, the swarthy Three had taken it to another level and he prided himself on his ability to kill using only his bare hands.

"Kamal Al Saud speaking," Three answered, using the codename he'd been assigned for this mission.

"Naylor here."

"Yes sir."

"Anything to report?"

"No sir, not a thing."

"Well stay alert, both of you." Naylor referred to Three and his fellow operative Fourteen who had both been sent to Thule. "There's a one-in-two chance our man will go to Thule first, so the odds are high he'll make an appearance sooner or later."

"Understood."

"And watch out for the woman, too," Naylor said, referring to Seventeen. "She may well be with him." Naylor ended the call and immediately resumed massaging his temple. His headache was worsening and as always he blamed Nine.

27

On arriving at Thule Air Base via Air Greenland and passing through the various US Air Force security checks, Nine's first port of call was his guest house in the tiny settlement of Thule. Then, after checking in and taking delivery of a rental car, his next port of call, quite literally, was the nearby Port of Thule.

Located as it was above the Arctic Circle, it was the world's northernmost deep water port. And, like all of Greenland's west coast ports and settlements, it was also ice-free in summer, which suited Nine just fine for what he was planning.

Driving through town to the port, he observed the charming and colorful houses that were home for many of Thule's seven hundred or so residents. The dwellings hugged the edge of the harbor and afforded their occupants unobstructed mountain and sea views. At this time of year, the only visible snow was on the mountaintops. Even so, Nine was pleased he was wearing his winter woollies, and he drove with the car's heater on full. It was only five degrees Celsius outside.

The skies above were never free of jet aircraft. There was at least one in sight at any given time, and the sound of fighter planes landing and taking off at the air base was constant.

Why on earth Omega had chosen Thule as the location for one of its secret medical labs, Nine could only guess. He assumed its isolation was one reason. No doubt the security afforded by the Air Force base was another.

Re-evaluating what he knew about the base, the former operative was aware it was home to the 21st Space Wing's global network of sensors that provided space surveillance and missile warning to the Air Force Space Command and the North American Aerospace Defence Command. It also served as a ballistic missile early warning site and since 2002 had been home to the 821st Air Base Group.

That knowledge didn't fill him with confidence. Nine had already had a taste of the tight security in force at the air base. He had a feeling finding his son – if Francis was even there – would be difficult enough. Secreting him off the base and away from Thule would be another matter. He had visions of being pursued by fighter planes or military helicopters intent on blowing them both to oblivion.

Nine was also aware of the strange events said to have occurred at or near Thule over the years. Conspiracy theories abounded.

In the early Twentieth Century, the tiny settlement inspired the underground Nazi occult organization known as the Thule Society. Its membership was rumored to include Adolf Hitler and numerous other Nazi leaders. Then in the 1950's, American soldiers wounded in the Korean War were hospitalized in Thule because the US Government considered its citizens weren't ready to see battle casualties so soon after World War Two. And when a B-52 nuclear bomber crashed and burned on the ice near Thule Air Base in 1968, the Pentagon classified all documents relating to the crash. Since then, media reports on America's northernmost Air Force base had been unaccountably few and far between.

Nine slowed as he neared a security gate at the entrance to the main wharf. Flashing the same security passes he'd used at the base, he drove onto the wharf, his destination a bright yellow boatshed at the far end.

Driving well within the ten miles per hour speed limit, he had plenty of time to observe his surroundings. In addition to the presence of commercial freighters, fishing boats and container ships in the harbor, there was a surprising number of pleasure craft at anchor. They included cabin cruisers, speedboats, schooners and even the odd racing yacht.

Nine felt slightly apprehensive as he pulled up outside the boatshed. This would be the first test of the loyalty and efficiency of Hells Angels biker Lars Khader. The big fellow had been ordered to book a fast, reliable boat to facilitate what Nine anticipated could be a hasty getaway from Thule.

Disembarking from the car, he walked to the edge of the wharf and looked down. There, tied up alongside, was a sleek

Albermarle sport fishing boat. Nine liked the look of her. Around thirty foot long, her markings indicated she was a 310 Express.

The former operative wracked his brains. Information filed away since his exhaustive studies at the Pedemont Orphanage slowly came to him: the craft's powerful inboard twin diesel engine had a range of three hundred and sixty-five nautical miles, and could maintain forty knots in heavy seas. He decided it'd deliver him to where he was going in good time.

Nine looked behind him as he became aware he was being observed from the boatshed.

A bearded, stocky, fiftysomething man greeted him from the boatshed's doorway with a friendly wave. "Alluu," he called out in Greenlandic.

"Hej," Nine responded in Danish.

Believing the stranger to be Danish, the seafarer switched to that tongue. "Are you here about the Albermarle?"

"I am."

"Come on in." The seafarer, who was in fact the boatshed's owner-operator, returned inside and motioned to Nine to follow.

Inside the boatshed, the man introduced himself as Hans Holdt. The transaction was finalised in double-quick time. Lars had already paid by credit card for the boat hire and for its fuel and provisioning, so all Nine had to do was sign the hire papers and insurance documents.

When Hans asked what he needed the boat for, Nine fobbed him off by saying he planned to use it to visit nearby Cape York, to the south, to take wildlife photos. Hans handed over the keys to the Albermarle and didn't question his customer any further.

Before departing, Nine asked, "What time does it get dark around here this time of year?"

Hans chuckled. "This is the land of the midnight sun my friend. The sun never sets this time of year."

Nine immediately felt stupid for asking. He knew he should have known that. *I must be slipping*. The former operative would never have needed to ask such a question once. He put it down to the heart pills he was on. They were taking their toll and he was aware he wasn't as sharp as he once was, mentally or physically. He covered his embarrassment with a smile. "Thanks for that."

The two shook hands and Nine hurried back to his car. Now that he'd finalized his escape route, he was ready to rescue Francis. *If he's here.* Nine still had no way of knowing if his son was even in Greenland. He'd find out soon enough. His next stop was Thule Air Base.

Driving back through town, Nine experienced chest pains. *Not again!* He pulled over to the side of the road and quickly popped a couple of pills. The pain subsided almost immediately, but the experience served as a timely reminder that he had to pace himself. It also left him feeling tired – so tired he could have easily fallen asleep right there and then.

Nine wasn't sure if it was the drugs causing his tiredness or the unrelenting stress he'd been under since Francis' abduction. *A bit of both perhaps.* Fighting against the tiredness, he resumed driving. Not to the air base, but to his guest house. He knew his limitations; he needed to grab some sleep before doing anything else.

Back at the guest house, he made a quick phone call to the air base's Customer Liaison Office to postpone his appointment by several hours. His contact there – a young airman assigned to guide him around the base – was most obliging. The airman was working the so-called night shift, so the rescheduled appointment wouldn't inconvenience him.

A desperately tired Nine then went to bed. Sleep came quickly.

#

The former operative woke to the shrill ringing of his alarm clock. He could easily have slept on, but he felt considerably more alert than when he'd crashed three hours earlier.

The clock told him it was eight thirty at night. For a moment Nine couldn't make sense of the sunlight that was streaming through a gap in the curtains then he remembered where he was and why he was here. *Francis!* He sprang from bed, splashed cold water on his face from a tap at the sink and hurriedly dressed.

Nine felt ready for whatever lay ahead. After repacking his travel bags and loading them into his rental car, he settled his account at reception then set off for nearby Thule Air Base to find his son.

As he drove, he recited his daily affirmation aloud.

I am a free man and a polymath.

Whatever I set my mind to, I always achieve.

The limitations that apply to the rest of humanity,

Do not apply to me.

28

From the upstairs visitors' lounge at Thule Air Base, Nine had a panoramic view of the base and its surrounds. The never-ending summer daylight facilitated flights by US Air Force jets twenty-four hours a day every day. This day, or night, was no exception: fighter planes were landing and taking off every few minutes. Even through the double-glazed windows, the sound of roaring jet engines was constant.

An attractive, uniformed receptionist had explained to Nine that his visit happened to coincide with scheduled Air Force manoeuvers. Nine had feigned interest in the activity, though his focus was on locating the whereabouts of the secret medical lab he knew to be somewhere on the base. The contents of the confidential file he'd uplifted on the orphanage at Thule Air Base had been very explicit, but they hadn't specified the underground facility's exact location.

Several large aircraft hangars on the far side of the base caught his attention. Using the zoom lens of his digital Canon single-lens reflex camera, he focused on the hangars, trying to identify anything that would point to the location of any facility that appeared to be off-limits to Air Force personnel.

A polite cough alerted him to the fact he wasn't alone. Nine turned to see he'd been joined by an eager young airman.

"Junior NCO Marty Williams," the airman announced stiffly, "at your service, sir."

Nine wondered whether he was about to be saluted. He extended his hand. "Hi Marty, I'm Johannes Petersson." He spoke English with a strong Danish accent. "Call me Jo."

Marty relaxed and shook hands with his opposite. "We spoke earlier, Jo. I've been assigned to look after you while you are here."

"Babysitter, eh?"

The Junior NCO grinned sheepishly. "How can I help?" Having been thoroughly briefed, he was already aware of the reason for Nine's visit – to photograph and report on how jet aircraft movements were impacting on Thule's wildlife for National Geographic.

Over the next five minutes, Nine explained how he needed to identify suitable vantage points he could use to take photos from when he returned the next day. He said his immediate focus was on establishing how aircraft movements were impacting on Thule's bird life, so he'd need access to parts of the base that offered unobstructed views.

Marty turned out to be a most obliging host. He said off the top of his head he could think of dozens of suitable vantage points.

"Are there any areas that are off-limits?" Nine hurriedly added, "I don't want to stray where I'm not welcome and get offside with the hierarchy."

"As long as you're with me, all areas are accessible except for one." He pointed to the same hangars Nine had been studying a minute earlier. "There's a Government facility behind the far hangar that's off-limits."

"Oh, what goes on there?" Nine asked innocently.

Marty shrugged. "We don't ask. Top secret apparently. Anyway, shall we make a start?"

"You bet." As Nine followed his guide downstairs and across a strip of tarmac to the main control tower, he celebrated the fact that at least he knew the lab's likely location.

Marty pointed up at the tower. "Best views around up there." It turned out he was right.

Over the next two hours, Nine and Marty visited almost every part of the base aboard an Air Force Land Rover, which Marty drove. At each location, Nine viewed his surroundings through his camera lens and diligently made notes in a shorthand pad.

Marty was impressed and showered his visitor with questions about his wildlife photography exploits, which Nine answered by lying effortlessly and tapping into his textbook-learned knowledge of wildlife photography. He did his best to appear continually enthusiastic, but his mind was on how to find Francis and secret him off the base without having every US Air Force jet north of the Arctic Circle after him.

It was after eleven by the time they reached the hangars that Nine was so interested in. Though the sun was now slightly lower in the sky and its brightness had dimmed, it was still broad daylight outside.

Marty conveniently parked the Land Rover in a parking space behind the closest hangar. Convenient because the car park was deserted and Nine was about to swing into action. Pointing at the far hangar to his passenger's right, Marty reminded him it was off-limits.

The former operative pointed at something else out the driver's side window. As Marty looked around, Nine's fingers closed around the vagal nerve in the young man's neck. Marty was asleep before he realized anything was amiss.

Working quickly, Nine tied and gagged the unconscious airman. He let the driver's seat down and rolled Marty onto the back seat, covering him with a tarpaulin he found in the rear of the Land Rover and securing him so he couldn't sit up when he regained consciousness. Then he climbed out of the vehicle and quickly walked toward the far hangar. He carried his camera in case he was seen and challenged. Fortunately, there were few Air Force personnel around at this end of the base.

No Entry signs greeted him as he reached the off-limits zone. Two security cameras he spotted caused him to lose valuable minutes as he was forced to circumnavigate around them to evade their gaze.

Nine found the hangar's main doors were closed, but a side-entry door was open with no guard in sight. A sign above the door read: *No unauthorized entry*. Nine slipped inside and immediately saw the hangar was home to half a dozen fighter planes. A quick visual inspection revealed he had the place to himself.

Sounds of activity reached him from outside the hangar's back wall. Keeping close to the near wall, he strode over to an exit door he'd noticed. Opening it just an inch or so, he saw an armed Air Force sentry standing just a few yards away. The sentry was at the top of a concrete stairway that led below ground. *Found it!* Nine was in no doubt the stairway led to Omega's medical lab for orphans.

Some thirty yards beyond the sentry were several low-lying blocks of apartments. Nine guessed they served as living quarters for the lab personnel. Like the entrance to the underground facility, they hadn't been visible from other parts of the base. Nine couldn't even recall seeing them when he'd flown into the base earlier in the day. He imagined considerable thought had been given to their location.

Even at this late hour, people were walking between the apartments and the underground facility. Nine noted many were dressed as lab technicians. Others – male and female – were dressed as nurses and medical orderlies. He also noticed an abundance of *No Trespassing* and *No Unauthorized Entry* signs along with a proliferation of security cameras in the area.

Nine was surprised by the amount of activity, here and elsewhere on the base, considering the lateness of the hour. He had to remind himself normal business hours didn't apply in the land of the midnight sun, nor did they apply to anything connected to Omega.

Three white-coated personnel approached the sentry. They showed him their passes then disappeared down the stairs.

Seconds later, two more personnel emerged from below ground, deep in discussion, and headed for the apartments. One could be heard complaining about the long hours they were working. The other one commiserated with his colleague, but reminded him how well they were being paid. Their accents gave them away as Americans.

If Nine had any doubt before that he'd found Omega's orphanage, he was in no doubt now.

The former operative felt his excitement rising. He realized he could be just minutes away from finding Francis. *Stay cool.* Nine reminded himself to remain totally professional. Now wasn't the time to get excited.

His first problem was how to get past the sentry. Closing the door quietly, he retraced his steps and left the hangar via the same side door he'd used earlier. He walked around the far side of the facility and soon spotted what he was looking for: an air vent leading below ground. It was exactly where he considered a vent should be.

Retrieving a screwdriver from the emergency kit he'd brought along, he quickly removed the steel grill covering the vent's opening. Sounds of activity from below carried to him. He found himself listening for the sound of Francis' voice.

29

Below ground, the air vent opened out into what appeared to be a large storage room. As soon as he confirmed he had the room to himself, Nine dropped silently down onto the concrete floor and took in his surroundings.

Shelves lining two walls were stocked with medical supplies, including prescription drugs and surgical instruments. Hospital-style trolleys and beds occupied most of the available floor space.

White coats hanging from pegs along the far wall caught

Nine's eye. Removing his heavy jacket, he selected one of the coats and slipped it on. He spent the next five minutes adopting the guise of a lab technician. There was nothing he could do about his ginger-dyed hair at short notice, but he removed his fake beard – pocketing it for future use – and made himself as presentable as possible.

Studying himself in the reflection of a stainless steel cupboard, he wasn't totally satisfied with the end result, but knew it would have to do. *At least I no longer look like the wild yeti of the Arctic.* He approached the door, opened it a crack and looked out. It opened into a brightly lit corridor.

Several white-coated technicians walked past deep in discussion. Nine identified American and British accents. He slipped out into the corridor and followed, taking care not to look directly at the security cameras he passed at regular intervals along the corridor.

Nine noted the technicians carried clipboards and other official-looking items. Empty-handed and feeling conspicuous, he looked out for something that would suffice. Nothing came to his attention.

The technicians slowed as they approached a large lab half way along the corridor. Nine hung back as they used their security cards to access the lab. Outside it, half a dozen white-coated personnel sat observing the activity inside through wide viewing windows.

Aware he'd attract attention if he continued to hover, Nine joined the observers, taking the last vacant seat. No-one gave him a second glance. They were too busy observing the activity inside the lab and making notes on their clip boards.

Nine noticed spare clipboards, pens and stationery on a shelf beneath the narrow bench in front of him. He grabbed a pen and clipboard then focused on what was happening on the other side of the glass. What he saw almost made him physically recoil.

The sights that confronted him took him back to his first visit, years earlier, to Omega's underground orphanage in the Black Forest. On that occasion, he'd witnessed macabre scientific experiments being conducted on children – dozens of children. Many of the grotesquely disfigured subjects were the failed results of Omega's first miserable attempts to clone the original Twenty Three orphans spawned by the Pedemont Project.

Nine had been horrified then and he was horrified now. In a lab that seemed to stretch half the length of a football field, scores of orphans were being subjected to scientific experiments conducted by scientists and medical personnel. The children ranged in age from around five to fifteen; the experiments ranged from bizarre to horrific.

Nine wanted to look away, but couldn't. He watched, transfixed, as scientists subjected a young girl to high-intensity shock treatment. The girl, who Nine assessed could be no older than seven, was as tall as the tallest man in the room. Her convulsions were such three orderlies were required to hold her down.

To one side of her, another little girl who had a full facial beard was injected with a substance Nine assumed to be growth hormones, while on the other side a young teenage boy who had six fingered hands screamed as orderlies strapped him to an operating table. Nine could only imagine what was in store for him.

As had been the case at the Black Forest orphanage all those years ago, many of the children were disfigured or had unusual physical features. Some were old before their time, others considerably younger than their years. One ten-year-old boy had a physique Mister Universe would be proud of while a young teenage girl had the mouth and nose of her unborn twin protruding from the back of her head.

Most of the children appeared to be in a trance-like state. Every now and then a nurse or orderly would flash psychedelic lights into their eyes to ensure they remained that way.

Looking around at his companions in front of the viewing windows, Nine saw they weren't remotely bothered by what they saw. *Another day at the office.* It was clear they'd seen it all many times before. Their manner was professional and detached as they observed the activities and recorded observations on their clipboards.

Nine returned his attention to the lab and was confronted by the surreal sight of two children levitating various objects, apparently through the power of their minds. The objects, which included a pencil and a ruler, floated in front of their eyes as scientists monitored their charges' progress. No-one seemed remotely surprised by the gravity-defying sight.

The lab was a study in motion as scientists and doctors conducted experiments, technicians entered data into held-held computers and voice recorders, and nurses and orderlies performed a wide variety of tasks ranging from the execution of basic medical procedures to the emptying of bedpans.

Nine scanned the orphans' faces, searching for Francis. *Where are you son?* There was no sign of the boy. Nine didn't know whether to be relieved or disappointed.

The former operative was so focused on looking for Francis he didn't immediately notice the reflection of a new arrival in the viewing window. It was only when the figure approached the window that Nine became aware of his presence. It was Number Three, one of his former Omega colleagues. Three stopped behind a technician seated two along from Nine.

To Nine's relief, the mixed-race operative showed no interest in him or any of the others. Three was too busy watching the levitation display beyond the glass.

The sight of the third-born orphan brought back a flood of memories for Nine. He had vivid memories of Three dating back to their years growing up at the orphanage in Riverdale, Chicago. Nine could still remember playing chess with his fellow orphan and going for training runs with him alongside Little Calumet River.

The former operative had a vision of Three giving One, the oldest and biggest of the Pedemont orphans, a bloody nose for mocking his Arab heritage. That had been one of the few times One had been bested in a fight. The incident reminded Nine that Three was an accomplished Teleiotes martial artist. He recalled Three was the only one of the orphans who had come close to beating him in the Teleiotes contests that were a regular event at the orphanage. Since those days, he'd heard that the operative had taken his fighting skills to a new level.

Observing Three's reflection in the viewing window, Nine promised himself he wouldn't take his fellow orphan on in a fair fight. He was relieved when the operative lost interest in what was going on in the lab and walked off down the corridor.

Nine gave it ten seconds then followed Three at a circumspect distance. Along the way he noticed a sign above a closed door. It read: *Control Office*. He made a mental note to return to it.

As they walked, Nine thought back to his days as an active operative and performed a quick mental stocktake of Three's abilities. As well as being highly accomplished in Teleiotes, he was an excellent marksman – almost as good as Seventeen. Of all the Pedemont orphans, Seventeen had been without peer as a sharpshooter. She'd proven that on the Guyana job.

Three had also earned a deserved reputation as the most ingenious of the orphan-operatives when it came to killing. He had devised some unique methods of terminating his targets over the years, and word of this had spread among his colleagues.

Nine didn't doubt that Three had refined his skills to even higher levels since he'd left Omega. He took it as a good sign that one of Omega's orphan-operatives, or elites, had been sent to the

Thule lab. *It could mean Francis is here.* Equally, he knew Naylor would have sent high level reinforcements to intercept him at the African lab, so he was aware he shouldn't read too much into Three's presence.

Either way, Nine realized he'd have to deal with Three and with any other Omega operatives who may be with him. Pedemont orphans would be a major obstacle to his plans if they weren't immobilized.

Whether or not Three was the only Omegan assigned to Thule Air Base was answered when the operative entered a room toward the end of the corridor. Before Three closed the door behind him, Nine caught a glimpse of Fourteen, a blond, Aryan-looking operative of Nordic descent. So now he knew at least two of his fellow orphans were at the base.

As Nine continued past the room, his mind was racing. He debated whether to charge in and shoot them both dead with the USP pistol he carried on him. That thought was dismissed almost immediately as he realized such drastic action would alert the entire base. He couldn't risk that. His strategy relied on remaining undetected.

30

Nine retraced his steps, vowing to sort the problem posed by Three and Fourteen later. He'd deal with them when they were alone and apart. Together, they presented too big a problem.

The former operative returned along the corridor to the control office he'd passed earlier. Testing the door handle, he found it was locked. That obstacle was resolved almost immediately when the door opened and a female technician emerged. Nine smiled at her and entered the office before the door had time to close behind the departing technician.

Inside, he found a controller seated before a line-up of computers and television screens. The controller, a middle-aged man, was monitoring activity in the lab. His attention was on the computer monitors and he wasn't aware he had company.

Nine checked the door was locked then drew his pistol and approached the unsuspecting controller who remained engrossed in the images on one of the monitors.

The first the controller became aware he wasn't alone was when he felt the barrel of Nine's pistol against the back of his head. Before he could utter a noise, a strong hand covered his mouth.

"One word and you're dead," Nine said quietly. "Understood?"

The startled controller nodded vigorously.

"Good." Nine removed his hand and moved around in front of the controller. With his free hand, he pulled out a photo of Francis and held it up before the controller's eyes. "This is my son, Francis Hannar. Is he here?"

The controller looked from the pistol in Nine's right hand to the photo in his left hand and then back to the pistol. Sweat rolled down his forehead and he shook with fear.

Nine waved the photo closer to the man. "This boy, have you

seen him."

The controller looked at the photo again then shook his head, indicating he hadn't seen Francis.

"Yes or no," Nine said losing his patience.

"No," the controller whispered.

"Look again!" Nine held the photo even closer to the man's face.

"No I haven't seen him!" the controller blurted out.

Nine felt his heart sink. He was reasonably confident someone in the controller's position would know all the lab's inmates by sight. "Where do you keep the registrations of subjects?"

The controller looked blank.

"Experimental subjects or orphans or whatever the hell Omega is calling them these days!" Nine snapped. "The children you people subject to these inhuman experiments." Nine looked pointedly at one of the television screens.

The controller glanced at the screen in time to see a white-coated scientist injected a dye into a small European boy whose skin had been turned black by a regime of such treatments. Now he understood what Nine was asking. "All registrations are filed electronically," he stammered.

"Show me." Nine waved his pistol threateningly.

The controller, who now shook more violently than ever, moved the mouse on his desktop computer and then typed in a password. Within seconds, a list of names appeared on screen in alphabetical order.

"Are these the children?" Nine asked.

The controller fidgeted nervously. In his haste to please the intruder, he realized he'd brought up the wrong list.

"Well?" Nine asked.

"No, they're the names of patients who have passed away."

The reality of what Nine was facing came home to him. Omega's experiments were high risk and right there, on the screen before him, was the proof. "My God," he muttered. "You people are no better than the Nazis." Nine rounded on the controller as if he was personally responsible.

"Please! I'm just following my employer's instructions."

"Don't give me that," Nine responded. He felt like pistol whipping the frightened man as he had Naylor. Instead, he remained as calm and detached as humanly possible. "Bring up the list of live patients." He put special emphasis on the word *patients*, and the sarcasm wasn't lost on the controller.

Within seconds, more lists appeared on screen. These, too, were in alphabetical order.

"These are the children currently undergoing treatment here," the controller said.

"Treatment!" Nine scoffed. He wanted to remonstrate with the man over his choice of words, but for the moment was fully focused on finding Francis' name in the lists on the screen. Nine scrolled through the lists twice, but found no mention of his son. Turning to the controller he asked, "Is there a list of recent arrivals?"

The controller nodded and brought up another list. "This is everyone who has arrived in the last month."

This list contained only six names. Nine saw at a glance Francis's name was not among them. *So he's not here.* His immediate reaction was almost one of relief. The thought of his son being interned here in this chamber of horrors had chilled him to the bone.

Then reality kicked in and he reminded himself if Francis wasn't here – as appeared to be the case – he'd be in a similar facility in Africa, and it would take time to get there. *Time Francis may not have. Or me for that matter.* Even allowing for a clean getaway from Thule, he estimated it would be a good three days before he'd arrive in the DRC.

Resigned to departing Thule Air Base without Francis, Nine looked directly at the controller. The poor man was convinced he was about to be shot. Instead, Nine gagged him using the controller's own handkerchief then trussed him up using computer cords. He tied him firmly to a protruding gas pipe so he couldn't move far.

Before opening the door, Nine looked back at the controller. "Following your employer's instructions is no excuse. You know that, don't you?"

The controller just looked at him, wide-eyed.

"Don't you?" Nine repeated, pointing his pistol at the man.

The controller nodded, indicating he did know that.

Nine concealed his weapon and slipped out into the corridor. Closing the door quietly behind him, he heard the familiar *click* as it self-locked. He hoped it would be at least half an hour before someone found the trussed-up controller. That would give him time to get off the base.

First, he needed to find one or both of his former colleagues, Three and Fourteen. He hoped his fellow Pedemont orphans may be able to reveal information the controller could not.

Nine retraced his steps yet again – this time back to the room where he'd seen the two orphan-operatives.

31

Standing outside the room, Nine quickly looked up and down the corridor. There was no-one in sight. He drew his pistol and then pressed his ear against the door. Not a sound.

Keeping his pistol concealed beneath his white coat, Nine knocked on the door. No answer. He knocked again.

"Coming." A voice came from inside.

Nine recognized the voice was Fourteen's. Even after all these years, he still recognized the voice of a fellow orphan.

The former operative sensed he was being viewed through the door's spy hole. He just hoped his technician's guise would stand up to the scrutiny of his fellow orphan. The door opened, indicating his disguise had stood up to initial scrutiny at least.

Fourteen was exactly as Nine remembered him, only older. The years had not been kind to the operative with the Aryan features. His once youthful Nordic look had been replaced by a hardness that probably reflected the life he'd led since graduating from the orphanage as a fully fledged operative.

"Yes?" Fourteen asked curtly.

The operative seemed annoyed to have been disturbed and Nine wondered if he'd been about to take a nap. He wouldn't blame him if he had been. After all, it had gone midnight.

"I work in Precinct Eleven," Nine said maintaining his strong Danish accent. "I have an urgent security matter I wish to discuss."

"Very well." Fourteen stepped aside "Come in."

Nine's eyes swept the room as he stepped through the doorway. He saw at a glance they had the room to themselves and immediately wondered where Three was. Behind him, Fourteen closed the door and indicated to Nine that he should sit. He obliged, sitting down on the nearest chair. Fourteen sat down facing him.

Surveying the room again, Nine could see it served as a day

room for the use of his former colleagues while they were at the base. There was a television set in one corner and a bookshelf in another. Unwashed coffee mugs could be seen in a sink in front of a coffee urn and newspapers lay strewn over a small table.

"Well," Fourteen asked, "how can I help you?"

Nine stood and handed his opposite the clipboard he'd picked up. He pointed to some doodles the clipboard's previous owner had left on it. "I've been keeping a record of the daily activities in the main lab," he said.

Fourteen frowned as he tried to make sense of the doodles. He was concentrating so hard he never saw the butt of the machine pistol that smacked against his skull.

Pocketing his pistol, Nine locked the door. He didn't want to be disturbed by Three, or by anyone else for that matter. The former operative pulled a telephone cord from the wall and used it to firmly tie the unconscious Fourteen's hands behind his back. Then he propped his fellow orphan up against the wall and waited for him to regain consciousness.

Looking at Fourteen, Nine reviewed what he could recall of

him. Of all the Pedemont orphans, Fourteen had been the most studious. What he may have lacked in physicality, he made up for with brainpower and ruthlessness. Nine recalled that next to Seventeen perhaps, Fourteen was the most ruthless of the orphans. Indeed their mentor, Tommy Kentbridge, had once nicknamed Fourteen *Mister Ruthless*.

A groan indicated the operative was coming to. Nine walked to the sink and poured cold water into a mug. He then threw the mug's contents over the groggy operative's face. Fourteen's eyes flew open as he regained full consciousness.

"Welcome back," Nine said.

Fourteen squirmed as he tested the bonds that secured his hands.

"No point in struggling," Nine cautioned. He spoke in his normal voice now. "I used an Axle hitch."

Fourteen noted the change in his assailant's accent. He now sounded American.

Nine continued, "I could have used a Barrel knot or a Constrictor knot perhaps, but they have their limitations." He recited almost verbatim a lecture Kentbridge had once given the orphans on which knots to use to restrain someone. "Or I could have gone for a Killick hitch or a Span loop, but they're not totally reliable either." As he spoke, he could see Fourteen trying to work out who his assailant was. "Then again, I could have--"

"Nine? Is that you?" Fourteen asked. Something about his assailant reminded him of the ninth-born orphan.

"Got it in one. Well done, Fourteen." Aware he'd already spent too much time at the air base, Nine knelt down in front of his former colleague. "Where's Three?"

"He went back to the barracks for some shut-eye."

Nine tried to assess whether Fourteen was lying. All the signs were he was telling the truth. He fished the photo of Francis from his pocket and held it up in front of the operative. "Have you seen my son here?"

Ignoring the question, Fourteen said, "Naylor said you'd probably show up."

"Yeah well there was a one in two chance I'd come here, so it wouldn't take Einstein to work that out."

"How's life outside Omega, anyway?"

"It's just fine thanks." Nine simultaneously held the photo closer to Fourteen's face and, with his other hand, released the safety catch on his pistol. "Don't make me ask again."

Fourteen could see Nine meant business. He looked at the photo and shook his head. "No."

"Do you know if he was sent here?"

"No. Naylor didn't tell us that in case this exact scenario eventuated."

Again, Fourteen seemed to be telling the truth. It made sense to Nine that Naylor wouldn't have told his operatives which of the labs Francis had been sent to. That way, the truth couldn't be prized out of them. Nine felt it would be a waste of time asking the next question, but he had to ask it. "Do you know where they sent him?"

Fourteen just shook his head.

Nine wasn't fazed. *I already know the answer anyway*. He was resigned to having to travel to the other orphanage in Africa. The former operative stood up and looked around.

"Over there." Fourteen nodded to a cushion on one of the chairs. He'd already deduced what Nine was looking for.

Nine picked up the cushion and knelt down beside Fourteen again. "Sorry I have to do this."

Fourteen shrugged. "I know. It ain't personal. It's business."

Resigned to what was coming, the operative closed his eyes as Nine placed the cushion against his head. Nine pushed the barrel of his pistol hard against the cushion and prepared to pull the trigger.

32

"You could try American Summit Camp," Fourteen said. His muffled voice could just be heard through the pillow.

"What's that?" Nine lowered the pillow, but kept his pistol trained on the operative.

"I said you could try American Summit Camp. It's a scientific station in the dead centre of the ice sheet."

Nine had heard of the station. He recalled it was established in the late Eighties to support the country's deep ice-coring efforts. "What about it?"

"I heard new subjects bound for the laboratory here in Thule are sometimes processed at a branch lab near the Summit Camp."

"How near?"

"Five miles south of the camp. It's signposted."

"Why are you telling me this?"

Fourteen didn't answer.

Satisfied he'd learned all he could from his fellow orphan, Nine returned the cushion to Fourteen's head and pushed the barrel of his pistol hard into the cushion once again.

This time, Fourteen didn't close his eyes. He just looked calmly at his fellow orphan.

Nine steeled himself to pull the trigger. He couldn't do it. Despite their differences, the Pedemont orphans were like family. They'd been brought up together as siblings and the boys looked on each other as brothers. Although they'd since all gone their own separate ways, there was still that bond between them.

With a mighty effort, the former operative forced all such thoughts from his mind. *You have to do what's best for Francis.* He steeled himself once more. This time he pulled the trigger.

The retort was muffled so efficiently it wouldn't have been heard unless someone was standing right outside the door. Fourteen sagged to the side, clearly dead.

Nine quickly checked for a pulse. There was none. He stood up and prepared to leave.

Looking down at the body, he said, "You're wrong Fourteen. This is very personal."

For a split second he wondered why the operative had told him about Omega's branch lab at American Summit Camp. *An attack of conscience maybe.* He decided his fellow orphan must have wanted to do one decent thing before he met his Maker.

Nine felt himself becoming emotional. He was suddenly filled with remorse. It felt like he'd just killed a brother. *Pull yourself together man!* He reminded himself that Fourteen had been trying to stop him finding his son, and he daren't risk leaving him alive as he'd have presented too big a threat.

As he left the room, Nine clung to the hope he may yet find his son in Greenland. Striding along the same corridor he'd trodden earlier, he debated whether to find and kill Three. He dismissed that idea almost at once. Every minute he delayed increased his risk of discovery.

A recurrence of the chest pains he'd suffered earlier caused him to pull up. The pains weren't as bad as before, but they were bad enough to cause him to lean against the near wall to support himself.

"Are you okay?"

An American woman's voice startled him.

Nine looked around to see a uniformed nurse hurrying toward him. "I'm fine," he assured her. "Something I had for dinner doesn't agree with me." He managed a smile.

"Well, if you're sure." The nurse walked on ahead.

"Thank you," Nine called after her. He quickly popped a couple of heart pills. As always, they did the trick. He cautiously resumed walking along the corridor and dared not think head to the day the pills no longer worked their magic.

The former operative passed a door that had previously been closed. Glancing through the doorway he saw a sign that read: *Children's Quarters. No unauthorized entry.* Nine hesitated. He knew he should keep moving, but here was an opportunity to verify once and for all that Francis wasn't at this facility.

33

Nine stepped through the doorway into a corridor leading to the advertised sleeping quarters. He strode along it, passing a group of nurses on the way. They took no notice of him. His white coat and clipboard seemed to be a passport to all areas underground.

A door at the end of the corridor opened up into a large dormitory. In the semi-dark, it appeared to be home to some twenty or more sleeping children. These were obviously children who were not currently being tested, poked, electrocuted or otherwise tortured. Nine guessed it was probably one of a dozen or more such dormitories on the premises. It reminded him the lab's young inmates probably never got to see daylight – not even in a land where the summer sun never set.

A burly English orderly appeared out of the darkness and

challenged Nine. "Who are you?" His accent signalled he was a Cockney.

"Anker Frevert," Nine replied falling back on his Danish accent. Recalling the name tag of one of the scientists he'd seen earlier, he added, "Professor Hipkiss asked me to check the sleeping patterns of the children in this room."

"Why?"

"Who knows why the good Professor wants anything? I just carry out orders."

The orderly chuckled. "You 'n me both, mate." He continued on his rounds.

Nine approached the nearest bunk and found a young girl fast asleep beneath the blankets. He woke her gently. Showing her the photo of Francis by the light of a pen torch he carried, he asked, "Do you know this boy?"

The sleepy girl studied the photo then shook her head. "No sir, I don't." She spoke in the gruff voice of a grown man.

Nine recoiled from her and hurried to the next bunk where he got the same answer – this time from a boy whose face and hands showed signs of recent burn marks. He repeated the exercise another six times, each time getting the same answer the first two children had given him. None had seen Francis.

Now convinced beyond doubt his son wasn't here, Nine hurried to remove himself from the premises. He felt sad for all the children he was leaving behind, but in truth there was nothing he could do. He'd need an army to help them.

#

Nine's departure from Thule Air Base was surprisingly uneventful. Surprising because he'd spent three hours impersonating someone else inside one of the most secure facilities in the Northern Hemisphere, and in that time had incapacitated three people – in one case permanently – and still hadn't been found out let alone apprehended.

The former operative had slipped back into the guise of Danish photo-journalist Johannes Petersson complete with fake ginger beard. As he drove his rental car from the base to the nearby port, he wasn't to know he'd had a freakish run of good luck that was set to continue for a few hours yet.

Firstly, the hapless airman he'd left trussed up in the back of the Land Rover and the frightened controller he'd left tied up in the lab's control office wouldn't be discovered until the day shift personnel reported for duty. That wouldn't be until eight in the morning, another five hours away. And secondly, Three wouldn't find Fourteen's body until the air base's alarms woke him from his slumbers and alerted him to the fact that there'd been a serious security breach.

If Nine had known that, he'd have relaxed a little. As it was, he drove to the port fully expecting to be pulled over at any second.

It was with some relief he arrived at the main wharf and saw his Albermarle charter boat ready and waiting for him. After passing through the security gate without incident, he drove to the end of the wharf and parked the car beside the same yellow boatshed he'd visited earlier. There was no sign of Hans, the boatshed owner, which suited Nine just fine.

The former operative quickly transferred his luggage to the boat then locked the car, placed the key in an envelope and slipped it beneath the boatshed's locked door, just as he'd arranged with the car hire firm. Then he returned to the Albermarle, cast off her mooring lines, fired up her powerful twin inboard diesel engine and motored out into the bay.

Ahead of him was a journey of some seventy-four nautical miles south to the small settlement of Savissivik.

Despite the early hour, Nine had plenty of company in the bay. The crew of a fishing boat returning to the port gave him a wave, and a crewmember aboard another fishing boat departing the port also acknowledged him. He noticed stevedores working the night shift also taking an interest in the Albermarle as she headed for open sea.

There was no doubt the Albermarle's departure had been noted and that would be duly reported. Sooner or later, someone would put two and two together.

Nine knew full well when the alarm finally went up at the air base, the authorities would act quickly to cut off all escape routes from Thule. And if they didn't, Three certainly would.

The former operative had estimated that traveling at near-maximum speed he had a journey of almost two hours ahead of him. *Plenty of time to be apprehended, or blown out of the water!* He just hoped he'd reach his destination before the balloon went up.

34

While Nine was cruising south from Thule along Greenland's ice-free west coast, Isabelle was preparing for sleep in the bedroom she shared with one of her host family's children in Tahiti. She was exhausted after another day of doing nothing in the tropical heat.

The day had gone like every other since Seventeen had joined her at the commune that was now home to them both. In the three days they had been together, they'd hardly shared more than a dozen words. Such was the animosity Isabelle felt toward the woman who had killed her parents. Most of the time had been spent keeping out of each other's way and staying out of the hot sun as much as they could.

Seventeen's only respite had been a daily visit to one of

Papeete's Internet café's to check the email account Nine had set up for her under an assumed name before she'd left Chicago. So far, after each visit, she'd had to report back to Isabelle that there was no word from her husband.

That had only served to depress Isabelle further. If that wasn't bad enough, the baby had been moving a lot of late, causing the Frenchwoman added discomfort on top of her other aches and pains.

As she lay in the dark, idly fondling the ruby that rested on her chest, Isabelle's thoughts were with her husband and their abducted son. When she wasn't thinking about them, she was thinking about her unborn child.

The nightmare that had begun with Francis' abduction one week earlier continued with no end in sight. Nine hadn't communicated with her and she remained beside herself with worry for him and their son.

Slowly, mercifully, sleep came to her.

Isabelle didn't know how long she'd been out to it when she awoke to find herself being shaken roughly by the shoulders.

"It's me, Jennifer."

In the dark, Isabelle recognized Seventeen's voice.

"We have to go," Seventeen said. She spoke quietly so as not to wake the child sleeping in a bed nearby.

"What is it?" Isabelle asked sleepily, sitting up in bed.

"We are in danger," Seventeen said simply.

"What?"

"I'll explain later. Get dressed."

Seventeen was in operational mode now. The Frenchwoman recognized the change in her immediately. She remembered how Nine became a different person when danger threatened.

"We leave in ten minutes," Seventeen said as she left the room.

Isabelle climbed out of bed, switched on a bedside lamp and began dressing. She always kept a change of clothes on top of a trunk next to the bed for just such an emergency, so it didn't take her long to dress. Then she retrieved her pre-packed travel bags from inside the trunk, turned out the lamp and headed for the door. Isabelle hesitated then walked over to the sleeping child. She kissed the child's head then left the room.

The Frenchwoman found a stranger waiting for her in the kitchen. It was Seventeen, though Isabelle didn't recognize her as the former operative was now disguised as a man. A fake stubble gave her normally smooth skin an unshaven look, and clever use of a prosthetic nose gave her a distinctly mannish appearance. Her face was partly concealed by a baseball cap which she wore low on her forehead. Beneath the cap, her hair was parted in boyish fashion, though that wasn't evident at the moment.

"It's me," Seventeen said.

Isabelle gaped at the woman as the realization set in it was Seventeen she was looking at. She became distracted as the sound of voices coming from outside reached her.

The back door opened and Chai's head appeared. He looked at Seventeen. "Your vehicle's ready," he said.

"Thanks Chai," Seventeen said.

Chai disappeared back outside.

Isabelle turned to Seventeen. "What is happening?"

"One of Chai's cousins works on a market garden a couple of

255

miles down the road. Chai just happened to call in to see her on his way back from Papeete and she mentioned some guy had called in earlier, flashing your photo and asking if anyone had seen a pregnant Frenchwoman matching your description. Chai didn't have to see the photo to know it was you."

Alarmed, Isabelle asked, "Where is the man now?"

"Chai's cousin said he drove back toward Papeete, but she said he mentioned he'd be back tomorrow. He's checking all the properties along the road."

"Can't we just hide out here?"

Seventeen shook her head. She had considered that, but dismissed it as she realized it was too risky. It would be different if Isabelle wasn't in the advanced stages of pregnancy. If that had been the case, they could take a tent and a couple of sleeping bags and hide out in the mountains. Given the life-threatening complications Isabelle had suffered in her last pregnancy, Seventeen agreed with Nine's assessment that it was important Isabelle remain close to medical facilities.

"So where are we going?" Isabelle asked.

"I'm still working that out. Firstly, we have to get away from here." Seventeen knew from the description given of the man who had been asking after Isabelle that it was Twenty Three. She was also aware that when he did resume his door-knocking quest the next day, someone would recognize the Frenchwoman.

Isabelle wanted to argue the point with Seventeen. She still didn't trust her. But something told her to follow orders for the moment.

"Okay," Seventeen said. "Say your goodbyes. I'll be waiting in the Jeep." She took Isabelle's bags from her and left the kitchen.

Isabelle followed Seventeen outside. She found Chai and other members of his extended Thai family waiting for her on the veranda. Tears flowed as Isabelle hugged her dear friends and thanked them for their hospitality. She had a special word for Chai. "Thank you, Chai. Sebastian and I will never forget your family's kindness." She kissed his cheek.

Chai placed his right hand on Isabelle's shoulder as if to bless her. "It is as my uncle would have wished." He referred to his uncle and Nine's long-time friend, the kindly monk Luang. He removed his hand and stepped aside to let Isabelle pass.

In the waiting Jeep, Seventeen reached behind her and opened the rear door as Isabelle approached. "Jump in the back," she ordered.

Isabelle did as she was told. She waved to her friends as the vehicle drove off. Up ahead, the Jeep's headlights illuminated one of Chai's brothers as he unlocked and opened the commune's front gate to allow the vehicle to pass through. Isabelle waved to him and then he disappeared into the darkness behind the Jeep as it accelerated away.

"Keep out of sight back there," Seventeen said. "I don't want anyone seeing you." She felt it unlikely anyone would see them let alone recognize them in the darkness, but didn't want to take any chances.

Isabelle lay down across the back seat. Looking up through the Jeep's rear window, she studied the stars in the night sky. She wondered where Nine was and whether he was looking at the stars at that moment. And she wondered if he'd found Francis yet.

35

It was now four in the morning in Greenland, and if Nine had looked skyward at that moment he wouldn't have seen stars – not even if they were normally visible in summer in the land of the midnight sun. The skies above were hidden behind dark clouds; a storm was brewing as the Albermarle continued her journey south.

Since departing Thule, the voyage had been uneventful. The permanent daylight ensured the west coast was always in sight, which made navigation relatively straightforward. All Nine had to do was ensure the coastline remained in sight, to port, and he'd reach his destination sooner or later. Already, he'd rounded Cape York, so by his reckoning Savissivik was only half an hour away.

An hour earlier, he'd called Hells Angels biker Lars Khader

on the boat's radio-telephone. Lars had confirmed the helicopter he'd chartered on Nine's behalf was already waiting for him at the pre-arranged venue. Nine was thankful the big biker hadn't specified that the venue was Savissivik. He and Lars were both aware the line they used was an open one and their conversation could be overheard by anyone else who happened to share their radio frequency.

Using the vaguest of terms, Nine had advised him the *consignment* he'd hoped to uplift at his last stop had not been found, but there was another possibility he needed to check out before leaving the country. He ordered Lars to relay that information to the chopper pilot and ensure that the chopper had enough fuel for an extended flight. Lars had assured him he'd relay that information to the pilot immediately.

Now, as Savissivik came into sight, Nine's thoughts turned to the next step in his mission to find Francis. From Savissivik, he'd do as Fourteen had suggested and fly to American Summit Camp, in the middle of Greenland's ice sheet, to see if his son was being held there. From there, he'd fly to Kangerlussuaq

International Airport. Where he went from there would depend on whether or not he was traveling alone or with Francis. He prayed it would be the latter.

#

Omega boss Andrew Naylor was in deep discussion with CIA Director and fellow Omegan Marcia Wilson. It was early in the morning and the meeting was in Naylor's office at Omega HQ. Marcia was there in the flesh this time, not in holographic form – such was the importance of the meeting.

"And there's been no sighting of him since?" Marcia asked. She was referring to the unexplained disappearance from Thule of the man posing as Danish photo-journalist Johannes Petersson. Neither Marcia nor Naylor had any doubt the man was Nine.

"Nothing," Naylor said. He continually massaged his temple to ward off the headache that was now a permanent and unwelcome companion during his waking hours. It served to constantly remind him of the rogue operative, and that did nothing for his already short temper. Gone was Naylor's earlier enjoyment in the challenge Nine was providing. Now he was just angry, frustrated and worried.

"This isn't good, Andrew." Marcia's tone was one of rebuke. It was as though she held Naylor personally responsible for Nine's actions.

"Christ, don't you think I know that?" Naylor said, glaring at his opposite.

Marcia had a cutting response of her own planned, but was interrupted by the ringing of a phone on Naylor's desk.

Naylor picked up the phone. "Speak to me."

"It's Kamal Al Saud," the voice said on the other end.

Naylor placed his hand over the mouthpiece and mouthed to Marcia, "It's Three."

This was the second call Naylor had received from Three that morning. Several hours earlier, the mixed-race operative had phoned, advising of the dramas that had occurred at Thule Air Base and at the underground lab. At that stage, Three had just discovered Fourteen's body and had not long learned of the young airman and the controller who had both been found tied up. He'd established that the Danish photo-journalist had been one of three outsiders to visit the base on official business that night and had effectively disappeared after leaving the base.

Naylor removed his hand from the mouthpiece and resumed talking to the caller. "Give me the latest." He flicked the speaker phone mode on so that Marcia could also listen.

"It looks like Petersson is our man alright," Three said. "The rental car he was using was left down at the port and I've established he chartered a boat, and the same boat was sighted arriving in Savissivik, a small settlement south of here, about an hour ago."

"Marcia Wilson here, Kamal. Was Petersson sighted?"

"Yes ma'am. He was seen boarding a private helicopter. No markings."

Naylor leaned forward. "Where'd he go?"

"Destination unknown, but the pilot of an Air Force jet reported that he sighted an unmarked chopper flying south east from Savissivik around that time."

"Your thoughts?" Naylor asked.

"If I had to bet, I'd say he's flying to Kangerlussuaq," Three ventured.

Naylor looked at Marcia.

"Makes sense," Marcia said to Naylor. "Our Mister Petersson came up empty-handed in Thule. Next stop the DRC."

"Not if I can help it," Naylor mumbled through gritted teeth. He flicked off the speaker phone and resumed talking to Three. "I don't want him leaving Greenland. Got that?"

"Yes sir."

"Miss Wilson already has some of the firm's people watching out for him at the airport at Kangerlussuaq, but I want you there, too. Pronto. And do whatever needs to be done to stop him. Understood?"

"Yes sir."

Naylor ended the call in no doubt Three knew what he meant. Nine wasn't to leave Greenland alive.

#

Several hours after departing the commune on the north-western side of Tahiti Nui, Isabelle and Seventeen arrived in the small tourist town of Taravao, on the south-eastern side. For want of a better plan, Seventeen decided they'd pose as tourists and stay at a motel until a safer alternative presented itself.

The former operative was still in the guise of a man. Until they moved on, she was resigned to maintaining the guise, and decided she and Isabelle should pose as husband-and-wife. That would help throw the bloodhounds off her scent, she hoped.

A *Vacancy* sign outside a three-star motel several streets back from the waterfront caught Seventeen's eye. The establishment was in darkness, and its proprietor – a grumpy, fiftysomething man – was even grumpier than usual over being woken in the middle of the night. A sweetener of a hundred dollar bill helped smooth him over.

Using a pretty convincing male voice and speaking in an even more convincing, clipped English accent, Seventeen told the proprietor his wife was poorly and needed peace and quiet. She stressed they wanted a self-contained unit and didn't want to be disturbed during their stay. The proprietor assured her he understood.

Under cover of darkness, Seventeen shepherded Isabelle into

their unit, which was conveniently located to the rear of the premises, away from prying eyes.

Inside the unit, the two women looked at each other for a moment.

Seventeen noticed her sister-in-law looked tired and stressed. "You okay?" She knew that was a silly question as soon as she asked it.

Isabelle nodded. "I need to sleep." She headed for the nearest of the two bedrooms.

Seventeen went to say something, but remained silent. She'd been about to advise Isabelle she wouldn't be able to venture outside the unit for fear of someone seeing she was pregnant. If they did, there was a very real risk her former Omega colleagues would eventually hear of it. However, she decided that bit of news could wait until morning.

The former operative was also resigned to having to continue her masquerade as Isabelle's husband. Something that didn't exactly thrill her to bits.

36

Rasmus Posse, the Greenlandic helicopter pilot ferrying Nine to American Summit Camp, couldn't believe the change that was taking place before his very eyes. Alongside him, in the passenger seat, Nine was transforming himself from Johannes Petersson, the ginger-haired Danish photo-journalist, to Andreas Olsen, a Greenlandic Inuit hunter.

Appropriate clothing and equipment for Nine's latest guise were already on board the chopper when it arrived in Savissivik to collect him. Biker Lars Khader had made sure of that, as per his client's very specific orders. Lars had also chosen the pilot carefully, using one he'd groomed to transport future heroin supplies to the network of pushers he'd set up throughout the country.

The Inuit disguise presented more of a challenge than most new guises posed for Nine. For a start, the distinctive gun-sight eyes and Eskimo-like features of the Inuits were extremely difficult to replicate, even for a superior shapeshifter like Nine.

In the confines of the chopper, it had taken him over an hour to complete his transformation. Even now, as the chopper approached the ice station, he wasn't totally happy with it, but it would have to do. His appearance wasn't his only concern. Nine was also very aware he didn't speak Greenlandic, the native tongue of the country's Inuit population. Of the many languages and dialects he'd mastered in the course of his years as an Omega operative, Greenlandic wasn't one of them.

Nine's answer to that particular problem was he'd pretend to be deaf. *Not ideal, but it'll have to do.* His attention was diverted when the pilot pointed to several low-lying buildings visible on the ice sheet several miles ahead.

"There's the Summit Camp," Rasmus said in Danish.

"I see it," Nine responded in kind. Looking at the camp, he

marvelled at how tiny and inconspicuous it looked against the vastness of the ice sheet – a mere speck on a canvass of blinding white nothingness that extended as far as the eye could see in every direction.

Nine knew American Summit Camp was one of several such research stations on the ice sheet. This particular one was operated by a US-based company in support of Greenland's deep ice coring effort. In winter, the station's population dropped to five, but at this time of year it accommodated up to fifty-five people. Three of the current residents could be seen moving around, like dots, between the buildings.

"Where's the laboratory building?"

"It will come into view soon. Ah, there it is."

At first, Nine couldn't see it. Then he was able to make out its outline against the glaring whiteness of the ice. It was a small building exactly where Fourteen had said it would be, five miles south of the ice station.

Nine studied the building and hoped he'd find Francis inside it. "Pity you can't drop me there."

Rasmus mumbled his agreement. He and Nine had already discussed the drop-off and pick-up arrangements. All visiting aircraft had to land at American Summit Camp where pilots and passengers had to undergo the same strict security checks that were in force at Thule Air Base.

"There's our reception party," Rasmus said. He pointed to a small group of Inuit hunters who had assembled on the ice just beyond the perimeter of the station. The snowmobiles that had delivered them to this remote location were parked nearby.

Nine studied the hunters and marveled at the fact that Lars' influence and long reach even extended out onto the ice sheet. Through a contact of a contact, the Hell Angels biker had somehow arranged for a group of Inuits to rendezvous with a foreigner in the middle of Greenland. Just how he had managed that, Nine couldn't even guess, but he made a note to congratulate him on his organizational skills when they next met.

The Inuits studied the chopper as they became aware of its approach. There were six of them. Their snowmobiles set them apart from other hunters in the region whose mode of transport was the more traditional dog sleighs.

The chopper descended rapidly toward a clearly marked helipad near the station's front entrance. Nine busied himself checking that he had all he needed for what he hoped would be a brief visit. The seats behind him were covered in pelts and furs that would soon come in handy. He was here, officially at least, to trade with the locals.

On landing, the pair disembarked from the chopper and walked to a small hut that served as the station's Arrivals and Departures facility. Nine did his best to walk naturally and to appear at ease, but the heavy clothing felt strange and the reindeer hide boots he wore felt cumbersome. He noticed the Inuits looking at him strangely.

The hut was manned by a friendly Texan who spoke with a Southern drawl and introduced himself as Randy. If he noticed anything strange about Nine, he didn't let on.

Rasmus did the talking, as he'd been instructed to. After introducing himself and his passenger, he handed over permits and paperwork that confirmed they were who they claimed to be.

Nine's documentation had been prepared and supplied courtesy of yet another of Lars' contacts.

The pilot explained that his passenger was deaf and had come to join his Inuit friends on a trading expedition to the nearby medical lab, and that seemed to satisfy Randy. If the official wondered how an Inuit could afford to travel by helicopter, he kept that to himself also.

Formalities over, Nine and Rasmus returned to the chopper. They waved the Inuit hunters over to them. The hunters fired up their snowmobiles and motored across the ice to join the new arrivals. Two of them towed a large sled that was piled high with hides and other items of trade. Another towed a spare snowmobile. Nine guessed that was his ride.

"So, we're all set?" Nine asked of his companion.

"Yep," Rasmus said. "I'll wait three hours then come looking for you if you haven't returned."

"Good. Don't leave without me." Nine was mindful of their isolation. They were in the middle of one of the world's most massive ice sheets and nearly three hundred miles from the nearest town. "And remember we may have to leave in a hurry."

Rasmus nodded. He'd already been thoroughly briefed by Nine during the flight, and by Lars before that. The pair ceased conversing as the hunters pulled up alongside them.

Slipping into his native tongue, Rasmus introduced the hunters to Nine and explained to them his Inuit friend was stone deaf. He stressed there was no point in trying to talk to him as he couldn't hear a word they said. They seemed to accept that, though they continued to look sideways at the man they'd been told was a fellow Inuit.

Nine endeared himself to the hunters when he climbed into the chopper and emerged moments later holding an armful of furs and pelts. He strapped them on to the sled that was already piled high with trade items.

The Inuits' faces lit up with smiles as Nine collected two more armfuls of furs. Little wonder as they knew they'd share the spoils between them after the items were traded.

This arrangement had been negotiated twenty-four hours earlier by another of Lars' contacts, an Inuit interpreter. The hunters, who were already en route to American Summit Camp from their hunting grounds, had readily agreed to cooperate. Their end of the bargain was they had to allow Nine to accompany them when they traded with the occupants of the nearby laboratory building.

37

The journey to the lab building took an hour. Uneven ice and the ever-present risks posed by hidden crevasses forced the hunters to drive slower than Nine would have liked. So it was with some relief that they finally arrived and parked outside the building's main entrance.

There was no sign of life within the inconspicuous looking, single-level building which, if Fourteen was correct, served as a branch of the Thule lab. Nine hoped the building hadn't been vacated. His concerns were allayed when a door opened and a tall, bearded, fiftysomething gentleman stepped outside.

"Hello there," the man shouted. He spoke Greenlandic, but his accent was distinctly American.

The man was joined by several fellow Americans – three

more men and a woman who all appeared to be in their thirties. They looked as though they'd been expecting to see the Inuits as they walked over to welcome the visitors.

The members of the two parties greeted each other like old friends, confirming that this was not the Inuits' first visit. They all conversed in Greenlandic.

When the woman tried to engage Nine in conversation, one of the hunters came to his rescue, explaining that Nine was deaf. The woman gave Nine a sympathetic smile and moved on to converse with the next hunter within earshot.

The trading that followed took another hour. It wasn't so much a trade as a straight buy-out by the Americans. They loved the furs and pelts on offer. Their items of trade were Greenbacks, and the Inuits were only too happy to receive the US currency.

During the trading, Nine surveyed the building and its surrounds. Movement inside the building indicated the presence of someone else. He wondered again if Francis was there.

When trading concluded, the two groups said their farewells. Nine and his Inuit companions drove off on their snowmobiles.

Before they'd gone a hundred yards, Nine motioned to the others that he was returning to the building they'd just left. Using hand signals, he indicated they should continue to American Summit Camp without him.

Mystified, the hunters chattered amongst themselves and gesticulated to him to follow them, but he held firm. Confused, they reluctantly continued without him.

Nine motored back to the building alone and parked his snowmobile right outside the front door.

The door opened and the same man who had first greeted the visitors emerged, looking puzzled. "Forget something?" He spoke English then remembered who he was addressing and repeated the question in Greenlandic.

"Yes," Nine responded in English. "I left my son here."

The man's surprise turned to shock when Nine pulled out his USP semi-automatic pistol from beneath his heavy coat.

Nine spun the man around, encircled his throat with his arm and held the pistol to the back of his head. "What's your name?"

"Stan Sinclair," the man stammered.

"Well Stan. Do as I say and I may let you live." Nine marched the frightened man back inside. "How many of you are there here?"

"Just the five of us," Sinclair said hoarsely as the pressure around his throat increased.

Nine had no way of knowing if his hostage was telling the truth. He removed the safety on his pistol. It made an audible *click* causing Sinclair to flinch. "How many?"

"Six counting our security officer!" Sinclair blurted out.

"That's better. Now where are they?"

"They're all in the dining room preparing for lunch."

"Let's join them, shall we?"

Again the frightened man nodded.

"You lead the way," Nine ordered.

Sinclair led Nine to the dining room. Sounds of laughter and lively discussion came from within.

"Open the door," Nine whispered.

Sinclair did as he was told and the pair entered the room. No-one noticed the new arrivals immediately.

Nine saw at a glance there were five of them. They were all sitting around a dining table and were about to start tucking into pizza slices that had just been microwaved.

The woman Nine had met earlier noticed the pair first. It took her a second or two to register that someone was holding her colleague at gunpoint. Then she screamed. Her startled companions looked around to see what had upset their colleague.

"Stay calm," Nine ordered. He released his hostage, pushing him toward the others.

The woman continued to scream.

Nine glanced at her plastic name tag. It read *Dr Sue Talbot*. "If you keep screaming I promise I will shoot you, Doctor Talbot." Nine pointed the pistol at her.

The doctor ceased screaming immediately and appeared close to fainting.

Nine surveyed the others. He noticed a big, strapping individual he hadn't seen before. Arnold Fisk was the security officer Sinclair had referred to earlier. Nine pointed his pistol directly at Fisk. "Hands on the table where I can see them."

Fisk did as he was told. Like the others, he seemed bemused that he was being threatened by an armed Inuit who sounded distinctly American.

Nine then walked over to the security officer. Frisking him, he discovered he carried a holstered pistol on him. Nine relieved him of the weapon. "Now why on earth would you need this at a scientific laboratory in the middle of an ice sheet?"

Fisk remained mute.

Looking at the others, Nine asked, "Who is in charge here?"

A sixtysomething man with a handlebar moustache raised his hand. "I am."

"And you are?"

"Professor Bernard Smythe."

"Very well, I shall start with you." Nine pulled out Francis' photo and handed it to the professor. "That's a recent photo of my son. His name is Francis Hannar and I have it on good authority he's being held here."

Smythe looked genuinely puzzled as he studied the photo. "I can assure you, whoever you are, he is not here. Nor indeed has he or any other child ever been here."

Nine couldn't determine whether the professor was lying or telling the truth. *He sounds convincing, but his body language tells a different story*. He waved his pistol at him. "Pass the photo around and let's see if it jogs anyone's memory."

Smythe passed the photo to Doctor Talbot who sat next to him. She studied it, shook her head and passed it to a colleague.

As the photo did the rounds, Nine studied the reactions and body language of each person. Each indicated they hadn't seen the boy, but it was Nine's assessment that they were covering up something. Running out of patience, he asked, "Where's the lab?"

"Out back," Smythe said.

"Let's go." Again Nine motioned with his pistol. "Everyone."

All six stood and filed out of the dining room, down a long corridor and through to the lab. Nine followed close behind, pistol ready.

The lab looked like any conventional lab. There was no sign of children or any other human guinea pigs.

Not convinced, the former operative decided to conduct a search of the entire premises. Looking around, he pointed to a closed door. "What's in there?"

"That's a storeroom," Smythe said.

Nine crossed the lab and tried the door handle. It was locked. "Who has the key?"

"I do," a senior technician said. He fished a set of keys from his jacket pocket, selected one key and unlocked the door. It opened up into a small, windowless storeroom.

Nine could see the room would suffice for what he had in mind. "Okay, everyone inside." As an afterthought he added, "And leave your cell phones here."

Smythe managed a nervous smile. "We have no need of cell phones here. There's no cell phone coverage on the ice sheet."

Nine reached inside his coat, pulled out his cell phone and saw immediately that there was no signal. Satisfied, he motioned to his captives to enter the storeroom. As soon as they were inside, he locked them in then embarked on a search of the premises.

Ten minutes was all it took to establish there were no

children being held on the premises. Any hope of finding Francis in Greenland had almost vanished.

Nine felt despondent and angry. Then a plan occurred to him – a last throw of the dice. Ignoring the sudden twinges of pain in his chest, he marched back to the storeroom, unlocked the door and looked inside. "Okay people," he announced, "I'm gonna question you one at a time. If I think anyone's lying, I'll kill them."

There was a collective gasp.

Nine pointed his pistol at Arnold Fisk. "You first."

38

The security officer did as he was told and joined Nine outside the storeroom. Nine could see by the expressions on the faces of the others that his new hard-line strategy was having the desired effect. He locked them in again then motioned to Fisk to lead the way back to the dining room.

In the dining room, Nine clipped his hostage over the back of his head, stunning him. The security officer fell to his hands and knees. Before he could recover, Nine tied him up using spare electrical leads someone had left in a bundle nearby. Then he walked through to the adjoining kitchen and re-emerged holding a tea-towel which he used to gag his hostage who had now regained his senses. "There now. Hope that's not too uncomfortable."

The security officer glared at him. His expression changed to one of fear and his whole body tensed as Nine aimed the pistol at his chest.

Nine fired a single shot into the ceiling then smiled at his bemused but relieved hostage. "That should do the trick."

Fisk, who was now hyperventilating, couldn't believe he was still alive. He was sure he should be dead.

Nine returned alone to the storage room. Unlocking the door, he looked in. He could almost smell the fear in the confined space. "Your security officer lied to me, so you now have one less mouth to feed."

That news was greeted by stunned silence. It was clear the lab workers believed their colleague was dead. They shrank back as Nine stepped inside the small room.

Nine's eyes rested on Doctor Talbot.

"No, please!" the doctor whimpered.

Nine reached forward, grabbed the frightened woman by the wrist and pulled her out of the storeroom. She screamed and struggled, but he held her firmly. Looking back at Smythe, he said,

"If she doesn't cooperate, I'll be back for you." He locked the others in again then dragged his unwilling hostage kicking and screaming to a conference room he'd come across during his earlier search of the building.

The former operative pushed Doctor Talbot inside the room, sat her down and pointed his pistol at her. She'd stopped screaming, but was now rigid with fear.

Nine hated what he was doing to her, especially if she and her colleagues were innocent, but he kept thinking of Francis. If she knew anything, she'd tell him, of that he was sure. *Be strong, lady. This will all be over soon.* Pulling his scariest face, he said, "I don't want to have to kill you, but I will if you don't tell me the truth. Do you understand?"

Doctor Talbot, who now shook violently, nodded. She most certainly did understand.

Nine held up the same photo he'd produced earlier. "Have you seen my son?"

The doctor shook her head. She was so frightened she was momentarily incapable of speech.

Nine released the safety on his pistol. The metallic *click* promoted his hostage to jump.

"We have had other children here!" Doctor Talbot blurted out. "But not for several months, and I've never seen your boy. Honest."

Nine could see she was telling the truth. Cross-examining her, he established that young subjects bound for Omega's lab at Thule were sometimes processed at this branch. The doctor stressed that it was a rare occurrence, and claimed she and her colleagues had no idea what awaited the children when they were transferred to Thule.

On learning this, the former operative felt the same crushing disappointment he'd experienced at Thule after confirming Francis wasn't being held there.

As a final act, Nine escorted the relieved doctor back to the storeroom and locked her in with the others. He would advise the people at American Summit Camp of their predicament once he was safely back in the air.

#

Nine didn't have long to wait before the chopper arrived to collect him. As soon as he was in the air, he ordered Rasmus to head for Kangerlussuaq International Airport. Then he used the radio-telephone to advise a bemused radio operator at the ice station that the Americans at the nearby lab building had somehow locked themselves in a storeroom and were in need of rescue. He didn't give the operator a chance to cross-examine him.

The former operative then called Hells Angels biker Lars Khader and relayed final instructions to him. These related to his upcoming departure from Kangerlussuaq.

Nine was aware Naylor would have heard of his exploits in Greenland by now and would have people looking for him at Kangerlussuaq and, indeed, at all six of the country's international airports. He had a feeling he may need backup. Hence the call to Lars. The irony of relying on a gang leader and drug pusher to watch his back wasn't lost on him.

Nine's thoughts were already on his next destination, Africa, and on his son. *Hang on Francis, I'm coming for you.* The macabre and shocking sights he'd seen at Thule ate away at him. He couldn't bear to think of Francis being thrown into such an environment, and he wondered how the boy was coping.

Another twinge in his chest reminded him of his ailing heart condition. Popping a couple of pills, Nine wondered if he was up to what lay ahead. He fully expected he'd be flying into a maelstrom in Africa. That is *if* he managed to depart Greenland in one piece.

Exhausted and dispirited, Nine lay back and closed his eyes as the chopper continued its flight south over the ice sheet. His last thought before drifting off to sleep was how Isabelle and Seventeen were getting on back in Tahiti.

39

Seventeen didn't like leaving Isabelle alone at the motel, not even for a minute, but there were times she had to venture out – for food and other day-to-day essentials, and to check her emails to see if Nine had made contact. This was one of these occasions.

The former operative was still in the guise of Isabelle's husband, stubble and all.

After purchasing food at a Taravoa supermarket, she then called in at a local Internet café. The result was the same as always: other than the usual spam, there was no email from her brother.

Seventeen returned to her Jeep and soon found herself driving past the township's picturesque boat marina. The road she followed took her up onto the isthmus that separated Tahiti Nui from the Tahiti Iti peninsula to the south. Friendly Tahitians waved at her as she drove along the windy road. Seventeen returned their waves with a masculine thumbs-up sign, in keeping with her latest disguise.

The Tahitians weren't the only people using the road. Every minute or two, a French Army truck would rumble past. Some carried uniformed soldiers and served as a reminder to tourists and locals alike that Taravoa was a military town and the old fort at the top of the isthmus was in use as an army training center.

Within minutes, the original stone walls of Fort Taravoa came into view, signalling to Seventeen that she'd reached the summit. Judging by the number of army trucks and personnel coming and going, there was some kind of training exercise underway.

As Seventeen looked for a place to park the Jeep, she reviewed what she knew of the fort. Her memory still wasn't what it once was, but it was improving by the day thanks to Nine's timely intervention. She recalled the French had built the fort during the French-Tahitian War of the 1840's if she wasn't mistaken. It was used to help subdue the last of the rebellious Islanders on the Tahiti Iti peninsula. During World War Two, it gained some notoriety when German residents were interned there.

Seventeen found what she was looking for – a parking spot that afforded glorious views over the township below. Disembarking from the Jeep, she strolled to a lookout to admire the views.

Just then a late model convertible passed by, catching Seventeen's eye. Its fire-engine red paintwork made it hard to miss. And its top was down so Seventeen caught a glimpse of the driver. *Fifteen!* It had only been for an instant, but Seventeen was sure it was her fellow orphan.

Fearing Fifteen was onto them, Seventeen jumped into the Jeep, started it up and headed back downhill. She drove fast and soon had the convertible in view.

A few minutes later, Seventeen held her breath as the convertible approached the turnoff leading to her motel. Thankfully, Fifteen continued driving south toward the peninsula.

Seventeen followed at a discreet distance for a mile or so until it was clear that her fellow orphan really was departing Taravoa.

The former operative returned to the motel. There, she found her sister-in-law looking at a small framed photo of Nine and Francis she was holding. Isabelle had obviously been crying.

"What's wrong?" Seventeen asked.

"Nothing," Isabelle lied. Knowing that Seventeen had gone to check her emails, she asked, "Anything from Sebastian?"

Seventeen shook her head.

"Something must be wrong," Isabelle murmured.

"No news is good news."

"You think so?"

"Definitely." Seventeen tried to sound and look more positive than she felt. "If Sebastian had bad news he'd let us know."

Seventeen's words had a calming effect on Isabelle. The look of despair on the Frenchwoman's face was replaced by hope. Seventeen realized that hope may be misguided, but she said nothing. Nor did she tell Isabelle she'd just seen one of the Omega operatives who were hunting them.

40

While Isabelle and Seventeen were making the most of a bad situation, the mixed-race orphan-operative Three was surveying outbound passengers in the Departures Lounge at Kangerlussuaq International Airport.

The Omega operative was looking out for Nine, and he wasn't alone. He had the assistance of three CIA agents whom Marcia Wilson had despatched from the firm's Berlin office at Naylor's request. One of them was currently with Three in the airport's upstairs Departure Lounge while the other two were downstairs, monitoring outbound travellers who were checking in.

The same scenario was being repeated at Greenland's other international airports. More Omega operatives had been called in to try to stop Nine leaving the country and they, too, were being supported by seconded CIA agents.

For Three, the mission had suddenly become personal. The termination of Fourteen back at the Thule Air Base lab had occurred on Three's watch, and he wasn't happy about that. He knew he was in Naylor's bad books as a result of what had gone down and was intent on redeeming himself.

While Three was looking out for Nine, he was himself being observed. Lars Khader had been watching out for a gentleman of Three's description arriving from Thule after Nine had called him from the chopper. It hadn't taken Einstein to deduce that the mixed-race traveller who arrived dressed in civvies aboard a US Air Force chopper soon after that call was Three.

The big biker had observed the operative studying other travellers at the airport and briefing three similarly dressed, fit-looking individuals at the same time.

Like Three, Lars wasn't working alone either. His network of *eyes and ears* extended to employees of Greenland's major airports – in particular the baggage handlers and airline ground staff.

Moving huge quantities of illegal drugs around the country required the cooperation of such people. Mindful of this, Lars had been busy in recent months lining the palms of people he thought could help him.

The time had arrived to call in a few favors. Because he needed to depart to meet Nine at another location, Lars had quietly recruited the services of several airport personnel who were in his debt. He had surreptitiously pointed out Three and the CIA agents, and asked his contacts to keep him informed of their movements by cell phone.

Now, as Lars awaited the arrival of Nine's chopper in a forest clearing on a farmlet on the outskirts of Kangerlussuaq, he was receiving calls every five minutes updating him on the movements of the mysterious men who were so keenly observing departing travellers at the airport.

One of the calls alarmed him. A barman working in the Departure Lounge reported that Three had departed the airport not long after Lars had left. The barman said a baggage handler had confirmed that the agent had driven off in a rental car, and he appeared to be in a hurry. Lars hoped there was an innocent explanation for that.

The familiar whirring of blades alerted him to the chopper's arrival. Low cloud cover hid the approaching chopper from view, but Lars estimated it would land within the next couple of minutes.

Whirring blades was the last sound Lars heard. He never even saw the arm that encircled his throat nor the hand that snapped his neck.

Three let his victim fall to the ground then stepped back to admire his handiwork. Lars had fallen awkwardly, his arms, legs and head splayed at odd angles. His sightless eyes stared up at his killer. Three thought he looked more like a rag doll than a Hells Angels gang leader.

The Omega operative almost regretted that he'd surprised his victim and hadn't given him the opportunity to make a fight of it. He guessed the big man would have given him a run for his money.

Lars would never know that Three had realized from the outset he was being observed at the airport. The operative had quickly identified Lars as the observer and had pointed him out to the CIA agents he was collaborating with.

When Lars had left the airport astride his Harley-Davidson, one of the CIA agents – a nondescript, thirtysomething man uncharitably referred to as *Shag* by his colleagues – had followed him to the farmlet. Shag had alerted Three who had joined him soon after.

The CIA agent placed the sniper's rifle he was carrying on the ground then tried dragging Lars into the nearby spruce trees. Grunting, he looked around at Three. "Help me, will you?" The big biker was a handful for one man.

Three helped Shag drag the body out of sight.

"What about the Harley?" Shag asked.

"Leave it where it is. He'll be expecting to see it."

Shag retrieved his rifle and re-joined Three under cover of the trees just as the chopper dropped below the cloud cover above them.

Three drew his pistol from a shoulder holster. "Remember, the passenger's mine." He had to shout to make himself heard above the sound of the chopper. "You take the pilot."

Shag nodded and the two professionals separated. They knew to follow protocol and establish a field of fire from opposite sides of their target.

Inside the chopper, Nine studied the terrain as the craft descended. He was no longer in disguise, having dispensed with his Inuit guise during the flight from the ice sheet. The forest clearing came into view and he drew out his machine pistol in readiness for the landing.

Nine saw the Harley, but there was no sign of Lars. He thought that odd as the biker had phoned him on his cell from the clearing five minutes earlier to advise it was all clear. He'd assumed Lars would be in the clearing with his bike.

Just before the chopper dropped below the treeline, Nine noticed a hundred yards or so off to his right two late model cars parked outside an old farmhouse. He found that odd, too, as Lars had assured him he'd come alone.

"I don't like this," Nine said aloud as the chopper continued its descent.

Rasmus slowed the chopper's descent and prepared to land. The craft's skids were now only a few feet off the ground.

Nine was growing increasingly concerned. Still there was no sign of Lars. *He should be here*. Then he saw it – a shadowy figure in the trees. Whoever it was, he was too short to be the biker. "Abort the landing!" Nine screamed. "Abort!"

Rasmus reacted quickly, jerking on the joystick, but he was still too slow to avoid the heavy calibre bullet that smashed through the front windscreen and lodged in his brain.

The chopper tilted over and began rising at a forty-five degree angle to the ground, its engine screaming. Nine tried to prize Rasmus' lifeless fingers from the joystick, but was powerless to prevent the chopper's blades striking the upper branches of the surrounding trees.

The out-of-control craft carved a path through the treetops until it ran out of steam. Its blades stopped turning and the chopper fell to the ground.

From Nine's perspective, the chopper's death-throes seemed to happen in slow motion. In reality, it was all over in a matter of seconds. In that short space of time however, the chopper had carried its passenger a good fifty yards from the forest clearing and from the killers waiting for him there.

Three and his companion had reacted quickly when the chopper crashed. However, the undergrowth was dense and it took them a couple of minutes to reach the craft's final resting place. When they arrived, they found the chopper upside down on the ground. Smoke rose from its engine and sparks threatened to turn the craft into a fireball.

The pilot's body could be seen through the smoke. Rasmus was still at the controls, strapped in his seat. There was no sign of Nine.

Three motioned to Shag to go one way and he went the other. The Omega operative was cursing. This was not going to plan.

When the chopper had struck the ground, it was only Nine's seatbelt that saved him from being thrown through the windscreen. The impact had left him dazed and winded. His ribs hurt – a result of the seatbelt's resistance to the centrifugal forces that had thrown him forward – and he wondered if he actually had broken a rib or two.

Nine's first thought had been to escape the smoking chopper before it burst into flames. He'd scrambled to extricate himself from the smoking craft. Safely on the ground, his next thought had been to evade whoever it was he'd seen waiting for him in the trees, and he'd sought to distance himself from the chopper as quickly as he could.

In the first couple of minutes, Nine had identified two people pushing through the dense undergrowth. It had been clear to him they were prepared to sacrifice stealth for speed in their haste to reach the downed chopper. Now there was only silence.

41

Nine knew they were coming for him and was grateful he had his machine pistol. He estimated he'd moved perhaps fifty yards from the crash site. His path had taken him toward the farmhouse he'd seen earlier. *What to do?* He debated whether to sit tight and wait for his quarry to show themselves or whether to keep moving. *Problems either way.* He decided to keep moving. The longer he delayed, the more time his quarry had to call in reinforcements.

The former Omega operative thought if he could get to the farmhouse without being spotted, he could possibly jump-start one of the cars he'd seen and get away.

Nine wondered what had happened to Lars. Logic told him the men who were now hunting him had dealt with the biker. *I could do with your help right now, my Viking friend.* He pressed on.

Movement in the undergrowth nearby warned Nine that he had company. Crouching behind a bush, pistol raised, he saw Shag approaching. The agent had his rifle at the ready and was literally tip-toeing through the forest to avoid standing on a branch or twig. He seemed oblivious to the fact that, in the still of the forest, he might as well be an elephant crashing through the undergrowth.

Nine debated whether to shoot the agent or try to subdue him quietly. He decided the latter too risky, so promptly killed him with three well-placed bullets.

Forty yards away, the burst of gunfire that shattered the silence immediately told Three where his quarry was. The lack of return fire also told him his back-up had been taken out of the picture. Now it was just him and Nine.

Three began moving toward the sound then pulled up when he realized Nine was coming toward him. He hid behind a tree and waited.

Nine realized he was making too much noise, but it couldn't

be helped. His intention was still to reach the farmhouse and make his getaway from there. To do that, he had to keep moving. He'd entered an especially dense patch of undergrowth and was having trouble pushing through it. In the process, he advertised his whereabouts loud and clear.

Three waited until his fellow orphan had passed his hiding place before revealing himself. "Freeze!" he ordered.

Nine pulled up. He didn't have to look behind him to know he'd been out-maneuvered.

"Drop the gun then turn around slowly," Three said.

Nine did as he was told. He smiled when he saw the orphan he'd grown up with all those years earlier. "Well, well. I should have known it would be you."

"You've been up to your old tricks, I see." Three returned the smile. It was a cold smile with little affection behind it.

The mixed-race operative's stance was relaxed and his demeanor casual, but Nine noted the pistol he held was rock-steady and pointed straight at him.

"Still causing problems for Omega I see, Nine," Three said.

"More than a few I hope." Nine continued to assess his opposite as he spoke. Three appeared to be as fit and dangerous as ever. Despite the exertions of the last few minutes, the operative appeared to be hardly breathing. That reminded Nine how dangerous the man could be. "What now?" he asked.

Three seemed ready to shoot Nine. He hesitated as another idea came to him. "Lead the way back to the clearing." He indicated with his pistol the direction Nine should take.

Nine set off. *What are you up to, Three?* The operative followed a prudent distance behind, pistol ready. As they walked, Nine looked for an opportunity to turn the tables. There was none.

They soon reached the clearing. Through the trees, Nine could see Lars' bike parked where he'd left it. Again he wondered where the big man was. Then he saw Lars' body just inside the treeline. He didn't need to inspect the biker to know he was dead. Lars' head was thrown at an unnatural angle to one side, his neck clearly broken.

"You'll see I found your friend," Three said matter-of-factly.

"If you're gonna shoot me, shoot me!" Nine snapped. He

hated Three at that moment.

Three shoved Nine toward a tree. "Spread," he said.

The former operative realized Three intended to frisk him. He did as asked, leaning against the tree's trunk and spreading his legs. Three expertly frisked him, confirming he was unarmed.

Three spun him around, pointing his pistol between Nine's eyes. "I have something better than a bullet planned for you, my friend."

Three ordered Nine to stand in the middle of the clearing. The former operative fully expected to be shot then and there. To his surprise, Three placed his pistol behind a tree then joined him in the clearing. It dawned on Nine that his fellow orphan wanted to kill him with his bare hands.

Nine's initial reaction was one of intense relief. Under normal circumstances he'd be dead by now. However, he soon recalled he wasn't in the best of health while Three looked as fit as ever. *I know who I'd put my money on right now.* Regardless, he clung to hope.

"Let's settle this the old fashioned way," Three said as he

went into a fighter's crouch and began circling Nine. The mixed-race operative was in his element now. This was what he lived for – pitting his speed and strength against a worthy opponent. The very thought of what was to come excited him. He crouched low, looking for an opening.

Nine's thoughts were very different to Three's. He was aware there was more than just his life at stake. Also at stake was Francis' life and possibly the lives of Isabelle and their unborn child. He was also remembered once again that he wasn't the fighting machine he once was. His heart condition had taken its toll. And if that wasn't enough, his injured ribs hurt like hell.

42

Three attacked first, feinting with a left hook while kicking out ju-jitsu style with his right foot. Nine just managed to avoid the blow, but he was too slow to dodge the right cross that followed. It clipped his jaw, stunning him for a second or two. If it had landed flush, it would have knocked him out cold.

That first exchange reminded Nine how deadly Teleoites was. The brainchild of their mentor, Tommy Kentbridge, it was a mix of all the martial arts – ju-jitsu, karate, boxing and judo included. His expertise in Teleoites had saved his life more than once, and had ended the life of at least half a dozen assailants during his operational years.

Nine didn't wait for Three to come at him again. He took the initiative and launched himself at his opposite, hurting him with a swinging elbow that connected above Three's eye and caused a nasty gash. Three subconsciously licked at the blood as it tricked down into his mouth.

Encouraged by his early success, Nine employed one of his favourite strategies, simultaneously throwing punches and kicking without let-up. Three was forced to back-peddle to avoid the blows. Picking his moment, he ducked beneath a punch and used his right foot to sweep Nine's legs out from under him. Nine went down hard and Three was onto him in a flash.

All Nine could do was cover up as Three rained blows down on him from all angles. He could feel his energy draining and wasn't sure how much more punishment he could take. Heart pains served as a warning that he needed to finish this quick if he was to survive.

Sensing Nine was fading, Three used a wrestling technique to get behind his opponent and employ a strangulation grip. He placed his left forearm across Nine's throat and, with his right hand, slowly tightened the grip.

Nine was struggling to breathe. He knew he'd be asphyxiated if he didn't escape the hold Three had on him. But try as he may, he couldn't dislodge the vice-like grip.

As he began to lose consciousness, he remembered the voice-commands used to activate and de-activate mind control in the orphans. "Mercury, Venus, Earth, Mars," he gasped, "Jupiter, Saturn, Uranus, Neptune, Pluto. Release me."

Nine could feel himself going as Three's grip continued to tighten. The voice-commands seemed to have no effect. *Has he been de-activated?* He repeated the planets' names over and over, clinging to consciousness in a desperate bid to survive.

Three suddenly released his grip. Nine struggled to his feet, gasping for air and fighting against the pains that now coursed through his chest. He looked at Three and saw the operative's eyes were glassy. Three seemed to be looking right through him and was obviously somewhere else at that moment.

As the heart pains threatened to overwhelm him, Nine fished out the pill bottle he always carried in his pocket and downed a couple of pills. Relief came, though not as fast as usual.

Afraid Three would snap out of his trance, Nine hurried to retrieve the pistol he'd left behind a tree. He returned moments later, pistol in hand. Three saw the weapon, but didn't appear to register that his life could now be measured in seconds.

As before, when he'd shot Fourteen, Nine had to contend with his conscience. The idea of killing a fellow orphan still repelled him, but again he had to put his family's welfare first. Three was trying to stop him saving his son.

Nine shot the operative at point-blank range.

#

Isabelle felt like she was going stir crazy. The Frenchwoman had been cooped up inside for three days now – a virtual prisoner in the motel she shared with Seventeen at Taravoa. She felt like an elephant, her lower back hurt, every joint ached and she was constantly tired. And the baby was making her presence known increasingly often.

Alone for the moment, Isabelle was sorely tempted to disobey her minder's instructions and venture outside for a stroll around the grounds. Before popping out to stock up on more food and provisions, Seventeen had left her with strict instructions not to so much as even look outside. She was paranoid Isabelle would be seen and her whereabouts reported to Fifteen or Twenty Three. The former operative had no doubt her fellow orphans would have set up a network of eyes and ears around Tahiti to help them in their search for Isabelle. After all, that's what she'd have done.

As the walls closed in on Isabelle, the temptation became too great. She *had* to venture outside, if only for a few minutes.

Dark glasses and a big sun hat hid her face, but the light cotton dress she wore did nothing to hide her pregnant state.

The motel's head cleaner, a large Tahitian woman, spotted Isabelle as soon as she stepped foot outside. She was walking between units, cleaning materials in hand, when she noticed the pregnant guest.

Noting the unit Isabelle had emerged from, the cleaner hurried back to the vacated unit she'd just finished cleaning. There, she used the unit's telephone to make a call.

43

At Omega headquarters, Naylor presided over another extraordinary board meeting. The meeting had been prompted by the news, relayed to him earlier that day by CIA Director Marcia Wilson that one of her agents and Omega operative Number Three had been found shot dead on a property on the outskirts of Kangerlussuaq, in Greenland. Worse, Nine had effectively disappeared since his exploits at American Summit Camp and before that at Thule Air Base.

Marcia was currently in the hot seat and she was being grilled by founding director Bill Sterling. Like his fellow directors, he wasn't happy about the mayhem Nine had caused.

"You had people at every airport in Greenland?" Sterling asked.

"At every international airport, yes," Marcia said defensively.

"And still you couldn't find one man or stop him leaving the country?"

"We don't know for sure that he has left Greenland."

"Would you bet against it?" Lincoln Claver asked.

"I wouldn't," Fletcher Von Pein said, jumping into the discussion. "We've known for a long time now the man's a human chameleon. If he doesn't want to be found, we know from hard-earned experience he probably won't be."

Sitting at the head of the table, Naylor was content to let the discussion run its course. He recognized his fellow directors were worried by recent events, and with good reason. They were all only too aware that Nine's actions could sink Omega's secret offshore medical laboratories and, if word got out, potentially destroy the careers of every person sitting around the table. So, he was content to allow his fellow directors to vent their frustrations for the moment at least.

Claver eyeballed Marcia. "So, assuming he has left

Greenland and is en route to our lab in Zaire, or the Democratic Republic of the Congo or whatever the hell they call it these days, what's the guarantee he won't make your people look stupid all over again?"

By now, Marcia was fair bristling. She looked to Naylor for support, but none was forthcoming, so she ploughed on. "For starters Lincoln, it's not only the CIA's people watching out for Nine, it's Omega's as well. We're all in this together. I've doubled my original number of agents in Kinshasa and have people at all the major airports in the DRC."

"And I despatched two more operatives to our lab there yesterday," Naylor added.

"Our elites I hope?" Sterling asked.

"Yes, two of our orphan-operatives were on assignment in South Africa," Naylor said, "so I sent them as back-up to the three already in the DRC. I believe they arrived in Kinshasa last night our time. They'll be arriving at our lab soon if they aren't there already."

"Well let's hope they're a bit more effective than their

colleagues were," Sterling said, referring to the Greenland disaster.

Naylor hoped so, too. He knew it was only the leverage Nine's son gave them that was stopping the rogue operative going public about the agency's illegal medical and scientific activities offshore. The repercussions if Nine went public didn't bear thinking about.

"Any news of the Frenchwoman?" Claver asked, referring to Isabelle.

"No, but two of our best operatives are on the case," Naylor said.

"Send another," Von Pein said. "Find Isabelle Hannar and that will bring Nine to heel."

Naylor concurred with that assessment, but his resources were already fully stretched with two of his orphan-operatives dead and a dozen others now pulled off important missions to join the hunt for Nine. And that wasn't counting the two in Tahiti hunting Isabelle. "I'll see what I can do."

Von Pein wasn't happy. "And what about the other woman?"

Again, Naylor knew who Von Pein referred to. He looked at

Marcia.

"There's been no sighting of Seventeen since she and Nine were seen driving from her home into the city," Marcia said. "I have my people looking out for her."

Naylor added, "We suspect she has gone to ground somewhere in downtown Chicago. She'll be found."

"So many goddamned loose ends!" Claver said. "How can one man cause us so many problems?"

Naylor had no answer. He'd been asking himself the same thing. Looking around, he could see by the worried expressions on the faces of his fellow directors that every one of them was aware things were starting to unravel.

Von Pein looked at his watch. "I have to be somewhere. Was there anything else?"

"Just the boy," Naylor said referring to Francis. He began collecting his files as he spoke to signal the meeting was drawing to an end. "Doctor Andrews informs me that testing of the boy has been postponed as he picked up a virus soon after arriving at the lab. The doc assures me it's only a flu virus, but they can't begin tests until he's a hundred per cent."

"What next?" Von Pein mumbled to himself as he took his leave and departed the boardroom.

The other equally disgruntled board members followed Von Pein, leaving Naylor alone. The Omega boss felt a headache coming on and began massaging his temple in a vain attempt to keep it at bay. He cursed the day the ninth orphan had been born.

44

As Naylor sat alone with his thoughts, Nine was about to cross Zambia's northern border into the DRC aboard a mini-bus.

After killing Three and the CIA agent in Kangerlussuaq, he'd departed Greenland in the guise of an African-American businessman. The elaborate disguise, which entailed blackening his skin, had taken some time to perfect, but he'd felt it necessary because of the numbers of Omega and CIA personnel he knew were looking for him.

Aware they'd be expecting him to arrive in the DRC by air, Nine had flown to Lusaka, in neighboring Zambia. From there, he'd taken a domestic flight to Solwezi, near Zambia's northern border with the DRC, and there he'd joined an adventure tour party of backpackers who were headed for the DRC's capital of Kinshasa.

Nine had forsaken his African-American guise in favor of traveling undisguised for once. He still traveled under a different moniker as he was aware the name *Sebastian Hannar* would set off red flags at any airport in the world. His ten traveling companions – all backpackers from as far afield as America, Holland, Japan and Australia – were young and adventurous. Despite the age gap, they accepted Nine immediately and welcomed him aboard their tour.

Now, approaching Zambia's northern border, Nine observed the crossing point with interest. It was marked by a large sign which read: *You are entering the Democratic Republic of the Congo*. Graffiti below it read: *Formerly the Belgian Congo, Congo Free State, Congo-Leopoldville, Congo-Kinshasa and Zaire*.

Armed guards in the uniform of the Army of Zambia patrolled the southern approach to the border crossing while their counterparts from one of the DRC's many military splinter groups patrolled the northern approach. The two factions were in stark contrast to each other: the former were smartly dressed and professional-looking while the latter were sloppy and decidedly unprofessional in their appearance and manner.

Observing the DRC soldiers as they swaggered about with AK47's slung over their shoulders, Nine thought they looked more like guerillas, or mercenaries at best. It didn't fill him with hope for what lay ahead.

This would be Nine's second visit to the DRC, though his first didn't really count. That had been a fleeting visit to its western seaboard where the DRC – or Zaire as it was then – meets the Atlantic Ocean. Arriving after dark on that occasion, and departing before dawn, he'd overnighted there en route to a mission in neighboring Angola.

Despite the armed presence on both sides of the border, the mini-bus crossed into the DRC without any problems.

The tour party's next stop was Kananga, a sizeable city to the east, and that's where Nine planned to part company with his young traveling companions. His destination was slap bang in the middle of the country – a dark, forbidding place referred to by explorers and historians of yesteryear as *the heart of Congo*. It was there he hoped he'd find Francis.

#

Seventeen thought she was imagining someone was observing her as she parked her Jeep behind the motel unit she shared with Isabelle.

A minute later, while unloading groceries from the vehicle's rear seat, the former operative became convinced she was being observed when she saw the head cleaner's reflection in the Jeep's side window. The big Tahitian woman seemed to be furtively watching her from the open doorway of the unit opposite.

When Seventeen turned around to look, the woman pulled back out of sight, confirming her suspicions.

The former operative tried to appear casual as she carried the groceries into her unit. Inside, she found Isabelle half asleep on a couch in the main room. Peering outside through a small gap in the curtains, she asked, "You awake?"

"Yes." Sensing something was wrong, the sleepy Frenchwoman sat up. "What is it?"

"We're leaving."

"What?"

"No time to explain."

Isabelle knew not to question Seventeen. Something was obviously wrong and now wasn't the time to ask questions. She immediately retrieved her pre-packed bag from her bedroom while Seventeen retrieved hers from a wardrobe.

The pair took only a couple of minutes to load their bags into the Jeep. As they drove out of the motel grounds, Seventeen noticed the head cleaner keenly observing their departure.

At the motel's front gate, Seventeen turned right and headed south toward the Tahiti Iti peninsula. A mile down the road, she executed a U-turn and headed north back through Taravoa, all the time checking the rear vision mirror to confirm they weren't being followed.

Isabelle wanted to ask why they were heading north, but she held her tongue. Seventeen had been giving her the cold shoulder ever since she'd admitted she ventured outside the motel for a stroll. The former operative had been furious at Isabelle over that transgression, and had directed a few choice words her way. Since then there'd been nothing. Only silence.

The Frenchwoman didn't know, but Seventeen had already put that behind her. She wasn't talking because she needed to concentrate, not because she was still angry. Seventeen knew their choices were limited. Tahiti was a surprisingly small island for anyone trying to hide. *What would you do, Sebastian?* She desperately tried to figure out a solution.

45

At the motel Isabelle and Seventeen had vacated minutes earlier, Fifteen interviewed the head cleaner. The big Tahitian woman advised him she'd seen the pregnant woman and her husband depart in their Jeep. She also gave him the registration number and told him which way the vehicle had gone.

Fifteen thanked the woman, paid her an agreed cash bonus and returned to his convertible. Driving south in pursuit of the Jeep, the African-American operative wondered who the man was masquerading as Isabelle's husband. He knew it couldn't be Nine as the description the cleaner gave indicated the man was too short to be his fellow orphan.

The operative also wondered why he hadn't seen the Jeep

when he was driving north from the peninsula to the motel. If the Jeep had been heading south, as the cleaner had said, he should in all likelihood have seen it. His gut told him the Jeep was traveling north, so he turned the car around and sped back toward Taravoa.

As he drove, he called Twenty Three on his cell phone. The call was answered almost immediately.

Fifteen quickly established that Twenty Three was at Atiue, a settlement on Tahiti Nui's east coast, south of Papeete. He advised him of the reported sighting of Isabelle and the man posing as her husband, and suggested that Twenty Three drive up the coast road to head off the Jeep the couple were traveling in. Before signing off, Fifteen relayed the Jeep's registration number to his fellow operative.

That done, Fifteen made some calls to contacts in the network he and Twenty Three had established, advising them of the Jeep and its likely whereabouts. On the other side of the island, Twenty Three did the same.

The net was closing.

#

Isabelle and Seventeen were still traveling north, but they were no longer in the Jeep. While Fifteen had been talking to Twenty Three, the fugitives had abandoned the Jeep in favor of a late model station wagon, which Seventeen had noticed parked in a layby overlooking the sea. The station wagon belonged to a fisherman who was fishing from the rocks below the layby.

Before jump-starting the station wagon's engine, Seventeen had driven the Jeep a short distance down a no-exit dirt track and hidden it in the dense rainforest. She hoped it wouldn't be discovered any time soon.

Having commandeered the station wagon, the former operative still had no set plan. Her problem was the island's interior was almost entirely uninhabited, so as far as she knew hiding places for Isabelle and herself were limited to the coastal towns and villages. She was sure if they remained on the coast, they'd be found sooner or later.

The solution to their problem came when they reached the small settlement of Papenoo, a popular surfing spot on the island's north coast.

Seventeen slowed the station wagon when she saw a roadside signpost pointing to a tourist lodge ten miles inland. A billboard beneath it advertised a vacancy at the establishment. The former operative turned off the coast road and headed for the lodge. Isabelle was unaware of the change of direction as she was fast asleep.

Looking at her sister-in-law, Seventeen noticed the ruby hanging from the silver necklace around her neck. It reminded her of Nine. He'd worn that same necklace for as long as she could remember.

Seventeen's memory was improving with every passing day. Since she'd been deprogrammed by Nine's friend in Chicago, fragments of past events, people and places had started coming back to her, like the pieces of a jigsaw puzzle. Some memories – like the killings she'd been involved in – she'd have preferred had remained buried.

The road they travelled followed the Papenoo River, Tahiti's biggest river. It cut through some of the most picturesque scenery on the island. High, craggy mountains rose up on both sides of the river valley and lush rainforest abounded. Every few miles along the road, spectacular waterfalls cascaded down the mountainsides.

As she drove, Seventeen decided it was time to stop posing as Isabelle's husband. That cover was blown now anyway. She was looking forward to being a woman again and being able to dress, talk and act like one.

Seventeen pulled over and set about changing guises while Isabelle slept on. Ten minutes was all it took. Making use of the spare clothes and disguise aids she had with her, she transformed herself into a chic tourist complete with fashionable shades and a decorative sun hat that wouldn't look out of place at the Kentucky Derby or the Royal Ascot even.

As Seventeen was adding the final touches to her new guise, Fifteen was driving through Papenoo in his convertible. He was still hoping to catch up to the Jeep he thought the fugitive pair were traveling in and didn't give the tourist lodge sign or signpost a second glance as he sped past them.

46

After Nine and his fellow backpackers crossed into the Democratic Republic of the Congo, they were faced with a full day's drive east to their first stop, Kananga. That's where Nine planned to part company with his newfound friends. While they went bungy-jumping at a new adventure tourism venture run by local tourist operators on the nearby Lulua River, he'd fly north in a chartered private helicopter.

Traveling in heat of Africa and in the confines of a mini-bus whose air-conditioning system had malfunctioned, every hour spent on the bumpy road was torturous for the tourists. For Nine, it was especially torturous as he knew every hour that passed was time he, or Francis, could ill afford.

Despite the need to find his son quickly, he'd opted to cross the border on land as he thought it a no-brainer Omega would be scrutinizing the passengers of all commercial flights arriving in the DRC. While he had supreme confidence in his shapeshifting abilities, he didn't want to push his luck any more than he had to. After all, he'd used just about every disguise in his repertoire.

The mini-bus arrived in Kananga just on dusk and therefore too late to connect with the private helicopter Nine had chartered earlier. He contacted the chopper pilot and organized an early morning departure then joined his young friends for dinner in a cheap restaurant on the ground floor of the backpackers' hostel they were overnighting at.

Nine only wished the circumstances had been different. He found his traveling companions stimulating company and enjoyed their sparkling conversation, but his family was never far from his mind. It was with regret that he made his apologies and retired upstairs for an early night.

In the privacy of the single room he'd been lucky enough to secure, Nine began studying the confidential file he'd printed out relating to Omega's secret medical lab in the DRC. He quickly established that the lab had been modelled on the agency's lab in Thule and its layout was almost identical.

According to the file, the number of patients – or *subjects* as they were called – fluctuated between one hundred and ten and one hundred and thirty. Alarmingly, this fluctuation was attributed to *an unacceptably high death rate*. The file went on to say: *Doctor Andrews is introducing measures to reduce the death rate to an acceptable level*.

Even though he'd read the file many times, its wording never failed to anger Nine. At the same time it frightened him, knowing that Francis was in all probability one of the subjects referred to.

Unlike the Thule lab, the location of this orphanage was clearly marked: it was situated on the grounds of an American Fortune 500 company's refinery on the Congo River, in the troublesome eastern province of Maniema. The company, Carmel Corporation, originally made its fortune processing raw diamonds sourced from throughout Africa, Canada and elsewhere. Since setting up in the DRC, the company was rumored to have more than quadrupled its huge profits. The reason for this could be summed up in one word: coltan.

Nine drew on his memory to recall what he knew about the precious metal. He recalled coltan was used for the production of tantalum capacitors, which were included in the manufacture of cell phones and other electronic devices as well as in high temperature alloys for air and land-based turbines.

While the file glossed over the many specialized uses of the metal, it did highlight some of the conflicts it and other precious metals had caused in the DRC. Ongoing conflicts had made exploitation of coltan ore problematic, and much of it was mined illegally and smuggled out of the country by militias from Rwanda and other neighboring countries. As a result, Congolese coltan represented only about a tenth of the world's total production even though the DRC was believed to have seventy percent of known coltan reserves.

Nine was aware the continued siphoning of coltan, as well as cobalt and diamonds, from the eastern Congo was part of a wider conspiracy to destabilize the country.

Why Carmel Corporation had opted to establish a refinery in

such a politically unstable and dangerous part of the world, he couldn't begin to fathom. He guessed the company must have reached some agreement with the Congolese Government that protected its interests and guaranteed the future of the refinery and the safety of its personnel. An unusual concession considering the company had been widely accused abroad of neglecting its corporate responsibilities by underpaying and abusing its Congolese labor force and polluting the Congo River.

To Nine's way of thinking, the problems surrounding the exploitation of coltan in the DRC epitomized the problems the entire African continent faced in capitalizing on the huge untapped wealth that lay beneath its surface. Corruption, political unrest and outside interference from non-African countries ensured the continent that should be the world's wealthiest remained the poorest.

Reading between the lines as he sifted through the file, it was obvious Carmel Corporation was yet another of Omega's many business interests. Although the agency's name never appeared in any company documentation, it would be pulling the company's strings and siphoning off the profits, of that he was sure.

Of special interest to him was the location of the refinery. It was on the Congo River and sited downstream from Kindu, a city of some two hundred thousand people. Nine planned to base himself in Kindu and travel from there to the refinery.

According to the file, the medical lab was a three-storeyed structure that adjoined Carmel Corporation's administration building next to the refinery. Photos showed that only one of those storeys was above ground, which meant the other two were below ground. Nine could imagine what went on there.

The fact that any part of the lab building was visible at all signalled to him that Omega considered it far removed from prying eyes and unlikely ever to receive the scrutiny of the West. *That could all change very soon.* As tiredness set in, he closed the file, swallowed another heart pill, then turned off the bedside lamp and prepared for sleep. Tomorrow, he planned to find his son.

47

Nine was in the air shortly after dawn. The chartered helicopter whisked him north from Kananga to Maniema Province. Its pilot, former South African Air Force flier Heinrich Schubert, followed the Congo River for the latter part of the flight, giving Nine his first glimpse of the mighty Congolese jungle.

The world's second largest rainforest after the Amazon was a sight to behold from the air. It seemed to stretch forever. And the river reminded Nine of the Amazon, too, as it wound its way like a never-ending python through the jungle.

Entering the skies above the city of Kindu, Nine ordered Heinrich to follow the Congo downstream and overfly Carmel Corporation's coltan refinery.

Some twenty miles downstream – or eleven miles as the crow flies – the refinery came into view. And there, adjoining its administration building, was the smaller building that supposedly accommodated Omega's secret medical lab. Nine's pulse quickened as he viewed the orphanage he believed Francis was imprisoned in. Even from the air it looked forbidding.

White-coated personnel could be seen walking between the smaller building and a nearby block of apartments. Nine assumed they were scientists and medical staff. The whole setup looked very similar to the lab at Thule.

Nine was concerned to see armed guards patrolling the grounds around the buildings and the refinery. There had been no mention of them in the file. He told himself he shouldn't be surprised. Omega had a major investment to protect in what was a very unstable region even by African standards.

The former operative retrieved a digital camera from an airline travel bag he'd acquired. Using its zoom lens, he snapped a dozen photos of the refinery and its surrounds.

"Want me to go lower?" Heinrich asked.

"No." Nine didn't want to attract the attention of people on the ground. "I've seen enough."

Heinrich turned the craft around and flew back over Kindu to a railway station five miles south of the city's outskirts. Seemingly in the middle of nowhere, it was surrounded by jungle. There wasn't another building in sight. Twenty or so Congolese commuters could be seen mingling with railways staff on the station platform. Nine wondered where they'd come from. He hoped the train they were waiting for would be arriving soon as he planned to be on it.

A minute later, the chopper landed on a bare patch of land behind the station. Nine disembarked, travel bags in hand, and thanked Heinrich. "Wait for my call. And don't be late."

"Ya." Heinrich knew what was expected of him as he'd been fully briefed by Nine. He'd also been well paid for his services to date and he expected to collect a healthy bonus before their arrangement was at an end. Heinrich threw a casual salute at his generous client and flew off.

Nine watched the chopper until it was just a dot in the sky. He had a feeling it would come in handy in the next day or two – as would Heinrich's military background.

The former operative had chosen this remote place to be dropped off because he didn't wish to draw attention to himself by arriving in Kindu by air. Nine was aware Europeans automatically attracted attention in this part of the world, but he hoped arriving by train would enable him to remain under the radar. He was in no doubt there would be people looking out for him in Kindu as well as at the orphanage downriver.

As he hurried over to the railway station to escape the heat of the sun, the Congolese looked strangely at the European who had appeared mysteriously amongst them. They couldn't understand why anyone would arrive at this isolated station by chopper to catch a train.

"Only white people do things like that," one middle-aged female commuter said to another. Like most Congolese, the woman spoke French. She happened to be within earshot of Nine.

Speaking French, Nine asked, "Excuse me Madam. Do you know when the next train to Kindu is due?"

"Very soon," the woman answered shyly.

"Thank you." Nine smiled and walked to a nearby ticket counter to buy his ticket.

Standing in line with other commuters, his mind was miles away. He was already planning his assault on the medical lab. Nine was glad he'd viewed it from the air. It had been a spur-of-the-moment decision to order Heinrich to overfly the refinery. The aerial reconnaissance had given him a good overview of the facility and would prove invaluable, of that he was certain.

#

The exclusive Papenoo River Valley Lodge in Tahiti's interior was a Godsend as far as Seventeen was concerned. Off the beaten track and away from prying eyes, it was in her opinion a far safer alternative to staying on the populated coast. The only drawback she could identify was it was toward the end of a no-exit road, so there was only one way out should she and Isabelle need to leave in a hurry.

The women were among a mere dozen guests staying at the lodge. It only catered for sixteen guests at any one time, so was near full capacity. The guests, who came from all over the world, were all moneyed people. They had to be: the tariff was well beyond the average tourist.

Each unit was self-contained and private, which suited Isabelle and Seventeen admirably for they could venture outside and have the run of a screened-off courtyard without fear of being seen by other guests or visitors. A well-stocked store on site meant that guests could purchase any foodstuffs and other essentials they may require without having to drive back to the coast on shopping expeditions.

For the first time since arriving in Tahiti, Seventeen was starting to believe she'd found the perfect hiding place for Isabelle and herself.

#

Having spent the day fruitlessly searching for some sign of the two fugitives, Twenty Three and Fifteen were spending the evening working the phones in their hotel room back in Papeete. They were phoning hotels, motels and guesthouses throughout Tahiti, asking if a pregnant woman had recently checked in with her male companion.

In every case, they left their cell phone number and asked to be called back if the couple showed up. A sizeable cash inducement was offered for any tip-off that proved accurate.

The two operatives were feeling confident. Recent events had confirmed that Isabelle was still on the island. The pair couldn't guess who the man was that she'd been seen with, but he didn't concern them.

Twenty Three and Fifteen had established a wide network of informants throughout Tahiti, and tomorrow they'd be joined by another elite orphan-operative. They were convinced Isabelle was fast running out of hiding places.

The Frenchwoman's capture couldn't come fast enough for the operatives – their Omega masters were becoming tetchy.

48

Nine was experiencing sensory overload as he was driven through the crowded, grubby back streets of Kindu. He was traveling in an old, battered Holden that belched smoke and barely passed for a cab even by Congolese standards.

Sitting in the back seat with the window wound down, Nine was assailed by the sights, sounds and smells of Africa. Colorful Congolese rubbed shoulders with other Africans on the congested streets as they peddled their wares or shopped in the numerous markets and roadside stalls. There wasn't a white face among them.

Old men and women sat gossiping in the shade of the frangipani trees that abounded in this quarter of the city while youths congregated in small groups in the middle of the road, forcing traffic to drive around them. The honking of irate motorists' horns competed with music blaring from car speakers and roadside stalls, creating a cacophony of sound.

Nine's cabbie, a middle-aged Congolese whose name tag read *Elvis Ndobo*, took the mayhem in his stride as he negotiated the busy streets. A photo of a homely, smiling African woman glued to the cab's dashboard signalled that Elvis was a married man.

The photo reminded Nine of his own wife. He quickly put Isabelle to the back of his mind: he had to remain focused for what was ahead.

Nine was heading for a bar that had a reputation for being the seediest drinking establishment in the city. He had it on good advice it was frequented by the kind of people he was hoping to meet.

The former operative had checked in to a hotel earlier that day. He'd opted to stay at a third rate hotel in a rundown quarter of Kindu because he was aware the people watching out for him would expect him to stay in plush premises in an upmarket part of town.

Nine had a plan he wanted to put into motion, but for it to work he had to have outside help. Unfortunately for him, the kind of people who could help him weren't listed in the telephone directory.

As he had no contacts or informants in the DRC, he'd gone out of his way to befriend an old Congolese janitor at the hotel who looked like he knew a thing or two about a thing or two. It turned out he'd chosen well: the old man had his finger on the pulse of life in Kindu and knew, or knew of, just about everybody who lived and worked in that quarter of the city.

When Nine asked the janitor where he could meet people who would be least likely to receive Christmas cards from the Congolese Army or Police Force, the old man knew exactly what kind of people the white guest was referring to and where he could find them. He had directed him to the bar Nine was now heading for. He'd also warned him to watch his back.

As the bar came into view, Elvis pointed it out to Nine.

"There it is, boss. The Taj Mahal." He spoke French, the predominant language of the DRC.

Nine noted there wasn't a trace of irony in the cabbie's voice. Studying the drinking establishment, he quickly established there wouldn't be a building in all of Africa less like the real Taj Mahal. It was basically a lean-to shack built in to the side of an abandoned warehouse. A weathered sign above the doorway read: *Sale price liquor all day every day*. In the doorway, a net curtain substituted for the door.

Congolese youths sat drinking bottles of beer in the gutter outside while other patrons came and went from the premises. The youths directed wolf whistles at two promiscuous and scantily clad teenage girls who emerged from the bar. Clearly intoxicated, the girls held onto each other for support as they staggered along the pavement in their high-heel shoes.

Elvis studied his fare in the rear vision mirror as he parked the car near the youths. "You sure you want to stop here, boss?"

"I'm sure," Nine grinned as he paid the cabbie and tipped him generously for good measure. "Buy your beautiful wife some nice perfume."

Elvis beamed at Nine and pocketed the cash. "You want me to wait, boss?"

"No need, thanks." Nine disembarked from the cab and watched as the cab drove off. Conscious the youths were observing him, he entered the bar. It took a minute or two for his eyes to adjust to its gloomy interior. The only illumination was from natural light that came from small windows along the far wall.

As his eyes adjusted, he could see the bar was half full. The patrons were all black males who appeared to have been drinking for some time. Prostitutes circulated among them, touting for business. A rowdy card game was in progress at one table. The hum of conversation could just be heard above the African harmonies that played over a radio. Conversation ceased as the patrons became aware of the new arrival.

Nine approached the bar. A surly barman looked him up and down and reluctantly acknowledged him. As the barman moved closer, Nine could see he had a wicked scar that ran from his forehead to his jaw – a legacy of a knife fight no doubt.

"What you want, man?" the barman asked.

"Give me a beer," Nine said.

The barman poured a tall glass of beer and placed it on the counter in front of the first white customer the bar had seen in more than a year.

Nine paid him then indicated he wanted a word. "I want to speak to someone connected with Lusambo's Mai Mai Militia," he said quietly. "Can you help me?"

The barman blinked once then stared hard at Nine. After what seemed an age he asked, "Who wants to know?"

"Someone who is prepared to pay a lot of money."

The barman looked thoughtfully at Nine then motioned to him to sit down at the nearest unoccupied table. Nine did as he was asked. The barman served another patron then disappeared into a room at the rear of the premises. He returned a minute later and advised Nine that he had sent for someone who may be able to help him. The barman warned him he may have a wait.

Nine was resigned to waiting. This was Africa after all. He proceeded to drink his beer, all the while aware the surly barman was observing him even as he served other patrons.

The barman's interest in him was understandable. After all, Nine had enquired after one of the most feared of the Congolese rebel groups operating in the eastern Congo.

Lusambo's Mai Mai Militia was named after its infamous leader, Captain Undu Lusambo, a former decorated officer in the Congolese Army. Nine had learned that much from the old janitor who had advised him that the militia's rebels may be the kind of people he was looking for.

Like the six other Mai Mai militias operating in the region, Lusambo's group was largely comprised of disenchanted combatants of the country's armed forces. Unlike the other militias and independent armed groups, Lusambo's rebels didn't attack villages or kill, rape and plunder innocent citizens. Their target was the Congolese Army whose soldiers had a deserved reputation for terrorizing the very people they were supposed to protect.

Nine's research had revealed that conflict minerals – gold, tin, cobalt and coltan included – were behind much of the violence that gripped the region. So it had come as no surprise to him that

Carmel Corporation's coltan refinery was located in the middle of the area controlled by Lusambo's militia. *That would explain the heavy presence of armed personnel at the refinery.* Nine downed his beer and ordered lemonade on ice. He wanted to keep a clear head.

49

Forty-five minutes and two iced lemonades later, a one-armed Rwandan entered the Taj Mahal via the back door. He looked at the barman who nodded in Nine's direction.

The Rwandan approached Nine. "My name is Christian," he said in halting English. "Come with me."

Nine drained the remains of his glass and followed Christian outside into the bright sunlight. An old van was waiting for them, its engine throbbing. Two of its side windows were cracked and small, round holes in the glass and in one of the door panels looked suspiciously like bullet holes.

Two big Congolese men sitting in the van's back seat jumped out as soon as they saw they had company. They marched up to Nine and, without introduction, began frisking him. As they did, he observed they were armed with dated, military-issue revolvers. He guessed the men were former soldiers.

In anticipation of being frisked, Nine had left his own weapon – a Luger pistol he'd purchased soon after arriving in the DRC – back in his hotel room. He had also left behind the black makeup kit he usually wore strapped to his chest.

Jules, the taller of the two men, removed Nine's wallet and the bulging money belt he wore around his waist. Opening the belt's zip, Jules found wads of US dollars inside. "What's this?" he asked.

"That's ten thousand American dollars," Nine said. "It's for Captain Lusambo. Call it a token."

"A token?" Oudry, the shorter of the two men, asked.

"A down-payment."

Jules threw the money belt and wallet onto the van's front seat then he and Oudry bundled their guest into the rear of the van. Nine ended up wedged between them on the back seat. Oudry produced a scarf and began to blind-fold him. Before the blindfold was securely in place, Nine saw Christian was behind the wheel.

He hoped the one-armed Rwandan had his driver's license.

The van took off and backfired as it accelerated jerkily along the street.

Twenty minutes later, the vehicle stopped in a screech of brakes somewhere in a relatively quiet part of the city. Two pairs of strong hands hauled Nine from the van and frog-marched him into a building.

When his blindfold was finally removed, he found he was sitting in a small, windowless room. Furnishings were sparse and there was no clue as to whether the room was inside a house or in commercial premises.

Facing him were the two Congolese men who had frisked him and a third man whom they addressed as *Prince* and who was obviously their leader. Shorter than the others, but built like a tank, Prince had a cruel face and a menacing presence.

The three men spoke Swahili amongst themselves. While Nine couldn't speak Swahili, he did speak the closely related Bantu language of Duruma – a result of time spent in Kenya on a mission – so he got the gist of what was being said. The men were speculating on who he was and were obviously afraid he could be working for the Government's security forces or the Police.

Nine wondered if Prince was in fact Captain Lusambo. That question was answered when the man addressed him.

"What business do you have with Captain Lusambo?" Prince asked in French.

"That is for his ears only," Nine responded.

Without warning, Prince slapped Nine's face hard with his open hand. The force of the blow drew blood and nearly felled the former operative.

"I asked what business you have with the captain!" Prince shouted.

"You already have my answer." Nine stood his ground and braced himself for the next onslaught.

Prince looked like he was about to explode. His right hand twitched above the handle of the large hunting knife he carried in a sheath on his hip.

"There's a lot more of that where it came from," Nine said hurriedly, looking at the money belt one of his escorts was holding.

"And I'm sure the captain wouldn't be happy if he didn't get to hear what I have to offer."

Nine's words had the desired effect. Prince conferred with his companions in Swahili. Opening Nine's wallet, he pulled out a business card and looked at the visitor. "Ted Williamson," he said reading the name on the card aloud. He looked at Nine. "Is that your real name?"

"It will do for now."

"And what do you do for a living, Mister Williamson?"

"I make people rich."

Again, this gave Prince something to think about. He reached a decision. "It will take a little time to reach Captain Lusambo."

"My offer has a twenty four-hour time limit."

Prince stared hard at Nine. "Where are you staying?"

"The Masonic Hotel."

Prince fired orders in Swahili to the others then turned back to Nine. "My men will take you back to the Masonic. You should wait there until someone comes to you with the captain's answer."

"Twenty-four hours, remember," Nine said.

Prince glared at him then nodded to his men who immediately blind-folded their visitor and marched him back outside to the waiting van.

Nine tried not to show his relief as he was bundled into the van. He'd taken a huge risk and he knew it. But it had been necessary. Now he could look forward to finding and rescuing Francis – he hoped.

50

While Nine was being chauffeured back to his hotel, one of his best friends going right back to his orphanage days was checking on security at Omega's medical lab at the coltan refinery downriver. Number Thirteen, a muscular Polynesian, had been the first of the orphan-operatives to arrive at the lab in anticipation of Nine showing up.

Naylor had chosen Thirteen to oversee the mission in the DRC. He'd also assigned four of his best male operatives to assist him, and Marcia Wilson had pulled in half a dozen of her CIA agents from Nairobi and Cape Town to provide backup. The firm's agents had been assigned to watch out for Nine in nearby Kindu while Thirteen and his fellow orphan-operatives remained at the lab as that was where the expected fireworks would happen.

Having just finished a briefing, Thirteen was starting his daily inspection of the grounds around the lab and the nearby refinery. He was accompanied by Twenty Two, one of the Pedemont graduates Naylor had sent to help him.

Both men were sweating profusely. A storm was brewing and the humidity levels rising. The pair were discussing Nine and the havoc he'd caused at Thule Air Base.

"He was the best of the best," Thirteen said, "and judging by recent events, he hasn't lost his touch."

"That's for sure," Twenty-Two said. "I still can't believe it has come to this, can you?"

"No, but ours is not to reason why."

"I know. It's to do or die."

The operatives continued their rounds in silence.

It was a typically hot day and the sun beat down on them mercilessly. Behind them, white-coated scientists and medical personnel walked between the lab building and an apartment complex behind it, while ahead of them, executive types came and went from Carmel Corporation's administration building.

Beyond the admin building, the coltan refinery was its usual industrious self. Congolese workers scurried to and fro under the watchful eye of armed guards. Trucks laden with ore arrived at the refinery every few minutes to empty their loads. Above them, the refinery's twin chimney stacks discharged smoke into an otherwise blue sky.

As the operatives continued their rounds, Thirteen felt confident he had the necessary manpower and resources to prevent any repetition of the events at Thule. Naylor had sent some of Omega's best male operatives to assist him. Each of them had unique skills and collectively they represented quite a force.

Twenty-Two was an excellent example of the caliber of operatives Naylor had chosen. He was probably the toughest and most aggressive of the operatives, and arguably the most accomplished martial arts exponent now that Three was dead.

The others were no slouches either. Four, a chess grandmaster who played in major tournaments when time permitted, applied his chess strategies to everyday life. He was a formidable operative who had never known failure in all his years with Omega. Eighteen, an operative of Asian heritage, was an explosives expert who had lost count of the number of people he'd terminated using explosive devices. And Twelve was a crack marksman who knew everything there was to know about weapons and armaments, and who, officially at least, had more kills to his name than any of Omega's operatives.

As for Thirteen, he was an all-rounder in every sense of the word, which was why Naylor had put him in charge of the DRC mission. While all the orphan-operatives were true polymaths, Thirteen was an expert in so many different fields even he had lost count. His golden-brown skin and easygoing Polynesian manner meant he was often underestimated, and that was something he didn't hesitate to use to his advantage when necessary.

Thirteen and Twenty-Two completed their rounds. Everything seemed in order. Before retreating indoors, Thirteen asked, "Have we overlooked anything?"

"Not that I can think of."

"I can't think of anything either, so let's get out of this heat."

The pair re-entered the lab building where they caught up

with the other operatives. They all adjourned to a private meeting room to compare notes and discuss their security arrangements.

Compared to meetings involving executive types in the corporate sector, any meetings between Omega's orphan-operatives were decidedly casual affairs. There was never a shortage of humor, everyone had a say and no-one actually chaired the meetings. Despite this, the operatives were professional and on the rare occasions they did meet, the business at hand was covered in double-quick time.

Today's spur-of-the-moment meeting was no different except the operatives were more subdued than usual. They couldn't help but wonder what had brought their lives to the point where they were planning to kill one of their own. Even though Nine had turned his back on them and the agency, he was still one of them – an Omegan, a Pedemont orphan, a brother.

They also wondered, when the time came, if they could kill one of their own.

What they didn't know was they were all under the influence of the insidious MK-Ultra mind-control program – just as their deceased colleagues at Thule had been – and when it came time to kill Nine, they wouldn't hesitate.

#

As the orphan-operatives waited for Nine to show up at the refinery, their six CIA colleagues were wearing down their shoe leather trudging the streets of Kindu looking for him. Knowing their target was a man of means who could afford to frequent the best hotels, the agents concentrated their search on the city's upmarket areas. That suited them just fine as the back streets and poorer quarters of Kindu were best avoided.

The storm that had threatened earlier arrived with a vengeance. It rained as it can only rain in the tropics, drenching the agents and making their job all the more tiresome.

51

Dusk had fallen and Nine had just about given up on hearing back from Lusambo's people. Since being returned to his hotel that afternoon, he'd waited on tenterhooks for news. Not a word. He was preparing to dine in the hotel restaurant downstairs when there was a knock on his door.

Nine answered the door cautiously and was pleased to see Christian standing there, dripping wet. The one-armed Rwandan was holding the wallet and money belt his companions had taken from Nine earlier.

Christian handed the items over. "You come now." He walked off toward the nearest stairwell.

Nine quickly checked the contents of the returned items. Predictably, the ten grand had been taken from the money belt, but the contents of his wallet were intact. He picked up a pre-packed airline travel bag and followed the Rwandan downstairs. Among other things, the bag contained the confidential file on the secret orphanage and prints of the aerial photos he'd taken earlier. He'd had them downloaded and printed off soon after arriving in Kindu.

Stepping outside, Nine was immediately drenched in the torrential rain. Through it, he could just make out Christian waiting for him on the other side of the street. He was in the same old van and was impatiently revving the engine. There was no sign of the Rwandan's two Congolese companions.

Nine ran across the road, dodging puddles, and climbed in beside Christian. He held on for dear life as his one-armed chauffeur gunned the accelerator and took off. The former operative could hardly see anything as rain lashed the van's windscreen.

Ten hair-raising minutes later, they arrived at a jetty on the river where a boat awaited them. Beyond it, the Congo disappeared into the darkness like some evil entity.

At first glance, the boat appeared to be typical of many of the craft that plied the river, transporting food and produce to the settlements that lined its banks. A converted passenger ferry, she appeared to be well past her used-by date and in a state of disrepair.

Closer inspection reminded Nine appearances could be deceiving. While the boat's exterior paintwork left a lot to be desired, her reinforced hull was strong – and presumably bulletproof – and judging by the sweet throbbing sounds coming from below deck, her engine was powerful. The vessel's crew were not typical of other Congo River boat crews either. Nine counted at least a dozen others already on board. In the darkness they were just shadowy figures. However, the way they conducted themselves and the automatic weapons they carried told Nine they weren't fishermen or traders. He assumed they were members of Lusambo's Mai Mai militia. At least he hoped they were.

Nine thought he recognized the two Congolese he'd met earlier, but couldn't be sure. None of the men seemed to notice the rain, which now fell heavier than ever. They were obviously used to it.

Christian escorted Nine aboard the boat. They were met by the skipper, a gangly Ugandan appropriately called Skipper. He exchanged brief words in an unidentifiable African dialect with Nine's escort before dismissing him.

As Christian departed, Skipper quickly frisked Nine and inspected the contents of the travel bag he carried. Then he motioned to one of his crew members, a young Zambian, to escort the white man below deck.

The Zambian led Nine toward the stern. As Nine followed, he looked over the near rail as one of the rebels shone a torch down onto the surface of the water. The torchlight picked up two pairs of luminescent eyes. *Crocodiles!* Nine reminded himself not to fall in.

Descending a ladder, he found himself in a large cabin adjoining the galley. There, he was met by two unsmiling Congolese who had evidently been assigned to guard him. They motioned to him to sit down. Despite the fact that it was dark outside and the cabin's windows had been blacked out with paint, one of the guards blindfolded their passenger.

Nine heard Skipper give the order to cast off. Moments later, he could feel the power of the current as the boat and everyone aboard her were carried downstream. Skipper, or someone, gunned the engine and the boat responded, showing an impressive turn of speed.

Just over an hour later, Nine heard the order given to douse all lights on board and to maintain silence. Then the motor shut down and the boat just drifted along in the current. The only sound was the relentless rain which hammered the boat's hull and deck.

Nine guessed they were passing the coltan refinery. That was confirmed when he heard the sound of machinery and other industrial noises coming from the far bank. Putting two and two together, he guessed his traveling companions didn't want to advertise their presence to the armed personnel stationed at the refinery. Those people would be allied to the DRC Armed Forces, or to the Government at least, and therefore no friends of the Mai Mai militias operating in the eastern regions of the country.

Five minutes later, the engine revved back to life and the boat resumed its journey downriver at full speed.

#

Just under two hours later, the boat pulled in to a jetty on the near bank. Several pairs of rough hands manhandled Nine up the ladder and onto the deck where he discovered the rain continued unabated. From there he was escorted off the boat and hoisted up into the back of an open-deck vehicle, which took off at speed along a muddy track that cut through the jungle.

Still blindfolded, Nine lost all track of time as the vehicle slid and bounced its way along the track. Every now and then he was struck by an overhanging branch or vine. Curses from others sitting nearby told him he had company. To Nine, the only redeeming feature of this part of the trip was the vegetation overhead formed a natural umbrella, keeping most of the rain at bay.

At some point the order came from the vehicle's driver to remove Nine's blindfold. One of Nine's traveling companions removed it immediately.

Nine saw he was traveling in an open-top, military-style Jeep. Three armed rebels sat with him in the back and he counted two more rebels up front, including the driver. The three in the back looked at him dispassionately. He guessed they'd just as soon slit his throat as deliver him to wherever it was they were going.

The former operative glanced at his watch. It was close to midnight. That didn't leave much time for what he had in mind.

52

Finally, the vehicle broke clear of the jungle and entered a clearing that was home to a force of a hundred or so rebels. Nine guessed they were members of Lusambo's Mai Mai militia.

The camp had a temporary look about it. Living quarters were comprised of tents that were lined up in rows, military fashion. An assortment of armoured vehicles and light artillery pieces were parked in between the tents. Camouflage netting covered the entire encampment, keeping it hidden from any aircraft that may be looking for it.

Through the rain, half a dozen sentries could be seen patrolling the camp's perimeter. There was no sign of the others. Nine assumed they were either sleeping or away on patrol. The camp itself was a quagmire of mud and slush.

The Jeep Nine travelled in stopped outside the biggest tent. It was in the center of the encampment. A towering, stern-faced Congolese man emerged from the tent, yawning. Two sentries standing guard outside the tent snapped to attention when they saw him.

Nine didn't need to be told that he was looking at Captain Undo Lusambo.

The captain motioned to the rebels in the back of the Jeep to bring the visitor to him and he disappeared back inside the tent.

Twenty seconds later, and mercifully out of the rain, Nine found himself standing before Lusambo. The captain was flanked by two lieutenants. A woman was fussing around at the back of the tent, boiling water over a gas stove. Lighting in the tent was supplied courtesy of kerosene lamps, which hung from the tent poles.

"Captain Lusambo at your service," Lusambo said in perfect French. "You will join me for tea I hope?" The captain threw a towel at his guest.

Nine was a little taken aback. "Ah, thank you, yes." He used the towel to dry his face and hair.

Lusambo dismissed his lieutenants then sat down on one of three folding chairs that had been set up. Smiling, he motioned to Nine to sit down. "And what should I call you Mister...Williamson?"

Nine had the good grace to look embarrassed as he sat down facing the rebel leader. "Ted Williamson's an assumed name. I am Sebastian Hannar." Even though it went against his training, he somehow felt it proper to use his real name. It felt good to not have to lie about who he was and he hadn't been able to do that for some time.

The two men stared at each other, each assessing his opposite. Nine was impressed by what he saw. At six foot seven, Lusambo made an imposing figure. Not even his loose-fitting camouflage fatigues could hide his strong physique, and his intelligent eyes appeared all knowing.

Lusambo was similarly impressed. He liked the look of this green-eyed white man who had risked his life to seek him out and journey to his camp in the middle of the night. The captain assumed Nine must have pressing business to attend to and looked forward to hearing what he had to say.

They were interrupted by the woman Nine had seen earlier. She held a tray supporting three mugs of tea and a plate of plain biscuits. A refined-looking, statuesque woman, she smiled lovingly at Lusambo who gave her a playful slap on the rump as he took one of the mugs from her.

"Meet Leila, my sweetheart, Mister Hannar," Lusambo announced proudly. He used the term *sweetheart* loosely: Leila was his wife, though Nine had no way of knowing that.

Nine nodded at Leila as he took the other mug of tea from her. He was immediately struck by her beauty and wondered where she came from. She was quite different to the Congolese women he'd seen.

Leila smiled politely and sat down on the other side of Lusambo. It was evident she was a party to all his business dealings.

Lusambo noted Nine's interest in his wife. "She is from

South Sudan," he said. He'd switched to English in deference to his wife for that was her second language behind Arabi. "She saved my life once and so I have devoted my life to making her happy." He squeezed her hand and she reciprocated.

Leila turned to Nine. "Are you married, Mister Hannar?"

"Please call me Sebastian. Yes I am married--"

"I'm sure Sebastian has not come all this way to discuss his home life, my dear," Lusambo interjected.

"Well, that's not quite true," Nine ventured.

The Lusambos looked at their guest, surprised.

Nine proceeded to tell them why he was there. Starting with Francis' abduction and ending with his arrival at their camp deep in the Congo jungle, he left nothing out.

When he'd finished, he opened the travel bag he'd brought with him and pulled out the confidential file on Omega's secret medical lab upriver from the camp. He selected a stack of grizzly photos of the lab's medical subjects – mainly African children – who had been disfigured by scientific experiments, and handed them to the couple who then studied them in silence.

Leila was clearly shocked by what she saw. Her reaction was one of a mother's compassion for her children. She expressed her horror at what was going on at the lab and her heartfelt sympathy for Nine's situation.

Captain Lusambo's reaction was totally different. He'd heard thousands of sad stories over his lifetime. Nine's story was sad, but almost everyone in Africa had a story as sad, or sadder. Lusambo just wanted to know where he and his militia fitted in to Nine's sad story, and how well they'd be paid. So he asked exactly that.

Nine explained what he had in mind.

53

Lusambo heard him out. When Nine had finished, the captain asked: "So let me see if I have this right. You want me and my men to risk our lives to attack Carmel Corporation's refinery upriver and rescue your son. Am I correct so far?"

Nine nodded.

The captain continued, "And will you pay us a hundred thousand Yankie dollars with another hundred thousand on top if we get your son out alive?"

Again Nine nodded.

Lusambo looked thoughtfully at Nine as he considered the proposal. He suddenly looked over his shoulder and shouted, "Arcel!"

One of the sentries Nine had seen earlier entered the tent. "Yes Captain."

Lusambo snapped an order at the sentry in Swahili. The sentry disappeared, returning a minute later with the two lieutenants who had been there when Nine had arrived. Lusambo then conferred with his lieutenants in Swahili, not realizing that Nine was able to follow the gist of their conversation.

Nine was able to deduce that Lusambo was relating his business proposal to the men and asking for their opinion. It seemed they liked the idea of adding one to two hundred thousand American dollars to the militia's coffers, but they didn't like the risks involved. *This is not going well*. Nine's hope began to fade when he realized Lusambo shared their opinion.

After a few minutes, the captain dismissed his lieutenants then turned to Nine.

"Let me save you the trouble," Nine said. "Your men think it's too risky and you agree with them."

Lusambo assumed Nine had just deduced that from their tone of voice. He didn't contradict his guest.

Nine asked, "Is it the money? I am open to negotiation."

The captain shook his head. "It's not the money. Even a million dollars wouldn't change anything."

Lusambo said the refinery was heavily defended by armed mercenaries hired by the Government. He went on to explain how the rebels couldn't match the mercenaries' superior firepower and how his men were largely limited to surprise hit-and-run raids on smaller targets. "Besides," he said, "the refinery is not a priority target for us. Even if we were able to over-run it, we could never hold onto it. The Government would send its troops in and we would be annihilated."

"But I'm not asking you to hold onto it," Nine said. "All I'm asking is for enough men to force our way onto the premises, find my son and get out quick. The whole thing could be over in fifteen minutes or less."

"I'm sorry Mister Hannar." Lusambo stood up, indicating the meeting was over. "I won't order my men on a suicide mission. Not for any amount of money."

Nine was beginning to feel desperate. He'd been relying on

securing the support of Lusambo's militia. He had no Plan B.

Sensing his despair, Leila touched his arm. "I am sorry, Sebastian. If my husband could help you, he would."

Realizing he was beaten, Nine stood up and faced Lusambo. He couldn't think of anything else to say. The captain's mind was obviously made up.

Lusambo handed the photos back to Nine.

"No you keep them as souvenirs," the former operative said.

Lusambo handed the photos to Leila then ordered his lieutenants to arrange for Nine to be returned to the boat that was waiting to take him back to Kindu. Turning back to his guest, he said, "I wish you well, my friend."

"And you," a disconsolate Nine said. He smiled at Leila and followed the lieutenants out of the tent into the rain.

One of the lieutenants blindfolded the visitor, then he and his comrade bundled him into the back of the same vehicle that had brought him to their camp. From the opening of their tent, Lusambo and Leila watched as the vehicle drove off.

The drive back to the boat seemed to take forever. Nine was

feeling even more disconsolate by the time he reached the jetty. Without the firepower the rebels could have supplied, he knew he didn't have a hope of even finding Francis let alone rescuing him.

Nine belatedly remembered the ten thousand dollars he'd paid Lusambo's men earlier as a down-payment for the militia's services. He put that out of his mind immediately. It seemed unimportant now.

As he boarded the boat, he felt as though he was in a trance. His mind and body were just going through the motions.

Minutes later, sitting alone, drenched and blindfolded in the darkness of the cabin below deck, he thought of Francis and silently wept.

54

As Nine was being ferried back to Kindu, Leila lay wide awake next to her husband in their jungle tent. Images of the disfigured children in the photos Nine had left behind kept running through her mind like some horror movie.

Finally, Leila arose from the bed mat and retrieved the photos she'd left on one of the folding chairs. After lighting a kerosene lamp, she sat down and began looking through the photos again.

"What is it?" Lusambo asked from across the tent.

"Nothing, dear. You go back to sleep."

Moments later, loud snoring told Leila that her husband had heeded her advice.

Leila cried tears of anguish as she studied the gruesome photos. The skin of one colored African boy had been turned white; the skin of a European girl had been turned black; another young African boy had the facial features of an old man and yet another had a third eye inserted in his forehead. The eye looked to be in working order though there was no way of knowing if that was the case.

Leila was about to return to bed when a photo of yet another young African boy caught her eye. She'd overlooked it earlier because it had been stuck beneath a larger photo. Leila lifted the photo up to the lamp and studied it closely. She let out a scream of recognition. "Sonny!"

Alerted by his wife's scream, Lusambo jumped to his feet, revolver in hand. "What is it?"

At the same time, the two sentries on duty outside the tent burst in, rifles at the ready.

"Undu, it's Sonny!" She held the photo up to her husband's face.

Lusambo snatched the photo from her and studied it by the

light of the lamp. He recognized the boy in the photo. It was Sonny, his nephew and his late sister's only child. The boy had been abducted and his mother raped and shot when another Mai Mai militia group had raided their village two years earlier. Sonny was seven when he was taken.

"Oh, Indu! We must rescue him!" Leila implored. "We owe that much to Grace." She referred to the woman who was Sonny's mother and Lusambo's older sister.

Lusambo didn't need convincing. He'd worshipped his sister until she'd been so cruelly taken from him. Grace had served as a substitute parent after their own parents had died in a malaria outbreak, working hard to ensure there was always food on the table for herself and her kid brother. She'd even put him through school using her own hard-earned wages.

Turning to the nearest sentry, Lusambo said, "Get word to Skipper."

The sentry knew his boss was referring to the skipper of the boat that was taking Nine back to Kindu.

"Tell him to get his passenger back here quick as possible."

The sentry left the tent.

Lusambo addressed the remaining sentry. "I'm calling a meeting in the war tent in ten minutes. Alert the men."

"Yes sir." The second sentry hurried off, leaving the Lusambos alone for the moment.

Leila looked up at her husband, her eyes full of hope. "God has returned Sonny to us." She buried her face in his chest.

"Not yet he hasn't," the captain said. He knew it would need a miracle to rescue his nephew, but he was prepared to die trying. He owed that much to Grace.

While the Lusambos were thanking God for giving them a sign the boy was still alive, in a nearby tent the camp's radio operator was talking to the boat's skipper via radio-telephone. "Yes you heard correct," the operator said. "The captain wants you to bring the white man back to camp. Over."

#

The boat had been chugging upriver for the best part of an hour. In that time, Nine had resigned himself to having to find another way to rescue Francis. His mentor's words kept coming back to him. *For every problem there's always a solution.* But try as he may, he couldn't think of one for this particular problem.

The first he knew something was up was when the boat suddenly turned around. Thirty seconds was all it took the boat to complete the turn. Now, aided by the current, it was speeding back downriver.

"What's going on?" he asked. Still blindfolded, he couldn't see a thing. "What's going on?" he shouted, louder this time.

Nine sensed a presence at the top of the ladder leading down into the cabin. Then a gruff African voice said, "Skipper says he has been ordered to return you to camp."

The former operative wondered if he was hearing things. "Say again."

"We are taking you back to camp."

Those words were music to Nine's ears and he inwardly rejoiced.

55

For Isabelle and Seventeen, two days had passed without incident since they'd checked in to the exclusive Papenoo River Valley Lodge in Tahiti's rugged interior. The lodge, which overlooked the river, gave them the privacy they required. And their enforced association had brought about a change in their relationship, too.

The change had been subtle at first. Monosyllabic responses had given way to full sentences and these in turn had evolved into full blown discussions. Their first discussion was more of an argument. It happened on their first night at the lodge and concerned the little matter of Seventeen terminating Isabelle's parents in France five years earlier.

Though Nine had explained that Seventeen had been under

the influence of MK-Ultra mind-control at the time and to this day had no recollection of the incident, Isabelle hadn't been able to forgive Seventeen. Nor had she forgotten how Nine's sister had mistreated her when she'd interned her in the CIA detention center after killing her parents.

As for Seventeen, she was still getting over the shock of learning of her past actions. Hearing that she'd killed innocent people had hit her like a bombshell, and she was grappling with learning how to live with herself. She never expected Isabelle's forgiveness.

It was Isabelle who had raised the delicate topic, asking her minder if she ever had flashbacks to her days as an Omega operative. Seventeen had advised her she did as, to the best of her knowledge, she had only occasionally been in a mind-controlled state. Isabelle had responded sarcastically, suggesting that was very convenient.

The argument that followed had been brief but vigorous. Seventeen had taken issue with the sarcasm and Isabelle had vented the anger she'd built up over the years since the loss of her parents.

Though painful at the time, the argument had cleared the air. It ended in tears with both women consoling each other.

Since then, they were rapidly become inseparable, and not only because they were forced to spend just about every minute of every day in each other's company. A true friendship was starting to blossom.

Isabelle recognized some of Nine's traits in her sister-in-law. Like her brother, Seventeen was compassionate and caring, and she had hidden depths that she only revealed to those she trusted.

The Frenchwoman also couldn't forget that Seventeen had put her life on the line to do Nine's bidding and come to Tahiti to protect her from the same people who had taken Francis. Isabelle knew enough about Omega to know they wouldn't hesitate to kill Seventeen if they thought she was preventing them from achieving their aims – whatever those aims were.

Now, as the pair enjoyed a drink beneath the shade of tropical almond trees in the private courtyard of their unit, they discussed the people who were always in their thoughts: Nine and

Francis. And as always, Isabelle became emotional when she talked about them.

"I just know something is wrong," the Frenchwoman said, fondling the ruby that dangled from the end of her necklace. "Sebastian could be dead!" Isabelle began sobbing. "Perhaps Francis is dead, too!"

"I'm sure nothing's wrong," Seventeen countered. She put a comforting arm around Isabelle. "I'll drive into town tomorrow to check my emails. There may be some good news." Her sister-in-law seemed encouraged by that. Seventeen added, "And if anyone can rescue Francis, Sebastian can." Her choice of words had a calming effect on Isabelle.

A movement in the Frenchwoman's swollen belly caused her to grimace. She clutched her tummy.

"You okay?" Seventeen asked.

"Baby moved," Isabelle smiled. "She has been doing that a lot lately."

"She?"

"Yes, it is a girl."

"Do you have a name for her?"

"Annette. After Sebastian's mother."

Seventeen felt tears welling up. "And my mother, too."

Isabelle hadn't considered that before. She reached out and touched Seventeen's arm affectionately. "Yes. After your mother, too."

#

As Isabelle and Seventeen talked and sipped cold drinks in the shade, just fifty yards away in the Papenoo River Valley Lodge's front office, a telephone rang. The call was answered by one of the proprietors, Fraulein Schmidt, a sophisticated German woman.

"La ora na," Fraulein Schmidt answered by way of an authentic Tahitian greeting, "this is the Papenoo Lodge. Can I help you?"

At the other end of the line, Twenty Three answered, "Yes this is Inspector Marcel, of the French National Police, in Papeete." He spoke English with a strong French accent.

The proprietor immediately reverted to fluent French. "Oui,

Inspector. How can I help?"

Responding in kind, Twenty Three said, "I am phoning to enquire whether a man and a woman have checked in there in the last couple of days. They are possibly traveling as husband and wife."

"Non. The only people who have checked in recently are two women."

"Ah." Twenty Three was about to hang up. He and Fifteen had been phoning accommodation establishments all over Tahiti for the past two days – all for nothing – and they were both running out of energy and motivation. As an afterthought he asked, "You're sure they are both women?"

"Oh, oui. They both look very feminine. One of them is pregnant."

Twenty Three suddenly became interested. He questioned Fraulein Schmidt further, noting the women's mode of transport, the registration number of their car and the names they had checked in under. Before ending the call, he asked the proprietor not to mention the phone call to anyone.

As soon as he was off the phone, Twenty Three checked with local gendarmes who confirmed that the registration number he'd been given belonged to a station wagon reported stolen on the north coast two days earlier.

56

It was nearing dawn before Nine was returned to Lusambo's militia encampment – too late for the night-time raid he'd hoped to organize on the refinery upriver. The former operative was convinced Lusambo had reconsidered his proposal. *Why else did he bring me back?* He was only seconds away from finding out.

The Mai Mai rebels' base looked quite different to how it looked earlier that night. Although it was still dark, the camp was now a hive of activity with rebels everywhere. For the first time, Nine noticed there were women among them. Several carried sleeping babies on their backs while tending cooking fires and performing other menial chores. Two women were armed and looked ready for a fight.

Many of the rebels appeared to be readying vehicles and equipment for an engagement. Others were stockpiling and cleaning weapons. The AK-47 was apparently the weapon of choice though there was an impressive collection of rocket-launchers, mortars and explosive devices in addition to the light artillery pieces Nine had noticed earlier.

Nine observed the rebels were a mix of ethnicities – not surprising given the DRC's huge population comprised some two hundred ethnicities – and nationalities. The majority were Congolese, but Nine had discovered a number of rebels were Rwandan, Ugandan, Sudanese, Zambian and, in one case, Angolan.

The first impression was they were a rag-tag bunch. Their camouflage uniforms were ripped and torn – and sodden of course – and their gear looked decidedly second-hand. However, Nine's assessment was they were battle-hardened warriors. They had a look about them that was reminiscent of Special Forces soldiers whose casual appearance and demeanour were often decidedly deceptive.

Although the storm had passed, light rain continued to fall and the camp remained a quagmire. Negotiating the muddy ground reduced the rebels to a sometimes comical study-in-motion as they tried to keep their footing and remain upright.

Nine was marched, slipping and sliding, to the militia's war tent where Lusambo and his lieutenants had been meeting since Leila's discovery that her husband's nephew was among the children interned at the medical lab at Carmel Corporation's refinery. Since that discovery, as Nine was about to learn, several rebels had identified long-lost young relatives among the photos he'd left with the Lusambos.

As he was escorted into the war tent, Nine could sense anger among the rebels. The incidence of missing children was a common occurrence in the DRC, and in most African countries for that matter. But this was different. Omega's medical lab was right under the militia's noses and the abducted children were being subjected to the most horrifying scientific experiments imaginable. The realization that some of the orphanage's subjects were related to the rebels made it personal, too. Lusambo's men wanted blood.

All eyes turned to Nine as the rebels became aware of his presence. Lusambo motioned to him to approach, and the two greeted each other warmly.

"I did not think we would meet again, my friend," the captain smiled.

"Me either, captain."

Lusambo then explained why Nine had been brought back. He said he planned to embark on a rescue mission to save Francis and the other children under cover of darkness the following night.

Nine's relief was tempered by the fact his plans had been delayed twenty-four hours. He had hoped to get to Lusambo in time for a raid on the lab that night, but that wasn't to be. The night was nearly over and the raid had to be carried out under cover of darkness. It would be far too risky to attempt it during daylight hours.

It was then Nine noticed Leila among the lieutenants assembled around Lusambo. He hadn't noticed her before as she now wore army-style fatigues complete with a military-issue pistol in her belt, and was hardly distinguishable from the other rebels.

Leila smiled warmly at him.

Nine also noticed the rebels were passing around the photos he'd left earlier of Francis and the other children. Francis' photo, and those of children the rebels had recognized, had been photocopied so that each rebel involved in the raid would have a set of the relevant images. It turned out seven more children had been recognized and, of those, five were directly related to the rebels.

The blood ties between the children and the rebels had played into Lusambo's hands. As soon as the children had been recognized, his men had fully supported his plans. Without their total support, any raid on the well defended refinery would be tantamount to suicide. Even with their support, it was a tall order. Lusambo's hundred-strong militia had been reduced to fifty. A quarter of his fighting men were over the border, in Rwanda, on another mission. Nearly as many again were bedridden as a result of an influenza epidemic that was sweeping the DRC's eastern regions and half a dozen were recovering from wounds received in a recent fire-fight.

Given the captain had to leave at least twenty rebels behind to defend the base in the event of attacks by Government troops or other militias – a not uncommon occurrence – that left only thirty men at his disposal for the planned raid on the refinery. Not good odds and he knew it.

For the next hour, Lusambo and his lieutenants grilled Nine about the medical lab and the people who were running it. The former operative told them everything he knew, and furnished them with the photos he'd taken of the lab and the refinery from the air. These proved invaluable to the men who were about to risk their lives attacking a facility which until now they'd deemed too well defended to breach.

The rebels took special note of the strength and location of the armed guards. After sometimes heated debate, they agreed on a plan of attack.

Nine was impressed by Lusambo's democratic leadership style. He obviously valued his men and their opinions, and ruled accordingly. Equally, the men knew who the boss was and deferred to him when tough decisions were needed.

The meeting concluded as the grey light of dawn arrived through the drizzle. Lusambo ordered his men to get some sleep and prepare to depart as soon as darkness returned. He then took Nine aside. "There's the small matter of ensuring our agreed terms are met," he said.

Nine knew instantly what he was driving at. The captain wanted to ensure his client kept his side of their arrangement. It would mean taking the rebel leader at his word, but there was nothing else for it. Nine drew his cell phone from his pocket. "I will text my funds manager at a certain Swiss bank and the first instalment will be transferred immediately to a bank account of your choice."

"As simple as that?"

"Yes. I should delay texting until it's normal trading hours in Switzerland."

Lusambo looked at his watch and did a quick calculation. "It will be normal trading hours there in exactly three hours."

Nine was impressed by the captain's general knowledge. "Correct."

Satisfied, Lusambo ordered a Ugandan rebel to escort Nine to a small tent that would serve as his private quarters for the day ahead. "You'll find some breakfast waiting for you in the tent," he said. "I suggest you get some sleep, too, my friend. You may need it."

Nine needed no encouragement on that score. He'd been suffering niggling little chest pains for the past hour or so and was nearly out on his feet. He knew he was in desperate need of sleep and just hoped his ailing heart would hold out long enough to rescue Francis.

57

Seventeen knew something was wrong as soon as she struck up a conversation with the Papenoo River Valley Lodge's proprietor. The normally engaging Fraulein Schmidt wasn't her normal cheerful self. From the moment Seventeen bumped into her, the proprietor had seemed tense and withdrawn.

The former operative had been walking to the lodge's store to purchase some items before it closed for the evening when she'd come across Fraulein Schmidt. Usually, whenever they saw each other they would chat for a while – often about places they'd both visited and sights they'd seen in Germany and elsewhere on the Continent.

However, on this occasion Seventeen had the impression the

proprietor was nervous and anxious to be on her way.

Like all Omega operatives, Seventeen was an expert at reading body language and picking up on other signs. After parting company with Fraulein Schmidt, every cell in her body told her something was wrong. Bypassing the store, she hurried back to her unit.

Isabelle knew something was up as soon as her sister-in-law entered the kitchenette. She was learning to recognize the signs. "Please don't tell me we have to move again."

"Afraid so." Seventeen told Isabelle about her strange encounter with the proprietor.

"She may be worried about something," Isabelle said in the proprietor's defence.

"I'm sure she is. I have a feeling she's worried about us."

"But we cannot keep--"

Interjecting, Seventeen said, "I think someone has got to her."

Isabelle was about to protest then thought better of it. She'd learned that Seventeen had a well-developed sixth sense for such things and she now trusted her.

"We have to hurry." Seventeen was mindful the lodge was at the end of a no-exit road and they would be trapped if someone was coming for them.

The two women quickly retrieved their bags and possessions, and loaded them into the stolen station wagon before climbing in. Not wanting to draw any more attention than necessary to their sudden departure, Seventeen disengaged the handbrake and allowed the car to roll silently down the driveway to the road before starting the engine.

Once out of earshot of the lodge, Seventeen gunned the accelerator and sped along the narrow, windy gravel road toward the main coastal highway some ten miles to the north.

The two fugitives had no way of knowing that at that very moment a red convertible was approaching from the northern end of the road. Fifteen was at the wheel and Twenty Three next to him in the front passenger seat. They were accompanied by their newly arrived fellow orphan-operative, Eight, who rode in the back seat. She'd arrived in Tahiti the previous day.

Of Asian heritage, Eight had attributes that complemented her colleagues. In particular, she spoke Tahitian fluently. Naylor had considered that a positive as the signs were Isabelle had bypassed conventional tourist accommodation in favour of hiding amongst the native people. That was the logical explanation for the Frenchwoman's disappearance since she'd been tracked to Taravoa. Having an orphan-operative on the case who could speak Tahitian would be a big advantage – of that Omega boss Andrew Naylor was sure.

Night was approaching as the station wagon Isabelle and Seventeen traveled in reached the top of a bluff high above the river. Despite the fading light, Seventeen drove with the headlights off so as not to draw the attention of her former colleagues if in fact they were on their way.

Seventeen drove as fast as she dared. As she nursed the car around a bend she saw an approaching vehicle – a red convertible. It was beginning its climb up the same bluff the station wagon was now descending and it, too, was being driven with its headlights switched off.

Though too far away to identify, Seventeen was in no doubt the convertible was the same one she'd seen Fifteen driving in Taravoa. "Damn!" She pulled over to the side of the road, out of sight of the oncoming car.

"What is it?" Isabelle asked. She hadn't seen the convertible.

"We have company." Seventeen could now hear the convertible. Its revving motor indicated it was traveling at speed.

Isabelle heard it, too, and was suddenly very afraid.

Seventeen was also frightened, but she pushed the fear to the back of her mind and focused on finding a solution – just as she'd been trained to do. *How long have we got?* She estimated the convertible would reach them within a minute, or ninety seconds at best. *We can't go back.* She had already deduced there was no point in returning to the lodge. It was near the end of the no-exit road and offered no escape route.

Looking ahead, Seventeen noticed a roadside picnic area just in front of a sharp bend. *That'll have to do.* She planted her foot on the accelerator and the car shot forward.

"What are you going to do?" Isabelle asked.

"Don't ask. Just hang on tight." Seventeen glanced down to ensure Isabelle's seatbelt was on. It was.

Seventeen drove into the picnic area and turned the station wagon so it was facing the road at a ninety degree angle. Then she waited, her foot resting lightly on the accelerator. Beside her, Isabelle closed her eyes and held her breath.

If she'd judged it right, the former operative knew the occupants of the approaching convertible wouldn't see the station wagon until they were too late. She was waiting at the edge of the road just before the tight bend. The other side of the road fell away to the river some forty feet below.

It would all come down to timing. If she didn't time it right, Seventeen knew she wouldn't achieve what she hoped to do, and that was ram the convertible and send it and its occupants plummeting down the cliff-face. In a worst case scenario, she was aware she could miss the other vehicle completely and drive over the cliff herself.

Seventeen and Isabelle tensed as the sound of the approaching convertible grew louder.

Just before the convertible rounded the corner, Seventeen had a horrible thought. *What if it's not Fifteen?* She remembered she hadn't actually identified the car's driver when she'd sighted it a few moments earlier. Logic told her it was Fifteen, but she couldn't be sure.

As the convertible rounded the corner, instinct took over. What followed took only a few seconds, but to Seventeen it seemed like an eternity. She simultaneously switched on the station wagon's headlights and revved the accelerator, ready for a fast take-off.

In the first second, she identified the familiar features of Fifteen in the driver's seat and Twenty Three next to him, and she noticed the woman with Asian features in the back seat; a second later she'd identified the woman as Eight, another fellow orphan; at the same time, she released her foot from the brake and the station wagon shot forward.

58

Isabelle screamed as the vehicle struck the convertible just behind the driver's door. In the headlights, she and Seventeen saw the startled expressions on the faces of the convertible's three occupants as the station wagon rammed them at full throttle.

The convertible didn't stand a chance. It disappeared over the side of the cliff, rolling twice before trees and shrubs arrested its fall a few yards from the river's edge.

Seventeen had managed to stop the station wagon a couple of feet from the cliff-edge. She looked at Isabelle. "You okay?"

White-faced, Isabelle nodded. She was too shaken to speak.

Seventeen reversed the station wagon into the picnic area then turned off the engine and grabbed a torch from beneath the dashboard. "You stay here." She jumped out and ran to the cliff-edge. As she ran, she drew a tiny pistol out from beneath her loose-fitting shirt. Although the 9mm semi-automatic pocket pistol had a limited range and only carried eight rounds, its small size made it easier to conceal and that suited Seventeen. She'd deliberately kept the weapon hidden from Isabelle, not wanting to alarm her any more than she already was.

Looking down over the edge of the cliff, Seventeen was disappointed to see signs of life around the convertible, which had come to rest on its side. It was now too dark to identify the survivors, but she saw a shadowy figure moving in the car's front seat and another staggering about a few feet from the car. The latter occupant had obviously been thrown clear.

Unintelligible groans came from the figure in the front seat. Seventeen couldn't tell if it was Fifteen or Twenty Three, but it was a safe bet it was one or the other. This was confirmed when a woman's voice was heard enquiring after the wellbeing of her fellow operative. Even after so many years, Seventeen was able to recognize Eight's voice. More groans from the operative still in the car signalled that he wasn't faring well at all. There was no sign of the third passenger.

Seventeen was surprised there were any survivors at all. Then she noted the drop from the road was more benign than she'd imagined. The ground sloped away toward the river, and trees and shrubs protruded from the cliff-face. She deduced the vegetation had slowed the convertible's fall.

Now Seventeen was faced with a decision: whether to try to finish off the survivors or make a clean getaway. She opted for the getaway as she was under no illusions her pocket pistol couldn't match the firepower of the weapons her fellow orphans would be carrying.

#

At his mansion in Saint Clair County, in Illinois, Naylor walked from his front door to his upstairs bedroom. The Omega boss had just seen off his family doctor who had made a house call at his request.

Naylor's headaches had worsened and had seen him confined to bed for most of the day. His doctor had dispensed prescription drugs during the visit and these had taken effect almost immediately to his patient's great relief.

The cocktail of drugs Naylor had been on for some days now also left him constantly tired. Hence his decision to take the day off work and stay in bed.

It was another hot summer's night and that only added to his discomfort. As he stripped and lay down naked beneath the whirring bedroom ceiling fan, Naylor was in no doubt that Nine was the cause of his continuing headaches. He cursed the ninth-born orphan yet again then tried to get some sleep.

Naylor was starting to doze off when his cell phone rang on a bedside cabinet. He snatched it up and put it to his ear. "Naylor," he snapped.

"Sir, it's Sue Lee calling from Papeete," a woman's voice informed him.

Naylor instantly recognized the codename his operative, Eight, was currently using. "Yes, Miss Lee." He sensed from her tone that bad news was coming.

Eight relayed to him the events of the past few hours,

explaining how an unknown person, or persons, had rammed the car in which she and her fellow operatives had been traveling. The crash had killed Fifteen instantly and left a badly injured Twenty Three hospitalized.

Two minutes was all it took for Eight to explain in detail what had happened. In that time, Naylor's headache returned with a vengeance. "Do you know who it was?" he asked.

"No, sir. It was dark and the vehicle came out of nowhere."

"Damnation!" Naylor cursed. He didn't think to ask after Eight's welfare. "Alright, I'll send reinforcements. Meanwhile, you stay on the case." Referring to Isabelle, he added, "I want that woman found." Naylor ended the call and flung his cell phone across the room. He then sat on the edge of his bed and began massaging his temple as he tried to figure out exactly who was helping the Frenchwoman evade her pursuers. He was in no doubt someone was helping Isabelle.

His former operative, Seventeen, came to mind. The seventeenth-born orphan hadn't been sighted since she and Nine had been seen together in Chicago, so Naylor knew it was possible she had flown to Tahiti to help Isabelle evade his operatives.

Naylor hadn't considered Seventeen before because he thought she was too fragile – mentally at least – to be of any use to anyone. Now he wasn't so sure.

59

Carmel Corporation's coltan refinery looked deceptively calm as Nine and the other members of Lusambo's raiding party studied it from the surrounding jungle. Refinery employees working the night-shift could be seen attending to a variety of mundane tasks while trucks came and went after delivering their loads of ore – all under the watchful eye of armed guards.

The twenty-two strong raiding party had arrived at the refinery just after midnight. Using an existing vehicle track, the raiders had driven to within a mile of the refinery then walked the rest of the way through the jungle so as not to advertise their presence.

Captain Lusambo looked at his watch. "They should be here

soon." He was referring to the ten rebels who were traveling by boat to the refinery.

The plan was to use the boat as a decoy, distracting the refinery's armed personnel long enough for Lusambo's main fighting force to access the refinery grounds, enter the medical lab building, and rescue Francis and the children who had been recognized in the photos Nine had supplied.

Before setting out from the rebels' base, Leila had pleaded with her husband to free all the children who were being held at the lab. It had taken some persuading by Lusambo to convince his wife that would be impractical. However, before leaving he'd had to promise her he'd do everything in his power to ensure all the children were freed and the orphanage closed down after the mission had been completed.

Now, studying the refinery and the adjoining lab building, Lusambo wasn't at all confident he could keep his promise. The facility was well guarded – he'd counted twenty armed guards and knew there could be twice that number on the premises – and it was strategically sited, making a surprise attack almost impossible.

All vegetation around the refinery had been cleared, leaving a grass belt fifty yards wide between the refinery's perimeter fence and the edge of the jungle.

Nine had reached the same conclusion: breaching the refinery's defences and rescuing Francis was going to be difficult. It was not a given anyone would survive the mission let alone rescue any children – not tonight or any time in the future.

Now, to add to the difficulties the raiders faced, the rain had stopped, the clouds cleared and a full moon lit up the night. The raiders would be seen as soon as they left the cover of the trees.

The sound of a boat's engine reached them. Its distinctive throbbing told them it was the boat they'd been waiting for.

"That's us," Lusambo confirmed. He turned to his rebels who were waiting in the trees behind and let out a long, low whistle. They immediately readied their weapons and prepared for the signal to move forward.

Looking at them, Nine saw most carried AK-47's. Three mortars and a rocket-launcher had also been brought along, and Nine was aware similar weaponry had been loaded onto the boat that was now approaching the refinery. The former operative was armed with a machine pistol Lusambo had loaned him, and a hunting knife one of the captain's lieutenants had given him.

Nine found he was having to keep a lid on his excitement. The realization he could soon be holding Francis in his arms was almost intoxicating. He couldn't think of anything else. *Please let him be here. And please let him be okay*. Nine daren't think of his son's condition. *Have the bastards experimented on you, Francis?* He pushed that thought out of his mind as soon as it entered.

"There it is!" Lusambo said.

At first Nine couldn't see anything. Then he saw the boat's shadowy outline against the moonlit reflection of the river.

A sudden commotion inside the refinery grounds signalled that others had also become aware of the boat. Night-time visits to the refinery by boats were a rare occurrence – and then only by appointment – so an unscheduled visit in a region notorious for militia activity was cause for alarm.

As Lusambo had hoped, his boat's arrival made it the center of attention among the guards and other personnel at the refinery.

A siren sounded and a dozen or so armed guards emerged from barracks adjoining the refinery's administration building. They marched in disciplined ranks through the refinery's manned security gates and down toward the jetty, which was now lit up like daylight courtesy of a spotlight located in a lookout tower.

Nine and Lusambo watched as the boat's crew tied the craft to the jetty, and Skipper, the boat's Ugandan master, disembarked. He carried a large bag, which Lusambo was aware contained goods that could pass for genuine items of trade.

As he'd been instructed to do, Skipper walked innocently toward the guards who were now only a few yards from him. Behind him, rebels disguised as common crewmembers began unloading similar bags onto the jetty as if anticipating a late-night trade.

To Nine and the others watching, the guards' actions and body language indicated they were annoyed rather than alarmed by the late night visit. Their weapons remained shouldered. It was obvious they'd fallen for the ruse and considered the visitors genuine traders.

As the guards reached Skipper they checked the contents of his bag and began remonstrating with him. Although they couldn't be heard from where Nine and the others were hiding, it was clear the guards weren't happy about being dragged out in the early hours to prevent unauthorized traders from entering the refinery grounds.

Skipper appeared to be doing a good acting job, trying to convince the guards his employer had gained permission for the visit. The gangly Ugandan even fumbled in his pockets, searching for non-existent paperwork to support his claim.

While this was going on, the ten rebels now on the jetty sauntered toward their skipper, bags slung over their shoulders. The guards started to become agitated when they noticed the men approaching, but still they kept their firearms shouldered.

A senior guard began shouting at Skipper, ordering him and his men to return to their boat. By this time, the rebels were only a few yards away.

Finally, Skipper motioned to the rebels that trading wouldn't take place that night. The rebels did their best to appear upset, just as they'd been coached to do earlier.

Watching them, Lusambo couldn't help but chuckle. He whispered, "I do swear my men are worthy of an Oscar nomination."

Next to him, Nine asked, "In what category? Best Supporting Actors?"

The captain looked at his client. "No." He grinned. "Special Effects."

Nine looked mystified.

"Keep watching," Lusambo said. He knew it wouldn't be long before the fireworks started.

60

own at the jetty, Skipper re-joined his men and they pretended to be resigned to returning to their boat. The guards turned and started retracing their steps to the refinery. Behind them, the rebels reached into their bags and pulled out an assortment of weapons.

One of the guards saw the danger, but was too late to save himself and his comrades. Half their number was cut down in the first volley of bullets. The others managed to un-shoulder their arms and loose off a few wild shots, but they, too, were quickly mown down.

Skipper had the presence of mind to order one of his men to deal with the spotlight that lit them up like sitting ducks. A rebel took aim at the spotlight, fired and missed. He fired again. Another miss. As Skipper berated his hapless sharpshooter, the rebel took aim yet again. Third time lucky. The bullet found its mark and the spotlight was extinguished.

While this was happening, Nine and the other raiders were already running across the open ground toward the barbwire perimeter fence behind the refinery. They somehow reached the fence without being noticed. Two rebels with wire-cutters cut an opening in the fence and the raiders entered the grounds. Still not a shot had been fired in their direction.

The rebels down by the jetty had already forced their way past the refinery's security gates, shooting dead the two guards stationed there. Now they split up and looked for vantage points from which they could lay down cover fire for Lusambo's main force.

In and around the refinery and the adjoining buildings, panic reigned supreme as guards, workers and other employees ran blindly, trying to escape the gunfire. To add to their confusion and fear, mortar shells began falling in their midst – a result of the mortar fire being directed their way by three rebels Lusambo had left behind at the edge of the jungle. On cue, the trio were expertly loading, firing and reloading the two mortars they'd brought with them.

The mortar fire was directed toward the front of the refinery so as not to endanger the rebels tasked with rescuing Francis and the other children. The downside of this strategy was the shells were landing within range of their comrades who had arrived by boat and who were now laying down diversionary fire. Two of them were killed and another wounded by mortar shell shrapnel in the first couple of minutes.

Lusambo had anticipated such casualties. He considered it inevitable collateral damage – regrettable but nonetheless inevitable.

As they neared the medical lab building, Nine and a small group of rebels split from the others and sprinted toward the building's main entrance. It was their job to force entry and secure the building's interior while Lusambo and the others set up a defensive cordon around the building. Once that had been achieved, Nine's group could locate and rescue the children.

Until now, no shots had been directed their way. The diversionary tactics the rebels had employed seemed to have worked a charm.

Elsewhere on the premises, Thirteen and his fellow Omega operatives had woken as soon as the siren had sounded in response to the boat's arrival. Their sleeping quarters were in different buildings: Thirteen and Twenty-Two were based in the lab building itself, Four and Twelve were based in the adjoining admin building, and Eighteen was based in one of the nearby apartment blocks.

Thirteen and Twenty-Two had walked down toward the jetty to investigate who the late night visitors were. They were still inside the perimeter fence when the shooting had started.

In the three chaotic minutes that had elapsed since then, the two operatives had sprinted back to the medical lab building where they found their Omega colleagues already waiting for them. That was as per the protocols Thirteen had established. The Polynesian operative knew that any attack on the refinery would be likely to have been organized by Nine, and therefore the lab building would be the target.

Those same protocols dictated that the operatives occupy pre-arranged defensive positions on the building's ground floor regardless of what may be going on outside the building. Should they be over-run, they'd retreat to the floors below ground one floor at a time. Each man knew what was expected of him.

Eighteen and Twelve waited, weapons at the ready, behind a heavy oak counter in the ground floor reception area while Thirteen, Four and Twenty-Two hid in separate rooms and vantage points behind reception.

Whatever was going on outside the lab building didn't overly concern the operatives. Their only concern was to protect Omega's investment – the medical lab – and to kill Nine if he showed up.

As Nine and his companions neared the building's entrance, their luck changed. Machinegun-fire felled one rebel and badly wounded two others, effectively reducing their number to four. The shooting came from a machinegun post at the top of the nearby admin building.

Nine and the others who were still in one piece found cover

beneath the lab building's entrance. Behind them, the two wounded rebels were shot dead as they tried to crawl away.

The survivors' respite was short-lived as more guards appeared from nowhere and directed shots their way. They were soon accounted for by Lusambo's men who then turned their attention to the shots coming from the machinegun post atop the admin building. Lusambo sent half a dozen of his men into the building to deal with that particular problem.

Taking advantage of the brief respite, Nine and his three companions entered the lab building's reception area only to be greeted by a hail of gunfire. The former operative recognized the tell-tale *rat-tat-tat* of machine pistols – a favoured weapon of Omega operatives in close-quarter combat conditions such as these.

Nine had never doubted he'd come face-to-face with more of his fellow orphan-operatives. He just wondered who Naylor had sent this time. Any misgivings he may have had about killing more Omega operatives vanished as he and his companions dived for cover to escape the withering gunfire.

In the confusion, Nine had been separated from his rebel comrades. He risked a quick look around the side of an upturned desk and caught a glimpse of two male figures on the other side of the reception area. They were crouched down at either end of the oak reception counter. Nine thought they looked familiar. Risking another quick look, he recognized one of the men. *Eighteen!* The operative's Oriental features were instantly recognizable even though Nine hadn't seen him in well over a decade.

Looking to his right, Nine saw that his three companions remained pinned down by the gunfire. They were sheltering behind large, steel filing cabinets to avoid the shots the two operatives continued to direct at them. It appeared the pair hadn't noticed their fellow orphan.

Nine caught the attention of the nearest rebel – a young Congolese man - and motioned to the two grenades hanging from his belt. The young rebel immediately unhooked one of the grenades and rolled it along the marble floor, bowling ball style, toward Nine. The former operative hoped its pin remained intact. It did. He scooped the grenade up and peeked around the corner of the upturned desk to ensure the two combatants were still where he'd last seen them. They were. One of them noticed Nine and directed gunfire his way. *Was that Twelve?* He thought he recognized him.

Nine pulled the pin from the grenade then threw it toward the two operatives.

"Grenade!" Eighteen shouted.

61

In the enclosed space, the explosion was deafening. It shattered every window in the reception area and blew a hole in the wall behind the reception desk. It also killed the two orphan-operatives instantly.

Nine's ears were still ringing as he raced over to check on the pair. The first body was unrecognizable as his face had been blown away. However, a tell-tale Chinese symbol tattooed on his forearm confirmed to Nine that it was indeed Eighteen. He'd been with him when, in a moment of rare rebelliousness, his fellow orphan had visited a tattooist in downtown Chicago and ordered the tattoo. That had been on Eighteen's sixteenth birthday. Their mentor, Tommy Kentbridge, had grounded them both for a month and threatened to beat them to within an inch of their lives if they did anything like that again.

Nine thought it was appropriate in a ghoulish kind of way that Eighteen had been killed by an explosion: he recalled the operative had once boasted he'd lost count of the number of people he'd killed using explosive devices.

The former operative hurried to check on the other body. One of the rebels, a scar-faced Angolan, was already standing over it.

"This one's dead, too," the Angolan said.

Nine saw at a glance he'd been right the first time. It was Twelve. The twelfth-born orphan's face was unscathed, but flying shrapnel had carved a large hole in his chest and there was only metal where his heart had once been.

Twelve's unmarked face looked innocent in death. Looking down at him, Nine had to remind himself he was looking at the operative who, arguably, had more kills to his name than any of Omega's operatives. Nine recalled his good friend Ten had told him Twelve was rumored to have terminated fifty-three targets. That had been six years earlier. *God knows how many he killed since then*. Nine guessed there had been many more.

The sound of running feet alerted the raiders to the presence of others on the ground floor. A bald Congolese rebel snuck a quick look around the corner of a corridor and saw three armed men running toward a stairwell at the far end of the building. He let off a burst of gunfire from his AK-47 in their direction before they disappeared downstairs. The bald rebel didn't know it, but the three were the surviving Omega operatives.

Thirteen had made the decision to relocate to the next defensive position – on the floor below – as soon as he'd realized he and his fellow operatives were up against some serious firepower. He hadn't bargained on facing grenades and AK-47's. Rather, he'd assumed – as had Naylor – that Nine would try to infiltrate the lab building on his own, just as he did in Thule. This was something else altogether.

On the ground floor, Nine and his companions began a room-to-room sweep of the floor to root out any other opposition and commence their search for Francis and the other children. They found the floor deserted. Anyone who may have been working the night shift had obviously fled as soon as the shooting started. Nine guessed they would be holed up in the admin building opposite.

Nor was there any sign of any of the children or any other experimental subjects thought to be interned in the building. That was no surprise either as the confidential files Nine had uplifted showed the ground floor was purely an admin floor, and the labs and the lab's subjects were accommodated on the two levels below ground.

The sound of continued gunfire and explosions outside told the men the fire-fight was continuing. From inside the building, there was no way of knowing if Lusambo's rebels were holding their own.

The three rebels with Nine then conferred on their next move. Nine noted the Angolan and the young Congolese rebel deferred to the bald rebel. He was older than them and seemed a natural leader.

Using hand signs, the bald rebel motioned to Nine and the young Congolese to descend to the next floor via the stairwell at the rear of the building. Baldie and the Angolan ran back to a stairwell they'd noticed near the front of the building.

The strategy made sense to Nine. They would access the floor below from opposite ends of the building and trap any hostiles between them.

As Nine and the young rebel descended the stairs, the former operative glanced at his watch. He saw twenty minutes had elapsed since the shooting started at the refinery. Lusambo had warned that the refinery would alert the authorities in Kindu as soon as the attack began. Armed reinforcements would be mobilized within twenty minutes and it would only take them another thirty minutes to reach the refinery by road. If the captain was right, Nine realized they had another thirty minutes before their escape route would be sealed off.

Nearing the bottom of the stairs, the former operative thought he saw a shadow flit across the floor just beyond the bottom step. *There it is again!* This time it was more discernible. The shadow was that of a man holding an automatic weapon. It was now motionless. Nine flashed a warning sign to the young rebel who hadn't yet seen the danger.

The gunman obviously wasn't one of the other rebels. Nine calculated there hadn't been enough time for Baldie or the Angolan to have reached this end of the building.

Noting the corridor's walls were concrete, the former operative silently stepped to his right and aimed his machine pistol at the far wall at an angle that was close to forty-five degrees. He planned to fire a burst from his machine pistol and hope a ricochet would hit the target.

Nine aimed and fired a long, sustained burst. His plan worked. At least one bullet ricocheted and struck the gunman – not fatally but sufficient to drop him. Before the gunman could recover, Nine was onto him, shooting him dead with another burst.

The gunman lay face-down on the floor. Nine rolled him over onto his back and immediately saw it was yet another fellow orphan-operative. *Four!* As with most of the orphans, Nine had never been close to the fourth-born orphan. However, he recalled spending many an hour playing chess with him at the orphanage. He also recalled that Four was the only orphan who could sometimes beat him at chess.

Gunfire and shouting from the other end of the floor startled Nine and his companion. It sounded as though a full-blown firefight was underway. The shooting intensified as the pair moved cautiously toward the sounds of conflict. Then silence. The pair quickened their pace. Before they'd gone far, the faint sound of crying children reached them.

The corridor they followed took them past labs and medical facilities – all unoccupied and apparently vacated in a hurry not that long ago. They came across a staff cafeteria where half-full mugs of still-steaming coffee and plates of uneaten food indicated the diners had also departed hurriedly.

Nine and the young rebel hesitated as they came to yet another corridor. A sign at its entrance read: *Children's Quarters: Authorized personnel only*. The sound of crying children was louder here. Some of them were screaming.

62

Nine could imagine how terrifying the continuing gunfire and explosions would be for any child. He was sorely tempted to check the quarters immediately, but he knew it was important to ensure the floor had been cleared of hostile forces first.

The former operative and the young Congolese rebel ran to the stairwell at the front of the building. As they proceeded, passing more labs, they noticed the sounds of conflict from outside had quieted. Nine hoped that meant Lusambo's rebels had gained the upper hand.

Before they reached the stairwell, they found three bodies whose number included Baldie and the Angolan. All three were riddled with bullet holes.

The Congolese rebel checked to ensure his comrades were dead. However, Nine was more interested in the third body. The gunman was lying on his back. He'd flung his arm across his face – his final act – so his identity was momentarily concealed. Nine reached down and pulled the man's arm away from his face.

The former operative recognized the man immediately. It was Twenty Two. Nine had clear recollections of clashing with him during their many Teleiotes sessions in the Pedemont Orphanage's gym. He remembered Twenty Two as one of the toughest orphans.

A noise alerted the pair to the approach of others descending the stairs. They waited, weapons at the ready, for whoever it was to arrive.

"Mai Mai!" someone shouted, using the mission's agreed codename.

Nine thought the voice was Lusambo's.

"Mai Mai!" the young rebel responded.

Lusambo appeared. He was accompanied by two other rebels. The signs of conflict were visible on all three. Their faces and uniforms were blood-flecked, and Lusambo himself had sustained a flesh wound in his left leg. Blood flowed from the wound, which appeared to be just above his knee and which made walking difficult.

The captain scanned the three bodies on the floor then conferred with Nine's young companion in Swahili. Nine understood most of what Lusambo was saying. It seemed the captain's rebels had secured the grounds around the refinery with the loss of five lives and another seven wounded. The two rebels lying at his feet lifted the militia's death toll to seven. Nine also deduced that most of the refinery's guards had holed up in the nearby admin building, but they were safely contained for the moment.

Lusambo turned to Nine. "Are there children on this floor?"

"Yes," Nine said. "A lot, if I'm not mistaken."

Lusambo ordered the two rebels he'd brought with him to return upstairs to prevent enemy forces gaining access to the elevator or stairwells. Then he, Nine and the young rebel began a room-to-room search of the floor they were on, secure in the knowledge someone was watching their backs.

As was the case on the floor above, there were no staff members. They'd all fled.

The search took the trio to the corridor leading to the children's quarters. It opened up into a maze of large rooms that could best be described as barracks – not too dissimilar to the sleeping quarters Nine had accessed at the medical lab at Thule. It was the same chamber of horrors as at Thule, only worse. The young inmates of this facility appeared to have been exposed to the same type of bizarre scientific experiments, but over a longer period.

All the children had been wakened by the firefight, and were highly distressed. The sight of strangers bearing arms in their midst caused even more distress.

Nine estimated there could be fifty children on this floor alone. He glanced at Lusambo. The captain was grim-faced. The photos hadn't prepared them for what they were seeing in the flesh. They recoiled at the sight of children displaying the most grotesque deformities imaginable. A once pretty, young girl had the facial features of a Neanderthal while a little boy was covered from head to foot in long hair. Worse was to come.

As the trio went from room to room, the two rebels constantly referred to the photos of the children they'd come to rescue, looking for a match.

Nine didn't need to do that. He was solely interested in finding his son. Desperate to locate Francis, he began shouting the boy's name. "Francis! Francis!" There was no answer. He ran ahead of the others, checking on the children in each room. As he went, he showed Francis' photo to children, asking them if they'd seen him. None had.

Behind him, Lusambo gave a shout of joy. "Sonny!" He'd recognized his nephew.

Then, in another room, the young rebel uttered a shout of recognition. He'd found a young girl who was the spitting image of a girl in one of the photos.

By now, Nine had already determined that Francis wasn't on this floor. He'd checked every room and was becoming increasingly desperate for some sign that his son was here. Without waiting for his companions, he raced for the stairwell leading down to the next floor.

As he descended the stairs, Nine didn't give any thought to the possibility he could encounter more resistance. It hadn't occurred to him that Naylor would have sent more than four elite operatives to stop one ailing, over-the-hill, former operative whose best days were most certainly behind him. All he could think about was finding Francis.

So it was a shock when a dark, muscular figure launched itself at him at the bottom of the stairs. Nine was quick enough to avoid the wickedly sharp blade that had been meant for his throat, but too slow to avoid the karate punch that knocked him to the floor and sent his machine pistol flying from his grasp.

63

Thirteen had opted to kill Nine silently rather than use his machine pistol and advertise his presence to one and all. Suspecting his fellow operatives had all been killed, the Polynesian operative didn't fancy his chances of fighting his way out of the building on his own. Not with so many Mai Mai rebels to contend with. Hence the decision to use his knife.

Though stunned, Nine had the presence of mind to roll over and over as soon as he hit the floor. That action saved his life. Thirteen had launched himself at Nine a second time, intent on finishing him quickly. His flashing blade missed its target again, striking the floor and jarring his wrist. He grunted in pain and cursed his fellow orphan.

Only now, as he jumped to his feet, did Nine recognize his attacker. "Thirteen!"

The Polynesian's eyes seemed glazed over and only registered fleeting recognition of the former operative. Nine identified the symptoms immediately. *MK-Ultra!* He'd seen the same glazed-over look in the eyes of Three and Fourteen when he'd clashed with them in Greenland, and in Seventeen's eyes before that.

In the precious seconds he'd bought himself, Nine had drawn his hunting knife from its sheath. He awaited Thirteen's next assault.

Breathing hard, the two orphans began warily circling each other, knives extended.

"You shouldn't have come here," Thirteen said.

"You shouldn't have tried to stop me rescuing my son."

Thirteen came at Nine, his blade flashing. Nine was forced to back-peddle before the onslaught. His head was still fuzzy from the initial attack and he desperately tried to clear it while parrying his opponent's blows.

Nine didn't see the knife-thrust that caught him. The blade sliced through his right shoulder, causing him to drop his knife. Crying out in pain, he automatically placed his left hand over the wound to prevent the blood from gushing out.

Thirteen followed up with a ju-jitsu style kick that felled Nine. As he prepared to finish the former operative off, a shot rang out and Thirteen fell to the floor, mortally wounded.

At first, Nine wasn't sure where the shot had come from. Then he saw the young Congolese rebel. Lusambo had sent him to assist after he'd seen his client run downstairs. The rebel was preparing to shoot Thirteen dead. "No!" Nine shouted.

Pushing himself painfully to his knees, Nine moved over to Thirteen. Blood was trickling from the operative's nose and mouth, and he was struggling to breath. It appeared he'd been shot thorough the lungs.

Nine cradled Thirteen's head in his hands. Blood from his shoulder wound dripped down onto the dying operative's face. "Where's my son?" he asked.

"Your son's not here," Thirteen gasped as his life rapidly

faded.

"Where is he?" Nine was becoming desperate. He could see Thirteen was barely alive. *Don't die on me now, you son of a bitch!* He shouted, "Where is he, man?"

Thirteen seemed to rally, as if making a conscious effort to communicate with another human being one last time. "At Omega's lab in Nevada," he whispered. His words were so faint, Nine had to put his ear close to his fellow orphan's mouth to hear.

"Where in Nevada?"

The light in Thirteen's eyes began to fade.

"Where in Nevada?" Nine shouted. *Stay with me!* He shook his fellow orphan.

"At Omega's new laboratory…at…Nellis…Air Force…Base." Thirteen exhaled one last time as his life expired. His final breath was accompanied by frothy, reddish-pink spittle that settled on his lips and chin.

Nine was left looking at Thirteen in disbelief. He was having trouble coming to grips with what he'd just heard. If the Polynesian operative had told the truth, Omega had sent Francis to a new secret lab at Nellis Air Force Base in Nevada – a facility Naylor hadn't mentioned and a facility that hadn't shown up in the confidential files Nine had accessed at Naylor's residence.

The former operative looked up the young Congolese rebel. His bemused expression indicated he hadn't a clue what was going on.

Nine didn't know it, but of all the operatives he could have questioned about Francis' whereabouts, Thirteen was the only one who knew. While Naylor had made a point of not divulging which Omega lab the boy had been sent to, for some reason known only to himself the Polynesian operative had made it his business to find out.

Nine was suddenly possessed with the need to find out if Thirteen had been telling the truth. Ignoring the pain in his shoulder, he pushed himself to his feet, recovered his fallen machine pistol and embarked on a desperate search of the floor he was now on.

The bottom floor was a virtual replica of the floor above. More barracks-like rooms accommodated another fifty or so kids.

All were African. Francis wasn't among them. Nor did any of them recognize Francis from the photo Nine showed them.

By now, the former operative was so despondent he felt like shooting himself. Shouts of alarm from a nearby room distracted him. He ran to investigate.

The young rebel had found half a dozen lab scientists and other staffers huddled together in a small office. They'd left their flight from the lab building too late to escape the gunfire that erupted after the rebels attacked so had opted to hide out on the bottom floor in the hope they'd remain undiscovered.

By the time Nine arrived, the staffers were cowering in fear before the young rebel who looked like he was ready to shoot them. Nine deliberately didn't do or say anything to alleviate their fears. Instead, he grabbed a middle-aged, female scientist and held his pistol to her head. "What's your name?"

"Madeleine Swindell," the frightened woman stammered. Her eyes swivelled from the pistol Nine held to the blood that now soaked his shirt and back to the pistol.

Nine noted her accent was American. He held the photo of

Francis up to her face. "Have you seen this boy?"

Madeleine shook her head. "No."

"Are you sure he's not here? His name is Francis Hannar and he's my son." He glared at Madeleine as if he held her personally responsible for his son's welfare. "Well?"

"I'm sure. He's not here."

Nine showed the photo to the other staffers for the same result. *Damn it! Thirteen was telling the truth*. The sinking feeling he'd experienced earlier returned tenfold. He pushed Madeleine back over to the others. "Where's the database of this facility's inmates?"

The staffers looked at him blankly.

"Patients!" Nine snapped. "Where can I find the database of your patients?"

"In the IT room on the ground floor," a senior scientist said.

Nine looked at the man's name tag. It read: *Professor Michael Lindsay*. "Take me there, professor," Nine said, motioning with his pistol for the man to lead him to the IT room.

Professor Lindsay jumped to his feet and led Nine upstairs.

As they proceeded, they passed rebels walking down, intent on finding more of the children they'd come for.

Half way up the stairs, Nine stumbled as sharp heart pains coursed through him. He had to grab the handrail to prevent himself from falling over.

64

"You okay?" Professor Lindsay asked.

Ignoring him, Nine focused on getting through the pain. He knew it would pass. It always did.

This time however, the pain persisted. Nine searched his pocket for his heart pills. He momentarily panicked when he couldn't find them then remembered he'd stored the small container of pills in another pocket. Locating the container, he opened it and popped two pills. They took a little time to work – longer than usual – but they worked eventually and the pain passed. Nine motioned to the professor to resume walking.

On reaching the floor above, Nine found Lusambo was holding his nephew, Sonny, and reassuring him. The seven-year-old looked confused and frightened, but otherwise okay.

Lusambo didn't know it, but he was in for a shock when he finally saw Sonny without his top. He would find burn marks all over his upper torso – a result of experimental electric shock treatment Sonny had undergone over the past two years.

Nine noticed three other young children in the care of the rebels. He recognized their faces from the photos, but only just. Each child now had deformities or unusual features that could only be the results of experiments gone wrong. One little African girl had white skin and all the other symptoms of an albino; another had a bone sticking out of her arm; and a young teenage boy had severely bowed legs and abnormally large feet.

Lusambo caught Nine's eye and pointed to his watch. Nine nodded. Time was running out fast and he knew it.

Nine jabbed Professor Lindsay with his pistol and motioned to him to keep moving. The professor led the way upstairs to the ground floor. There, all seemed quiet outside. It was evident the rebels had secured the refinery grounds. Nine knew that would all change when the reinforcements arrived from Kindu.

Professor Lindsay led Nine into a large office that accommodated the lab's IT Department. Without waiting to be asked, the professor entered a password into one of the computers and brought up a list of all the lab's patients. They were in alphabetical order, as they had been at Thule.

Nine pushed the professor aside and scrolled down the hundred odd names on the list. As he feared, Francis' name wasn't there. He turned to Professor Lindsay. "Where's the list of recent arrivals?"

The professor took over the mouse from Nine and accessed a list of seven children who had been admitted in the past month. Again, Francis' name wasn't among them.

Nine felt totally defeated. He'd come on another wild goose chase, of that there was no doubt. The realization he'd been well and truly duped hit him. Frustrated, he raised his head and shouted, "Damn you, Naylor!" Thirteen's dying words came back to him. He looked around at Professor Lindsay. "How many orphanages does Omega have around the world?"

"Only one other that I know of."

Nine pulled the professor to him and rammed the barrel of his pistol into the man's open mouth, chipping two of his teeth as he did so. "I'm only going to ask you once more. How many of these horror chambers does Omega have?"

The professor's eyes bulged as he pleaded for his life. "Please, I'm telling the truth." His words were muffled.

Nine withdrew the barrel from the terrified man's mouth.

"I can show you," Professor Lindsay said quickly. He immediately accessed another file on the computer. It was headed: *Confidential: Icon Corporation's Medical Laboratories*.

Nine recognized *Icon Corporation* as codename for the Omega Agency.

The professor scrolled down the first page, revealing two labs only: the one he and Nine were currently in and the one at

Thule. He looked up at the former operative. "There was one in Germany, but I understand it was closed down recently."

Nine sensed instinctively the professor was telling the truth – or the truth as he knew it at least. *And therein lies the problem.* He wondered whether Thirteen knew something the professor didn't, or whether the operative's final words had been the delusional ramblings of someone whose brain had been scrambled by MK-Ultra.

Three shrill whistle blasts followed by three more echoed throughout the ground floor. Nine recognized that as the pre-arranged signal for the raiders to depart. He pointed his pistol at the professor once more. "I should shoot you now," he hissed. God knows he was tempted to pull the trigger.

Professor Lindsay cowered before the pistol. "Please. Don't kill me!"

"Go back to your lowlife friends in your rat hole downstairs," Nine ordered.

The frightened professor took off before Nine had a change of heart.

Alone now, a myriad of thoughts flashed through the former operative's mind. He wondered if Francis was dead then banished that thought as quickly as it occurred. *What to do?* Assessing his options, he quickly reached a decision: he would go to Nellis Air Force Base in Nevada. *There's no other choice.*

As Nine departed the IT room and hurried to re-join the departing rebels, Thirteen's final words were etched on his mind. That was all he had to go on – the dying words of someone who was undoubtedly in a mind-controlled state at the time. It was a tenuous lead and he knew it.

65

Seventy-two hours after the dramatic event she and Seventeen had experienced in the Papenoo River valley, Isabelle was feeling safer than she'd felt in a while. She was staying with a Tahitian family in a small settlement well off the beaten track in the island's rugged interior.

After Seventeen had rammed the convertible her former Omega colleagues were traveling in, she and Isabelle had continued to the north coast highway in their stolen station wagon. Then, at the first settlement they'd come to, they abandoned the station wagon and hired a rental vehicle. From there, they'd returned to the same Thai commune they left nearly two weeks earlier, but only after they'd stopped at an Internet café to check their emails. As usual, there was no word from Nine, which only served to depress Isabelle further.

While Seventeen had reservations about returning to the Thai commune, she'd done so out of desperation: she had no more ideas. If there was one thing recent events had taught her it was that Tahiti was a small island with few hiding places for two women on the run. Especially for a pregnant woman who was now only two weeks from her due date.

Chai and the other members of his extended family had proven as accommodating as ever, hiding the fugitive pair in their midst as they'd done previously. However, Seventeen knew that was only ever a temporary fix and had looked for a more permanent long-term alternative.

It was Chai who came up with the solution. He'd had dealings with elders from the indigenous settlement that was now home, for the moment at least, to Isabelle. The settlement – one of the few in Tahiti's interior – was populated by around fifty indigenous people. They eked out a living, growing tropical fruit and selling it to markets on the coast.

Affectionately referred to by local islanders as *Pomareville*, after the settlement's respected Pomare family, it was only accessible by four-wheel drive vehicle and was so small it didn't feature on any maps. Pomareville was effectively off the grid with no cell phone coverage, few visitors and no reliable power supply. Its only electricity was generated locally and used by those families who could afford it.

Isabelle had initially resisted the idea of relocating there. Memories of her difficult birth when Francis had arrived were still fresh and she wanted to be near modern medical facilities when her daughter arrived.

Seventeen persuaded her otherwise. The former operative had pointed out that Omega would find Isabelle if she remained on the coast, and when they found her they would take her daughter just as they'd taken her son.

Isabelle had needed no more persuading. She couldn't bare the thought of losing a second child to Omega.

Chai had chimed in with some positive comments, too. He'd assured Isabelle the Tahitian midwives at Pomareville were highly experienced when it came to delivering babies. They had to be for their settlement was some distance from civilization.

So it had been decided: Chai would drive Isabelle under cover of darkness to the settlement while Seventeen returned to Papeete to attend to other matters.

Isabelle's relocation to the interior had taken place the following night. Chai had driven extra carefully as the windy, hilly road they followed degenerated to a rough dirt track before they were even halfway there. He'd had visions the bumpy ride could bring on the baby.

They had arrived at the remote settlement in one piece and, after introducing Isabelle to her host family, the Pomares, Chai returned to his commune outside Papeete.

Now, as Isabelle began her third day at the tiny settlement, she was feeling as content as any woman who had been separated from her husband and son could feel. Her host family, and the other villagers, had accepted her as one of their own. While they didn't know Isabelle's circumstances, they sensed she was in need of love and care, and lavished these upon her in true island fashion.

#

While Isabelle was hiding in Tahiti's interior, Seventeen was staying at a hotel in Papeete. She'd checked in under the guise of a Belgian forensic anthropologist who was supposedly in Tahiti to study skeletal remains of the island's ancient peoples.

Seventeen's latest disguise had entailed dying her blonde hair black, darkening her fake tan so that her skin was now nut brown and changing her blue eyes to brown through the use of colored contact lenses. For good measure she had added a faint scar that ran down one side of her forehead – the result of a supposed attack by a chimpanzee whilst on assignment in Uganda should anyone ask.

The former operative's decision not to accompany Isabelle to her new hideout had been one based on common sense. She'd reached the conclusion that nothing would be achieved by staying with her sister-in-law. Rather, it was time to be pro-active and take the fight to Omega. This way, she could check her emails regularly, too.

Seventeen wasn't sure if Nine would approve. But he wasn't here and she had to make her own decisions.

If there was one thing she was sure of, it was that Naylor would send someone to replace the two operatives she'd put out of commission and to assist Eight who, it seemed, had escaped the car crash unscathed. Instead of waiting for them to find her, Seventeen planned to find them.

Since the incident in the Papenoo River Valley, Seventeen had learned that Fifteen had been killed and Twenty Three seriously injured. She'd tracked Twenty Three to Papeete's main public hospital where, for the first forty-eight hours, he'd been on life support. There, she had seen Eight and tracked her to the hotel she was staying at.

Seventeen planned to keep Eight under surveillance. She was sure the operative would be contacted by the reinforcements Naylor was sending. In other words, Eight would lead her to them, so it suited her to let the operative live a while longer.

As for the injured Twenty Three, she had other plans for him.

66

As Isabelle and Seventeen adapted to their new routines in Tahiti, Naylor presided over yet another urgent meeting of Omega's board. It had been called at short notice at the insistence of several of Naylor's fellow directors.

The directors were alarmed by recent events – in particular the Mai Mai militia's attack on the agency's medical lab in the DRC and the subsequent incident that had seen two operatives put out of commission in Tahiti.

It was a full meeting with everyone in attendance, although CIA Director Marcia Wilson was once more present in holographic form only.

Naylor had planned to take more sick leave. His headache of

a few days earlier had returned with a vengeance. However, he knew it wouldn't be a good look for the board chairman not to be present at an urgent directors' meeting, so he'd forced himself to attend.

Like Naylor, the other directors were horrified at the thought that Nine had wreaked so much havoc at the DRC lab, especially coming so soon after the events in Greenland. They were in no doubt Nine was behind the latest attack even if no-one had actually seen him. No-one still alive that is.

The directors were also alarmed that someone had attacked the three operatives in Tahiti, putting two of them out of commission. That was the last straw as far as they were concerned.

It was founding member Fletcher Von Pein who expressed what everyone was thinking. "What the hell's going on in this agency?" the elderly banker asked. He was looking directly at Naylor and it was obvious to everyone that's who he was directing his criticism at.

Naylor squirmed and tried to ignore his pounding headache as Von Pein let fly.

"The last two weeks have been a comedy of errors. First, an over-the-hill operative with a heart condition uplifts confidential information from right under our noses. Then he breaks into our Arctic facility and kills two of our best operatives." Von Pein paused for effect then continued. "A few days later, rebels attack our facility in the Congo, killing not one, not two, but five of our operatives."

"No prizes for guessing who was behind that," fellow director Bill Sterling ventured.

Naylor went to speak, but Von Pein continued right over him. "And if all that's not enough, we learn someone is hunting our people down in Tahiti." He looked accusingly at Naylor. "Correct me if I'm wrong, but the agency's wheels seem to be falling off."

All eyes around the table were now on Naylor. The besieged Omega boss knew exactly what his fellow directors were worried about. Naylor shared their fears. He, and they, were worried that news of Omega's underground medical labs, and the unsanctioned and unspeakable experiments being conducted inside them, could leak to the outside world. They were in no doubt they'd each be vilified and probably imprisoned for life if news did get out.

For once, Naylor decided honesty was the best approach – for the moment at least. "First, let me summarize what we know. We know it was Nine who drove Seventeen from her house in Chicago and she hasn't been seen since. And there's little doubt it was Nine who infiltrated the lab in Greenland and killed our people there."

The other board members looked restless. Naylor was telling them nothing they didn't already know.

Naylor continued, "We all know Nine was behind the attack on our lab in the DRC. The European gunman sighted with the rebels could only have been him."

"And was Nine behind the attack on our people in Tahiti as well?" fellow director Lincoln Claver asked.

"In a way I suspect he was," Naylor said. "I believe he arranged for his sister to fly to Tahiti to protect Isabelle Hannar."

"But before he was killed Fifteen reported the Hannar woman was with a man who claimed to be her husband," Claver said.

Marcia chose that moment to enter the discussion. "Don't forget all our orphan-operatives are masters of disguise. That goes for Seventeen, too."

"Yes I believe that was Seventeen disguised as a man," Naylor agreed.

"So what are we doing about that situation?" Sterling asked.

"Two more operatives are on the way to Tahiti now. They're under orders to find and kill Seventeen, and then locate Missus Hannar."

"I'm surprised we have any operatives left," Von Pein said with more than a touch of sarcasm. Before Naylor could respond, Von Pein asked, "So where does all this leave us, Andrew?"

"It leaves us with some collateral damage, but that's all."

"You're joking, surely? What about the risk of Nine going public with what he knows?"

"He won't do that," Naylor responded confidently. "Not while he believes there's any chance his son's still alive. And sooner or later, he'll make a mistake. Then we'll have him."

"Well I hope you're right," Von Pein said, "for all our sakes. What about the boy?"

"The boy is still safe and sound at our new lab in Nevada and, as far as we know, Nine doesn't even know it exists."

"As far as we know?" Sterling asked.

"I never told him about it and it wasn't mentioned in any of the files Nine accessed at my place."

"Who else knows about Nellis?" Claver asked.

Everyone present knew he was referring to Nellis Air Force Base, the site of the secret lab in Nevada.

"Besides us and Doc Andrews, no-one except for the lab staff who work on site. And they're employed under the usual confidentiality conditions and security restraints."

Again, everyone present knew what Naylor meant by that. It was common knowledge among the directors that Omega's employees were extremely well paid, but they were also under threat of death if they broke any of the strict terms of their employment.

"Just what security arrangements are in place in Nevada?"

Von Pein asked.

Naylor looked at Marcia, or at her holographic image at least.

"We sent Operatives One and Ten to Nellis a week ago," Marcia said. "They're stationed at the lab on base."

"Is that sufficient given what has gone down at the other orphanages?" Sterling asked.

"I believe so," Marcia said. "As Andrew alluded, it's highly unlikely Nine even knows of the Nellis lab's existence."

As Marcia spoke, Naylor was watching Von Pein. He thought the ageing co-founder was about to explode. His face was turning crimson red and his expression was furious.

Von Pein could contain himself no longer and he jumped to his feet. "For Christ's sake!" He thumped the table with one massive fist. "Haven't we learned anything?" He glared at Marcia's image then looked at Naylor. "We've been trying to second-guess Nine every step of the way, and every step of the way he has made fools of us!"

"Fletcher's right," Claver said. "We can't blindly assume this rogue orphan doesn't know about Nevada. We should assume he does and send more troops immediately."

Listening to the debate, Naylor realized Claver and Von Pein were right. He also realized for the first time in his life he could be losing his touch. Five years ago he'd never have made the mistakes he had in recent times. He'd totally underestimated Nine and now they were all paying the price. He could feel his lazy eye beginning to twitch and his headache was worsening. "Yes you are right. I will send more operatives immediately."

That seemed to pacify the other directors for the moment. The discussion returned to Nine's son.

"What progress is being made with the boy?" industrialist Hank Smythe asked.

"According to Doc Andrews, Francis Hannar is almost back to full health and will soon be ready to commence stage one in the cloning process," Naylor said.

"At last a smidgeon of good news," Von Pein sighed.

Ignoring him Naylor said, "I spoke to the doc last night and he said it was looking good to start testing the boy within forty-eight hours."

67

Nine slept almost the entire final leg of his long-haul flight from Cape Town to Los Angeles. His sleep was punctuated by nightmares of hideously disfigured children. He'd probably have slept the entire leg if his British Airways flight hadn't struck turbulence as it began its approach to Los Angeles International Airport.

Now awake, the former operative felt as though he was on auto-pilot – much like the passenger jet he travelled in had been on for much of the flight. Since departing Africa without Francis, he'd just been going through the motions. He felt physically and mentally exhausted, and disconsolate at not finding his son.

His bandaged right shoulder hurt like hell, too – a constant reminder of his knife fight with Thirteen.

What made his current state of mind worse was that he still wasn't convinced he wasn't on another wild goose chase. He only had Thirteen's word that Francis had been sent to a new secret lab in Nevada – the word of someone who was in a mind-controlled state at the time.

For maybe the twentieth time since departing Cape Town, Nine reviewed his final hours in the DRC. They played over and over in his mind like a bad movie.

After he and the Mai Mai rebels fled Carmel Corporation's refinery, they'd endured a frantic drive through the jungle as they were pursued by government troops sent from nearby Kindu. Then after losing them, they'd arrived safely at their base where Leila and other women took charge of Sonny and five other children the rebels had rescued from the lab. Leila had also attended to Nine's shoulder, treating the knife wound and efficiently dressing it.

The chopper Nine had called in was waiting for him at the rebels' encampment and he'd been flown back to Kananga, in the south of the country, where he'd joined a tour group of British backpackers and crossed safely into Zambia. There, he'd caught a flight to Cape Town where he'd connected with the British Airways flight he was now on.

Aware Omega and the CIA would still have people looking out for him at the main international airports, Nine was traveling in the guise of a South African university professor visiting America on business. His latest disguise was a convincing one despite the fact he'd slipped into it in a zombie-like state before checking in for his flight.

His exertions during the raid on the refinery, combined with lack of sleep and a cruel travel schedule before and since that event, had left him feeling fragile. His shoulder hurt, too, but that was the least of his problems. In the past two weeks, he felt he'd aged a hundred years. His weak heart continued to trouble him and he could tell he was on borrowed time.

As the *Please fasten your seatbelt* sign lit up above him and the plane began its final descent to LAX, Nine's thoughts turned to the next stage in his odyssey to find Francis. He was clinging possibility there was a secret lab in Nevada and his son was there. *He has to be!* That was all he had to go on. He couldn't bring himself to consider what he'd do, or what he'd tell Isabelle, if Francis wasn't there.

Nine was aware he always had the option of going public with the information he had on Omega's secret orphanages. Leaking the confidential files to the likes of mainstream media outlets, government watchdogs, key politicians and law enforcement agencies would certainly expose Omega. It would also result in the closure of the labs and undoubtedly end the careers of Naylor and his cronies in spectacular fashion, but it wouldn't return his son to him.

The former operative knew as soon as news of the labs' existence broke, Omega would go into damage control. They would act fast to destroy all evidence the labs ever existed. And that evidence would include the children interned in those same labs.

#

While Nine's plane was preparing to land at LAX, Seventeen was parked in her rental car outside Papeete's upmarket Hotel Tiare Tahiti. She'd been observing guests coming and going from the hotel's front entrance for the past two hours, hoping to sight her fellow orphan, Eight.

Within the confines of the small, nondescript Honda vehicle she'd rented, Seventeen was sweltering in the heat. She was still in the guise of a Belgian anthropologist. Perspiration threatened to ruin her carefully-applied, nutmeg brown tan and she would have loved to be able to languish in the hotel's swimming pool whose sky blue waters she could just make out to one side of the hotel.

Seventeen was thinking about taking a break when she caught sight of a familiar figure. *Eight!* The Omega operative wore dark shades, but even they couldn't hide her Oriental features. Besides, Eight was tall for a woman of Asian heritage and she generally stood out in a crowd. Seventeen estimated her fellow orphan was as tall as she was.

The former operative watched as Eight jumped into a waiting cab. Seventeen started the engine and followed the cab at a discreet distance. As she'd hoped, the cab traveled to Fa'a'ā International Airport.

Seventeen watched as Eight disembarked from the cab and

entered the airport's International Arrivals terminal. Quickly parking her car, she followed Eight inside. A glance at the flight arrivals board told her an Air Tahiti Nui flight had just arrived from Chicago. She assumed whoever Eight had come to meet would have been on that flight.

The former operative didn't have long to wait. Two familiar figures emerged through Customs. Seventeen saw them even before Eight did.

Omega operatives Seven and Nineteen were traveling as themselves and were instantly recognizable. Seven, a muscular African-American male, hardly seemed to have aged in the eight years since Seventeen had last seen him. He still looked as youthful as ever even though she recalled he was her age. Seventeen wondered if he was still adept at terminating targets by garroting them. She recalled that had been his preferred *method of termination*, as he'd called it.

Nineteen, a mixed-race man of similar age, hadn't worn as well as his traveling companion, but he, too, looked in top shape and as foreboding as ever. One of the tallest of the Pedemont orphans at six four, he had a menacing persona. Of all Seventeen's former colleagues, Nineteen was the one who frightened her the most. She had always sensed an evil presence in the man.

Only now did Eight notice her colleagues. She hurried forward to greet them.

Seventeen observed the three operatives engage in the briefest of formalities before Eight led them outside. As had been the case when the female operative arrived, the latest arrivals traveled light with only one small travel bag each. They evidently didn't expect to be in Tahiti long.

Outside the terminal, Seventeen watched as the three walked to a rental car bay where a small fleet of shiny cars sat glistening in the sun. There, Eight spoke briefly to an attendant who handed over a set of keys and pointed to a late model Renault parked close by. Seven and Nineteen piled into the vehicle's back seat while Eight accompanied the attendant into a small office to sign the rental agreement forms. That done, she returned, climbed in behind the wheel of the Renault and drove off.

As Seventeen had done earlier, she followed at a discreet

distance. Eight led her straight back to Hotel Tiare Tahiti. Rather than stopping outside the establishment, Seventeen drove on by – a precaution in case any of the operatives were watching for a tail. Knowing them, and knowing the exhaustive training they and all Omega's operatives had undergone, she was aware they would always be on guard.

Seventeen didn't need to stop anyway. She now knew who her targets were and where they were staying, so would deal with them later. Meanwhile, she had other business to attend to.

The former operative headed for the public hospital where Twenty Three was recovering. She planned to deal with him before he could recover from his injuries and once again become a threat to Isabelle and herself. Then it would be another one down and three to go.

68

After arriving at LAX, Nine flew by chartered plane to a private landing strip on the outskirts of Las Vegas and checked into a budget motel nearby. He'd chosen to base himself in *Sin City* because of its close proximity to Nellis Air Force Base.

Nine had also forsaken his South African guise in favour of a rosy-cheeked, bespectacled and slightly overweight tourist from Devon, in the south of England. His newly acquired paunch was courtesy of a small cushion he'd stuffed down his singlet. It was crude, but effective.

Since departing Los Angeles, he'd forced himself to put the disappointments of his failed African sojourn – and his Greenland and German visits before that – to the back of his mind and fully focus on what he needed to do in Nevada.

Nine was aware he was seriously disadvantaged. He had not a shred of information about Omega's lab at the Air Force base. Unlike the agency's offshore labs, its specific whereabouts, layout, access and security arrangements were a mystery to him. He wasn't even sure the lab existed, though he wasn't dwelling on that possibility for the moment.

The former operative reminded himself that for every problem there's a solution. *That's right, isn't it, Tommy?* Holding onto his mentor's oft-quoted mantra, he reviewed his immediate plans while eating a meal in the privacy of his motel unit. He was aware he needed to familiarize himself with Nellis Air Force base and its surrounds, but first he had more pressing priority.

Nine caught a cab to a downtown realtor's office. There, he took out a short-term lease on a fully self-contained, private, ground-floor apartment that had caught his eye in a local real estate flier. While he didn't inspect the apartment in person, he could tell from the photos it would meet his requirements: it would serve as a safe house, away from prying eyes, for Francis and himself. For security reasons, he didn't plan to move in until after he'd rescued his son.

After lunch, armed with a camera and determined to give his best impersonation of a tourist, Nine joined a group of foreign tourists who were about to depart by coach to Nellis Air Force Base. It was the day's last scheduled tour of the facility and Nine had been fortunate to obtain one of the last available tickets for the three-hour excursion.

Before boarding the air-conditioned coach, the tour guide advised Nine and his fellow passengers they would have to leave their cameras behind. Cameras were not allowed onto the base.

The former operative had a window seat toward the rear of the coach. As luck would have it, he was stuck next to a garrulous Australian woman who proceeded to tell him everything she and her equally garrulous chubby daughter had done since arriving in the US. Nine tried to feign interest, but it was a struggle and he had to resist the temptation to tell the woman to shut up.

Looking out his window at the vapor trails left by fighter jets in the blue skies above, Nine was taken back to his time at Thule

Air Base, in Greenland. He wondered now, as he'd wondered then, what the significance was of locating secret orphanages at US Air Force bases.

As the coach neared Nellis Air Force Base, Nine surveyed its layout and began to take more interest in the tour guide's patter. The guide, an enthusiastic twentysomething Hispanic woman, addressed her captive audience from the front of the coach.

"Nellis is under the jurisdiction of Air Combat Command and is home to the Fifty Seventh Wing, *our* Air Force's biggest composite flying wing," the guide gushed. "It includes F-15 Eagle and F-16 Falcon Aggressor air and space squadrons to help keep *our* citizens safe."

Nine was amused the way the guide personalized everything about the base – as if she had some ownership of, or a stake in, the base and its squadrons.

"Ten thousand personnel are assigned to the base and to the NTTR," the guide continued. "NTTR stands for the Nevada Test and Training Range, which facilitates training for military ops for *our* people."

Surveying the base, the first thing that struck Nine was it seemed many, many times busier than Thule Air Base. Fighter planes were landing and taking off every thirty seconds while others taxied in readiness for take-off and still others queued to await their turn to roll onto one of the many runways in use. The noise of jet engines almost drowned out the tour guide's patter even though she was now shouting into her microphone.

The coach slowed as it approached a manned security gate. A uniformed guard motioned to the driver to stop. The guard exchanged pleasantries with the driver through the driver's open window then requested an inventory of his passengers. The driver handed a list of names to the guard.

Nine had expected as much. Similar security precautions had been in force at Thule Air Base. However, he didn't expect what happened next.

A distinguished looking man wearing civvies emerged from a nearby guardhouse. Nine couldn't see him clearly as the sun was in his eyes. He guessed the man was around his own age, and by the look of him he kept fit. The man walked purposefully toward the coach.

Nine suddenly recognized him. *It's Ten!* The tenth-born orphan had been his best friend at the orphanage. They had been like brothers. Nine remembered him as the orphanage's practical joker. Each had been the butt of many a practical joke over the years and each had been reprimanded by their Omega masters many a time for their unsanctioned tomfoolery.

Now wasn't the time for nostalgic reminiscing, however. Nine could see that Ten was in the process of boarding the coach. He could feel his heart racing.

As he'd done every day since Naylor had sent him to the base to watch out for the rogue operative, Ten had boarded each and every tour coach – morning and afternoon – to check its passengers. Starting at the front of the coach, he slowly walked down the aisle, studying the faces of each passenger.

Nine hoped his rosy-cheeked English tourist guise would pass muster. In support of his disguise, he engaged the Australian woman next to him in a discussion about her homeland, using his best rural Devon accent. By the time Ten reached them, Nine was telling the woman about a visit he'd made to Ayers Rock in the heart of Australia.

The former operative could feel Ten's eyes on him and he prayed he wouldn't be recognized. His heart was beating faster than ever.

Ten continued on down the aisle, leaving Nine and the Australian woman deep in conversation.

As Ten completed his inspection of passengers and disembarked from the coach, Nine silently thanked his old tutors at the Pedemont Orphanage for giving him the ability to shape-shift and adopt believable disguises at will. His pulse returned to normal, but he was left with a feeling that resembled heartburn. It was a new sensation and Nine didn't like it one bit. He tried to put it out of his mind.

Ten's presence at the base confirmed to Nine the likelihood that it was home to a secret medical lab. *And if that's the case, Francis could well be here!* Nine wondered how many other operatives Naylor had sent to the base. He thought it probable Ten was alone. After all, Naylor couldn't know that his rogue operative was aware another Omega lab existed.

69

Seventeen returned to Papeete's main public hospital after dark. Her visit earlier that day had been cut short by the unforeseen appearance of the newly arrived Seven and Nineteen who called in to check on the progress of their injured colleague, Twenty Three.

For this late night call, which was well after official visiting hours, Seventeen had disguised herself as a nursing sister. As she'd hoped, security was lax as she strode through the hospital's main entrance, small bag in hand, and entered the first ladies' restroom she came to.

Emerging from the restroom a few minutes later minus the bag, she took an elevator up to the casualty ward. Night shift personnel were thin on the ground and that suited her as she didn't need any witnesses for what she planned to do.

There was only one junior nurse on duty in the ward. Keeping out of her way, Seventeen quietly walked through the ward, looking for Twenty Three's bed. She found it half way down the ward.

Twenty Three had a private room to himself. Seventeen took that to be a sign of the severity of his injuries. She wondered why Omega hadn't had him admitted to a private clinic and assumed it must be because public hospitals' operating facilities in French Polynesia were superior.

One look at Twenty Three confirmed he wasn't in good shape. The operative, who was fast asleep, was bandaged from head to foot. He was connected to half a dozen tubes and also to a heart monitor whose digital graph showed a decidedly irregular heartbeat.

For one moment Seventeen debated whether to go through with what she was planning. It was obvious Twenty Three wouldn't be a threat to Isabelle or herself for a very long time – if ever. In fact, judging by his heartbeat, she deduced he may not even survive his current injuries.

Seventeen cast her doubts aside. As well as removing any future threat, no matter how faint, she wanted to send a message to Omega. That message was that there was a price to pay for what they'd done. By becoming the hunter instead of the hunted, she also knew she would divert some of Omega's focus from Nine and Isabelle to herself. And that could just be enough to enable her brother and sister-in-law to prevail and to be reunited as a family.

Footsteps behind Seventeen alerted her to the approach of the same junior nurse she had seen earlier.

"Excuse me, Sister," the junior nurse said in French.

"Yes Nurse?" Seventeen answered brusquely as she looked up from a borrowed chart she'd been pretending to consult.

"It's my break now. Is it alright if I take half an hour?"

"Certainly Nurse, but don't be late."

"No Sister." The nurse smiled and marched off.

As soon as the nurse's footsteps had faded, Seventeen closed the door to Twenty Three's room then pulled a portable screen across so that it would hide her and the patient from anyone who paid an untimely visit to the room.

Seventeen then picked up a spare pillow from a bedside chair and stood looking down at the youngest of the Pedemont orphans. Memories of Twenty Three came flooding back to her – memories of events and moments she hadn't thought of in years. Like the times their mentor, Tommy Kentbridge, had bullied the young boy during Teleiotes training sessions at the orphanage in an effort to toughen him up; and the time she had tipped hot soup over him after he'd teased her at the orphanage's dinner table when they were both young teenagers.

For one awful moment, she wondered if she could do what she was about to do. Then she thought of Nine and Isabelle and their missing son.

The former operative placed the pillow over Twenty Three's face and held it firmly down. Twenty Three's fingers clawed at her face as he woke and tried to draw breath. He showed surprising strength for one so badly injured, but his struggles lasted for less than a minute.

Seventeen removed the pillow. She didn't need to check

Twenty Three's pulse. He was clearly dead. The flatline graph on the bedside heart monitor confirmed that.

Two tubes had been dislodged from Twenty Three's arm, so Seventeen quickly reattached them before returning the pillow to its original position on the chair and pulling the portable screen back.

Taking one last look around the room to ensure it was as she'd found it, Seventeen quickly left the ward, descended the stairs to the ground floor and entered the same ladies' restroom she'd used earlier. Retrieving the bag she'd left hidden in one of the cubicles, she changed back into the guise of the Belgian anthropologist. Then she departed the building, bag in hand, and walked to her rental car.

Driving back to her hotel, Seventeen pulled up alongside a rubbish bin and threw her borrowed nursing outfit into it.

Later, as Seventeen reviewed the night's events in the privacy of her hotel room, she hoped hospital staff would assume Twenty Three had died in his sleep.

However, she was in no doubt Omega would know Twenty

Three had been the victim of foul play. Sooner or later, the deceased's colleagues would learn of the presence of the mysterious nursing sister, and they would put two and two together.

Seventeen smiled at the thought. *And so it begins.* She was actually starting to enjoy herself.

The former operative hadn't felt this stimulated in a long time. Not since her days as an active operative. It was what she'd always know she'd been born to do.

#

In her refuge at Pomareville, in the middle of Tahiti, Isabelle couldn't sleep. She found the island's humidity worse at night for some reason. And the nightmares she'd been experiencing since Francis' abduction were becoming more frequent, so sleep was difficult at the best of times.

Added to that, the baby was suddenly very active. She could feel her moving in the womb. "Be patient, little one," Isabelle murmured.

As if in response to her mother's voice, the baby stopped

moving. Isabelle smiled to herself, arose from her bed and wandered outside to get some air. Sitting down on a comfy chair just outside her dwelling, she began softly singing a French lullaby while fondling the ruby that hung from her necklace.

Singing to her unborn child brought her pleasure – as did the thought of giving birth to a baby sister for Francis.

Thinking of Francis reminded her of the dreadful position she and her small family had found itself in. As she did every waking minute of every day, she wondered how her son and husband were faring. *Have you found him yet, Sebastian?* She prayed that her boys would be returned to her soon.

70

After a quick visit to a suit hire firm in downtown Vegas, a smartly dressed Nine walked through the palatial entrance of Planet Hollywood Resort and Casino, one of the hottest gaming facilities on the famed *Strip*, at the southern end of Las Vegas Boulevard.

It was the morning after Nine's tour of Nellis Air Force Base and he was now in the guise of a Hispanic playboy complete with greased hair, dark shades, fake moustache and genuine overnight stubble on his face. Gone was the heartburn of yesterday and his shoulder wound had ceased to trouble him. He was feeling more like his old self.

In keeping with his new guise, he'd checked out of his modest motel on the outskirts of town earlier that morning and checked in at the Paris Las Vegas, a swanky hotel and casino a few doors along from Planet Hollywood.

Excited tourists mingled with hardened gamblers inside and outside the casino that was synonymous with gaming, night life and good times in the city. Working girls and women on the prowl for a good time gave Nine the eye as they arrived for some early action.

Nine had spent the previous evening in his motel room researching the Air Force base online on a rented laptop. The five hours that had taken proved to be time well spent. Accessing archived media reports on the base, he'd quickly discovered references to rumors of the Mob's involvement in construction activity on the base in recent years. One name kept cropping up: Al *Madman* Ricca, boss of the Las Vegas branch of the Chicago Syndicate, or *the Outfit* as it's usually referred to.

Ricca, it seemed, had single-handedly taken control of much of Nevada's construction activity since relocating from Chicago to Las Vegas in 2007. After acquiring a stake in half a dozen casinos on the Strip, he'd turned his attention to construction, acquiring a number of lucrative building contracts.

For Ricca, the move to construction was a logical one. He'd qualified as an engineer before finding himself involved with the Mafia in Chicago, so he was able to talk the talk when dealing with other engineers and builders. Nevada's construction sector also offered huge opportunities – legitimate and otherwise.

It was the *otherwise* that appealed to Ricca.

When tenders were called to construct a multi-million dollar, high-tech, subterranean facility at Nellis Air Force Base, the anticipated large number of companies tendering for the hugely lucrative contract never eventuated. Several competitors announced their intention to tender, but they never followed through. Ricca's company mysteriously ended up being the only one to officially tender for the job. Rumors of threats, stand-over tactics and heavy-handedness were rife, but never proven.

Before, during and after construction, various journalists speculated on what the subterranean facility was being used for, but this, too, was never clarified.

One press statement in particular caught Nine's eye. It read:

When asked to comment on the purpose of the new facility, construction boss Al Ricca said he didn't know. "Even if I did know, I couldn't say. My contract with the Air Force stipulates I can't talk about the facility."

Nine was sure Ricca would have a fair idea what the facility was being used for, and he was in no doubt the mobster would have intimate knowledge of its exact location, its layout and how to access it.

The former operative had made contact that night with Ricca's underboss – an unsavory wiseguy known as Johnny *The Rat* Colosimo – at another casino the Outfit had connections with on the Strip, and had requested a meeting with Ricca for the following morning.

Knowing the people he was dealing with would check him out first to ensure he wasn't with the Feds, Nine had adopted the guise of one Miguel Carrera, a New York heavy of Puerto Rican descent – a creation of Omega for one of Nine's long-forgotten missions. He'd been confident his guise would still stand up to a background check, and so it had proven.

Now, as Nine waited in the downstairs lobby of Planet Hollywood, he was feeling refreshingly confident. Since his wasted trip to the DRC, Thirteen's dying words had been proven correct – in part at least. Nine had confirmed the likelihood of an underground lab at Nellis Air Force Base, and he thought it a reasonable assumption that Francis was being held there. Certainly Ten's presence at the base confirmed something was up.

Across the lobby Colosimo, the wiseguy Nine had met the previous evening, caught his eye. Colosimo turned and began walking up a flight of stairs. The underboss was almost at the top of the stairs when Nine caught up to him. They walked in silence to the end of a long corridor where two hard-looking suits stood outside a closed door, doing their best not to appear conspicuous. They quickly and efficiently frisked Nine. The taller of the suits then opened the door and stood aside to let Nine and the underboss in to what turned out to be a conference room.

Inside, Nine found himself face to face with Ricca. A big, jowlish individual, he sat conversing with his accountant, a nervous, pasty-faced, fortysomething man.

Ricca dismissed the accountant as soon as he saw Nine. "Mister Carrera, please join me," he said, motioning for Nine to sit down. The big man nodded to Colosimo who closed the door behind him and took a seat next to his boss.

"Call me Miguel," Nine said as he sat down facing the two men.

"Okay Miguel and you can call me Mister Ricca." Ricca and his underboss chuckled. "I hear you have a deal I won't be able to refuse."

Realizing Ricca didn't believe in small talk, Nine got straight to it. "I want information about the subterranean facility you built at Nellis Air Force base."

"What sort of information are we talking about?" Ricca asked.

"A copy of the architectural plans would be a good start along with security specs, the location of access and egress points, details of personnel numbers, that sort of thing. Oh, and your best guesstimate of what the facility is being used for."

"And in return?"

"One hundred grand. Cash."

Ricca sneered. "You're joking, right? My stake in this casino alone returns me a hundred grand every day. I'd need five hundred grand minimum for information like that."

Nine wasn't fazed. He'd expected resistance. "Okay I can go to a hundred and fifty."

"Like I said, five hundred minimum."

Nine stood up as if to go. "I was prepared to go to two hundred grand, but I can see I'm wasting my time." He left the room without saying goodbye. Retracing his steps down the long corridor toward the stairwell, he hoped he hadn't blown it. A shout from the meeting room door behind him told him he hadn't.

"Carrera!"

Nine turned to see Colosimo motioning to him to return to the meeting room. It seemed the negotiations were still live.

Walking back to the room, Nine wasn't unduly surprised he'd been called back. It was no secret the construction sector was battling in the present economy and he'd heard whispers that Ricca's business interests had suffered setbacks of late. The mobster had obviously decided that two hundred grand for a little information wasn't to be sneezed at.

Nine's earlier confidence had returned. *Hang on Francis. It won't be long now.*

71

Seventeen wasn't surprised to see Seven turn up at Papeete's main public hospital the day after she had fast-tracked Twenty Three's passing, though she had hoped the muscular African-American operative would be accompanied by his Omegan colleagues. That would have given her the opportunity to terminate all three remaining operatives in one hit. Now she'd have to content herself with crossing just one more off her list for the moment.

As she'd done when she visited the casualty ward the previous night, Seventeen had dispensed with her Belgian disguise. She was now in the guise of a hospital grounds person – complete with green cap and overalls, which she'd uplifted from an unlocked storage shed – and, in keeping with her new persona, was picking up rubbish in the hospital's outdoor car park.

Seventeen had spotted the late model Renault rental car as soon as it entered the hospital grounds. From beneath the peak of her cap, she watched as Seven parked the Renault in between two other cars in the middle of the car park. The operative climbed from the car and strode toward the hospital's main entrance.

As soon as Seven entered the hospital, Seventeen walked over to the Renault, picking up discarded papers as she went and placing them in a rubbish bag she carried. The car park was half full, but apart from a visitor parking his car some distance away and a skateboarder weaving around the stationery vehicles she had it pretty much to herself.

Seventeen quickly checked that no-one was looking then drew a small tool from her rubbish bag and deftly used it to access the vehicle's front passenger door. Satisfied she hadn't been observed, she slipped inside the car, closing the door softly after her.

Sitting as low as she could inside the vehicle, Seventeen retrieved more items from her bag. Among them was a small but powerful car bomb, which she'd been up half the night assembling. The former operative placed the device beneath the driver's seat then tied the fuse to the driver's door handle.

Moving cautiously so as not to prematurely detonate the bomb, she opened the front passenger door and climbed out, closing the door gently behind her. She then strolled casually over to a rubbish bin on the far side of the car park and emptied the contents of her bag into it.

Seventeen knew she should depart the scene, but something made her stick around. She didn't want the death or injury of some innocent bystander on her conscience. Though the bomb she'd rigged was only small, it was powerful enough to kill or maim anyone in the immediate vicinity should it explode.

The former operative had first-hand experience of the destructive powers of such improvised explosive devices. She'd become familiar with their assembly and use while working alongside CIA personnel during America's occupation of Afghanistan and Iraq prior to that.

Seventeen busied herself picking up rubbish when she saw

Seven emerge from the hospital. As the operative walked toward his vehicle, the skateboarder Seventeen had observed earlier chose that moment to send his skateboard flying into one of the cars parked next to Seven's Renault. It appeared the skateboard had scratched the door of the neighboring car.

The skateboarder, a pimply teenage boy, was inspecting the damage when Seven joined him. Though Seventeen couldn't hear what was being said, she imagined the discussion had to do with the mishap. She watched, heart in mouth, as Seven handed the skateboarder a pen and a piece of paper for the boy to leave his name and address for the owner of the damaged car. The boy obliged, leaving the paper beneath one of the car's windscreen wipers.

To Seventeen's consternation, the skateboarder hung around as Seven approached the Renault. She daren't wait any longer. "Hey!" she shouted.

Both Seven and the skateboarder turned and looked at her as she strode toward them.

"You!" she pointed straight at the skateboarder and spoke

French in keeping with the nationality of most of Papeete's workers. "This is not a skating rink. Now get out of here before I report you." She made sure she kept her head down so her cap would hide most of her face from Seven.

The skateboarder stared at Seventeen insolently. For one terrible moment the former operative thought the boy was going to disobey her. To her everlasting relief, he thought better of it and skated off.

Seven caught Seventeen's eye. "Teenagers," he said sympathetically.

"Tell me about it," Seventeen laughed as she turned and walked away. Just before she'd turned, she thought she caught a look of recognition in her fellow orphan's eyes. She continued walking, but could feel Seven's eyes boring a hole in her back.

Seven had a feeling he'd seen the grounds person before, but he wasn't able to place her as he fumbled for his car key. He found his key and recognized the woman almost at the same instant. Almost but not quite. As Seven realized the grounds person he was looking at was Seventeen, he depressed the remote on the key.

Seventeen felt the blast of the explosion from where she was, and she was a good thirty yards away. She spun around and was relieved to see the skateboarder was unharmed, and thankfully no-one else appeared to be in the immediate vicinity.

At first she couldn't see the Renault. It was hidden behind a cloud of smoke. The smoke cleared almost immediately and she saw Seven, or what was left of him, lying a few yards from the burning car. Both were unrecognizable. The operative had been reduced to a smoldering, charcoal carcass and the Renault had been reduced to a skeleton of white hot steel.

People converged on the car park seemingly out of nowhere. They included hospital staff and visitors. Several screamed when they realized they were looking at the charred remains of a body.

Seventeen took advantage of the sudden chaos to slip away. Her first port of call was a unisex restroom where she removed her green cap and uniform, leaving only the shirt and shorts she was already wearing. She still wore the same hikers' boots, but they complemented her current outfit.

Now bearing no resemblance to the grounds person who had

entered the restroom a few moments earlier, she emerged from it and walked to the rental car she'd left parked outside the front of the hospital. As she walked, her thoughts were already on the next operatives on her list.

72

Naylor's day had not ended as well as it had begun. That morning, Ten had called him and advised there hadn't been any sign of Nine anywhere near Nellis Air Force Base, nor anywhere in Nevada for that matter. It appeared the rogue operative hadn't learned of the existence of Omega's latest orphanage.

Shortly after that, the Omega boss had received another call from the base – this time from Doctor Andrews who reported that Francis was now fully recovered from his recent ailment and testing was about to begin.

That good news had been undone by the phone call Naylor received just as he was about to depart his office for home. Nineteen had called from Papeete to advise it seemed Twenty

Three's death was suspicious and, on top of that, Seven had been assassinated by a car bomber.

The escalation of activity in Tahiti confirmed to Naylor's mind that Seventeen was indeed in Tahiti. It also prompted him to suspect that Nine could have returned there to be with his wife and to help Seventeen protect her.

Naylor was tempted to send still more operatives to Tahiti to squash the resistance once and for all. He decided against doing that for the moment. Recent events had seen Omega's orphan-operatives reduced in number, leaving the agency under-resourced for the first time since its Pedemont orphans had graduated as fully fledged operatives. The remaining operatives were all engaged in vital missions around the globe and Naylor couldn't pull them away without very good reason. He just hoped his two operatives still operational in Tahiti were good enough to resolve the problem on their own.

#

Sitting down for dinner with her extended Tahitian family on a rug on the floor of their home, Isabelle felt strangely at peace for the moment – strange because she was aware she should be up the wall with grief and worry over her abducted son and her missing husband.

Despite the undeniable precariousness of the situation, the Frenchwoman had a strong feeling all would end well. She couldn't explain the feeling, not even to herself, but it persisted.

Looking around at the islanders who had taken her in without question and given her sanctuary, Isabelle was overflowing with goodwill toward them. The generosity they'd shown left her humbled. Though they were not wealthy in material terms, they wanted nothing from her in return.

As at all mealtimes, the Pomare family home was overflowing with children of all ages. They were lovingly watched over by parents, uncles and aunts, and by two sets of grandparents. Official head of the busy household was Manoa Pomare, a physically strong man with a stern countenance. However, everyone in the settlement knew the real boss was Atea, his wife and the family matriarch.

Larger than life – in every sense – Atea was the one who

family members and villagers turned to when something needed doing. She was also the settlement's most experienced midwife and in that capacity had formed a close relationship with Isabelle, fussing over her and ensuring that she was well and rested.

Though the villagers spoke Tahitian te roa, their native tongue, when in each other's company, out of respect to Isabelle they spoke French when she was around. In return, she made a conscious effort to master key words and phrases in their language. Her efforts bordered on hilarious, though the villagers never let on.

Isabelle sensed the baby was coming even before the pains began. A warm sensation that began in her belly gradually spread to her extremities. That was followed by a tingling sensation and then her waters broke. "Atea," she murmured.

No-one heard her above the sound of laughing children.

"Atea!" Isabelle shouted. The laughter stopped and all eyes were suddenly on the Frenchwoman. "Baby's coming."

Atea's big, round face creased into a smile. "Baby's coming!" she shouted, echoing Isabelle.

The matriarch swung into action, shushing the children and

chaperoning Isabelle through to a bedroom at the rear of the dwelling. Two aunties accompanied Atea. The three Tahitian women knew what to do: between them they'd delivered at least a hundred babies over the years.

73

Seventeen wasn't letting up in her mission to hunt down her fellow orphans. She felt she had momentum going her way now and wanted to maintain that momentum before they could get to Isabelle.

The former operative had been observing the front of Hotel Tiare Tahiti from her rented Honda since dusk. Her plan was to somehow isolate Eight and Nineteen, and pick them off one at a time, as she'd done with the others.

Seventeen, who was still in her Belgian guise, was under no illusions about what she was up against. Nor did she doubt how it would end. She'd been around Omega long enough to know it could only end one way: with her death. For every operative she incapacitated, Naylor would send two more in their place.

Ultimately, her luck would run out. She knew that, but it was a price she was prepared to pay.

For the first time ever, she felt she had a real purpose in life. She had her brother to thank for that. Nine had pulled her from the dark abyss she'd fallen into. *Or was pushed into more like it!* And she'd had a taste of what it was like to be part of a real family.

Seventeen felt she was indebted to Nine, and if it meant sacrificing her life to protect his wife and baby to repay that debt, so be it.

The former operative tensed as two familiar figures emerged from the hotel's entrance and hailed a cab. She observed Nineteen open the cab's rear door for Eight and jump in the front seat. Eight was about to climb into the cab when she received a call on her cell phone.

Seventeen watched as the female operative motioned to Nineteen that he should go on without her. The cab drove off, leaving Eight alone on the sidewalk. Still talking on her phone, she re-entered the hotel.

That was the opening Seventeen had been waiting for. She

climbed from her car and hurried after Eight. The former operative stepped into the lobby just in time to see her target enter an empty escalator. She watched as the lift buttons signaled that Eight had an uninterrupted ride to the fifth floor – the hotel's top floor.

Seventeen crossed the lobby and caught another elevator. This one was near-full of Japanese tourists who had entered it in the basement. It soon became apparent they were staying in rooms on different floors.

The journey to the fifth floor seemed to take an eternity. After four stops to permit the tourists to access their individual rooms, the elevator finally delivered Seventeen to her destination.

Now, alone on the fifth floor, she wasn't sure what to do. For a start, she hadn't a clue which room her target was in.

The answer came almost immediately when a door halfway along the corridor opened and Eight reappeared. She was still talking on her phone as she walked back to the elevator. Seventeen noted she was speaking in Russian, but the former operative was certain she had been speaking English when she'd first emerged from her room. It was obvious Eight didn't want anyone to understand what she was saying.

As Eight approached, Seventeen pressed the elevator's *Down* button to make it appear she'd been waiting to descend. She prayed they'd have the elevator to themselves.

The two women nodded to each other as they waited for the elevator door to open. When it opened, Seventeen waited for her unsuspecting companion to enter the elevator first then followed her inside and pressed the *Down Button*.

Standing close to the door with her back to Eight as they began to descend, Seventeen listened as the operative continued her conversation in Russian.

"Yes, sir," Eight murmured. "I'm confident we can handle the situation."

Seventeen deduced Eight was talking to Naylor, or to an Omega superior at least. She wondered if the discussion was about sending more reinforcements to Tahiti.

"No they still don't know what type of explosive device was used," Eight said. "The gendarmes are still looking into that."

Watching the operative with the Asian features talking

behind her in the reflection of the shiny elevator door, Seventeen could see she was engrossed in her conversation. With her right hand Seventeen reached for the pistol she carried in her open shoulder bag while with her left forefinger she hit the *Stop* button. The elevator stopped with a jerk midway between floors three and two. Seventeen muttered her annoyance in French and pretended to push the *Down* button in an attempt to restart the elevator.

"Hold on one second, sir," Eight said into the phone. Switching to French and speaking to the back of Seventeen's head, she asked, "What's the problem, Madam?"

"It seems to have stalled," Seventeen said.

"Let me see--"

As Eight stepped forward to help, Seventeen spun around, pistol raised. It was just as well she turned when she did. A second later and she'd have been dead.

Eight had become suspicious of the woman in front of her just before she stepped forward. By the time the former operative had spun around, Eight had drawn her own pistol and was preparing to use it.

74

Seventeen saw Eight's pistol in time and reflexively grabbed the operative's right wrist, pinning it to the elevator's rear wall before a shot could be fired. Eight had reacted similarly, grabbing Seventeen's wrist and holding it so the pistol was pointed away from her. As they'd been trained to do, the two flailed at each other, striking with their feet and knees.

A savage knee to the stomach winded Seventeen, forcing her to double over, gasping for breath. At the same time, Eight smashed the former operative's right wrist against the elevator wall, causing her to drop her pistol.

Now unarmed, Seventeen was fighting for her life. As they continued to flail at each other, a karate-style, stiff-fingered jab of Seventeen's found its mark, striking Eight's Adam's apple.

Momentarily unable to breathe, the operative dropped her pistol and tried in vain to suck in a breath of air.

Seventeen swept Eight's feet from under her and looped the strap of her shoulder bag around her opponent's throat. Before the operative could recover, Seventeen crossed the strap over and pulled it tight.

Eight, who still hadn't recovered from the jab to her Adam's apple, flailed her arms about in desperation as she sought to get air to her lungs. Her eyes bulged and her face turned bright red as Seventeen inexorably tightened the strap. Finally, the operative's eyes glazed over and she became motionless.

Seventeen maintained the pressure on her victim's throat for another twenty seconds to ensure she was dead. Then, breathing hard, she released the strap and stepped away from the body. She thought she might faint and had to lean against one wall to recover.

Studying her reflection in the elevator's door, Seventeen almost didn't recognize herself. Blood from scratches on her face had mingled with sweat, leaving streaks in her fake tan; she had a black eye and blood also oozed from a cut lip. As for her blouse, it was bloodied and torn, and her dress looked even more disheveled than her hair, which now resembled the Wreck of the Hesperus.

Thinking quickly, the former operative tidied herself as best she could. She then retrieved both pistols – hers and Eight's – and placed them in her shoulder bag.

Eight's discarded cellphone caught her eye. Wondering if the other party was still on the line, she picked the phone up and put it to her ear. There was no dial tone, which made her suspect someone was indeed still at the other end.

Lightening her voice to mimic Eight's as best she could, she said, "You don't have to worry about the target any more, sir." She gambled that the other party was Naylor and she hoped he'd believe the target she referred to was herself.

There was a long silence. Finally, Seventeen heard a voice she recognized.

"What is the status of the target?"

It is Naylor! Seventeen smiled to herself. "The target has been retired, sir."

"Permanently?"

"Yessir. Permanently."

Seventeen heard Naylor breathe a sigh of relief. Anxious to avoid being found out, she said, "Someone is coming, sir." She spoke with urgency. "I must go."

The former operative ended the call, cutting Naylor off. She hoped she had deceived him into believing he'd been talking to Eight. Of course, she knew he'd find out sooner or later that he had been tricked, but until then she prayed her former boss would delay sending reinforcements to Tahiti.

#

Seventeen had no way of knowing, but nearly six thousand miles away in the den of his mansion in Illinois, Naylor was quietly celebrating. The Omega boss had fallen hook, line and sinker for his former operative's ruse and firmly believed Seventeen was dead.

Even though he had his trick of the moment awaiting him naked in his bed upstairs, he indulged himself by pouring a stiff brandy from his liquor cabinet and raising his glass in a silent toast.

The brandy combined surprisingly well with the Viagra he'd taken earlier. Suddenly excited and remembering what awaited him upstairs, Naylor drained the glass and hurried off to pleasure himself.

#

Fifteen hundred miles away, in his room in Paris Las Vegas, Nine was making final preparations to breach Omega's secret lab at Nellis Air Force Base. The table he sat at was littered with the architectural plans and drawings he acquired that morning from Al *Madman* Ricca. He'd been studying the plans, taking particular note of the tunnels and pipes that would provide him with access to the underground lab.

Nine considered the two hundred grand the plans had ended up costing him money well spent. They were extremely detailed – right down to the exact location of every nut and bolt – and they pointed to the facility being a series of interconnected labs and medical rooms.

Ricca had confirmed the facility was a medical lab, though he claimed he never knew who its intended patients were.

However, he did reveal he'd learnt that some specialist personnel were recruited from international drug company *KaizerSimonsKovak* to work in the new facility. That had caught Nine's attention because he was aware *KSK* was an Omega-owned company.

Nine's plan was to access the facility just before midnight. That was only two hours away, so he knew he needed to get moving.

The former operative was under no illusions about the difficulties that lay ahead. Accessing an out-of-bounds facility that didn't officially exist on heavily guarded Air Force property would be hard enough, but freeing a five-year-old boy – assuming he was even there – and secreting him out of the state and out of the country amounted to his most difficult assignment yet. And he knew it.

Still, he clung to his mentor's slogan: *For every problem, there's a solution.* He was working on a solution at that very moment.

On a brand new smart phone he had purchased that

afternoon, he saved two emails he'd typed out. The first contained new instructions for his attorneys in Europe; the second contained detailed information about Omega and its illegal medical labs, and was addressed to American law enforcement agencies, high profile politicians and international news agencies. He planned to send the emails as soon as he found Francis, his rationale being that the inevitable furor they'd create would provide him with the smokescreen he needed to secret his son out of the country.

Without warning, the heartburn Nine had experienced earlier returned. What began as a dull ache quickly progressed to sharp pains. He hurried to his bedroom to retrieve the container of heart pills he'd left there. Before he even got to it, he remembered he'd run out of pills. He'd intended to use his last repeat prescription to purchase more at a drugstore in the hotel's retail arcade earlier, but hadn't got around to it.

Nine shook the container to check. *Nothing!* He cursed his forgetfulness.

The pain wouldn't subside. Nine feared he was having another heart attack. Frightened and unsure what to do, he staggered over to the telephone on his bedside table, picked it up and dialed reception.

Nine momentarily blacked out. When he opened his eyes, he found himself on his hands and knees. The telephone was on the floor beside him. Somewhere through the fog in his brain, he could hear a concerned woman's voice asking, "Hello? Are you alright, sir?"

Nine picked the phone up. He gasped, "Send someone to room ten eleven plea…" He collapsed face down on the carpet.

"Hello? Hello?" The concerned receptionist got no answer.

75

The shrill ringing of the bedside telephone jarred both Naylor and the hooker lying next to him awake.

"What is it?" the sleepy young woman asked.

"Go back to sleep." Naylor picked up the phone. "Yes?"

"Sir, this is Dan Abernathy."

Recognizing the name as the codename Omega operative Number Nineteen was currently using, Naylor sat up in bed, suddenly alert. "Go on."

"I have some bad news," Nineteen said. "Sue Lee was found dead in our hotel this evening."

Naylor thought he was hearing things. He recognized *Sue Lee* as Eight's codename. Mindful that he'd been speaking to her only a few hours earlier, he asked, "How did she die?"

"She was murdered. Strangled."

Naylor rubbed his temple as his all-too familiar headache returned. The realization that he'd been duped was starting to set in. "What was the time of death?"

"Around seven forty-five pm, Tahiti time."

That confirmed it for Naylor. He had been duped. He recalled that the telephone discussion he'd assumed had been with Eight had been around that time. He could feel his blood pressure rising. "I don't believe this!" he suddenly shouted. "I send five elite operatives to find one pregnant lady, and some slip of a woman terminates four of them!"

The hooker lying next to him cowered beneath the sheet as her client vented his fury over the phone.

The Omega director gradually calmed down. Controlling his anger, he said, "I'm sending more reinforcements. They'll be there within twenty four hours."

Naylor ended the call then speed-dialed a number. He was calling Ten, one of four operatives he'd dispatched to watch out for Nine at Nellis Air Force Base.

After a short delay, a sleepy voice came on the line. "This is Frederick Schlanger," Ten answered using his current codename.

"This is Naylor. I have new instructions for the two new arrivals."

Ten realized the Omega boss was referring to operatives Twenty-One and Six who had arrived at the base only the previous day.

"They are to leave immediately for Tahiti."

"Immediately, sir? They're sleeping right now."

"Immediately!" Naylor snapped. "Our man in Papeete needs their assistance and it's urgent. Understood?"

"Understood, sir."

"Good. Their orders and flight tickets will be awaiting them when they check in at McCarran," he said referring to Las Vegas' main international airport.

"Yessir."

Naylor ended the call then speed-dialed his PA, a renowned heavy sleeper. Resigned to having to wait for her to wake, he fumed over the latest news from Papeete. Eight's murder confirmed to his way of thinking that Seventeen wasn't working alone. He didn't believe the former operative could cause so much mayhem on her own. The more he thought about it, the more he was convinced Nine had returned to Tahiti. To his mind, that justified pulling operatives out of Nevada and sending them to Papeete.

"Hello, this is Susan," the PA finally answered.

Naylor instructed her to immediately book Business Class seats for operatives Six and Twenty-One on the first available flight to Papeete. Hanging up, he lay back and ruminated on recent events.

Since Nine had accosted him in his home, Omega's twenty-one remaining elite orphan-operatives had been reduced by over half to just ten. Naylor still couldn't quite get his head around that. For the best part of two decades, the agency's elites had proven time and again they were without peer in the murky world of espionage as they heaped success upon success in high stakes missions around the world. How two washed up former operatives could cause so much mayhem was a mystery to him – more so given one had a known heart condition and the other was until recently a verifiable nutcase.

If there was one thing Naylor was sure of, it was that his beloved agency was starting to unravel. He knew it and his fellow directors knew it. All were unhappy and there had been whispers that at least two of them were considering resigning from the board, no doubt to distance themselves from Omega.

The fear remained also that Nine had been wired when he'd broken into Naylor's home. Regardless of that, the Omega boss thought there was little doubt Nine would have downloaded the confidential files he'd accessed on his computer or, worse still, emailed them to a third party. Either way, he knew there was a very real possibility that Nine would release damaging information into the public domain – information that could sink Omega, or at the very least make life exceedingly uncomfortable for its directors.

Naylor clung to the hope that the rogue operative wouldn't risk doing that as long as Francis remained in Omega's custody.

#

Isabelle smiled joyfully as Atea handed her newborn baby to her. She couldn't believe that just three hours after going into labor, she'd given birth to a healthy, beautiful girl. Compared to Francis' traumatic birth, which had nearly cost her, her life, this birth had been very straightforward.

Sitting up in bed, Isabelle kissed her daughter's cheek. "I name you Annette Nicia Hannar," she whispered lovingly. The Frenchwoman knew Nine would approve. Their daughter had been named after Nine's mother, Annette, and after Isabelle's birthmother, Nicia.

Overcome by emotion, Isabelle began crying. Atea and her midwife helpers cried, too. Theirs were tears of joy while Isabelle's were tears of joy and sadness – sadness that her husband and son couldn't be here to enjoy the moment.

#

Seventeen just wanted to sleep. It had already gone midnight. Since terminating Eight, she had checked out of her old hotel and into a new one under a new guise. The suntanned Belgian anthropologist had evolved into a pale-skinned, freckled, red-headed New Zealand tourist. Strategic use of makeup and fake freckles had helped conceal her black eye and other bruises, and dark red lipstick had helped hide her split lip.

The former operative had spent the past two hours tending her cuts and bruises, and trying to improve on her new disguise. She was making hard work of it. The nonstop events of recent days had caught up with her. After so long removed from the world of espionage, she felt out of condition and craved sleep. However, sleep was a luxury she couldn't afford right now.

Seventeen was mindful that, if he hadn't already, Naylor would be sending more personnel to Papeete soon. She knew there was a good chance Nineteen was still alone and so there wouldn't be a better time to terminate him than right now, before the inevitable reinforcements arrived.

76

For a minute or two, Nine couldn't work out where he was when he woke. Nor could he make sense of the tubes and cords that connected him to machines and drips beside his bed.

The former operative wasn't aware he'd suffered another heart attack in his hotel room ninety minutes earlier, or that quick thinking by the hotel receptionist and the prompt, expert attention of medics had saved his life.

It wasn't until a uniformed African-American nurse entered his room that he worked out he was in a hospital. "Where am I?" he asked weakly.

"You are in the cardio ward of Spring Valley Hospital, sir."

Now it was coming back to Nine. "Did I have a heart

attack?"

"You've had an episode of some kind. The doctor will be with you shortly." The nurse hurried off – presumably to fetch the doctor.

Nine glanced at his left wrist only to see his watch had been removed. He hadn't a clue what the time was or how long he'd been here. Tiredness and an inability to focus on anything for more than a few seconds told him he'd been heavily sedated.

Another few moments passed before he remembered the reason he'd come to Las Vegas. "Francis!" He tried to sit up, but didn't have the strength, so he tried again.

The nurse chose that moment to return. She was accompanied by the duty doctor, a distinguished looking man of about sixty. The nurse hurried to restrain Nine. "Where do you think you're goin'?" she asked. She forced him gently back down onto the pillow. "You're not goin' anywhere."

Nine didn't argue. He was in no state to resist.

The patient noticed the doctor was now studying his chart at the foot of the bed. "What's the verdict, doc?"

The doctor continued reading. "One moment," he answered without looking up.

Turning to the nurse, Nine asked, "What time is it?"

The nurse consulted her watch. "It's eleven thirty. Why, you got a date?"

Before Nine could respond, the doctor walked around the bed, grabbed Nine's wrist and stood motionless as he assessed his pulse.

"You've had a heart attack, Mister..." he consulted the chart he was still holding, "Carrera."

Only then did Nine remember he was still in the guise of New Yorker Miguel Carrera. "How serious?"

"Serious enough to recommend surgery in the next forty-eight hours." Before Nine could object, the doctor added, "Until then it's complete bed rest for you." He emphasized the word *complete* to stress the importance of what he'd just said.

Nine nodded even though his immediate plans didn't remotely fit with the doctor's. The doctor excused himself, advising that a nurse would check in on him every half hour or so.

He then departed with the nurse.

As soon as the former operative was alone, he took stock of his situation. Whichever way he looked at it, he knew it didn't look good. He'd hoped to be on his way to Nellis Air Force Base by now and into the medical lab by midnight.

Commonsense told him he should at least rest up in hospital for a day or two to recover from his latest heart attack. He knew he'd be no use to Francis dead. Then flashes came to him of the disfigured children he'd seen in Omega's orphanages overseas. That decided him. *I have to get Francis tonight.* He was aware that every day's delay – every hour's delay – exposed his son to more risk.

To mentally prepare himself for what he was about to do, he quietly recited his daily affirmation.

I am a free man and a polymath.

Whatever I set my mind to, I always achieve.

The limitations that apply to the rest of humanity,

Do not apply to me.

Nine reminded himself to recite his affirmation daily. He'd

been neglecting to do that of late.

Finally, he sat up. Removing the tubes and cords from his body, he gingerly climbed out of bed and walked slowly to a wardrobe on the far side of the room. Opening its door, he was relieved to see his clothes, shoes, watch and wallet had been stored there.

Changing quickly back into his own clothes, the former operative then stepped out into the ward. He could hear two nurses talking softly in a room nearby, so he walked toward the exit at the opposite end of the ward.

Nine was heading for the nearest elevator when he noticed a sign above a door. It read: *Pharmaceutical Dispensary. No unauthorized entry.* A quick look around confirmed no-one else was present. Nine opened the door and entered the dispensary to find he had it to himself for the moment. He eventually found what he was looking for – heart pills that matched the medical name of the pills his specialist had prescribed in Papeete. Nine pocketed two small containers of the pills and quickly left, aware he could well be walking to his own death.

#

Two hours after discharging himself from hospital, Nine was poised to enter the medical lab at Nellis Air Force Base. He was still feeling weak, but a hundred per cent better compared to how he felt earlier. The sedatives he'd been given had worn off and he was mentally sharp at least.

The former operative had dispensed with his latest guise. He was content to be himself for the moment as he wanted to be instantly recognizable to Francis.

Nine had made good use of the past two hours. From the hospital, he'd returned to his room at the Paris Las Vegas and retrieved his gear, including his smart phone and the all-important architectural plans of Omega's underground lab at the Air Force base. Then he'd loaded his gear into a rental van he'd hired and had driven to a disused warehouse that backed up against the base's rear perimeter fence.

Studying the warehouse, Nine estimated it was less than twenty feet from the fence. The rusted lock on the building's backdoor proved no match for him and he quickly gained access.

Then, by the light of his pen torch, he descended a flight of stairs to the basement.

The entrance to the disused service tunnel he was looking for was exactly where mobster Al Ricca said it would be – six feet from the rear wall. It was concealed beneath a dozen planks that had been laid across an opening in the basement's concrete floor.

Nine removed the planks one at a time, and slowly so as not to overdo it. He was very aware he needed to pace himself. Even so, the effort took its toll and he had to sit down for a minute to regain his breath.

Slightly re-energized, he stood up and descended the dozen or so steps that led to the tunnel entrance. Guided by the architectural plans and drawings he'd obtained from Ricca, he began walking along the tunnel. After half a dozen steps, he noticed a red stripe painted on the tunnel ceiling. He guessed it marked the location of the base's perimeter fence above.

As he'd done before breaking into Omega's orphanage in the DRC, and in Greenland before that, he made a conscious effort to quell the excitement he could feel building in his gut. That was no easy task. This mission felt different somehow. He really believed

Francis was here.

77

The fire Seventeen started in Hotel Tiare Tahiti's unoccupied basement was safely contained in a trash can she had strategically placed below an air conditioning vent. However, the night-shift staff didn't know that when smoke billowed from a vent in the establishment's ground floor reception area. They immediately sounded the fire alarm.

Moments later, loudspeaker announcements on all five floors of the hotel advised guests to vacate their rooms and assemble on the pavement outside the front entrance as per hotel regulations. The announcements were in French, English, Japanese and Chinese.

Seventeen waited for the first twenty or so sleepy hotel guests to assemble outside before joining them. Observing their faces as she looked for Nineteen, she noted half them hadn't changed and were still in their nightwear.

The former operative had had to resort to such measures as she hadn't a clue which room Nineteen occupied. She figured this was one way to force her fellow orphan to show himself. Then she planned to terminate him.

Twenty minutes later, Seventeen still hadn't sighted her target among the hundred and eighty odd guests and staff who had assembled outside. When a senior fireman emerged from the hotel and advised the guests they were free to return to their rooms, Seventeen hovered near the entrance, looking for some sign of Nineteen.

The former operative would have been perturbed if she'd realized Nineteen had suspected the fire could be a ruse and had remained in his room on the hotel's fourth floor. When the fire alarm had sounded, he'd stepped out onto his unlit balcony and looked down at the street below. While he hadn't seen anyone he recognized, the mixed-race operative did see Seventeen's Honda Avis rental car parked in front of the hotel. He remembered seeing it earlier when he and Eight had hailed a cab. It had been in a different parking space then.

Now, from the darkness of his balcony, Nineteen kept the car under observation. He knew to look out for Seventeen as Naylor had advised him and the others that he suspected it was the blue-eyed, blonde operative who was hunting down her fellow orphans.

Nineteen didn't have long to wait. After the last of the guests had returned inside, a tall, redheaded woman approached the Honda. Nineteen didn't recognize her as she climbed into the driver's seat, but he estimated she was about Seventeen's height and age.

As the Honda drove off, Nineteen noted its registration number.

In the car, Seventeen was going through a checklist in her mind as she drove back to her hotel. She knew there could be any number of reasons why she hadn't seen Nineteen at Hotel Tiare Tahiti. *He could have chosen to ignore the fire alarm, or perhaps he checked into another hotel after Eight's murder, or his search for Isabelle has taken him out of town. Or he could have been disguised as someone else and I didn't recognize him!* It was the last possibility that worried her the most. She reflexively checked her rear vision mirror.

#

Fifteen minutes after setting off along the tunnel leading into Nellis Air Force Base, Nine had lost count of the number of twists and turns he'd taken. It was a maze of pipes and tunnels. The former operative had also lost all sense of direction and if it wasn't for the detailed plans he consulted every minute or two, he feared he could become permanently lost.

Nine was aware the base was supposedly connected to, or even part of, the fabled *Area 51*. Like most other Americans, he'd heard the rumors surrounding Area 51 – such as its anti-gravity machines and other suppressed technologies and inventions. He had no idea whether there was any truth in the rumors. Whether the US Government secretly worked in collaboration with extraterrestrial civilizations was of no concern to him anyway. All he cared about was finding his son.

Finally, he saw lights ahead. Nine doused his pen torch and

hurried toward them.

The last tunnel he'd entered delivered him to the rear of a storeroom. Shelving along three of its walls was lined with jars. Closer inspection revealed the jars were filled with human fetuses. Viewing windows in the far wall opened out into a laboratory and that was where the lights were coming from.

Nine walked quietly over to the window and saw two white-coated lab technicians cleaning medical equipment, emptying test-tubes and performing other night-shift duties. Bypassing the lab, Nine walked down a long corridor leading to still more labs. Along the way he came to a familiar sign. It was identical to the signs he'd seen at Omega's other labs, and it read: *Children's Sleeping Quarters. Authorized personnel only.*

Following the arrow, he opened the first door he came to and saw it accommodated a dozen or so sleeping children. They slept in bunks that were two high. Nine was just tall enough to view the children sleeping in the top bunks.

Using his pen torch, he checked each child and quickly ascertained Francis was not among them. Even so, the faces were disturbingly familiar. He'd seen children almost identical to these in Omega's other secret labs. Many of them featured the same range of deformities and signs of medical experimentation.

The next two dormitory-style rooms revealed more children for the same result. Then in the next dormitory, Nine was in for a shock.

This dorm was occupied by a dozen teenage boys. Checking the first boy – a Polynesian – the former operative noticed a photo pinned to the wall just above the boy's head. It was a photo of Thirteen, one of the operatives he'd encountered in the lab in the DRC. Thirteen looked about eighteen years old in the photo.

Shining his torch on the sleeping teenager's face, Nine felt as though Thirteen had been reincarnated. The boy was the spitting image of the now deceased operative.

On the wall beside the next boy was a photo of Fourteen, the Nordic-looking operative Nine had shot in the lab at Thule Air Base. The boy asleep next to the photo was a Fourteen-lookalike. *So, Omega's cloning of us original orphans continues!* Nine knew he was witnessing the handiwork of Naylor, Doc Andrews and others inside Omega.

As Nine came to the next bunk, the teenager woke. The boy sat up with a start and looked straight at him. Nine thought he was looking in a mirror. *It's me!* The teen's startling green eyes stared into the blinding torchlight as if trying to make sense of it. A shock of long, dark hair framed a pale face. Nine felt as though he'd gone back in time.

Sure enough, on the wall next to the boy, was a photo of Nine. He remembered when and where it was taken, and who took it. His mentor Tommy Kentbridge had taken it at the orphanage on Nine's sixteenth birthday.

"Who are you?" the sleepy teenager asked.

"I'm no-one of interest," Nine said. He pulled out a photo of Francis and showed it to his teenage lookalike. "Have you seen this boy?" He made sure his face remained in shadow so as not to alarm the teen.

The teenager nodded and pointed to a door. "You could try the next dorm."

"Thanks." Nine walked to the door, leaving the puzzled teen

to go back to sleep.

Opening the door, his eyes were drawn to a dark-haired boy asleep on a lower bunk not six paces away. Nine hurried to him. He shook the child gently. The boy turned to him. "Francis!" Nine whispered. He felt his heart leap – in a good way this time.

"Papa?" Francis looked wide-eyed at the shadowy figure behind the torch.

"Yes it's me, son." Nine grabbed his son and hugged him tight.

"Is Mama with you?"

"No, but I'm going to take you to her." Nine held Francis out at arm's length and inspected his face. Apart from looking stressed and a little drawn, he appeared to be in good health.

The first Nine knew he was in trouble was when he felt the cold, steel barrel of a pistol pressed against the back of his head.

"Hello Nine," the man holding the pistol said. "They warned me you may show up here."

Nine recognized the voice. It belonged to his fellow orphan, Ten.

Noting the alarm on Francis' face, Nine said, "Don't worry, son. Everything will be alright." He cursed that he'd been so intent on finding Francis he hadn't remained alert.

Someone behind Ten turned the dorm's light on, revealing yet another familiar face. It was the first-born orphan, One, a huge Native-American the other orphans had always referred to as *Numero Uno*. He, too, held a pistol. The biggest of the orphan-operatives at six foot six, he had a deserved reputation for being a good friend and a bad enemy.

Numero Uno and Nine had also once been friends, but no more. Looking into the big operative's eyes – and into Ten's – Nine could see no sign of friendship. Nor could he see any recollection that they'd ever been friends.

The realization hit him that they were in a mind-controlled state, just as their colleagues in Greenland and the DRC had been, and just as Seventeen had been until recently. He knew then that he could expect no favors from them. And, for the first time since setting out to find his son, he could taste defeat. It tasted bitter.

78

Nineteen had been driving around Papeete's hotels, motels and guesthouses looking for Seventeen's rental car ever since he had sighted it outside his hotel after the hoax fire alarm. He was about to give up and go back to bed when he saw it. The car was parked outside a modest hotel several streets back from the waterfront, and its registration number tallied with the number he'd written down.

The mixed-race operative parked his vehicle around the corner, checked to ensure his pistol was loaded then made his way on foot to the hotel. Posing as an undercover gendarme, he entered the hotel and flashed a fake identity card at the night-duty receptionist. Speaking fluent French, he said, "Mademoiselle, I am looking for the driver of a Honda Avis rental car parked outside your hotel." He recited from memory the car's registration number.

The receptionist, a teenage girl who looked to be asleep on her feet, consulted the hotel's guest book. Yawning, she confirmed the car was being driven by New Zealand tourist Shelley Bycroft who was staying in room 101.

Nineteen requested and received a spare key for that room. He thanked the receptionist and headed for the stairs.

In room 101, Seventeen was having trouble sleeping. What little sleep she'd managed to get had been disrupted by nightmares. She kept seeing the faces of Eight and the other Omega operatives she'd killed.

Terminating her fellow orphans had affected her more than she initially realized. Killing was different to how she remembered. Previously, as a working operative, she'd killed without compunction, and she'd been good at it. But this was different.

Even though she'd never formed friendships with her fellow orphans – and in fact had been the least popular of any of them – she found terminating them akin to murdering her brothers and sisters, and it was starting to take its toll.

Seventeen climbed out of bed to make a cup of coffee when she heard a floorboard creak outside her door. A glance at the door confirmed someone was there. A motionless shadow could be seen in the narrow gap between the carpet and the bottom of the door.

Retrieving her car keys, cell phone and loaded pistol from a bedside table, Seventeen quickly slipped into a T-shirt and a pair of shorts. She then placed two pillows end to end on the bed and pulled the top sheet over them. Satisfied they could pass for a sleeping person, she then hid behind curtains that separated the room from an outside balcony.

Seventeen didn't have long to wait. The telltale *click* of the door lock signaled that the intruder had unlocked the door. Peering through a tiny gap in the curtains, Seventeen recognized Nineteen as soon as he crept into the room. The sight of him sent a cold shiver up her spine. The man frightened her. He reminded her of a tall, foreboding undertaker or hangman – someone well versed in the ways of death.

Nineteen tip-toed to the bed, reached out and prepared to pull back the top sheet. At the same time, a slight gust of wind outside caused the curtains Seventeen was hiding behind to flutter, attracting the operative's attention.

Two gunshots rang out simultaneously. Seventeen's shot caught Nineteen in the right shoulder, causing him to drop his pistol; his shot caught Seventeen in the collarbone, shattering it; the impact of the bullets dropped both operatives to the floor.

Despite the severity of her wound, Seventeen was able to climb over the balcony rail and clamber one-armed down a fixed fire-escape to the ground. She was already halfway to her car before Nineteen had retrieved his pistol and made it out onto the balcony. He managed to squeeze off two hurried shots before Seventeen jumped into the relative safety of her car, started the motor and sped away.

Nineteen hurried from the room, descended the stairs five steps at a time and ran to his vehicle. He planned to give chase and finish off the former operative once and for all.

One block away, Seventeen knew she was on borrowed time. She was badly wounded, bleeding heavily and close to losing consciousness. The former operative also knew she couldn't outrun anyone in her little four-cylinder Honda. Not for the first time, she wondered why she'd rented such a gutless vehicle. *So much for wanting to remain inconspicuous.*

One block later, she spotted a car parking building. Checking her rear vision mirror to ensure there were no cars following her, she switched off her lights then drove through the building's entrance and continued up to the third level. There, she parked the Honda between two other cars, turned off the ignition and waited with baited breath.

Five minutes passed. After ten minutes, Seventeen knew – or hoped – she was in the clear.

Since entering the building, she'd been considering her options. They were exceedingly slim. Still bleeding and lapsing in and out of consciousness, she knew she needed help, and she needed it fast. She retrieved her cell phone and speed-dialed the number for Chai, Nine's Thai friend. "C'mon, Chai! Wake up."

Finally, the young Thai answered. "Jennifer?" Even half asleep, he'd recognized Seventeen's phone number.

"Chai, I need your help!" Seventeen managed to tell him where she was before losing consciousness.

#

Isabelle lay on her side in bed, staring at baby Annette who was asleep in a bassinette next to her. Moonlight flooded in through the open door and window, casting shadows on Annette's angelic features.

Tired as she was, Isabelle hadn't been able to sleep since giving birth. Nor had she let Annette out of her sight.

As always, her thoughts turned to Nine and Francis. How she wished they were here to share in her joy.

Thinking of her boys tempted her to phone Nine. In the excitement, she'd forgotten there was no cell phone coverage in this remote part of Tahiti. Rolling off the bed, she walked to a cupboard and retrieved her cell phone. Before speed-dialing Nine's number, his words came back to her. *Don't phone me under any circumstances. They will be monitoring our calls.* Putting that out of her mind, she punched in his number.

The *No Signal* notice came up instantly on her phone,

reminding her there was no coverage. Disappointed, she returned the phone to her cupboard and wandered outside. The night air refreshed her. The Frenchwoman marveled at how her body had changed since giving birth. Beforehand, she'd found the nights hot and unbearable. Now they were bearable at least.

Isabelle wondered yet again if Nine had found Francis, and if so when she would see them again. She'd heard nothing from Seventeen and the waiting was becoming unbearable.

79

Nine's fellow orphans looked on as a uniformed security man tied the former operative to a chair in an office that served as their temporary headquarters while they were based at Nellis. When he'd finished, the security man looked at Ten who dismissed him with a curt nod.

Ten and One weren't taking any chances. After apprehending Nine, they'd clapped a set of handcuffs on him and pulled a hospital restraint jacket over his shoulders. Though under the influence of MK-Ultra, they remembered how resourceful and determined their former colleague was.

Tight restraints weren't Nine's only problem. The heartburn he'd experienced just before his latest heart attack had returned with a vengeance. He desperately needed to swallow a couple of the heart pills he'd brought with him, but they were in his pocket and he couldn't access them. Realizing it would be pointless asking his former colleagues for their help, he gritted his teeth, determined to ride out the pain.

Now alone, the three orphans just looked at each other. This was a new experience for all of them. Once as close as brothers, they hadn't shared each other's company for a decade or more.

Observing his surroundings, Nine noticed his backpack was now lying against the wall. He thought of the smart phone inside it and wished he had sent the two emails stored in its memory banks when he'd had the chance. *Wrong decision.* He'd debated whether to send them as soon as he'd found Francis, but had decided to delay for some reason that seemed unimportant now.

It was Ten who chose to break the ice first. "Why did you turn your back on us, Nine?"

"By *us* I assume you mean Omega?" Nine asked.

"You know damn well who he means!" One grumbled. "He means us. Your brothers."

"I got tired of being ruled by others," Nine said. "By people who couldn't care less about any one of us."

"Those people you referred to gave us life and nurtured us," Ten said reproachfully.

"They nurtured us for their own ends," Nine responded. "Those ends being to further their own New World Order agenda and to line their own pockets."

Ten and One looked at each other and raised their eyes to the ceiling as if to say they were dealing with someone who had lost the plot.

Assessing the operatives, Nine considered them as nothing more than strangers compared to the two orphans he'd been raised with. Ten, who had been his closest friend, had always joked around and pulled pranks, while One had never been slow to join in the fun – not that there was ever a lot of fun at the Pedemont Orphanage. Now, thanks to MK-Ultra, the pair were all business and seemed to have no recollection of their earlier friendship.

Looking at his former colleagues, Nine asked, "What happens now?"

"Now we wait," One said. "The boss is phoning back with

instructions."

Nine guessed *the boss* he referred to was Naylor, and he had no doubt what his instructions would be. The former operative considered it was time to level the playing field a little. *I need to split these two up*. He looked up at them. "You don't think I came here alone do you?"

One chuckled. "You always work alone, Nine."

"I used to. No more, though. I'm too old to be the lone wolf."

One and Ten glanced at each other. Then they looked back at Nine, trying to establish whether he was telling the truth.

Nine stared at them poker-faced. In the ensuing silence, a plan was starting to form in his mind.

Ten turned back to his associate. "I better go look around just in case this fool isn't joking."

"No, you stay here," the big Native-American said. "I'll do it. I need to stretch my legs anyway." With that, One left the room intent on conducting a search of the premises.

Now alone with his former best friend, Nine wasn't about to delay putting his plan into motion. He began talking about the old days at the orphanage when the two of them used to kick around together, getting up to all sorts of mischief. In the course of the one-way conversation, he cautiously dropped in the odd word from among the code words used to induce mind-control under MK-Ultra. "Do you remember that time *Mercury* that we raided that orchard across the road from the orphanage, *Venus*?" he asked, emphasizing the planet names.

Ten didn't appear to notice anything strange about Nine's question. He just shook his head disinterestedly.

Nine continued, "I still chuckle *Earth* when I remember how you *Mars* gave that orchardist such a fright he fell into that trough *Jupiter*."

Ten still showed no indication that Nine was speaking oddly. Nor did it appear that he had any recollection of childhood events.

Nine grew bolder, dropping the names of more names planets into his conversation. "Then there was the time *Saturn* and *Uranus* hid *Neptune's Pluto* in the *Mercury* garden and then found it in time for *Venus*."

Now Ten showed a spark of interest. The glazed-over look in

his eyes was fading as his one-time friend continued to reminisce aloud.

While Nine was aware the planetary names were the voice-prompts that Omega used to induce mind-control in its operatives, he was also aware prolonged repetition of those same prompts had the opposite effect. After all, that was the technique his FBI friend had employed to help him and, more recently, Seventeen, to diffuse the voice-prompts. It had also saved his life when he'd clashed with Three in the forest in Greenland.

By now, Nine's heartburn had subsided and he was able to concentrate on reciting the planets' names over and over. "Mercury, Venus, Earth, Mars, Jupiter, Saturn, Uranus, Neptune, Pluto."

Mindful that One could return at any moment, Nine gambled that he'd done enough to bring Ten out of his mind-controlled state. He then reminded his old friend of an incident he personally would never forget. "Remember that time you nearly drowned in the Little Calumet?"

Now emerging from the influence of MK-Ultra, Ten recalled

the incident his fellow orphan referred to. He and Nine had snuck away from the orphanage for a swim in the nearby Little Calumet River. It had been a hot summer's day and he'd nearly drowned when he was struck by cramp. Only Nine's intervention had saved him. "I remember," he murmured.

Nine could see he was getting through to his opposite. He kept talking, reminding Ten of fleeting happy moments – in amongst the many unhappy moments – they'd shared together as boys. As he talked, he could almost see Ten's mind racing as he pieced together fragments of his forgotten past.

Ten slowly joined in the discussion, adding his own thoughts and memories. His whole demeanour had softened. He was fast becoming the friend that Nine remembered.

Out of the blue, Nine asked, "Ten, will you help me rescue my son?"

Before Ten could reply, the door opened and One reappeared, dashing Nine's hopes of recruiting his old friend as an ally.

"As we suspected," One said, "he came alone."

"No surprises there," Ten said.

Nine observed that Ten appeared to have reverted to his former cold self. He wondered if the operative had slipped back into his mind-controlled state. Nine didn't have long to wait before that question was answered.

80

Ten pointed to a file on a desk just behind One. "Pass that file to me will you, Numero Uno?"

As One turned to pick up the file, Ten reversed his grip on the pistol he was still holding and whacked his fellow operative over the head with it. The blow felled the big fella. Even though it had been a solid blow, it hadn't knocked him out. The second blow did, however.

Ten quickly checked One's pulse to ensure he was still alive. He was.

"He always was a tough one," Nine observed.

"Yep," Ten grinned. "What now?"

"Get me out of these restraints and put them on Numero Uno."

Working quickly, Ten removed the bindings from around Nine and un-cuffed him. Then, as Nine had suggested, he slipped the hospital restraint jacket over One and cuffed him to a protruding pipe. As One began to come round, Ten gagged him using a spare tea-towel.

"Can we leave him here?" Nine asked.

Ten nodded. "We are the only ones who use this room, and I have the only key." Ignoring One, who was now glaring at him, Ten added, "I doubt anyone will have any reason to come looking for him for several hours."

As Ten double-checked One's restraints, Nine retrieved his container of pills from his pocket and popped two of them for good measure. His heartburn had subsided, but he didn't want a repeat of it. Then he retrieved his smart phone from his backpack and immediately accessed the emails he'd filed in it. Before sending them, he looked at Ten. "I have something I have to do. Can you get my son?"

"Sure thing."

Ten hurried from the office, leaving Nine alone with the

trussed up Native-American operative.

Sitting down at the nearby table, the former operative opened the first of his carefully formulated emails. It was addressed to US intelligence and law enforcement agencies, high profile politicians and international media. The latter category included Reuters and other news agencies, CNN and other major television networks, Time Magazine and similar publications, major daily newspapers throughout America as well as smaller, independently-owned media outlets with no links to the mainstream news agencies.

Intelligence agencies on the list included the FBI and NSA, but not the CIA who worked hand-in-glove with Omega as Nine knew only too well. *They'll find out soon enough*. Politicians on the list included the Vice President and Governors of selected states.

The email, which would be accompanied by the two confidential files that Nine had downloaded from Naylor's computer, also contained examples of Omega's activities going back twenty years. It catalogued contract killings and other criminal business practices complete with names, dates, places and times. The names included all Omega's orphan-operatives and, most damningly, all the directors on the agency's board.

Skimming the email one last time, Nine clicked *Send*. Watching it go gave him great pleasure. The former operative then posted the explosive information on various social networks including Facebook and Twitter. He was confident it would soon go viral.

Ignoring the impotent glares Numero Uno continued to direct his way, Nine then opened the second email. An exact copy of the first, it was for his European attorneys and contained new instructions for them. Those instructions included a directive to immediately forward the email to appropriate agencies, media and politicians throughout Europe.

After skimming this email, he clicked *Send*. As soon as the *Message Sent* notice appeared, Nine felt he could relax slightly. *Let the games begin*. He was aware the emails and their damning attachments would put the Omega Agency in the public spotlight for the first time in its history. They would also ensure Naylor and his fellow directors would be put to the proverbial blowtorch.

The former operative's motivation for sending the emails was to put Omega into a state of disarray and give his former masters more to worry about than trying to stop him finding Francis. He hoped that with an ounce of luck it would be smooth sailing from here on – for Francis and himself, and for Isabelle and Seventeen.

Nine had been so involved with rescuing his son, he hadn't thought about his wife in a while. He suddenly felt guilty and wondered whether the baby had arrived yet.

The former operative's thoughts were disrupted when Ten returned holding Francis.

"Papa!" Francis beamed.

Nine took his son from the operative and hugged him tight for the second time that night. "Hello, boy." The happy father found it hard to contain himself. He felt like dancing around the room and laughing with joy.

"I knew you'd find me," Francis said.

Nine couldn't help himself: the floodgates opened, and he cried as he'd never cried before.

An anxious Ten placed a hand on his friend's shoulder. "We need to get outta here."

Nine pulled himself together. He looked intently at his fellow orphan. "You sure you want to do this?"

Ten grinned. "It's too late to back out now, isn't it?" He looked pointedly at his trussed-up colleague.

"I dunno what to say, bud."

"Don't say anything. Just get me and the boy outta here." As an afterthought Ten added, "I assume you know how to do that?"

Nine winked at him knowingly then turned back to Francis and kissed his cheek. "I need you to be very quiet for me. Can you do that, son?"

Wide-eyed and no longer sleepy, Francis nodded.

"Good boy." Nine turned to Ten. "Let's go." Still holding Francis, he picked up his backpack and hurried from the office. He didn't even spare One a glance as he departed. In the corridor outside, he dropped his smart phone into a wastepaper bin – a precaution against Omega finding him as a result of tracing the emails he'd just sent from the phone.

Ten followed. Before closing the door behind him, he looked back at the big Native-American. "Don't go anywhere, Numero Uno," Ten said. The last sight he had of One was him glaring at him as the door closed. Ten locked the door after him and hurried after Nine.

81

Members of the same Thai family who had sheltered Isabelle and Seventeen previously were now anxiously gathered around Seventeen as their family doctor, also a Thai, probed the former operative's flesh with a scalpel. He was looking for the bullet that had smashed her collarbone.

While the wound wasn't life-threatening, it was messy and Seventeen was bleeding quite heavily. The operation was being performed under local anaesthetic, so the patient was fully aware of what was happening.

Seventeen knew she was lucky to be alive. Nineteen had come close to killing her in her hotel room, and how she'd subsequently evaded him in her little Honda rental car she wasn't quite sure.

After phoning Chai from the car parking building just before she'd passed out, the Thai had arrived within the hour and transferred her, unobserved, into the back of his Land Rover. From there, he'd driven Seventeen straight to the family commune where the doctor, an elderly man who reminded her of Confucius, was already waiting for her.

The doctor gave a little exclamation as he found the bullet. Clasping it with a pair of tweezers, he withdrew it and held it up triumphantly for all to see. Chai and other family members nodded in appreciation of the doctor's skill. They and the doctor then conferred, speaking their native tongue in hushed tones.

"What is it?" Seventeen asked.

Chai approached her. "The doctor says your collarbone has been splintered. He wants us to get you to the hospital."

"No hospital, Chai," Seventeen said firmly.

Chai nodded. He seemed perplexed – frightened even – but didn't say what was bothering him.

Seventeen guessed what was on the young man's mind.

While she was at the commune, she was putting Chai's family at risk. They were all very aware there were people in Tahiti who wanted her dead and who wouldn't rest until she was. Anyone found giving her shelter was putting themselves in obvious danger. Seventeen reached out to Chai. "Can you take me to Isabelle's village?"

Chai's face immediately lit up. He liked the sound of that. "Yes," he said.

"Good. We can leave now if you like."

"Are you sure?" He wasn't certain Seventeen should be moved so soon after being operated on.

"Well, as soon as the good doctor here has stitched me up."

Chai quickly conferred with the doctor again. The doctor nodded and immediately began stitching his patient's wound.

#

In CNN's Los Angeles newsroom, cadet journalist Randy Jenkins was racing to finish typing a local news story before his shift ended. It was his last stint working nights and he was looking forward to resuming normal daytime shifts.

This particular shift had been busier than usual as the duty editor was away and Randy was having to check his superior's incoming emails from time to time, to ensure nothing newsworthy slipped through the cracks.

The familiar *ding* from the duty editor's computer in an adjoining office alerted the young journo to the arrival of yet another email. Annoyed at the latest disruption, he walked next door to check it.

Randy had to read the email twice before it dawned on him it was no ordinary news story. While he'd never heard of the email's sender, one Sebastian Hannar, the cadet could tell he was looking at a potentially explosive scoop.

Senior journalist Darren Henderson chose that moment to check on Randy. The deputy editor had asked Henderson to keep an eye on the lad, so he made a point of looking in on him every half hour or so. "Everything okay?" he asked.

"You better look at this," Randy said.

Picking up on the excitement in the young man's voice, Henderson looked over Randy's shoulder at the email. He did a double take as he digested the email's opening paragraph. "What the hell?"

"My sentiments exactly," Randy said.

Henderson pushed the young cadet aside and studied the email's contents. By the time he opened the first of the two attachments, he was shaking with excitement.

Similar scenes were being played out at that very moment in newsrooms, intelligence and law enforcement agencies, private offices and even in a few private residences around the world.

#

At CIA headquarters in Langley, Virginia, the firm's Director Marcia Wilson was reading the same email. It had been forwarded to her by an FBI mole her agents were cultivating. She, too, was shaking. But it wasn't because she was excited. Marcia was horrified, frightened and alarmed all at the same time.

#

In the White House Oval Office, in Washington D.C., the President received an urgent phone call from his Vice President. Not trusting the fact he'd called over the secure line, and fearful others could be listening, the Vice President simply said, "Omega is about to go into receivership."

The President knew immediately what his Vice President was talking about. The coded phrase he'd used meant that Omega's cover was blown and they were finished.

82

Naylor was dictating correspondence to his PA in his office at Omega's HQ when his phone rang. His PA answered it. The caller was one of the agency's directors, Scott Henderson, a New York-based publishing mogul.

The PA handed the phone to her boss. "It's Scott Henderson, for you."

Naylor took the phone. "Hello Scott."

"We need to talk privately," Henderson said.

Naylor waved one hand dismissively at his PA and she quickly left the room. "What's up?" He flicked a switch so that Henderson was on speakerphone.

"I take it you haven't heard the news?"

"What news?'

"Turn on CNN. Now."

Naylor didn't like Henderson's tone. He had a foreboding feeling as he pressed the TV remote on his desktop. The wall-mounted television screen flickered to life and the Omega boss watched as a female reporter delivered a news report live to camera.

"Repeating this breaking news," the reporter said, "allegations have been made that a secret American organization believed to be a major player in the New World Order is behind a raft of criminal activities spanning the past 30 years."

Naylor sat bolt upright in his chair. He suddenly felt dizzy and close to collapse.

The reporter continued, "The organization named at the center of the allegations is the Omega Agency whose headquarters are said to be in a subterranean facility in the state of Illinois. The allegations have been made by a Sebastian Hannar, who claims he is a former employee of the agency. If proven to be correct, the allegations could prove disastrous for the current Administration."

Naylor watched and listened in stunned silence. He could

feel another headache coming on and his lazy eye was starting to twitch uncontrollably. His worst nightmare was coming true.

"Mister Hannar has provided information to CNN that would seem to support his allegations," the reporter continued. "CNN's lawyers are investigating the legal ramifications of releasing details of the allegations. Until their findings are in, we are limited in what we can say. However, we can say the most concerning of the allegations are to do with clandestine Omega Agency-run medical laboratories. Mister Hannar alleges these facilitate unsanctioned scientific experiments on children who are either orphans or who have been forcibly removed from their natural parents. We understand law enforcement officials are en route to the laboratories named to investigate these particular allegations now."

"Are you watching this?" Henderson asked.

Naylor was so transfixed and engrossed by what was unfolding on screen he'd forgotten his fellow director was on the other end of the line. In their separate offices, they watched as photos of themselves and the other Omega directors appeared on screen. The reporter named the directors, giving prominence to

Naylor and fellow director Marcia Wilson.

"Andrew Naylor, said to be one of the original founding members of the agency, has been named as chairman of Omega's board, while fellow director Marcia Wilson is none other than the current Director of the CIA," the reporter said. "Omega's whistle-blower claims Miss Wilson's involvement with the secret organization represents a conflict of interest that threatens the very security of the United States."

Naylor had seen and heard enough. He switched his television set off and tried to marshal his thoughts.

"What the hell are we going to do, Andrew?" Henderson asked.

Naylor couldn't think straight. This was a worst case scenario and, truth be known, he hadn't planned for it because he never believed it would come to this. Now that it had, he could feel himself slipping into panic mode.

"Andrew?"

Pulling himself together, Naylor said, "Stay by your phone. I'm going to organize a conference call right now. It's imperative we are all on the same page when the media vultures descend on us." The Omega boss ended the call then began massaging his temple. His headache was becoming intolerable.

Naylor pressed a buzzer beneath his desk. A moment later, his PA looked in.

"You called, sir?"

"Organize an immediate conference call involving all the directors. No exceptions. Tell them it's urgent."

"Yes sir." The PA hurried to do Naylor's bidding. She could tell by the look on his face he wasn't exaggerating when he said it was urgent. Something was up. Something big.

83

Following the same underground route and consulting the same plans he'd used to access the lab at the Air Force base, Nine had reached the disused warehouse outside the base's perimeter fence in less than fifteen minutes. The return journey had been incident-free except five minutes into it Nine had to ask Ten to carry Francis as the boy was becoming too heavy for him. Ten saw that something was ailing his friend, but hadn't said anything.

Dawn was breaking as they emerged from the tunnel into the disused warehouse. Nine cautiously led the way to the rental van he'd left parked outside. Opening its rear door, he looked at Francis. "Can you be a good boy and lie down on the seat?" He didn't want anyone seeing his son in case the word was already out that Francis had been taken from the lab.

Francis, still wide awake, nodded. He was starting to enjoy this new adventure with his hero.

The former operative lay Francis down on the rear seat. "Good boy." He turned back to Ten. "I'm sorry I had to get you involved in this."

"Listen, old friend," Ten said sincerely. "You opened my eyes back there. I don't know what I was thinking." It was clear he didn't have a clue he'd been in a mind-controlled state, and Nine didn't have time to explain it to him. "Anyways, I'd rather die a free man than live like a robot."

"My thoughts exactly," Nine grinned. Then he grew serious. "Listen, we have to part company here. I will--"

"You don't have to explain," Ten interjected. "I'm already ahead of you." The operative knew exactly why Nine was suggesting they split. He tapped his right forearm, indicating he hadn't forgotten the miniature microchip embedded in it. Like Nine, he was very aware he could be tracked at any time by his Omega masters. "I'll get it removed first thing."

"Make that a priority. They'll be looking for you as soon as they know you've bailed."

Ten nodded. He understood. By his reckoning he had a couple of hours before anyone would notice he or Francis had gone missing. The big danger was someone could find One in the meantime, but there was nothing he could do about that. Either way, he knew he had to act fast.

"Where will you go?" a concerned Nine asked.

"To the first medical clinic I find open in Vegas."

"Okay, I'll give you a lift into town then we really must separate."

"Sounds good."

The two jumped into the van and drove back toward Las Vegas. Much as Nine felt grateful to his friend, he couldn't wait to part company because of the danger Ten's microchip presented to himself and to his son. He knew someone at Omega could be watching Ten's movements at that very moment on a computer screen. And if for any reason they were suspicious, they could arrange for the operative to be apprehended, or worse, by someone on the ground in Las Vegas in no time at all.

As if reading Nine's mind, Ten pointed to cab parked in a cab rank up ahead. "Drop me there."

"You sure?"

"Yup."

Nine pulled up opposite the cab rank and held his right hand out to Ten. "I'll never forget what you've done for us."

"Me either," Ten grinned.

"As soon as you've attended to that microchip, get off the grid and stay off it. Got that?"

"Got it."

"That means no credit cards, no phone calls, no contact with anyone you know."

"Yes mother."

"And never be yourself again. Get into disguise and stay in disguise."

"Don't you have somewhere you should be?" Ten grinned mischievously at Nine then turned around and winked at Francis. Jumping out of the van, he slammed the door shut, banged the side of the van twice with the palm of his hand then waved Nine on his way.

As Nine resumed driving toward downtown Las Vegas, he observed his friend in the rear vision mirror and silently wished him well. At that moment, Ten was where he had been five years earlier when he'd fled Omega and gotten off the grid.

The distant howl of sirens reached Nine through the van's open window. It came from the direction of Nellis Air Force Base. No sooner had he heard it than more sirens shattered the early morning calm. Seconds later, three police cars sped past, sirens howling and lights flashing. They were heading toward the base. *And so it begins*. Nine guessed his emails had already set new events in motion.

Moments later a CBS News van sped past. It was also heading toward the base, leaving Nine in no doubt his emails were behind the sudden activity.

84

The Omega Agency's board was in disarray. That much was obvious even before the urgent conference call Naylor had requested got underway. Marcia Wilson had resigned from the board as soon as the media storm broke; Naylor's longsuffering PA tasked with organizing the call advised her anxious boss that two other directors had gone to ground and couldn't be contacted, another had ended up in hospital with chest pains and yet another – founding member Bill Sterling – had committed suicide.

Marcia's resignation wasn't unexpected. In her capacity as Director of the CIA, her involvement with Omega had become untenable since she and the agency had so publicly been linked. There was already widespread speculation that she would soon be relieved of her post at the CIA and may face criminal charges. Similar rumors and speculation swirled about Naylor and, indeed, around all Omega's directors.

When the conference call finally got underway, pandemonium ruled with the directors all talking over each other and demanding answers. The one question they were all asking was: *How could this happen?*

Naylor took it upon himself to restore order by shouting over his fellow directors and demanding silence. When he finally had their attention, he summarized the current situation as succinctly as he could. Naylor didn't attempt to guild the lily. He knew they were caught up in the worst situation possible, but now was not the time to panic. The Omega boss insisted his fellow directors remain professional to the end and look to limit the damage.

"Andrew is right," founding member Fletcher Von Pein said. "None of us are going to come out of this looking good. It's all about damage control now."

"I agree," Lincoln Claver said.

"Yes," Scott Henderson added. "If we don't sing from the

same song sheet the media will crucify us."

"I think that ship may have sailed already," Von Pein groaned. "The public will demand scapegoats and the media will be happy to oblige."

A gloomy silence descended as the directors considered Von Pein's prediction.

Naylor chose that moment to re-enter the discussion. "Alright people, here's how it is." Omega's chairman launched into a twenty-minute monologue, summarizing the limited options the board had and suggesting what needed to happen to ensure that the directors could survive the maelstrom that was most assuredly coming their way.

In that twenty minutes, Naylor demonstrated why he was chairman of the board. He also gave his fellow directors hope – hope that they could survive, or avoid going to jail at least.

Naylor advised that a restructuring of Omega's no-longer-secret medical laboratories was already underway. That was the first instruction he'd given. He said the children and other experimental subjects of those labs were already being quietly transferred to foster families whose cooperation had been ensured through the longstanding payment of a generous annual retainer.

That news was greeted by a collective sigh of relief from everyone listening.

To their relief, the directors also learned that a revamp of the agency's headquarters was underway. Omega's personnel – from the most senior manager to the most junior clerk – had their cover stories in place after having been fully briefed by Naylor, and the agency's IT specialists were in the process of destroying incriminating electronic files. Fortunately, Omega was a paperless organization, so there was no physical paper trail of any of its activities – good, bad or otherwise.

High on the list of urgent proposals Naylor put to the board was that Omega's remaining operatives be terminated immediately. He said he considered them loose canons who knew too much. "One talkative operative could be the straw that broke the camel's back."

When his fellow directors reacted favourably to that proposal, he then explained how the operatives' deaths could be expedited quickly and efficiently without risk of any comeback.

"What about Nine and Seventeen?" Claver asked.

"I think it's patently obvious," Naylor said with more than a hint of condescension in his voice. "They represent the biggest risk of all. Especially Nine."

"But the media spotlight will be on them as soon as they surface," Claver complained.

"He's right," Von Pein said. "We can't risk doing anything that could link us to them."

"I realize that!" Naylor snapped. "Our Ukrainian friends are already working on a solution."

Naylor's fellow directors knew that he referred to members of the Ukrainian Mafia he'd been using on occasion to provide solutions for problems Omega's fully stretched operatives couldn't handle. The *problems* usually involved the assassination or removal of a target. As always, Naylor had contacted the Ukrainians via a middleman, a Berlin-based Russian diplomat, so there was no direct link between them and Omega.

"And what about the boy?" young Scott Henderson asked,

referring to Francis.

"He's of no interest to us now," Naylor said grimly. The Omega boss tried not to think of the lost opportunities – and lost megabucks – that Francis represented. He'd had high hopes the scientific testing planned for the boy would have fast-tracked Omega's cloning program. Now those dreams had turned to dust. The silence that followed confirmed to Naylor his fellow directors basically agreed with everything he'd said so far. "Now gentlemen, any questions?"

Everyone spoke at once, barraging the chairman with questions.

It was young Henderson who asked what was uppermost in the minds of all. "What do we say when the media get hold of us?"

Those board members who hadn't yet been pestered by reporters knew that was unlikely to last given the intense media scrutiny Omega was now coming under, not to mention the fact they'd been named in Nine's emails.

Naylor sympathized with their concerns. He and Marcia had already been hounded by the press even though the story had only broken a couple of hours earlier. "It's imperative you don't speak to the media," he cautioned. "You say you are not at liberty to comment because the agency's chairman is handling all media enquiries at this point."

"Which begs the question," Von Pein interjected, "what will you say to the media?"

"I'm still trying to work that one out," Naylor said honestly. "Stay on the line if you would when we finish up here. I want to run a few things past you."

"Sure thing."

"Anything else?" Naylor asked.

There were no further questions for the moment. The chairman of the board had summarized the situation well, highlighting the immediate priorities and spelling out how Omega as an organization, and the directors as individuals, could best limit the storm that was surely coming their way.

85

As the conference call Naylor had ordered came to an end, and as Nine and Francis made good their escape from Nellis Air Force Base, Seventeen was being helped out of Chai's Land Rover by members of Isabelle's adopted Tahitian family at Pomareville, in the middle of Tahiti.

Seventeen had survived two uncomfortable hours in the back of the vehicle as Chai had driven along one of the roughest roads on the island to reach their destination. The local anaesthetic the doctor had given her before removing the bullet from her collarbone had worn off early in the journey, causing the former operative considerable pain.

Now, as Manoa and other strapping members of the Pomare te opu fetii, or family, carried Seventeen toward Isabelle's dwelling, the dressing around the wound had turned pinkish, indicating the wound was bleeding despite the stitches. Manoa's wife, Atea, supervised the men as they carried Seventeen through the doorway and onto a spare bed in the main room.

Isabelle, who had finally managed to fall asleep with baby Annette in the next room, woke with a start when she heard voices. Climbing off her bed, the Frenchwoman hurried to investigate and got the surprise of her life when she saw her sister-in-law. "Jennifer!" She hurried to Seventeen's side. "What happened to you?"

Seventeen shook her head weakly. "I'll tell you later." She didn't have the strength to go into the ins and outs of her near-death experience.

"Any word from Sebastian?"

Looking at Isabelle, Seventeen could see her eyes were full of hope. She shook her head.

Isabelle looked crestfallen.

Seventeen reached out and touched Isabelle's hand. "How's my little niece?" she asked.

Realizing one of her hosts must have mentioned she'd had a girl, Isabelle smiled. "She is beautiful!"

"Let me see her."

Atea intervened. "You can see the baby later," she insisted, waving one fat forefinger at Seventeen and looking every inch the matriarch of the Pomare te opu fetii. "For now you rest."

Seventeen didn't intend arguing with the big Tahitian woman, so she just lay back on the pillow.

"Quite right," Isabelle agreed. "You get some sleep and Annette will be here when you wake up."

Seventeen nodded, but Atea wasn't finished yet. She insisted on checking the visitor's wound. Expertly removing the soiled bandages, she studied the wound and the stitches that covered it. Sure enough, blood was leaking from the wound.

Atea snapped an order at her husband who hovered nearby. Manoa hurried from the room and returned a couple of minutes later with several palm fronds, which he handed to Atea. She selected one of the fronds and folded it several times so that it was just big enough to cover the wound. Then, using the other fronds as a dressing, she wrapped them around Seventeen's chest and tied them so they were as secure as any bandage. "Now you can sleep," she ordered her patient.

Seventeen needed no encouragement. She hadn't had a good night's sleep since arriving in Tahiti. That, combined with the painkillers the doctor had given her earlier, meant she was well overdue for a decent sleep.

Atea shepherded the others from the room, leaving the two guests alone. Seventeen closed her eyes as Isabelle sat down beside the bed. The Frenchwoman began humming a lullaby and stroking her sister-in-law's hair.

As she dozed off, the last thing Seventeen heard was the sound of Chai's Land Rover starting up. Their loyal Thai friend was preparing to return home. Seventeen vowed she would thank him for helping her as soon as she had the chance.

The former operative had no way of knowing, but she would never get the chance to thank Chai.

#

Just over an hour after leaving Seventeen and beginning his

return journey, Chai had to brake suddenly as his Land Rover crested a rise in the bumpy, one-way, dirt road he was negotiating. Another four-wheel drive vehicle was approaching at speed from the opposite direction.

There was no room to manoeuvre as there was a high bank on one side of the road and a big drop on the other. If both vehicles hadn't braked when they did, they'd have collided for sure. As it was, they stopped only a few yards apart.

The driver of the other vehicle looked as surprised as Chai felt. A thirtysomething mixed-race individual, he could be seen collecting his wits as he got himself together after the near miss. Chai noted also that the driver had been driving one-handed and his right shoulder was heavily bandaged.

The young Thai wasn't to know that the driver was Nineteen, the operative who had not so long ago tried to kill Seventeen. Nor could he know that an hour earlier Nineteen had visited his family's commune outside Papeete.

Nineteen had learned of the Thai family's connection with Seventeen and Isabelle soon after arriving in Tahiti. After he'd had his shoulder wound attended to, he visited the commune and threatened to harm family members if they didn't tell him where the two women were. He'd been bluffing as he hadn't a clue whether or not they knew of the pair's whereabouts. The bluff hadn't worked and he'd been forced to shoot Chai's elderly grandmother in the foot to encourage the family's cooperation. That had the desired impact and frightened family members had readily told him where Chai had just taken Seventeen and where he'd taken Isabelle before that.

The first that Chai knew something wasn't right was when Nineteen disembarked from the vehicle holding a pistol in his left hand. Chai immediately threw the Land Rover into reverse and gunned the accelerator. Fast though he was, he wasn't as fast as the bullet that pierced the windscreen and lodged in his forehead.

Still accelerating, Chai unknowingly drove over the edge of the embankment.

Looking over the edge, Nineteen watched as the Land Rover bounced off rocks and trees on its way to the bottom. The vehicle burst into flames as it finally came to rest on its roof.

Satisfied, the operative returned to his vehicle and resumed driving toward the settlement that harbored the people he was looking for.

86

While Isabelle watched over Seventeen, and Nineteen drove ever closer to their Tahitian hideout, Nine sat looking at Francis who at that moment was asleep in an apartment in downtown Las Vegas.

The drive from Nellis Air Force Base had been uneventful. After dropping Ten off on the side of the road, Nine had driven straight to the same apartment he'd taken a short-term lease out on earlier. The ground floor apartment had its own private courtyard and an underground garage with internal entry, which meant he could access it without being observed.

On arriving at the apartment, Nine had hugged Francis until the boy complained he couldn't breathe. He'd then subjected his son to a full physical, inspecting him for any signs that he'd been experimented on or otherwise tampered with. To his great relief, Francis appeared to be in good health – physically at least.

Mentally, it was another matter. Francis seemed withdrawn and nervous. Nine had been prepared for that. He knew the boy had been through a traumatic experience, being forcibly abducted and then interned with strangers in an underground laboratory. The former operative clung to the fact that children were resilient and time was a great healer.

Although ecstatic to be reunited with Francis, Nine was aware his mission wasn't over. He still had to return his son safely to the arms of Isabelle. That would mean departing Las Vegas, and then America, unobserved.

Nine was very aware he would still be on Omega's most wanted list despite the media scrutiny the agency was now under. He knew his former masters couldn't afford to allow him to live to testify against them in court.

Taking one last look at his son, Nine wandered through to the main room and turned on the television. Flicking through the channels, he was delighted to see that every commercial channel was screening news flashes on the Omega Agency and the allegations that swirled about it. *Bingo!* His emails had had the desired effect.

Nine watched with interest as live footage of Naylor's mansion was screened from rural Illinois. Half a dozen news teams and their vehicles could be seen parked outside the front gate, and a man who claimed to be Naylor's gardener told reporters his boss was away and so was not available to comment. *Talk your way outta this one, Naylor.*

Another channel screened live shots from Nellis Air Force Base and archived aerial shots of Thule Air Base, in Greenland, and Carmel Corporation's coltan refinery in the DRC. Speaking off screen, a reporter advised viewers that these were the sites of Omega's alleged medical labs. The live coverage from Nellis showed scores of international media representatives assembled outside the base's front gate. In the skies above, at least three news helicopters could be seen at any one time.

Nine flicked over to CNN News in time to see thirty or more news teams assembled in front of a disused hydro dam a few miles from Naylor's residence. The former operative immediately recognized it as the location of Omega's underground HQ. He turned the volume up as a male TV reporter spoke to camera.

"Behind me is the old Roxburgh Hydro Dam that provided almost twenty per cent of southwest Illinois' electricity needs until Harmony Power Corporation unexpectedly closed it down forty years ago," the reporter said. "Since then, if the allegations made by the mysterious Mister Sebastian Hannar are proven correct, it has served as the gateway to a shadowy underground organization whose activities, and influence, defy belief and could sink the current Administration."

Nine had heard enough for the moment. He turned the television off and sat down in the nearest comfy chair.

While happy about recent developments, he remained worried – and for good reason. His heart was rapidly giving out on him. The heartburn he'd experienced earlier had returned and the pills he'd been popping were becoming less effective.

Nine was aware he must act fast if he was to get Francis to safety. His son was his first concern. Then, and only then, could he have the operation the doctors had said could save his life.

#

A subdued Naylor watched the televised coverage of the morning's events alone in his office at Omega HQ. He'd been a virtual prisoner there since the world's media had assembled outside the security fence that surrounded the old hydro dam above ground. The newscast included earlier footage showing a shocked Marcia Wilson being escorted in handcuffs from CIA headquarters in Langley by two FBI types.

"Doug Cassidy is ready for you now, sir," Naylor's PA said over the intercom system from her office next door.

"Thank you." That was what Naylor had been waiting for. He switched off the intercom and hurried from his office. There, waiting for him in reception, was his fellow director Scott Henderson. Omega's protocols dictated that the board's full blessing was required and at least two directors had to be present for what was about to happen.

Naylor and Henderson were walking toward the nearest elevator when the older man remembered he'd left his cell phone in his vehicle, which was parked in the car park above ground. He asked his PA to retrieve it for him then resumed walking.

The pair entered an elevator and descended three floors in silence to what was effectively the basement. The elevator doors opened out into Omega's IT department. It comprised sterile rooms with computers wall to wall. The computers were manned by white-coated IT technicians who, not surprisingly, also looked subdued. Like their boss, they were also very aware of the media furore going on in the world outside.

Naylor and Henderson were met by Omega's youthful IT manager, Doug Cassidy, who, at that moment, looked the most subdued of anyone. That didn't surprise Naylor. After all, Cassidy was aware he was about to be asked to commit murder.

Cassidy led the two directors to a private suite at the end of a long corridor. As Naylor had asked, they had the suite to themselves. Its solitary piece of furniture – a desk – supported a laptop computer connected by power cords to half a dozen miscellaneous pieces of high-tech electrical equipment.

"Lock the door, Doug," Naylor ordered.

A now white-faced Cassidy closed and locked the door.

"Okay," Naylor said, "you know what to do."

"Are you sure about this, sir?"

Naylor didn't respond. He just directed a steely glare at his subordinate.

Cassidy had his answer. "Yes, sir."

Naylor and Henderson watched as Cassidy walked over to the laptop and accessed the Internet. After entering a password, ten red dots appeared on screen. They were overlaid on a map of the world. Both directors were aware each dot represented a surviving Omega orphan-operative whose whereabouts was immediately obvious. At a glance, they could see the operatives were currently spread over three continents and, in one case, in Tahiti.

For Naylor, the ten red dots symbolized Omega's failure. It wasn't that long ago there were twenty-one dots on screen every time he'd looked at it and Twenty Three dots before that when Nine and Seventeen had been active operatives. Turning to Cassidy, he asked, "Can you reach them all in one hit?"

"No sir. It has to be one at a time."

"Okay, let's get on with it." To Naylor the dots didn't represent human beings. They represented money. Big money. Giving them life through the Pedemont Project's ground-breaking artificial insemination program and then raising them as future operatives in the orphanage, had cost Omega many millions of dollars. However, every single orphan had returned many millions more and helped Omega achieve its dream of establishing a New World Order.

Cassidy was shaking as he prepared to carry out Naylor's orders. After making several adjustments to the equipment on the desktop, he manoeuvred the laptop's cursor until it rested on one of the red dots on the screen.

"Who is that?" Henderson asked. The dot he was looking at was one of two that appeared to be joined. Their location showed they were in, or above, the Pacific Ocean, just north of Tahiti.

"That's Operative Number Six," Cassidy said.

"Where's he now?"

"She. Six and Twenty One are flying to Papeete," Naylor said. "I pulled them out of Nellis Air Force Base to go help

Nineteen find the Frenchwoman and her baby in Tahiti." In his mind's eye, Naylor could picture the red-headed Six. She and her identical twin sister Five were the only twins to result from Omega's Pedemont Project. Like her sister, Six was a first class operative.

Cassidy looked around at Naylor as if hoping for a reprieve. There was none. Resigned to carrying out his orders, the IT manager clicked on the red dot that represented Six.

87

The dot immediately disappeared, leaving only nine dots visible.

"One down, eight to go," Naylor said dispassionately.

"That quick?" Henderson asked.

"That quick." Looking at Cassidy, Naylor said, "Explain it to him, Doug."

Cassidy almost looked relieved that he had an excuse to delay completing his macabre assignment. "Yes, sir." Turning to Henderson he said, "This equipment enables us to send a signal to a computer-controlled laser machine we've installed on top of the old hydro dam above us. In turn, it transmits a strong electrical signal to the microchip embedded in the forearm of the target – in this case Number Six – overloading the microchip's capabilities and precipitating a fatal electric shock. Death is immediate."

"Sounds unbelievable," an incredulous Henderson said.

"Until recently it would have been," admitted Cassidy. "A year ago we gained access to equipment our Military have been using for the past four years. They developed it to interfere with the communication systems of foreign satellites."

"Incredible."

Naylor was becoming impatient. "Let's keep moving."

"Yes sir." Cassidy moved the cursor to the next dot on screen.

#

The Business Class cabin in the Air Tahiti Nui Airbus A340 that Six and Twenty One were traveling in from Los Angeles to Papeete was in an uproar. Six had just returned to her seat as the Airbus began its descent to Papeete's Fa'a'ā International Airport when she collapsed.

In the seat next to Six, Twenty-One checked his fellow operative's pulse. He barely had time to register surprise at being unable to find a pulse when he suddenly clutched his heart and slumped down in his seat.

A Tahitian hostess who had observed both incidents hurried to assist the two passengers. Finding them both dead, she began screaming, spreading alarm amongst the other passengers.

#

In a private medical clinic in downtown Las Vegas, Ten waited his turn to see the duty surgeon. He'd debated whether to do what Nine had confided he'd once done and remove the microchip from his forearm himself. Never one for the sight of blood – especially not if it was his – he'd opted to have the microchip surgically removed by a professional.

Ten was gambling that his Omega masters wouldn't be looking for him yet. It was a gamble he was about to lose.

There was only one patient in front of him when his heart received the fatal shock. Ten was dead before his face hit the carpet. He would never know that at the Air Force base down the road, Numero Uno, the big Native-American operative, was about to meet the same fate.

Over the next few minutes, similar events took place in other parts of the world.

In South Africa, Omega operatives Sixteen and Twenty died while on a mission in Cape Town; in Switzerland, Five died on a mission in the Swiss Alps; in Italy, Eleven died whilst between assignments in Rome; and in the Canary Islands, Two died in her sleep.

#

In Tahiti, Nineteen had been observing the settlement that was home to Isabelle and Seventeen for the past couple of hours. After dealing with Chai, he'd driven to within half a mile of Pomareville and covered the remaining distance on foot so as not to alert anyone of his presence.

Nineteen knew he'd come to the right place: within an hour of arriving he'd spotted Isabelle. She'd ventured outside her dwelling with her new born baby and was still there now, sitting in the shade of a tree.

The operative was observing from the cover of the rainforest, which encroached on the settlement from all sides. He'd brought a hunting rifle with him. His plan was to terminate Seventeen, and Isabelle, too, if necessary, and then abduct the baby. Once back at his safe house in Papeete, he would await Naylor's instructions on how to transfer the baby to Omega's medical lab at Nellis Air Force Base. That was the plan anyway.

Nineteen tensed as he sighted Seventeen. She emerged from the dwelling and walked over to join Isabelle in the shade.

It was an easy shot for Nineteen. He estimated the distance to be no more than a hundred yards. Even so, he was nervous about taking the shot. He knew the rifle's recoil was going to give his wounded shoulder hell.

Just before Nineteen could take the shot, Atea and the other two midwives who had helped deliver Isabelle's baby converged on the two women to admire little Annette. They ended up in Nineteen's line of fire. Cursing, he lowered his rifle and waited for another opportunity.

The opportunity never came. As was the case with his fellow orphans, he never knew what hit him. Death was instantaneous.

Nineteen was the last of Omega's active orphan-operatives to die that day. Of the original Twenty Three Pedemont orphans, only Nine and Seventeen remained. And they were on borrowed time if Naylor was going to have his way.

The Omega boss left Henderson talking to the IT manager and returned to his office. On his way in, his PA advised him she'd retrieved his cell phone from his car as requested and had left it on his desk.

In his office, pulsing light from his cell phone signalled that he'd received at least one call in his absence. Retrieving the phone, Naylor found there were in fact five messages. Four were from journalists requesting interviews. He deleted those then accessed the remaining message. It was from Nineteen.

The now-deceased operative advised Naylor that he'd just discovered where Isabelle was hiding out and said he was on his way to deal with the situation. He also confirmed that Seventeen was with the Frenchwoman. Before ending the call, he named the settlement that was now home to the two women and he specified its location.

Cursing, Naylor deleted the message. He wondered whether Nineteen had gotten to Seventeen before he'd been terminated.

88

"Why do I have to dress as a girl, papa?" Francis asked. He was trying to understand why his father was dressing him up in girls' clothes.

"Because we have to make sure the bad people don't recognize you," a patient Nine explained as he fitted a wig of long black hair to his son's head.

"But I don't want to be a dumb girl!" Francis complained.

Nine ruffled the wig. "Then be a bright girl then," he chuckled as he draped a sari around the boy.

Francis couldn't see the funny side. He just wanted to be reunited with his mom and wasn't in the mood for fancy dress.

Nine could sympathize. He'd just about had it with disguises for one lifetime and he, too, couldn't wait to be reunited with Isabelle. One last time, he'd told himself.

The former operative had decided to adopt the guise of a Sikh businessman holidaying with his Sikh daughter. He was aware if Omega was still looking for him, they'd expect him to be traveling with his son.

When he was satisfied with Francis' disguise, he set about establishing his own. Within ten minutes he looked every inch a Sikh complete with turban and sari plus a fake bushy moustache. He and Francis then stood in front of a full-length wall mirror, studying their new guises. The late afternoon sun was reflected in the mirror, dazzling them, so Nine pulled a curtain across.

Francis laughed hilariously when he saw himself for the first time.

Nine then grabbed Francis and steered him downstairs to the garage. The pair had an appointment to keep on the outskirts of Las Vegas and Nine didn't want to be late.

#

Dusk was approaching when Nine stopped his rental van

outside a stately home in an especially luxurious part of town. He and Francis had an appointment with the homeowner. The appointment had been made on Nine's behalf by mobster Al Ricca for the princely sum of fifty grand.

After being admitted through a security gate, Nine led Francis up a concrete path to the house's front door. They were still in their Sikh disguises. As they walked, Nine asked, "Now remind me who you are?"

"Daya," Francis answered without hesitation. Nine had been drilling the boy on his girlie cover for the past hour.

"And what does that mean in English?"

"Kindness."

"And where are we from?"

"Um…the Punjab."

"Yes, but without the um next time."

"Sorry papa."

"And remember, only speak if spoken to."

"Yes papa."

Nine rang the front doorbell. The door was answered by a

nondescript, middle-aged man whose accent betrayed him as a New Yorker. He introduced himself as *Hymie* and, without waiting for his visitors to introduce themselves, led them down a hallway to the back of the house.

Hymie was the Chicago Outfit's go-to man for false passports in Nevada. He'd been doing that all his working life and was one of the best around. What set him apart from the vast majority of his peers was he'd never been to jail – a big advantage for the likes of Ricca who used his services frequently. That meant Hymie could pretty much name his price. For a few hours work – as this job would be – he'd quoted twenty grand. Ricca had been happy with that, adding his usual exorbitant percentage on top. So everyone was content.

Fifteen minutes was all it took for Hymie to shoot the necessary passport photos and glean the personal details required from Nine.

"How long before they're ready?" Nine asked.

"Three hours tops," Hymie said. "Where shall I deliver them?"

"You won't. I'll collect them at nine tomorrow morning."

"I'll be here."

"I hope so," Nine said, sending a steely look that told Hymie he'd be very unhappy if he wasn't here at that time.

89

That night, back in the apartment, Nine cradled a sleeping Francis in his arms on a sofa as he watched TV. Surfing the channels, he paused every now and then as something caught his attention. *The Omega Agency story*, as the media had named it, was still dominating the news.

Nine had an early night planned as he and Francis had a big day coming up. After collecting their new passports first thing in the morning, they would be flying to Los Angeles on a private air charter flight Nine had organized. From there, they would depart America for good.

The former operative was about to retire to bed when an ABC news item caught his eye.

A male presenter announced that a series of unexplained

deaths of American citizens had caught medical experts by surprise and had led to speculation the incidents were somehow linked to the Omega Agency story. "In one incident, two apparently healthy adults – a man and a woman – dropped dead within a minute of each other on a flight to Tahiti today."

Passport photos of the pair filled the screen. Although he hadn't seen them in over eight years, Nine recognized them immediately as fellow orphans Twenty-One and Six.

The presenter continued, "Then, in near-identical circumstances, two men dropped dead in Nevada – one in Las Vegas and the other at Nellis Air Force Base just outside Las Vegas." Photos of Ten and One appeared on screen. "It was the Air Force base fatality that prompted speculation the deaths could in some way be connected to the Omega Agency story that has been dominating world headlines since it broke this morning."

Nine couldn't believe what he was seeing. His fellow orphans were dropping like flies. The news that Ten was among them hit him came as a cruel blow. He was saddened to learn his old friend hadn't survived or ever experienced freedom.

The presenter continued in the same vein as photos of six other Omega operatives appeared on screen. Nine recognized them all instantly.

When the news item finished, Nine switched off the set and digested what he'd just learnt. The former operative sensed Naylor was behind the unexplained deaths. *He has to be.* There was no other explanation. If he had to bet, he thought all Omega's orphan-operatives would have met the same fate. He just hoped Seventeen wasn't among them.

Putting himself in Naylor's shoes, he figured the Omega boss would have realized his orphan-operatives knew too much. *He couldn't risk them talking, so he had them killed. But how?* Logic told him it had something to do with the microchip embedded in each. *That could explain why I'm still alive. And hopefully Seventeen, too.* Regardless, he was aware Omega had access to the latest equipment, drugs and medicine, and killing its own operatives at long distance wouldn't have been too difficult.

Nine flirted with the idea that he was now off the hook. For a moment he was tempted to surround himself with media and front up to the police, or the appropriate authorities, and put Francis and himself in their hands. After all, his name had been mentioned in just about every news story that had aired in America that day. *Omega wouldn't dare touch me, or Francis, if I handed myself in.*

Then common sense prevailed. He knew there were no guarantees where Omega was concerned. Their tentacles were far-reaching. Thinking on it further, he deduced that Omega would want him out of the picture at all costs. *They don't want me testifying against them. The same goes for Seventeen.* His thoughts went out to his sister.

#

That night, while Nine and Francis slept, two thirtysomething Ukrainians were boarding a late Air New Zealand flight that would take them from Los Angeles to Papeete. Ivan Pasternak and Yuriy Borkovsky were low-level soldiers with the Ukrainian Mafia. They'd been sent to America to provide the muscle for a drug deal when they received an order to drop everything and fly to Tahiti. The order had come from Andrew Naylor's Berlin contact via their capo in Kiev.

Their mission was to kill Seventeen then to wait for Nine to show up and kill him, too.

Neither they nor their capo knew who their client was.

#

Next morning, a Sikh gentleman and a young girl sat patiently waiting for their flight in the Departure Lounge at LAX. Their newly acquired passports said the gentleman was Doctor Kuljit Panesar and the girl was his daughter, Daya.

After collecting their passports in Las Vegas, Nine and Francis had flown to Los Angeles by private air charter without incident and in plenty of time to connect with their international flight.

The irony of traveling as a doctor in his condition wasn't lost on Nine. His health wasn't getting any better and he knew he should be under a doctor's care at that very moment. He popped two heart pills to alleviate the chest pains that were now a permanent part of his life.

As the pair waited, Nine did something he'd been putting off doing for weeks: he phoned Isabelle. The former operative was aware the call could be delayed no longer. He'd been putting it off because he knew there was a chance Omega's sophisticated electronic surveillance equipment would intercept any such attempt to contact Isabelle, or Seventeen for that matter. For the same reason, he'd avoided emailing them or contacting them by any other means.

The call couldn't be delayed because Nine had to activate the next part of his plan to reunite his family. He was gambling that Omega would be in such disarray it wouldn't pick up one quick phone call. The recorded voice of a Verizon Wireless employee advised that the number was currently in an area that did not have cell phone coverage.

Disappointed, Nine then speed-dialled Seventeen's number. *C'mon sis. Answer.* He got the same result.

"Who are you calling, papa?" Francis asked.

"Just a friend," Nine lied. Frustrated, the former operative pocketed his phone. He realized there could be several reasons why he couldn't get through and hoped the non-responses didn't mean that Isabelle and Seventeen had struck trouble.

Anxious to get a message to the women, Nine led Francis to an Internet kiosk. There, he quickly set up a free email account under an assumed name and sent a cryptic email to temporary email addresses he'd set up previously – one for Isabelle prior to his departure from Tahiti and one for Seventeen prior to her departure from Chicago.

The email read: *All is well. Both parcels are in transit. ETA in V is 48 hours from now.*

Watching the email go, Nine was confident the recipients would realize the *parcels* referred to himself and Francis, and *V* referred to their agreed mutual destination: Vanuatu, the remote South Pacific island nation to the west of Fiji, near Papua New Guinea.

90

In the dwelling they now shared in Pomareville, the women Nine had been trying to reach were enjoying a late breakfast together. Isabelle was recovering well from the trauma of giving birth and Seventeen's wound felt considerably less painful than it had the previous day.

Baby Annette lay sleeping in a bassinette next to the table.

Neither woman knew of the major news story that had broken the previous day and was still dominating world headlines. Daily newspapers didn't arrive at the remote settlement until the day after their publication, and the power generator had been down for the past twenty-four hours, so the villagers hadn't been able to watch TV or listen to the radio. Nor had there been any visitors to the settlement in over a day.

Effectively, that meant a news blackout was in force at Pomareville.

As if telepathically prompted by Nine's attempts to reach them, the two women were talking about him at that very moment.

"How will Sebastian know where to contact us when he finds Francis?" Isabelle asked. "I mean for all we know he could be trying to contact us now."

"He would contact Chai's family," Seventeen said. "If there was any news, we'd have heard." Seventeen could see by the look on her sister-in-law's face that comment hadn't cheered her up. She hurriedly added, "I'm sure we'll hear something soon."

"I hope so--"

The honking horn of an approaching truck interrupted their conversation.

"I'll see what's happening," Seventeen said. She hurried outside to check.

Emerging from the dwelling, Seventeen saw Manoa's old flat-deck truck approaching the settlement. The big Tahitian was driving and he was still honking the horn, indicating something was up. Seventeen hoped he had some good news.

As the truck drew close, Seventeen could see Manoa had a passenger. It wasn't until the truck stopped close by that she identified the passenger as Chai. She gasped when she realized her Thai friend was dead. His lifeless body had slumped forward, leaving his forehead resting against the truck's windscreen. Seventeen ran to investigate.

"What is it?" The voice was Isabelle's. She'd ventured outside to investigate just as Seventeen was helping Manoa unload Chai's body from the truck.

"Stay there!" Seventeen ordered.

The former operative noticed the bullet hole in the middle of Chai's forehead as she and Manoa gently laid the young Thai on the grass. "He's been shot!" she whispered. Turning to the Tahitian, she asked, "Where did you find him?"

"About an hour's drive from here."

"Anyone else around?"

Manoa shook his head. "I noticed a four-wheel drive rental vehicle parked off the track about half a mile back, but there was no sign of its driver."

That worried Seventeen. The former operative considered it almost certain the vehicle's driver was connected with Chai's murder. She immediately thought of Nineteen. *It has to be him!* Seventeen looked around at the rainforest and shuddered at the thought her fellow orphan could have her in his sights right now.

A shadow announced Isabelle's arrival. The Frenchwoman took one look at Chai's lifeless body and broke down. Seventeen stood up and comforted her.

Over the next few minutes, villagers emerged from their homes and crowded around the small group. They, too, were shocked to learn that Chai had been shot.

No sooner had they recovered from their initial shock when shouts of alarm reached them from the nearby rainforest. Three village boys sprinted out from the trees some hundred yards distant, shouting and waving their arms.

Manoa went to greet them. They led him back into the trees to show him what they'd found.

Seventeen turned to Isabelle. "We have to leave," she

ordered. "Get the baby ready." She ran after Manoa before Isabelle had time to answer.

Isabelle wasn't about to argue. She could sense the sudden danger, and her only thought was to protect Annette and relocate her to a safe place.

On the edge of the rainforest, Seventeen caught up to Manoa and the three boys as they stopped to inspect an object. Pushing them aside, she saw the object was in fact a man. He was lying face-down on top of a powerful hunting rifle and appeared to be dead.

Seventeen used her foot to roll the body over. She recognized Nineteen immediately. The mix-race operative's sightless eyes stared up at her. Disconcerted, Seventeen knelt down and quickly closed her fellow orphan's eyes. She then checked his head and upper body for some sign of a fatal wound. There was none.

"How did he die?" Manoa asked.

Seventeen just shrugged. She hadn't a clue. All appearances suggested the operative had died of natural causes. Seventeen was in no doubt the bullet she assumed was still in the rifle's chamber had been meant for her. A quick check confirmed the bullet was still in the chamber.

Manoa ordered the boys to return to the settlement. He then turned to Seventeen. Glancing at the body, he said, "He came for you, didn't he?"

"Yes I'm afraid he did."

"We better get back." The worried Tahitian began walking back to the settlement. He clearly wasn't happy about the day's developments.

"Manoa, wait!"

The Tahitian waited while Seventeen pulled Nineteen's rifle from his lifeless hands and recovered an automatic pistol from his belt. She slung the rifle over her shoulder then pushed the pistol through her own belt. Before leaving, she quickly searched Nineteen's pockets and found the keys to his rental vehicle. Pocketing them, she joined Manoa and they began walking back to the settlement.

"Isabelle and I will leave now," Seventeen said.

"Thank you," a relieved Manoa mumbled. He considered the

continued presence of the two women a threat to the safety of his people and had been about to order the pair to leave. Seventeen had saved him considerable embarrassment without realizing it, or so he thought.

In fact, the former operative realized it was not the island way to order guests to leave at the first sign of trouble, but she understood: Manoa had to put the safety of his people first.

As they neared the others, Manoa said, "There is something else I must show you."

Seventeen wondered what was coming next as Manoa led her back to his truck. Reaching inside, he pulled out a copy of *Les Nouvelles de Tahiti*, Papeete's daily newspaper. He'd picked it up earlier. "I think this will interest you."

The former operative looked at the front page and saw at a glance it was entirely devoted to the breaking Omega story. Photos of the Omega operatives who had died mysteriously within minutes of each other took up half the page. Seventeen guessed that whatever had caused the deaths had killed Nineteen also. She also assumed it was Naylor's handiwork and wondered if all her fellow orphans had met the same fate.

91

Ukrainian Mafia soldiers Ivan Pasternak and Yuriy Borkovsky had wasted no time after their flight touched down at Papeete's Fa'a'ā International Airport. They'd collected the hire Jeep that had been booked on their behalf and, after checking in to their waterfront hotel, had set off for the remote Tahitian settlement known as Pomareville.

Though low level soldiers, Ivan and Yuriy were useful. They were tough and resilient, and they knew how to handle the small arsenal of weapons they'd collected on arrival. They were also ambitious – especially Yuriy who had a couple of years on his younger partner. Both aspired to higher posts in their organization.

Their capo back in the Ukraine had assured them the

information for their current assignment had come from an impeccable source. So it was with some confidence that they proceeded to carry out the first part of their mission – to find and terminate Seventeen, and to capture Isabelle to use as bait to lure Nine out of hiding.

The pair had good reason to be confident about their source of information. Their capo's Berlin contact had never let them down before.

As Yuriy slowed to avoid a fallen branch on the rough vehicle track neither he nor his passenger could have guessed their targets were driving toward them at that very moment.

#

Nine and Francis were asleep in the Air New Zealand 747's First Class compartment when a hostess came by with a lunch trolley. They looked so peaceful the hostess opted to let them sleep on. Lunch could wait.

Had he been awake, Nine would have appreciated the hostess's thoughtfulness. He was exhausted and his overtaxed heart needed rest. In Francis' case, the unusual hours he'd been keeping since his rescue had tired him out, too.

The pair had fallen asleep as soon as the airliner had departed LAX. They would sleep until it landed at Honolulu International Airport for a scheduled one-hour stopover before continuing on to Fiji, their next stop.

Across the aisle from Nine, an American business traveler watched a live CNN News report on the television monitor set into the back of the seat in front of him. It showed a US Government vehicle collecting Naylor from the car park above the Omega Agency's subterranean headquarters in Illinois.

Speaking to camera, a reporter advised viewers that Naylor had been summonsed to a meeting at the White House to answer the recent allegations that had been made against him and against the agency, and to explain the true purpose of the medical laboratories Omega was allegedly operating around the world.

Several seats behind Nine, another passenger – a Canadian businessman – pecked at his meal as he read that day's issue of the *Los Angeles Times*. Its news pages were almost exclusively devoted to the Omega Agency story. Other passengers were similarly engaged.

Since it broke, the story had taken on a life of its own. One news story led to another as the world's news agencies, television networks and newspapers tried to outdo each other in the competition to be first with the news.

No stone was left unturned. The details that whistleblower Sebastian Hannar had provided in his two bombshell emails had given journalists plenty of ammunition. They still had to earn their money and use their investigative skills to get to the truth, but with a little digging they were unearthing information that would keep their audience intrigued for a long time yet.

The airing of information was also having, and would continue to have, far-reaching ramifications for many, many people.

Most affected were the Omega Agency's directors and senior staff. They were now being interviewed separately by senior FBI officials. At least those who were still available were. Yet another director, founding member Fletcher Von Pein, had been hospitalized after a failed suicide attempt, another two directors had ended up in medical care with stress-related complaints and several senior staffers had done runners, fleeing the country under assumed names.

As a result of the pressure now being applied by the FBI and others, some Omega staffers were singing like songbirds, revealing all they knew about the agency and its nefarious business dealings.

#

While Nine and Francis winged their way toward Hawaii, Naylor was flying toward Washington D.C. aboard an FBI-chartered Hawker 800 private jet. He shared the jet's luxury passenger cabin with three senior FBI officials who at that moment were interviewing him.

The four men were sitting around a round table that was fixed in the middle of the cabin. Controlling the questioning was Senior Agent Stephen Dalby, a craggy-faced veteran of the bureau whose exemplary record commanded instant respect amongst his peers.

Dalby didn't hold back as he questioned Naylor. "When did the unsanctioned experiments on children begin at the Thule Air

Base laboratory?"

Naylor bristled. "As I've already said, there were no experiments on children, sanctioned or unsanctioned, at Thule." The Omega boss wasn't just upset by the line of questioning. He was also upset because Senior Agent Dalby had been recruited by him personally and had been developed over many years as an Omega mole within the bureau. What irked Naylor even more was that he knew he couldn't accuse Dalby of wrongdoing without incriminating himself in the process.

Dalby knew exactly what Naylor was thinking as he continued to question him. He found the whole situation faintly amusing as well as highly ironic. "Oh, really?" He referred to a file he was holding. "Yet your senior physician, Doctor Andrews, contradicts you."

Naylor felt his stomach drop.

Dalby continued, "Doctor Andrews said, and I quote, the Thule laboratory was the second one to be built after the Black Forest orphanage opened. He said, like the others, the Thule lab's patients were almost exclusively children."

Naylor glared at his mole as he rattled off one accusation after the other. "The good doctor also said none of the experiments had ever been sanctioned by any medical authority."

The Omega boss felt like he was about to throw up. Everything around him started spinning. "Excuse me!" he stammered. He stood up and bolted for the restroom cubicle at the back of the cabin.

Behind Naylor, the three officials grinned at each other. They were enjoying themselves.

The first any of them realized there was a problem was when Naylor burst out of the restroom cubicle and hurled himself at the cabin's exit door.

Dalby was the first to react. "Stop him!"

The official nearest the door lunged at Naylor, but was too slow. Naylor pushed the door open and was sucked through the opening.

In the cabin, the three officials had already forgotten about the recently departed. They were too busy hanging onto fixtures in around them to ensure they weren't sucked out too.

92

Isabelle grinded the gears as she drove Nineteen's four-wheel drive hire vehicle along the track leading away from Pomareville and back to civilization. Seventeen sat beside her, cradling the hunting rifle and the machine pistol she'd taken from her fellow orphan. Baby Annette slept on in a bassinette jammed on the seat between them.

Seventeen had chosen to ride shotgun in case Nineteen hadn't been working alone when he'd come after them. She figured in the event they were ambushed or pursued, she'd be of more use if she wasn't behind the wheel. After an hour of Isabelle's driving, she was wondering if she'd made the right decision. Her sister-in-law seemed to be trying to run over every bump and pothole along the way.

Rounding a corner, they were confronted by a rare straight stretch of track. It extended for about a hundred yards.

"Gun it," Seventeen ordered.

Isabelle accelerated and the vehicle shot forward. She braked almost immediately when a Jeep came into view. It was coming toward them at speed.

"Don't stop!" Seventeen ordered.

Isabelle kept driving, but at a much slower speed. "Who could that be?" she asked.

Seventeen could hear the fear in Isabelle's voice. "Stay calm and just keep driving."

As the two vehicles approached, the women could make out two men in the front of the Jeep. They had no idea these were Ukrainians who were coming for them. When the vehicles were about fifty yards apart, the Jeep stopped and the passenger, Ivan, jumped out. He motioned for the approaching vehicle to stop.

"Slow down, but for God sake don't stop," Seventeen said as she considered the situation. She estimated there was just room for their vehicle to squeeze pass the Jeep.

Isabelle slowed until only a few yards separated the vehicles.

"Go!" Seventeen shouted.

Isabelle accelerated and the vehicle shot past the Jeep. A startled Ivan only just had time to jump aside.

Looking back, Seventeen saw Ivan reach into the Jeep and pull out an automatic weapon. He lifted it to his shoulder.

"Keep your head down!" Seventeen screamed.

Both women ducked as a burst of gunfire shattered their vehicle's rear windscreen. Annette started crying, prompting Isabelle to look down at her.

"Keep your eye on the road!" Seventeen yelled. "I'll watch out for Annette." The former operative quickly checked the baby. "She's okay."

"Who are those people?" a terrified Isabelle asked.

"I don't know." Seventeen was wondering the same thing. "Never seen them before." She knew they weren't Omega orphan-operatives. Looking around again, she saw the Jeep was now turning around to chase after them.

Though Seventeen didn't know the two men pursuing them,

one thing was clear: she and Isabelle were still being hunted even if Omega, as an organization, was finished and even if all the agency's orphan-operatives were dead.

"They are gaining on us!" Isabelle said, checking her rear vision mirror. "What do we do?"

"Keep driving. I'm thinking." Seventeen went into a daydream state for a split-second – just as the Pedemont orphans' mentor Tommy Kentbridge had taught her and all his young charges to do many years earlier. Then an answer came to her. "Let me out around the next corner!" she ordered.

As Isabelle steered around the next corner, she slowed to allow Seventeen to jump out. The former operative was clutching the rifle and the machine pistol as she jumped.

In the side mirror, Isabelle watched as her sister-in-law rolled over before scrambling to her feet and waiting for the Jeep to appear. Common sense told the Frenchwoman she should keep driving, but she slowed the vehicle to a stop and waited to see what happened. Beside her, Annette was still crying. "Don't worry, little one," Isabelle crooned. "Everything will be alright."

While Isabelle consoled her baby, Seventeen stood in the middle of the vehicle track, legs astride and rifle raised, as she waited for the Jeep to appear. The leap from the vehicle had jarred her wounded collarbone, causing white hot streaks of pain to course through her. But Seventeen ignored that. She knew she'd only get one shot before the Jeep would be onto her.

A second later, the Jeep rounded the corner.

Seventeen lined up the driver, Yuriy, in her sights. What followed took less than a second, but to Seventeen it seemed more like a minute. She slowed everything down. Her breathing, her heart rate, even her thinking process – just as she'd been drilled to do over and over by her Omega instructors. Exhaling, she gently squeezed the trigger, sending one well-placed bullet into Yuri's brain.

Then everything sped up. The Jeep slammed into a tree, sending Ivan flying through the front windscreen and disappearing into the undergrowth. A fireball then erupted, engulfing the Jeep and its driver.

Ignoring the relentless pain of her wounded collarbone,

Seventeen raced to find Ivan in the undergrowth. She didn't expect to find him alive. It was her assessment few could survive an incident like the one she'd just witnessed. When she found Ivan, he was still alive, but only just. Bloodied and broken, and only semi-conscious, his limbs stuck out at odd angles from his torso, and shattered bones protruded through the broken skin of both arms and one leg. He was also struggling to breathe.

Kneeling beside Ivan, Seventeen asked, "Who sent you?"

The injured man managed to smile at Seventeen and then spat a mouthful of bloody phlegm into her face.

Seventeen wiped the phlegm away then calmly reached down and squeezed one of Ivan's broken arms. He screamed in agony. Ignoring his screams, she repeated the question.

"I can't understand you!" Ivan gasped in Ukrainian.

Seventeen couldn't understand him, but she recognized Ukrainian when she heard it. She'd never learnt Ukrainian. Switching to Russian, which she spoke fluently, she repeated her question.

"Our capo!" Ivan responded in kind.

"Who told him about us?" A screech of brakes alerted Seventeen to the return of Isabelle. The Frenchwoman had driven back when she'd seen what happened. Looking around at her, Seventeen shouted, "Stay there!" She turned back to Ivan and squeezed his broken arm again.

The injured man's screams prompted Isabelle to disembark from the vehicle and investigate what was going on. She was horrified by what she saw. "What are you doing?" she asked.

Seventeen stood up and grasped Isabelle by both shoulders. Looking into her eyes she said, "I'm doing what I do best. Now you go back to the vehicle."

Isabelle took one last look at the injured man then did as she was told.

Turning back to Ivan, Seventeen was alarmed to see he was fading fast. She knelt close to him again and repeated her earlier question. "Who told your capo about us?"

With his dying breath, Ivan gurgled, "His Berlin contact...an American diplomat."

Seventeen knew beyond doubt now that Naylor had put a

contract out on her and probably Nine as well. She recalled her former boss had installed a mole in the American Embassy in Berlin a couple of years earlier. She'd had reason to use the diplomat's services while on her last assignment for Omega. So the Ukrainian's dying words had a ring of truth to them.

The former operative digested this revelation as she returned to the waiting vehicle. It struck her that she'd always be looking over her shoulder, no matter where in the world she was.

She now had a decision to make.

By the time Seventeen reached the vehicle and jumped in beside her sister-in-law, she'd made up her mind. She would get off the grid – just as Nine and Isabelle had five years earlier and just as they were planning to do again.

93

On arriving back in Papeete, Seventeen left Isabelle and baby Annette in the hire vehicle they'd borrowed then walked down the street to an Internet café she'd spotted. The former operative wanted to check her emails.

Inside the café, Seventeen quickly accessed a free computer. She entered her password and user name then waited. It seemed to take forever. When the inbox finally opened, one email stood out from all the spam. Seventeen recognized Nine as the sender and immediately clicked on the email. When it opened, she quietly read it aloud under her breath. "All is well. Both parcels are in transit. ETA in V is forty-eight hours from now."

Seventeen almost cried out with joy. She noted the email had been sent only that morning. The former operative couldn't wait to advise Isabelle of the good news, but first she had to reply to Nine. Typing fast, she wrote: *We 3 OK. Mother & daughter are doing well. See you in V.*

After sending the email and closing out of the account, Seventeen hurried outside. The sudden activity aggravated her wounded collarbone, causing her to grimace and reminding her she should inspect her stitches and change the dressing soon.

Isabelle guessed Seventeen had good news even before she reached the vehicle. She'd spotted her sister-in-law as soon as she emerged from the Internet café. Seventeen had beamed at her and flashed a thumbs-up sign her way as soon as she saw her.

The former operative ran to Isabelle's open window, reached through it and hugged the Frenchwoman. "Sebastian and Francis are fine! They are on their way to Vanuatu now."

Isabelle dissolved into tears – tears of unbridled joy.

#

In an Internet kiosk in the transit passengers' lounge at Honolulu International Airport, Nine had to force himself to stem

656

back tears as he re-read Seventeen's email. Turning to Francis, who sat next to him, he said, "I have some news for you, young man."

"What, papa?"

"You now have a sister. Mom had a little baby girl."

Francis' face creased into a grin. "What's her name?"

"We'll find out soon. Mom and your Aunt Jennifer will tell us in good time."

Francis was delighted to learn he now had a sister. He was looking forward to seeing her – and his aunt, too. Nine had told him about Seventeen and how she may soon be living with them.

Father and son were still in their Sikh father-and-daughter guises. More than once, Nine had to quietly remind Francis to keep his voice down in case any eavesdroppers should overhear him. Fortunately, the boy's voice was far from breaking, so Nine was reasonably confident no-one would realize Francis was in fact a male.

As Francis chattered away, an Air New Zealand announcement caught Nine's attention. An airline representative advised passengers that the flight to Fiji had been delayed three hours due to a technical problem.

That wasn't what Nine wanted to hear. He could sense his ailing ticker was fast fading and he just wanted to reach his final destination and be reunited with Isabelle as soon as he could. The heartburn he'd experienced of late was now with him permanently and he feared he could go into cardiac arrest at any time.

In his present condition, flying didn't agree with him either. He guessed it may have something to do with altitude, or perhaps it was the stress of flying. Whatever it was, his heart didn't respond well to it.

A painful twinge in his chest caused Nine to grit his teeth.

Francis noticed something was wrong. "What's the matter, papa?"

"Nothing, son." Nine forced himself to remain cheerful for Francis' sake. "Feel like something to eat."

"Oh, yes!"

"Good. Follow me. And remember, act demure like the little girl you are supposed to be." Nine led Francis by the hand to the nearest food kiosk.

"What's demure?"

"Think of your mom. She's demure."

Ten minutes later, as Francis tucked into a hamburger, Nine sipped a mug of coffee as he absentmindedly watched a news broadcast screening on a wall-mounted television set. He came alert when a photo of Naylor filled the screen.

"Papa," Francis asked.

"Shhh! One minute, Francis." Nine listened as the presenter advised viewers that the Chairman of the Omega Agency, Andrew Naylor, had jumped to his death from a private jet earlier that day.

Normally, such news would have delighted Nine. Now, with so much going on in his life and so much to look forward to, Naylor's suicide meant nothing to him. His only regret was that his former boss would never stand trial for the evil he'd perpetuated. Turning back to Francis, he asked, "Now, what is it, son?"

Francis asked if he could have an ice-cream sundae to follow his burger.

"Sure you can." Nine ruffled Francis' hair then remembered

the boy was wearing a girl's wig. He checked that no-one was

looking then quickly readjusted it.

94

While Nine and Francis filled in time in Honolulu, Isabelle and Seventeen were putting in motion their plans to depart Papeete. They'd been busy since arriving back in the capital and there was still much to do.

After Seventeen had finished checking emails at the Internet café, her first priority had been to quit the four-wheel drive hire vehicle they'd borrowed. The former operative was aware its smashed rear windscreen was attracting attention and the vehicle provided a traceable link between her and the deceased Nineteen. She parked it in a waterfront hotel car park then caught a cab back to the backstreet motel where she'd left Isabelle and Annette.

Seventeen's next priority had been to confide in Isabelle her decision to accompany the Frenchwoman and Annette to Vanuatu. That news had been well received by Isabelle who couldn't imagine being separated from the former operative – especially not before she was reunited with Nine and Francis.

The mood had been upbeat since Seventeen received Nine's email. For Isabelle, knowing that she and her boys would all soon be reunited was a dream come true; baby Annette's arrival was the icing on the cake.

Though Seventeen was encouraged by recent developments, she remained cautious. The Ukrainian incident of a few hours earlier reminded her that these were still dangerous times. Seventeen didn't know for sure whether all Omega's orphan-operatives had been taken out of the picture. And even if they had been, there was no way of knowing whether more contract killers were on their way. For all she knew, they could already be in Tahiti.

Isabelle, who was breastfeeding Annette, noticed her sister-in-law seemed worried. "What's wrong, Jennifer?" she asked.

Seventeen wanted to shield Isabelle from any further stress. She was mindful that the Frenchwoman had been through a lot since Francis' abduction and didn't want to load more stress onto her. However, she realized this time she had no choice.

Over the next ten minutes, Seventeen explained to Isabelle the risks they still faced and what they needed to do to keep their rendezvous with Nine and Francis in Vanuatu. To her relief, Isabelle stoically accepted the fact they weren't yet out of the woods. The longer she spent with the Frenchwoman, the more substance she realized she had. She'd come round to the firm belief that Isabelle was a worthy wife for her brother.

As for Isabelle, she realized she now looked on her sister-in-law as a true friend. That revelation had come as a shock to her. A few weeks earlier she hated Seventeen and could never have envisaged growing to like the woman who had terminated her parents. However, she was wise enough to know the Seventeen of today was a different person to the one who had been operating under the mind-controlled influence of MK-Ultra. The old Seventeen would never have risked her life to help protect her and help reunite her with Nine and Francis.

Isabelle suddenly hugged her opposite.

"What was that for?" a surprised Seventeen asked.

"Just for being here for us," Isabelle said.

The two women shared a tear as they hugged each other.

When Isabelle pressed against Seventeen's wound, it reminded the former operative she needed to change the dressing. Ever the professional, she broke away, saying, "Okay, we have a lot to do."

Isabelle smiled and resumed feeding Annette as Seventeen went to the bathroom and inspected her wound. Relieved to find it was healing well and the stitches remained intact, she changed the dressing then re-joined Isabelle and began making final preparations for their departure from Tahiti.

#

Next morning, Isabelle and Seventeen travelled to Fa'a'ā International Airport in separate cabs. They were now unrecognizable, having adopted different guises the previous afternoon.

Isabelle, who was nursing a sleeping Annette in the back seat of one cab, was in the guise of a plump, matronly, new mom complete with puffed-out cheeks and padding that added quite a few extra pounds. An unflattering hairstyle combined with light brown hair dye administered by Seventeen had rendered the Frenchwoman unrecognizable even to herself. The only concession she made to her old self was she still wore the ruby and silver necklace Nine had left with her.

In the other cab, Seventeen was in the guise of a French tomboy complete with a GI-style haircut, a nose ring, fake tattoo, hikers' boots and mannish attire.

The former operative had deemed it safer that she and Isabelle travel to Vanuatu separately. She knew if anyone was still looking for them, they'd be expecting to see two women traveling together. Both were aware the baby was a complication, but there was nothing they could do about that.

To allay Isabelle's fears, Seventeen had told her their enemies would be looking for a pregnant woman as they had no way of knowing she'd already given birth. Isabelle knew her sister-in-law was putting a positive spin on things, but she didn't let on.

The women were flying to Vanuatu via New Caledonia. Isabelle was supposedly going to show off her new baby to family living in the South Pacific island nation's capital Port Vila while Seventeen was posing as a documentary filmmaker on a scouting expedition.

The pair hadn't had a spare minute since checking into their backstreet motel the previous afternoon. In between tending to Annette's needs, they'd changed into their new guises – a drawn-out, sometimes-hilarious, two-hour exercise. Then they'd checked out of the motel and separately checked into an upmarket, downtown hotel under assumed names.

After dark, they'd gone by cab to an underworld contact Nine had referred Seventeen to before she left Chicago. Bruce Zhi was a Chinese migrant on the payroll of Hong Kong's 14K Triad gang. Nine had used the man's unique services whilst on assignment for Omega eight years earlier.

Zhi had relocated to Papeete three years ago. His mission was to establish safe houses in Tahiti and elsewhere in the Pacific

Islands for 14K triads who were attracting too much heat from Asian law enforcement agencies. One of his special skills was forging passports, and that's why Seventeen and Isabelle sought him out.

Nine had paid the triad in advance, and the entire process ended up being quick and painless for the two women. Zhi had taken their photos and secured their details that night, and then hand-delivered the false passports to their hotel early the next morning.

#

Three uneventful hours later, Isabelle checked Annette's baby restraints in the seat next to her as the Air Tahiti Nui airliner lifted off. Mother and daughter were flying Business Class; Seventeen was up front in the First Class compartment.

Isabelle was fortunate to have a window seat. The Frenchwoman was able to view Tahiti and its outer islands as the aircraft headed west toward New Caledonia. She looked at the northern horizon for a glimpse of her beloved Marquesas Islands even though she was aware they were too far away to see.

Isabelle's emotions were in turmoil. Sad to be leaving French Polynesia and the memories and friends she'd made there over the past five years, she was happy beyond words to know she'd soon be reunited with Nine and Francis, and she had a healthy, beautiful baby girl.

#

While Isabelle, Annette and Seventeen were leaving Tahitian airspace, Nine and Francis were still waiting to depart Honolulu. Their three-hour delay had ended up an overnight delay as Air New Zealand engineers grappled to resolve the technical problem that had struck their aircraft. The airline had put the affected passengers up in an airport motel.

Normally, Nine would have taken such a delay in his stride, but this was different. His condition was deteriorating with every hour, and every hour's delay increased the likelihood that he wouldn't survive long enough to be reunited with Isabelle or see their new baby daughter.

Nine's heart pains were recurring with frightening regularity. He knew he should seek medical help immediately.

95

Thirty-six hours after departing Tahiti, Isabelle and Seventeen had their first real argument. Their Air Tahiti Nui flight to New Caledonia had been uneventful, as had the brief stopover there and the final leg aboard a Qantas plane to Port Vila, in Vanuatu. The women had expected Nine and Francis to be waiting for them when they arrived at Port Vila Airport. Instead, they learned that flight delays had put the pair behind schedule.

Putting that disappointment behind them, Isabelle and Seventeen had rented a comfortable beachfront villa on the outskirts of town. They'd dispensed with their disguises and had thankfully reverted to being themselves, albeit under false names – although Seventeen had still been left with her unflattering GI-style haircut.

Under normal circumstances, their stay would have been an enjoyable one. However, the latest delay was getting on their nerves – especially Isabelle's. She couldn't wait to see her husband and son.

So, as the hour of their delayed arrival neared, Isabelle insisted on traveling to the airport to greet them. Seventeen opposed that, explaining it would put Nine and Francis at risk if anyone was still tracking them.

Isabelle fired up and argued heatedly with her sister-in-law until sanity finally prevailed.

"We must wait for them to come to us," Seventeen said soothingly. "Otherwise we could be putting them in danger." She knew that was unlikely, but didn't want to take the risk.

Close to tears, Isabelle asked, "How will Sebastian know where to find us?"

"I left a note for him at the airport's Information Office. He knows to call in there as soon as he gets through Customs."

Isabelle relaxed. She realized Seventeen was right.

"I'll check the flight," Seventeen said. The former operative immediately phoned the local Aircalin office and confirmed the flight Nine and Francis were to connect with in Fiji had departed on schedule.

#

For Isabelle, the next three hours were unbearable. She passed them making small talk with Seventeen, pacing up and down the villa's shady veranda, and feeding and changing a fretful Annette. Like her mom and aunt, the baby wasn't comfortable in Port Vila's oppressive heat and humidity.

Seventeen was first to see the cab as it pulled up outside the villa. "They're here!" she called out.

Isabelle, who was holding Annette, handed the baby to Seventeen then ran down the veranda's front steps to greet the cab.

At that very moment, light rain began falling, but the Frenchwoman didn't even notice. Behind her, Seventeen remained on the veranda with Annette. She wanted to give her sister-in-law and brother some space.

In the cab's rear seat, Nine and Francis had changed out of

their Sikh guises. No-one was happier about that than Francis who was enjoying being a boy once more.

Nine was first to spot Isabelle approaching. She looked even more beautiful than he remembered. "There's your mom," he said, fighting back tears. He opened the near door for Francis to let him scramble over him and run to his mother.

"Francis!" Isabelle shrieked when she saw her son.

Francis ran straight into her arms. Crying with joy, Isabelle swept him off the ground and showered him with kisses.

Nine wanted to join them, but he couldn't. The invisible band that had been tightening around his chest since he'd disembarked from the plane was now so tight he could hardly breathe. He suspected he was going into cardiac arrest.

Using the last of his strength, he reached forward and tapped the cabbie's shoulder. "I am feeling unwell," he muttered. "Would you help me out?"

The cabbie, an elderly Melanesian man, climbed out of the cab and helped his ailing passenger from the rear seat onto the grassy kerb.

Only then did Isabelle see Nine. Realizing something was wrong, she released Francis and hurried over to her husband. "Sebastian!"

Nine began to topple over. He was too heavy for the cabbie to hold, but the old man was able to cushion his passenger's fall and lay him gently down on the grassy strip alongside the cab. The cabbie then returned to the front seat and called for an ambulance on his radio-telephone.

The light rain that had begun earlier was still falling and the grass was now wet, but the ailing Nine didn't even notice that. Before he knew it he was in Isabelle's embrace. She was kneeling beside him, cradling his head in her loving arms and kissing his forehead.

"My darling!" Isabelle murmured. "What is wrong?"

"Nothing's wrong…sweetheart." Hiding his pain behind a smile, he reached up and stroked his wife's beautiful face. "Everything's exactly as it should be now."

"What's wrong with papa?" Francis asked.

Nine recognized his son's voice. Sensing he didn't have

long, he grasped Isabelle's arm. "Help me sit up!" he muttered through gritted teeth.

Isabelle looked around at the concerned cabbie who was now hovering close by. "Help me, will you?"

Together, Isabelle and the cabbie propped Nine up so he was sitting, his back resting against the side of the cab.

Without waiting to be asked, Francis went to his father's side and sat down beside him. It was then Nine saw Seventeen approaching. He could see she was holding a tiny bundle in her arms.

Seventeen stopped just short of Nine and lowered the tiny bundle into her brother's arms. "Sebastian, meet your daughter, Annette Nicia Hannar."

Nine looked at his daughter's face in wonderment then held her to his chest. "Annette," he whispered. A solitary tear rolled down his cheek as he was reminded of Annette Hannar, the mother he'd never known.

Seventeen stepped back to allow Nine to enjoy a loving reunion with his small family. She had no idea what was ailing her brother, but she had a bad feeling. He didn't look well.

Nine could feel himself slipping away. The chest pains that had gripped him earlier had been replaced by a numbness and he was finding it even harder to breathe. Everyone around him looked worried and seemed to be talking to him, but he couldn't hear what they were saying.

Despite his precarious physical state, Nine felt an amazing calmness descend – almost as if he was in a state of euphoria. *I did it!* The ninth-born orphan had achieved what he'd set out to do and rescued his son from the very people who had so cruelly taken his own childhood away. He had also lived to hold his daughter in his arms, he'd been reunited with Isabelle, his soul mate and one true love, and he'd seen his long-lost sister once more.

Thinking on all that, Nine knew he'd die a happy man.

As if on cue, the rain stopped and the clouds cleared, allowing a shaft of sunlight to break through. A beautiful rainbow formed directly above the small gathering.

Only Nine noticed it. But that wasn't the last thing he saw. The last thing he saw was his mother's ruby dangling from the silver necklace around Isabelle's neck. He reached up and touched

it. As always, its touch brought him comfort.

Epilogue

After Nine's tragic passing, Isabelle and Seventeen made their home in Aneityum, the southernmost island in Vanuatu. With its remote location, tiny population and fledgling tourism industry, it was effectively off the grid, which suited the two women just fine.

Isabelle considered Aneityum an ideal environment in which to raise Francis and Annette. Reminiscent of the tropical island she and Nine had fled to in the Marquesas Islands, it was paradise. Its coast was ringed by reefs and lined with white sand beaches, coconut palms and pine forests, while its rugged interior was mountainous with superb views out over the blue Pacific.

Isabelle and Seventeen used local builders to convert an old church into a guesthouse conveniently located between two of the biggest settlements on the island. Business was slow with few visitors, but that didn't worry them. Nine had left Isabelle very well looked after and Seventeen had a few dollars of her own salted away. Besides, there was little to spend money on at Aneityum and the women were more interested in the lifestyle anyway.

For Seventeen, her new life was a dream compared to the horrors of her previous one. Working with Isabelle, babysitting her sister-in-law's children and being an aunt to her niece and nephew served as a daily reminder of the promise she made to her brother – that she'd look after his family and keep them safe.

Francis re-adapted to island life as if he'd never left it. He made friends with the Melanesian children almost immediately and quickly picked up their language and customs. Baby Annette, too, thrived in her new surroundings, endearing herself to the local island women with her cute looks, engaging smile and impish manner.

Isabelle and Seventeen only ever visited Port Vila to pay their respects to Nine who was buried in a private cemetery overlooking the picturesque bay. Sometimes they'd visit alone, sometimes together and at other times with the children. They always found it a moving experience. Nine had left a hole in their hearts that could never be filled.

The fallout that resulted from the emails Nine sent out far and wide exposing Omega never touched the former operative's loved-ones. Once they reached Vanuatu and got off the grid, they effectively became removed from the outside world and all its politics and perils.

The detailed, incriminating, explosive emails resulted in more suicides, stress-related deaths and sackings as well as accusations that went as far as the Oval Office and beyond. Casualties included the Omega Agency, its secret medical labs and every surviving director and senior staffer within the organization. Beyond the agency, casualties included senior intelligence agents in the CIA, the FBI and the NSA, high profile politicians, respected judges, magistrates, lawyers and law enforcement officers, and many more.

Although the emails had the immediate results Nine had

hoped for, the status quo had returned inside two years. New splinter groups – reminiscent of Omega in its infancy – formed, intent on accumulating wealth and power; soldiers of First World countries continued to occupy mineral-rich Third World nations under the pretext of protecting the oppressed; the oppressed in those same places and in other mineral-rich nations continued to starve while their leaders grew fat; and people in high places continued to accept bribes while people lower down the ladder continued to offer bribes.

However, none of that touched on the lives of Nine's loved-ones.

On the fifth anniversary of Nine's passing, Isabelle, Seventeen and the children visited Nine's burial plot as they did every anniversary. It was a day not too dissimilar to the day he died: light rain fell as it had done that terrible day five years earlier.

Had Nine been looking down at his loved-ones, he'd have glowed with pride. Ten-year-old Francis was a chip off the old block with his shock of long, black hair, his startling green eyes and a frame that was tall for his years; five-year old Annette was already a miniature model of Isabelle with her mom's dark, cascading locks, caramel skin and hazel-flecked eyes.

As for the love of Nine's life, Isabelle had become even more beautiful with the passage of time. The faint ageing lines on her face and even more faint tinges of gray in her hair gave her that special beauty of a mature woman in her prime. Her beguiling eyes still sparkled, though they were now tinged with a sadness that hadn't been there when Nine knew her.

Isabelle hadn't remarried. She'd had one or two opportunities – once when she'd dated an Australian bureaucrat who visited Vanuatu's outer islands periodically and once when she was befriended by a New Zealand Red Cross official who was based at Aneityum for a year – but had never taken those opportunities up. Her heart was always somewhere else.

Seventeen, too, had aged well. She'd discovered a joie de vivre she'd never known before Nine and then Isabelle and the children had come into her life. That self-discovery had manifested in laugh-lines around her mouth and eyes – lines she'd never had before.

Tugging at Seventeen's hand, little Annette asked her aunt to read aloud the memorial dedication engraved at the top of Nine's headstone.

Seventeen, who was the last of the original Pedemont orphans, tried to keep the quaver out of her voice as she did as her niece asked. "Here lies Sebastian H. Beloved son of Annette, loving husband of Isabelle, father of Francis and Annette Nicia, and brother of Jennifer." Seventeen paused to clear her throat. "Born in the year Nineteen Eighty. Died August ten, Two Thousand and Sixteen."

While Seventeen read the dedication aloud, Isabelle was silently reading an italicized inscription engraved at the bottom of the headstone. The sad Frenchwoman thought the inscription's wording couldn't be more appropriate for her beloved Sebastian.

The inscription read:

I am a free man and a polymath.

Whatever I set my mind to, I always achieve.

The limitations that apply to the rest of humanity,

Do not apply to me.

THE END

If you enjoyed this novel, the authors would greatly appreciate a review from you on Amazon.

Other books by Lance & James Morcan follow over page...

Other books by Lance & James Morcan published by Sterling Gate Books…

CONSPIRACY THRILLERS:

The Ninth Orphan (The Orphan Trilogy, #1)

The Orphan Factory (The Orphan Trilogy, #2)

CRIME THRILLERS:

The Me Too Girl

The Heathrow Affair

ACTION-ADVENTURE:

High Country Contract

The Dogon Initiative (The Deniables, Book 1)

HISTORICAL FICTION:

White Spirit (A novel based on a true story) Into the Americas (A novel based on a true story)

World Odyssey (The World Duology, #1)

Fiji: A Novel (The World Duology, #2)

NON-FICTION:

DEBUNKING HOLOCAUST DENIAL THEORIES: Two Non-Jews Affirm the Historicity of the Nazi Genocide

THE ORPHAN CONSPIRACIES: 29 Conspiracy Theories from The Orphan Trilogy

GENIUS INTELLIGENCE: Secret Techniques and Technologies to Increase IQ (The Underground Knowledge Series, #1)

ANTIGRAVITY PROPULSION: Human or Alien Technologies? (The Underground Knowledge Series, #2)

MEDICAL INDUSTRIAL COMPLEX: The $ickness Industry, Big Pharma and Suppressed Cures (The Underground Knowledge Series, #3)

THE CATCHER IN THE RYE ENIGMA: J.D. Salinger's Mind Control Triggering Device or a Coincidental Literary Obsession of Criminals? (The Underground Knowledge Series, #4)

INTERNATIONAL BANKSTER$: The Global Banking Elite Exposed and the Case for Restructuring Capitalism (The Underground Knowledge Series, #5)

BANKRUPTING THE THIRD WORLD: How the Global Elite Drown Poor Nations in a Sea of Debt (The Underground Knowledge Series, #6)

UNDERGROUND BASES: Subterranean Military Facilities and the Cities Beneath Our Feet (The Underground Knowledge Series, #7)

VACCINE SCIENCE REVISITED: Are Childhood Immunizations As Safe As Claimed? (The Underground Knowledge Series, #8)

SHORT STORIES BY LANCE MORCAN:

Mr. 100%

A GLADIATOR'S LOVE

BROOKLYN BANKSTER

ONCE WERE BROTHERS

THE LAST TASMANIAN TIGER

www.ingramcontent.com/pod-product-compliance
Lightning Source LLC
Chambersburg PA
CBHW030837030726
47495CB00005B/1267